RISING FROM DUST

LIGHT FROM APHELION - BOOK I

MARTINE CARLSSON

Rising from Dust
Light from Aphelion - Book 1
Copyright © Martine Carlsson 2016
Cover and layout: Nellie C. Lind
Second edition
ISBN: 978-91-983923-5-7

ALL RIGHTS RESERVED

This book may not be reproduced or shared in any way without the author's written permission. The book is a work of fiction. Part from one character, the other characters, names, places, and incidents are the product of the author's imagination.

ABOUT THE AUTHOR

Martine Carlsson lives in the middle of the Swedish forest. She is French and graduated librarian and historian from the University of Liege. She takes her inspiration from the nature around her, from her roots in Brittany, and from fascinating parts from the European history. Therefore, it is not uncommon to read in her stories about forest creatures meeting peculiar characters in a detailed, historical-based background. She enjoys writing fantasy, especially a mix between harsh realism and magical wonders. Rising from Dust is her first novel and the first volume of the series Light from Aphelion.

PROLOGUE

"Does anybody hear me?"

The trees loomed over him, dark, and tall. A chilly wind blew through their brown leaves. Between the branches, the sky was grey, nearly white. His bare feet ran through the dead leaves, sinking into the spongy ground. His heart hammered in his chest. Brambles gashed the side of his legs. Dried boughs of pine trees brushed through his long hair. Selen climbed over logs, hurting his toes on rocks. He didn't know if something chased him, but he ran nonetheless. Flee. It had been his first thought. He glanced at the forest around him. Mossy boulders. Giant ferns. Thickets. What kind of nature was this?

"Ow!" Something had cut his sole. Selen stumbled and fell. The small stones and wooden sticks hidden in the soil peeled his white, naked body that was already crusted in mud. The earth, cool and wet, sucked out his energy. His arms clenched around his chest. He shivered. His teeth shook.

"Where am I? Please, anyone?" Selen whispered with a sob.

He felt the urge to dig in the ground and bury himself in it. Yet, he could not. With such a wind, he would freeze to death. Selen dragged himself up and kept on running.

A structure appeared through the branches. Leaning against a trunk, Selen observed the house. *Such a small place must belong to a shepherd or a hermit*, he thought, *if it is occupied*. There was no light, no smoke from the chimney, and no animals in the yard. Covering his intimacy, he walked towards the door. Would someone even answer? Considering how frightful he looked and his nudity, he wasn't even sure if he would open to himself. He glanced behind him at the dark woods. It scared him to think he might have to walk back to the forest. Why had he woken up there? He knocked and waited. Nothing. Selen tried the doorknob. The old wooden door squeaked.

"Hello?"

The room was empty of life. Selen stepped inside. He traced a finger on the rustic table, creating a hill of dirt. He looked around. Plenty of jars and pots stood on the shelves. Was this witchcraft? Carefully, he approached one shelf and pulled out a book. In it, he saw pages that were filled with drawings of leaves and roots.

"Herbalism."

He shut the book in a cloud of dust and progressed with his investigation. The hearth was cold, as was the whole shack.

"No one has lived here for a while," he sighed.

He knew it also meant no food. Therefore, he couldn't stay here. He searched the jars and found alcohol. Selen sat down by the table and bent his leg. The transparent liquid burned his foot, cleaning the fresh wound. His face twitched with pain. Limping, he moved towards the trunk near the bed. It was filled with clothes. They were moth-eaten, brown rags, but it was better than nothing. He chose a brown tunic and pants that didn't look too damaged. With a white cloth, he dressed his wound. Even with a bandage, it was torture to put the old boots on. Once dressed, he sat on the bed.

How had he ended up here? What was this place? He tried to remember the day before. Or the week before. In vain. Nothing came to him, not even the glimpse of a familiar place. He felt panic overtake him. His heart raced. His breathing hastened. This wouldn't help. Selen tried to reason. He had clothes and a roof. What he needed now was food. Maybe there were other houses nearby.

He went back outside. In front of the shack, grit and mud formed what looked like a trail. Maybe it led to a village. Selen followed it. He still had no idea where he was.

The forest opened into a valley. In the middle of it stood a charming, little village with red houses. Surprisingly, all were made of wood. As Selen approached the first habitations, he saw an old couple coming his way. Both of them were wrapped up in warm coats. The woman had a headdress and carried a basket. At least they looked like him; he couldn't be too far away from home. Selen smiled at them.

"Hello! Would you…"

The old man gave him a black look, pushed the woman inside a house, and closed the door behind them. *What a peculiar couple*, Selen thought. He progressed through the street. There were carved, wooden signs fixed on some of the front walls, indicating shops. Selen heard the ting-a-ling of a bell. A blond woman in a woolen cloak stepped out of the nearest shop. He approached her.

"Excuse me, I…"

She shrieked and raised her arms in protection. Selen raised his hand to calm her, but she stepped back.

"Leave me alone!" she yelled.

She spoke his language.

"Go away, you monster!" a man shouted from the other side of the street.

Selen was puzzled. He was no monster. He had mud on him and his hair was a mess, but his face was clean. Why would no one talk to him? If they spoke the same language, how was it that he didn't recognize anything of this place? He felt lost and perturbed. All he wanted was an explanation. He heard noises coming from a house. He stepped forward. It was music. The house was probably a tavern. A bad feeling crept inside him. Yet, if he wanted answers, a tavern would be the best place to go to.

Carefully, he opened the door. The warmth from the interior felt like bliss on his frozen body. He stepped inside. The smell of beer and bread made his belly rumble. Under the glow of chandeliers hanging from the ceiling, benches and tables were aligned in rows. Customers sat here and there, and a bard played in a corner. Selen raised his hand shyly.

"Hello."

The music stopped. The strong, bearded men sitting at the bar turned around. Their glances froze Selen's blood in his veins. Their disgust couldn't have been clearer. Selen knew it was too late to run away.

"What the hell is that?" one of them grunted.

They rose from their stools and approached him.

"I got lost and I need some help," he muttered.

"It talks like a girl," the man with the red beard sneered. "Girls should not have pants on. And what's on your face?"

A girl? Selen thought, confused. The men were giants. Judging by the strength of their arms and the nastiness in their eyes, Selen knew nothing good would come out of this. Wherever he was, no words could convince brutes. Waiting for his fate, he stood, petrified, hoping someone would react. Whatever their animosity, he had done nothing to deserve it. One man moved behind him and pulled at his hair.

"Ow!" Selen exclaimed as his head was tossed backwards.

"It's real hair!" the man exclaimed. "Freak. How can it look like this?"

"But, why…" Selen muttered, massaging his scalp.

"That's no girl," the red beard growled.

The man behind him grabbed his arms and pulled them backwards, while one of his companions ripped off Selen's tunic. Selen was terrified and glanced around, but no one reacted. Some men even approved.

"Seidr," the red beard mumbled, gazing at his chest. Whispers of alarm rose around him.

The red beard punched Selen in the chest. The intense pain in his ribs made Selen bend over. He hoped no one would hit his face. One blow from these men and his head would be crushed. He felt pain in his back and fell to the ground.

"Disgusting ergi!" one man shouted.

Feet kicked him in his abdomen. Selen cringed as the blows fell on him from all sides. His body burned. *Please, don't let them kill me*, he thought. *I did nothing wrong.*

"Let's burn the ergi at the stake!"

The proposition was welcomed by roars.

"Stop this nonsense!" a voice shouted.

The blows stopped. A powerful grip dragged Selen to the side. A blond man with a thick beard looked at him.

"Who the hell are you?" the man asked, staring at Selen.

Short of breath, Selen did not reply. He already fought hard not to sob.

"Don't bother with that, Rodrick. It's just an ergi," one of Selen's assailants exclaimed. "He didn't even challenge me to deny it. Look at the color of his hair, look at the marks on his forehead. This witch-harlot is cursed by the spirits."

"Or blessed by them," Rodrick snapped to the brute. "What are you good at?" he asked Selen. Dumbfounded, Selen only gaped. "Your work. What can you do?"

Selen understood. "Heal. I can heal. I am good with herbs." He was not sure about it, but if it could save his life, he would give it a try.

Rodrick turned around. "A physician. Do you think we have enough of them in the village to burn him? The man may be a stranger, but he is useful."

"I won't touch his charms," the man grunted but calmed down. The man with the red beard spat in Selen's direction. Rodrick pulled Selen up by the arm. Selen groaned. His head swirled. The blond man took a piece of bread from a table and pushed it into Selen's hand.

"Please…" Selen moaned. "Where am I?"

"Run. Now," Rodrick said, looking Selen in the eyes.

Still trembling with fear and pain, Selen staggered out of the tavern. Once outside, the tears ran down his cheeks. His hands clenched around his throbbing chest as he ran away.

Winter had been long and dark in the Frozen Mountains. Selen looked at the grey clouds that approached from the north. It was time to go back home before the storm came. A chilly wind already blew through his long hair. A shiver ran through his body. He tugged his woolen cloak closer around him. He had been out all morning, picking some of the first thimbleweeds. He looked down again. With the tips of his fingers, he brushed the snow from the delicate, white flower. He snapped the stem and laid the white star on top of the others in his basket. It would have to be the last one for today.

He rose and whistled. Above the crown of the pine trees, a familiar shadow showed up. The hawk uttered a piercing screech. Selen raised his hand. The bird flew down towards him. Its flapping wings blasted icy air on Selen's pale face. Selen's eyes narrowed. The bird landed on his outstretched arm. Delicately, Selen put the leather chaperon on its head and laced the jess around his wrist. He picked up the basket with the flowers and walked to the trail. With cautious steps between the thick tree roots and slippery stones, he headed back home.

The shack stood in the middle of a clearing in the forest. The small building had proven comfortable and could be kept warm during winter. He had cleaned the rudimentary furniture. The shelves were still covered with mason jars, clay pots, and books, but the recipients were no longer empty. Last-season plants, which were tied to drying racks, hung from the ceiling. Selen put the basket on the table and started a fire in the hearth. His boots were damp with clotted snow, and his hands and feet felt frozen. When the wood burned, he knelt in front of the fire and let the blaze warm his body. He closed his eyes. He could hear the sheep bleat behind the door. It would soon be time for the first lambs to be born. This year again, he had managed to store enough hay for them to last through winter. He stretched. He could not fall asleep, not now. He had balms to prepare. Selen grabbed some thyme and sage from one of the racks and ground them together.

    He had planned to travel to the village in a few days. There would be peasants and housewives suffering from a cold of some sort. There were no lack of customers during winter. Selen would never forget the incident that had nearly cost him his life four years ago. Beaten and upset, he had returned to the shack and made it his home. To occupy his time, he had read the books on the shelves and noticed that he already knew a bit about herbalism. Progressively, Selen had learned to take care of himself and to live on his own. He had never returned to the tavern. The villagers and he had come to a tacit agreement. He would live in the wilderness, and they would leave him alone. As long as he did not mix with them, some people in the village could even show sympathy for him, especially the ones who needed his help. Selen was the only person around with medical knowledge. He could prepare balms, tinctures, and fix minor wounds. From time to time, he would sell his products at the market to buy the few things he could not make himself. Yet, his services as a physician were barely appreciated. No one had ever come to his shack, and no one ever would. They had despised him from the start. Selen had understood that it was his knowledge and usefulness that kept him alive. Therefore, though he sometimes missed seeing other people's faces, he did not mind loneliness. It was always better than to endure others' cruelty. His life was basically survival, but he had no other choice.

    Selen took the bowl with the herbs infused in oil and strained the mixture. Greasy drops ran down his wrists. He wiped his hands on a cloth. With skilled moves, he poured the oil into jars. The golden substance turned light green as it cooled down. He mixed melted wax into it. When he was done, he placed the jars on the windowsill. While he put down the last one, he gazed outside. The top of the birches bent in the wind. The sky was grey and heavy. Soon, it would snow again. He could see the shape of the mountains on the horizon, the peaks standing white and tall, like teeth biting the sky. Even the nature around was a display of coldness and solitude. He sighed and felt a spark of pain in his chest. It grew stronger. His heart was burning again. He needed to lie down. He moved to his bed and stretched on it.

Selen looked at the wooden beams on the ceiling. He took deep breaths and expired long. The pain calmed down. As he relaxed, he lost himself in thoughts.

These last weeks, he had not been feeling well. He was constantly nauseous. His sleep was restless, haunted by weird nightmares of monsters and fights. They were always blurry, but they felt so real, so frightening. He often woke up in the middle of the night screaming and panting, the bedsheets damp with sweat. The dreams haunted him during the day, as well. He hoped he was not becoming mad. People living alone in the wilderness often tended to turn a bit strange over the years, and his case was also special.

He did remember the last four years, but that was all. Nothing had explained why he had woken up naked in the middle of the wilderness. Maybe the nightmares were a reminiscence of his past, but why were they happening now? Had something changed? He had lived the same monotonous life for years now. Maybe it was not related to him. He did not know a thing about the outside world. Could there be a disease spreading? To think he could be dying of some infection alone in the wilderness tore his heart to pieces. Selen felt tears come to his eyes. He shifted on his bed and curled under the warm blanket. Would this be his life until he died? He refused such a fate.

Selen had had thoughts about leaving. He longed to go south. He could not explain why. Though he was lonely, he had all he needed here; a roof, his animals, his herbs, and enough work to put food on the table. Still, the call was stronger. It grew in his chest like a fire. Every day, he felt more and more like a bird before the migration. He, who had never left his forest. His walks would now take him on unexplored trails. He could stay out for hours watching the pink sun above the glowing white peaks. What lay beyond the Frozen Mountains was a mystery to him. Yet, the pain in his heart filled his chest, and he looked at the horizon with hopeful eyes.

Two days passed. The bags waiting against the front door were full with food and potions. Selen saddled his rustic dray horse. It had not been an easy decision, but leaving was his only choice. He would head to the village and keep on moving south. He harnessed the bags on the horse and added a second blanket. The sheep had food for five days and should make it until someone came for them. The most painful decision had been to free the hawk. The bird had been his only friend for three years. He had found it, nursed it, and cherished it like a child, but he did not dare to take it with him on the journey. Prey birds were a symbol of the higher class, to which he did not belong. Moreover, it would not survive down south. It would either be killed by a man's hand or by disorientation. Selen had taken him to the river, far enough away from the house. He had removed the small chaperon and delicately unlaced the jess from the bird's ankle. The hawk had waited a few seconds, as if tasting its new freedom, before taking flight and disappearing above the naked tree tops.

Selen hesitated before locking the door. He put the key back in his pocket, got on his horse, and rode away.

The village was silent, as it was in late winter. The only sounds were the dropping of the melting snow and the snuffling of the horse. The red wooden houses looked deserted except for the reflection of a candle through a window here and there. Smoke rose out of the chimneys like a forest of stunted trunks. A door opened. An old woman came out and gazed at him with a scornful look. She spat in his direction and disappeared around a corner.

Selen kept on riding. He halted by a house near the river. The construction was a bit larger than the others with a sloping roof on the side, covering what looked like a smithy. Selen dismounted, took out a leather pouch from his bag, and knocked at the door. A tall, bearded man in a dusty leather apron opened.

"Dear gods, if it's not our local hermit. It has been ages since we last saw you here in Fjolsta, Selen. What can I do for you? Are you here to sell me some potions?" the man asked, laughing. The blacksmith crossed his dirty arms over his chest, revealing the protruding muscles under his shirt. The man had always been amiable to him, and Selen knew he could trust him.

"Actually, I am here to say goodbye," Selen said with a sad face. "Still, master Dalin, I need a last service. Would you buy my last stock of products? I can make you a price on it. I have no time to sell it myself. And I need the money."

The blacksmith looked at Selen and frowned. "I could, indeed, but why do you need money so eagerly?"

"I intend to journey south," Selen answered. "More, I don't know myself."

"South, you say," Dalin grunted. "You must have stayed too long in your forest. There is bad news coming from that way. Some men talk about war. There is nothing good for you down there, Selen."

"I'm sorry, but I won't turn back," Selen said. War sounded bad, but he would not die in his shack. He handed the pouch with his products to the man. "I also give you my key. My sheep are yours, and so are my belongings if I don't come back in a few months. There is nothing of great worth, I fear."

"Wait here," Dalin said. The blacksmith left the door and disappeared inside the house.

A few minutes later, the man was back, his arms full of provisions. "Let me give you these. You will need food to cross the Frozen Mountains. And try to stay away from the road when things look bad. Men like you are easy prey," Dalin said with a concerned look.

"I think I can watch over myself," Selen answered, taking the provisions and a small pouch full with coins, "but thank you very much for the food…and for my sheep." Selen smiled and turned away.

"Fare well!" the blacksmith exclaimed. "And may the gods be with you."

Selen filled his bags, got on his horse, and waved back. Heading south, he crossed the village in silence. From a roof above his head, a flock of crows took to the air, squawking.

The pink-red sun beamed above the horizon. A flock of birds rose from the edge of the woods. Selen sat on a stone with his flask of water in his hand. He was weary. It had taken him two weeks to cross the Frozen Mountains. With the rising spring temperatures, the roads had been turned to swamps. Some rivers had proven to be impossible to cross, thus forcing him to make detours through rocky slopes and deep copses. He had been obliged to make many breaks to let his horse rest. The poor beast had panted most of the time and had been close to hurt itself on many occasions. Selen had not met a single traveller. Neither had he seen a tavern or a shack to take shelter. The road south was barren of human life. The nocturnal dampness and the rain had made his clothes so unbearably wet and cold that he had had to keep a fire going at every bivouac to partially dry them. He had also been too exhausted to be disturbed by nightmares, falling instantly asleep where he had laid down his head. Fortunately, he had enough food to last for weeks and could harvest roots or trap a hare if needed.

The Frozen Mountains were behind him now. The forest that stretched to the horizon was full of promises. The burning he felt in his heart was like a beacon leading him through the elements. Something strong called him. He was sure he had made the best choice. He gazed south at the bright kingdom of Trevalden and sighed with high expectation.

Selen got up and mounted. It was time to resume his journey south and wind down the mountains.

The vegetation was a mix of deep pine and birch forests and tall grass prairies.

The horse had no difficulty following the trail. The journey promised to be more pleasant. Even the freezing wind had turned into a light breeze. Except for the chanting of the birds, the south slope of the Mountains looked deserted. Here and there, Selen could see a farm in a glade. Most looked like they had been abandoned for years. The few people he saw fled at his sight. He spotted ruins of old watchtowers but no trace of a village. It seemed as if no one wanted to live south of the Mountains. Yet, the path got broader and turned from a grassy trail into a muddy road.

The first refugees appeared in the morning. At first, it was isolated men wearing rags and a bag with their last belongings. They avoided him and moved in utter silence, like ghostly figures. Selen wondered if they would dare to cross the Frozen Mountains, or if they would head west and take the road to the Windy Isles. He interrupted his thoughts when he saw the first families. The lucky ones traveled by cart. The others wandered in groups, sometimes dragging an old, scrawny mule behind. Mothers pulled crying children. They looked starved, worn-out, and dirty. The refugees looked at him with wild eyes. Selen, who had never seen so much misery, watched them go by with utter shock. Moved by compassion, he dismounted from his horse and gave some of his food and water to the poorest families, who mumbled a few words of thanks in return. Yet, as the road went on, and the flow of unfortunate men and women grew larger, Selen became overwhelmed by the number. He understood with genuine sadness that he could never help them all. Some desperate souls even tried to grab at his horse. He felt forced to quicken his mount's pace.

Later on the road, Selen saw a cart pulled by an old nag. The couple on the seat didn't look better than their horse, but at least they looked aware. Selen took the chance to glean some information. "You there," Selen called. "Where are you from? What happened back there?"

"How can you not know?" the grumpy, old man answered with reproach in his voice. "You better turn around, young maid. It's war down there."

"War against whom?" Selen continued, trying to block the road for the cart and ignoring the old man's mistake. "Please, tell me. I came all the way from the other side of the Mountains."

"It's King Agroln. He is sending troops to take over the north. The south is already in flames," the old man explained. "There are creatures and outlaws going through the villages, burning houses. We have lost everything," he mumbled, looking down. "You don't want to see this." The man shook the reins, and the horse pulled the cart again. Selen watched them disappear around the curve. He kicked his mount.

He wondered now if it was wise to go south. Still, he did not need to ride much further. The warmth in his heart radiated. Whatever was calling him, he drew nearer with each step. The first drops of rain were falling on his hood when he glanced ahead and saw the top of what looked like a tavern.

Louis had left the city of Neolerim, capital of the Iron Marches, two weeks ago by the road leading west. The saddlebags on his horse were packed with food. He had purses filled with money hidden under the saddle and under the blanket. It was his first long journey, but he was determined to reach the north of the kingdom of Trevalden without incident. It had not been as easy as he had planned to travel with all these refugees flocking from the west. Every night for a week, he had slept against the trees in the woods, some hundred yards away from the road. The taverns were crowded with disoriented families, ready to pay a fortune for a bowl of soup and a piece of bread. In every village he had crossed, wounded and beggars agglutinated on the houses' porches. Still, the worst had been the road itself. Some carts had been pulled over and abandoned where the axle had broken or where the mount had died. It attracted scavengers, everything from crows to wild dogs.

Of course, the inhabitants of Neolerim had been informed of the war in Trevalden. It had been going on for four years now, ever since King Wymar Lambelin had been poisoned. The old king had been the last one of his house. Rumours said it was one of his counselors who had poisoned him. Other rumours said the queen had done it. A long, bloody war for the throne had followed, a conflict that people who lived east, in the Iron Marches, had vaguely heard of. But now that the north of the realm had been struck, refugees poured into the Iron Marches.

Louis watched them pass by with pity and reproach. He could not understand why such an amount of people fled instead of joining forces. What were their lives worth outside their kingdom anyway? They would never survive the harsh life in the Iron Marches. Only barren hills and dry, rocky mountains lay ahead. Many refugees were already exhausted by the journey. Half of them were incurably sick, while others had lost their minds.

He had crossed Trevalden's border ten days ago. The forest where he was now showed the first signs of spring. With its mild climate, Trevalden was a more pleasant place to live in than the Iron Marches. Louis hastened his mount's pace.

The call he had felt inside his chest these last weeks had been the spark he had needed to motivate him to travel west. He would not turn back. This burning in his heart, which had been so warm and comforting in the beginning, had turned into fire. Besides, the world was changing in the west, and he wanted to be a part of it. He could not stand to live in the city any longer. His life as an archivist bored him to death. Maybe this journey would also be an opportunity for him to learn about his past. Four years of intensive work in the city archives never shone the glimpse of a light on his memories. Whatever lay ahead, the journey excited him.

Around him, the uninterrupted flow of the refugees moved faster. They all hoped to cross the forest before nightfall. Like a migrating flock, the weaker were prey to all that roamed along the path. Louis heard a cry that was unusual among the multitude of whines, like a call of distress. Curious, he pulled his mount around the slope. A cart pulled by an ox stood in a glade. A few yards away from it, a man lay in a pool of blood with arrows stuck in his back. His aggressors, two men in filthy clothes, manhandled a young boy. Louis assumed the dead man had been the father. Without a second thought, Louis dismounted, drew his sword, and approached the men. They were too busy with the child to notice his presence. As he moved closer, he heard their conversation.

One of the two bandits took the young boy by the wrist. "Now, tell us where his money is, or I'll open your dear pa to check his guts," the taller man said.

The child stood mute with a horrified look on his face.

"Maybe we should roast him? Isn't that what your brother used to do, Bran?" The man pushed his dagger closer to the boy's throat.

"'You don't spoil good merchandise,' he also used to say. And what I see here is worth some pieces of gold," Bran replied.

"And where do you hope to sell it, genius? There are only more of them around," the tall man objected.

"I know a few men in a tavern nearby who would not mind some entertainment," Bran sniggered.

"As you wish, your—"

The man's head bent down when Louis ran his sword through his back. Louis pushed his sword out as Bran turned around. The blow was swift, and the blade cut clean. When Bran's head touched the ground, the eyes were still frozen with disbelief. The man's body collapsed on top of it.

Louis knelt and took the boy by the shoulder. "Are you unhurt?" he asked.

The boy did not answer. Instead, he grabbed Louis's long brown hair and cried in silence. Louis bore the child onto his saddle and brought him back to the flow of people. He halted near a group of families passing by.

"You there," he called out to a man who looked to be the oldest, "this boy's father has been killed. You will help me bury him."

Louis's voice was firm, but he did not shout. The man and his relatives looked at him suspiciously. The women felt concerned by the tears running down the boy's face, but no one dared to move without the old man's approval.

Louis sighed. So much for compassion. "You can keep the man's cart. Just don't make me have to force you." Louis reached for his sword. Should they still refuse to move, he would not hesitate to use it. The threat and the opportunity to loot convinced the men of the group.

The families followed him into the glade. Louis was pleased to see that they headed to the man and not to the cart. At the site of what had happened, the refugees showed more will to perform the task. Louis dismounted and helped them dig the grave with tools found in the cart. Once the work was done, Louis turned to the child.

"You will have to stay with the others. It seems they are good people after all," he said. "Where I go is no place for a child." Louis put the boy on a cart with other children and kept on moving west.

"Whatever I am looking for, it's hidden here," Louis said and looked at the sign of the Wounded Owl Inn. It was time he arrived. His heart inflamed his lungs. His hands in his gloves were moist, and his vision had blurred a few times.

The place was built with white stone, and judging by the thickness of the ivy that grew on the north wall, it had probably stood there for a hundred years. The inn was big, with a long red tile roof and half-timbered walls. Louis looked at the stained-glass windows of different colors. Only rich taverns in cities could afford such luxury. To be so impressive, this place was probably the only resting spot on the main road for miles. He walked towards the porch. Like a moat around a castle, the inn was circled by a stream, which also could have been waste waters. A stone bridge connected the alley to the entrance gate.

A young lad in dusty outfits approached him. "Should I take care of your horse, my lord?"

"I'm no lord, but yes, you can," Louis answered. As he dismounted, his head spun. He closed his eyes a few seconds. "How big is this place?"

"You have the stables at your right, over there. On the left is the inn. Though, I think the inn is full for the night. There is an inner garden that you can reach from the west side of the main room. This gate is the only entrance," the lad explained.

So, that door would be the only exit should he meet someone nasty inside the inn. Louis was not reassured at all. "Thank you. That will be all." Louis gave the lad a coin, handed him his horse's bridle, and headed to the inn's main door across the inner yard.

As Louis pushed the door, the smell of tobacco and cabbage fried in grease with onions welcomed him. He put a hand on his mouth. The tavern was crowded with all kinds of folk, each more suspicious and shabby looking than the other. The customers' loud chatting covered the distant sound of a bard's lute. His eyes narrowed when he stared at the faces. Under his cloak, Louis reached for the pommel of his sword. No eyes crossed his. No one reacted to his presence. Still, it was here, somewhere.

The heat in his chest was suffocating. He pushed his hood back. The terrible smell made his stomach contract again. In search for some fresh air, he noticed the open door on the other side, the one that led to the inner garden. He took a few unsteady steps towards the doorframe and leaned against it. The cold air of the evening felt wonderful on his face. The garden was full of colorful flowers. This enchanting place was a stark contrast to the main room of the tavern. Someone sat in the alley.

The pain in his heart stopped. The nausea left him. Could the something he was after be a someone? Louis approached with his hand on his sword. "Whoever you are, turn around and show yourself," Louis commanded.

The person in front of him rose slowly and turned, pushing his hood back. The pain Louis had felt in his heart came back stronger than ever, but it was another kind of pain this time. The man had long hair the color of lilacs cascading down his back to his thighs. His face had the most delicate features Louis had ever seen. But above all, it was the man's eyes that caught his attention. He had eyes of the purest green, expressing the most infinite kindness. Louis was drawn out of his amazement when the man opened his plump, curved mouth.

"My name is Selen. I've been waiting for you," the man said with a smile and a hint of a blush.

The burning in his chest had almost choked Selen. He had found refuge in the garden, among the plants and flowers, where he felt safe. He had sensed the man approach behind his back. It had been too late to think about grabbing a weapon. Now, he felt ridiculous even to have conceived that idea. The man who stood in front of him took his breath away. Heat rose to his cheeks. During all these years, Selen had never seen anyone with such deep blue eyes. He stood mesmerized. To escape the man's strong gaze, he forced his own eyes to wander to the brown locks of the man's long hair and to his full lips, a sight that only made him blush more. Was it he who had summoned him here? He tried to fight his embarrassment and spoke. "My name is Selen. I've been waiting for you." It was the first thing that came to his mind. He knew at once that his words sounded foolish. He should have said something more neutral, or asked the man's name. He bit his lip and waited.

There was a moment of silence. "I'm Louis," the man finally answered. "Who are you? And why did you call me here?"

"I never called you here. You called me," Selen said, startled.

"I don't understand," Louis said, looking disconcerted. "I came all the way from the Iron Marches because something pulled me here, and I see no one else in this garden."

"And I came from the Frozen Mountains," Selen replied, "but there is nothing here. Except you."

"There must be more to it. I think we should talk and sort it out," Louis proposed. "Should we sit in the tavern? I don't want to stay exposed here in case it's some kind of trap." He looked around.

"I suppose the company of rogues, marauders, and mercenaries is more reassuring," Selen said. He had avoided the tavern until now. Maybe if he were accompanied, no one would want to bother him. He threw his hood over his head and entered the tavern, followed by Louis.

The room was noisy and smelled like old smoke and beer. It was better not to ask about the stains on the tables and the benches. Selen was pretty sure that blood was one of the substances. He did not want to know about the others. Selen shrank, lowered his gaze, and walked through the crowd. They managed to find a round table in a corner. Selen sat on a stool.

"How did you find your way here?" Louis asked.

"I have felt pain in my chest for some time now. Not as a sickness, but as something calling me, telling me to go south." Louis leaned closer over the table, turning his head slightly. Selen tried to talk a bit louder. "Eventually, I could not resist anymore, and I travelled across the Frozen Mountains. This mysterious force dragged me here to this tavern." Selen made a quick gesture with his hand. He was disappointed. "I thought it was some kind of quest," he said. "I thought that someone wanted to meet me, that I was meant to do something important."

Louis looked at him with surprise. "But you don't need a call for that if it's what preoccupies you. Anyway, we don't even know if our pain is over. Maybe there is more to come."

Selen looked at Louis. The man had smiled at him. Besides, until now, he had not even stared at him with distaste. "What do you think it's all about?" Selen asked. "Could it be related to the war?"

Louis gazed at him. It felt as if his eyes pierced his soul. Selen barely held his look and squirmed.

"I suppose I can tell you. I have had nightmares these recent months, always about some beasts, and, I'm not sure, but…a dragon," Louis said. "I don't know if you can understand. I have amnesia. I don't remember anything about my past. I worked as an archivist in Neolerim in hopes of finding answers. But whatever I read, it never brought me anything. Then, the nightmares began and the pain. I had hoped that I could learn who I am."

Selen could not believe what he had heard. "That's it!" he exclaimed. "This is the link between us," he whispered. "I have amnesia too…and the nightmares. They seem so real. Whatever called us here, we were bound to meet." Selen felt an intense excitement. After so many years of loneliness and questioning, he finally had found someone he had something in common with. Moreover, Louis did not look like everyone. Selen felt lucky. "So, do you think we should head south?" he asked. He would as well have followed east, west, or back north. He wanted to learn more about Louis.

"I had planned to go south, but it means travelling in the middle of a land at war. I have no equipment. I hate to say it, but I guess we will have to find some on corpses," Louis answered. "Do you have food? There is not much left to buy, I fear, not for a good price."

"I gave most of it to the refugees I met," Selen said. He realized now that his generosity would probably mean some days of abstinence for him. At least Louis did not voice the disapproval shown by his expression.

"That was most kind of you," he said instead. "Can you fight?" Louis asked in a dubious voice.

"I can use a stick and a spear. I also know by which end to hold a sword," Selen said. He hoped he did not sound too pathetic. He was not bringing much to their journey by now. "Can you?"

"I think I am pretty good," Louis answered with a smirk.

"But, you are an archivist?" Selen frowned. "You should barely see sunlight."

"Sometimes the archives close, and you have to do something with your time, like learning to defend yourself," Louis said. "I could teach you."

Selen would love that. "So let's do it right now," Selen said. He got up and pushed his way to the door.

Louis saw Selen jump up and rush outside the tavern. Dumbfounded, he followed him out. The man's motivation startled him. Was all this a game for Selen, or did he just crave adventure? They walked together through the inner courtyard.

"We can train in front of the inn. I think I saw a merchant standing there. He probably has a sword you can buy," Louis said.

They arrived in front of the stand. A round man in a brown shirt and an apron saluted them. Axes and swords of different qualities were on display. Louis picked one, judged the balance, and observed the blade. He tested a few of the finest swords.

"Try one of these," he said to Selen.

"I don't need such a nice blade if I can barely use it," Selen told him.

"Your equipment may save your life. Never spare on it," Louis insisted. Selen picked a one-handed sword. "Does it fit your hand?"

"Yes, it fits it." Selen twisted his wrist. The blade glittered in the last ray of the evening light.

Louis turned to the merchant. "How much for this sword?"

"Two gold coins," the man answered while lighting a lantern on the table.

Selen took out his purse, but Louis held his hand. "You're kidding, right?" He stared at the merchant with defiance.

The man shrugged and frowned at him. "It's a fine sword."

"I'm sure there is a profusion of fine swords down south. One only need to bend his knees and pick one." He made a sign for Selen to leave. "Come."

"One gold and four silver," he heard the man say as they left.

Louis smirked. He turned around and took out his purse.

"No. It's mine." Selen put a hand on his arm. "I pay." Selen counted out the coins. Louis wondered if he also had given his money to the refugees. The purse was nearly empty.

They went to the sandy alley on the other side of the inn. It was quiet, though a bit gloomy in the shade of the trees.

"This is a nice place to train," Selen said.

"Indeed." No one could see them from the tavern, and it was all that mattered. Louis stared at Selen. His hood fell over his brow to the top of his eyes. "Won't you push back your hood? It's not raining. Or do you hide yourself from someone?" Louis chuckled.

"I do."

Louis turned serious. He had meant it as a joke. There was no one but them outside. "I hope it's not from me." Slowly, Selen pushed back his hood. Louis smiled. "If we journey together, I want to see your face. Besides, you have no reason to hide yourself." Selen pinched his lips. His eyes shone.

Louis drew out his long sword and moved in place. Selen raised his sword. Louis engaged with a blow aimed at Selen's shoulder, and he deflected the attack easily. Louis swung his sword and aimed for Selen's hip. Selen blocked and pushed the blade away. To test Selen's reflexes, Louis made a feint at Selen's legs, but he raised his sword diagonally and aimed for the flank instead. The metal clattered as the weapons crossed on their flat. Louis was pleased to see that Selen could defend himself well. He decided to increase the speed. Louis's blows and thrusts became more violent, until he felt pain in his arms. Selen intercepted every move and never let him complete his blows. Yet, Selen never engaged.

"Why don't you attack me?" Louis asked, slightly irritated.

"Do I need to?" Selen replied.

"It's the whole point with the training."

To force him to react, Louis swung his sword in a downward blow and stepped forward, reducing the space between them. Unable to raise his sword properly, Selen made a counter-cut on the flat, pushed, and slipped in Louis's broken defense. Louis saw Selen twist around him and disappear behind his back. He swiveled, but too late. The push Selen gave him with the flat of his sword surprised Louis. Though he managed to block the blow, he lost balance and fell.

"Why did you lie to me?" Louis rose, his hand brushing his hip. He felt cheated. He never mingled with folk. Yet, Selen had seemed so guileless that, for once, he had considered opening himself to someone. Could he have been wrong?

"I didn't lie to you," Selen said, startled.

"You said you have never held a sword. Yet, you fight like a knight."

"I have not touched a sword in four years. I can't explain…" Selen stopped and bent. He staggered, his mouth gaping and his eyes wide open. One of Selen's hands reached for his chest.

"Are you all right?" Louis asked, worried.

Selen fell to his knees and screamed with pain, his hands crossed on his ribs.

"Selen!" Louis shouted. He ran to him, knelt, and held him up. "What is wrong?"

"I felt it again," Selen sighed. He looked pale and nauseous. His breathing was forced. "The pain in my heart. I felt it again. Something, or someone, is coming."

"Was it as strong as when we met?" Louis questioned, his hands still holding Selen. He wondered why he had not felt it too. Maybe Selen was more sensitive, or maybe they didn't feel it at the same time.

"No. I feel better," Selen answered, "but I would guess it's coming towards us, from the south."

"It's too late to search for it today. We will head south tomorrow." Louis looked around, but no one had seen Selen's faintness. "We should go back to the inn before it gets pitch black." While steadying Selen, Louis's gaze faced Selen's. Louis noticed they were of equal height, and that they stood awkwardly close. He took a step back, but he still held one of Selen's arms.

"I am fine. The pain is gone. Thank you." Selen smiled. "I did not lie. I swear." With such kindness in his voice, Louis could not imagine that the man was or had been a warrior. Yet, his fighting skills proved otherwise.

They went back to the inner courtyard. Louis headed to the stables, but Selen stopped him.

"Where are you going?" Selen asked.

"I'm going to sleep near my horse. I don't know if you noticed, but the inn is full," Louis said, nodding towards the noisy inn. By the uproar coming from that direction, it was clear that most of the guests were drunk and in a joyful mood. The stables smelled of horse dung, but at least it was quiet in there.

"You could share my room," Selen said in a low, timid voice.

Louis gave him a surprised look. He tried to look into the man's eyes, but Selen avoided his gaze.

"I would love to," Louis answered.

They weaved through the crowd in the main room, went up the steps, and entered Selen's room. The place was small and narrow but relatively clean, with a little table and a single window. The room smelled of dry hay.

They removed their boots, and Selen took off his tunic. "The mattress is small, but I can sleep on the floor if you wish," Selen said, facing the crudely constructed bed. Louis wondered if Selen had suggested that they share the narrow bed, or if he had heard what he wanted to hear.

Louis looked at Selen's hair. It glittered in the moonlight. Almost hypnotized by this ethereal sight, he approached Selen and ran his fingers through his hair that reached down to his thighs. Delicately, he put his lips on Selen's left shoulder. The fragrance of his skin reminded him of the forest mixed with the scent of flowers. He felt Selen's skin twitch under his lips. Louis heard him take a sharp intake of breath. Selen turned around with a stunned look on his face. Shame flooded Louis, and he pulled away.

"I'm sorry, I shouldn't..." Louis said, looking down, but before he could finish his sentence, Selen threw his lips onto his and put one arm around his neck. Selen's move was so straightforward that it surprised Louis. Yet, the touch on his lips was so innocent that he did not pull away. Louis laid a hand against the side of Selen's head and kissed him back. The feeling of relief and desire that overwhelmed him was intoxicating. Louis forgot everything: the call, the amnesia, and the monsters. All his thoughts were now on Selen. He stopped to observe Selen's face and knew his candor was genuine. They smiled at each other. Louis kissed him again. He pushed Selen back gently and took the initiative to remove his own clothes. He waited for Selen to do the same. Awkwardly, Selen removed the rest of his clothes. Louis saw by the way Selen shrank his shoulders that he felt shy, even insecure. Louis smiled at such a lovely and silly gesture. He took one of Selen's hands in his and admired his enchanting beauty. The man was graceful, but in contrast to his face, there was nothing feminine about his body. Louis felt heat fill him.

He led Selen onto the bed and laid down on top of him. The contact of their naked bodies was heady. Selen's mouth reached for his. Louis put his lips on Selen's. As their first kiss had been rough, this one was careful, tender. The light touch sent shivers through his nerves, but yet not as strong as when Selen's hands closed around the back of his head. In Selen's arms, he realized how lonely he had been until now. Louis wondered if Selen shared this feeling to have given way to his emotions with such haste. He hugged him tightly. Louis's lips parted slightly, and his tongue grazed

Selen's teeth. Selen's mouth opened and welcomed him.

When Selen waved that he had no air to breathe, Louis grazed his lips from Selen's mouth to his cheek, trailing a line to his chest. Gazing down, he saw Selen's arousal, but when he looked again into Selen's intense, green eyes, he saw fear.

"I don't think I have ever…" Selen whispered.

And I had hoped it, Louis thought with relief and decided to show the same sincerity. "I don't remember either, but I will try not to hurt you."

He kissed him again and grazed his hands on Selen's soft, white skin. He would be gentle and slow, ignoring the ache in his lower parts. He went down Selen's body and traced the shape of his delicate muscles with his lips, down to his groin. The moisture that pearled on his skin tasted of salt and honey. As he pleasured him, he sensed Selen's long fingers on his head, gripping his hair. Louis heard how he tried to hold back his moans. Selen did not last. He screamed out his pleasure as he came. His grip on Louis's hair eased, and his breathing calmed down. Louis moved slowly upwards. Selen's eyes were wide open, but his eyelashes twitched. Louis smiled and kissed him passionately.

While they tasted each other, Louis moistened his fingers and prepared Selen for more. He looked into Selen's eyes, searching for any sign of doubt, but the fear was gone. When he felt him ready, Louis's left hand ran down Selen's back and grabbed one of his cheeks. Selen's long, muscular legs closed around his waist, and he disappeared into a world of pleasure.

5

Selen felt lips kiss his. He opened his eyes slowly.

"We have to pack our things," Louis said with a smile. His companion was already dressed and ready to depart.

Selen was relieved to see that what had happened last night had not been a dream. He had had but little hope that Louis could have such inclinations, let alone be interested in someone like him. It sounded too good to be true, and it almost made him cry. However, he did not want to put words to his feelings yet. Years of persecution had taught him to be wary of the human nature. He just hoped that Louis would not leave him. He raised his head, still feeling drowsy, and looked out the window.

"It's barely dawn. Do we need to leave so early?" Selen groaned.

"I want to be gone from here before the charming assembly sleeping nearby notice it was just us in this room. You were not really…quiet," Louis chuckled. "Besides, we have a potential enemy coming at us," he added seriously.

Understanding the threat, Selen gave up arguing. He got up, got dressed, and packed. They slipped outside the silent inn and made for the stables. No one was to be seen. They fixed the bridles and saddles, attached the bags, and pulled gently on the bits to move the horses to the porch. Once outside, they got on their horses. Selen realized that this was going to be a long day.

The way leading south was still clear of people. "I see you do not hide under your hood anymore," Louis said.

"Considering all you have seen of me, a hood would be a bit pointless." Selen flushed.

"But why did you hide? You are a bit different, but you are no monster."

"You would be surprised to know that you are the first one to think that way," Selen responded. He would nearly thank Louis for that, for bringing him the warmth and comfort he had so much longed for. Yet, pity was the last thing he wanted of him.

"You mean that your look is unusual in the Frozen Mountains as well?" Louis asked.

"I had to live in the wilderness," Selen answered. His mouth twitched. He hoped it was the last question.

"I'm sorry."

And there it came. To be seen as a victim irritated him. All he did was to survive. He had no choice. The world hated him, and he had been unable to adapt, partly because he was useless, and partly because he refused to be someone else. "Please, don't be. I don't want…"

"Commiseration?" Louis said. "What would you say my life was in Neolerim?"

Selen had thought about it a bit. With his beautiful look, Louis must have had an intrepid life in a rich world full of pleasures. Until last night, Selen would have added a world with women. Now, he considered it less probable. Only the fact that he was an archivist had given Selen a little hope to get his attention. Archivists were usually calm and austere. "I would say, popular."

Louis laughed. "Do you see me as a brat? I could take it as an insult."

Selen was relieved to have guessed wrong. "No, I prefer you as an archivist."

"Please, stop. I don't need your commiseration," Louis said. They both grinned. Louis closed his eyes and put a fist to his chest. He grimaced with pain.

"Louis? Is something wrong?" Selen stopped his horse and laid a hand on his friend's arm.

"I can feel him now," Louis said. "He's probably coming right at us."

"Should we ride straight to him, or should we plan something?" Selen inquired.

"What do you propose?"

"I can follow the road through the bushes. If it's someone on their own, I may surprise him."

"You may. If it's someone on their own," Louis stressed. "What if it's a group?"

"I thought you were good at fighting," Selen exclaimed, joking. He turned his head to Louis and smiled. "I am good at hunting." He attached his reins to Louis's saddle, dismounted, and disappeared through the thickets.

Selen made his way through the copses, always keeping an eye on the road. Fortunately, the bushes were thick enough for him to hide, but not enough to prevent him from passing through or under. He felt that they were drawing near. He heard a shout coming from the road. Selen climbed up a tree and moved closer for a better view. A hooded man stood on the side of the road with a bow in his hand. Selen saw that the man had not pulled the bow string.

"Tell me who you are and where your friend is," the man said. Selen crawled silently on the branch to move even closer.

"I travel alone," Louis answered.

"Don't take me for a fool," the man snapped back. "Who would travel with two saddled horses? And you still haven't answered my question." The man's fingers twitched on the string.

Holding on to the branch, Selen swung his body down and fell on the man's back, blocking him between his legs. The hooded man landed heavily on the ground. He twisted onto his back but froze when Selen pressed his dagger against his chin.

"Show yourself!" Selen ordered. The man pushed his hood back, revealing a young face behind shaggy, long, brown hair. Selen could not help but notice that he had the largest blue eyes he had ever seen. It gave the man a mischievous but cordial look.

"Will you hurt me?" the man asked. He looked at Selen's hair. "What a peculiar hair color."

The man's remark threw Selen off-balance for a moment. "We won't hurt you if you tell us why you attacked us," Selen said.

"I felt you come my way. It was just a precaution. I can explain, or maybe you can."

Louis joined them, his sword pointed at the man. "Do you have a horse?" his friend asked.

"I left it by the river. I can show you the way," the man answered.

Selen lowered his dagger and got up. He held out his hand to the man, who grabbed it. Selen pulled him up onto his feet.

They walked together to a quiet place along a river and sat down on the grass while the horses grazed a few yards away.

"You felt us come your way?" Louis asked.

"Yes, it sounds ridiculous, I know," the man responded, massaging his back.

"We felt you too," Selen said.

"So I'm not crazy," the man exclaimed. "Do you dream too?"

Selen nodded. "Yes. Can you tell us a bit more about you? Where are you from?"

"I am a fisherman from Kilcairn in the Windy Isles, but I sold my boat to make this journey," the man said with sorrow. "Where are you from?"

"I am from the Frozen Mountains," Selen answered. "There is a weird question I would like to ask you. Do you have amnesia?"

"It is not a weird question. I suppose that, if you ask, it means that you have it too. I woke up four years ago on the beach with no memory of my past. For reasons I can't explain, I felt secured near the sea. So I walked to the closest haven and searched for work. I found some on the docks. I unloaded ships until I could afford to rent my own boat."

"Do you have a family?" Louis asked.

"No. I lived a solitary life between my boat and my cabin." Selen could understand the sadness on the man's face. They all had lived alone.

"And then you have the dreams," Selen said kindly.

The man nodded. "Two months ago, the dreams compelled me to travel. I had an uneventful journey, though I think I was lucky."

"How so?" Louis asked.

"I walked across the northern border of the Ebony Forest. I had heard from tales that it was enchanting, so I was curious. Still, the place was gloomy and unsafe, and I got a strange feeling that something watched me."

"Something you could see?" Selen asked.

The man shook his head.

"What do we call you?" Louis asked.

"My name is Lissandro," the man said, "but you may call me Lilo." He smiled.

"My name is Selen, and this is Louis," he said and nodded towards Louis. "I'm confused, Lilo. You say you have dreams. Do you mean nightmares?" Selen asked. "I have only seen monsters, and Louis has even seen dragons."

"Actually, I think it's neither," Lissandro answered. "I think it is visions."

"You mean that what you see, or what we see, is real?" Louis asked.

"I think it is, yes. For example, I didn't know your faces, but I knew you were two. This is why I waited for you on the road. I was afraid you would try to kill me," Lissandro told them. "As for the monsters and the dragon you think you saw, Louis, I have heard tales about them," he carried on. "Some refugees came my way as well. Some talked nonsense, but many of them mentioned ugly beasts coming from the woods and attacking villages. I think that at least this part is true. Then, one refugee told me that he met a man coming from the south who pretended to have seen a dragon, but the refugee had called him a liar."

They all stayed silent for a while. Selen looked at Louis, who frowned, his eyes fixed on the ground. If Lissandro was right, they faced great danger. What was their role in it anyway? He felt the cool grass through his fingers and looked up. The sky was pure blue. The warm rays from the spring sun caressed his face. Could there really be a war going on nearby?

"Why us? What do we have in common?" Louis asked, eventually.

"Well, we are men. At first look, we are around the same age. We all suffer from amnesia, but I don't have arabesque tattoos on my forehead." Lissandro smirked, looking at Selen.

"Wait," Selen interjected. "We have had amnesia for four years now, right? What happened four years ago?"

"The death of King Wymar Lambelin," Louis answered, "and the beginning of the war in Trevalden."

A silence fell. Even the forest had turned quiet.

"It means this is our destiny," Selen said. Mixed feelings grew inside him. He felt the weight of responsibility on his shoulders for something he still could not explain. Yet, he was excited that his life had finally moved forward.

"So we should go south," Louis said. "Lilo, do you have visions about it? Something that could help us?"

"Actually, I have," Lissandro answered. "There is another reason why I did not meet you at the inn. I have had visions about some kind of giant ritual stone the first inhabitants of Trevalden used to worship their gods. This is where I had intended to go before I felt you. I think that there may be something there for us."

"What do you think, Louis?" Selen asked. He was ready to go south, but he would not take the risk to voice his opinion before hearing his friend's. Going south was one thing, going south alone was completely different.

"We have no choice," Louis said, resolute. "It is our call. It means that, one way or another, something in the future will depend on our actions. It is war. We may die. But if we don't go, it may turn worse."

"That sounds reassuring," Lissandro said sarcastically. "Anyway, I'm in."

"I'm coming too," Selen said.

"We should keep moving," Lissandro said, "and preferably not on the road. It may be hard for the horses to cut across the woods, but it will be safer. Who knows what we will meet on our way from now on."

They got up and went to their horses. Selen looked back at the glade where they had sat. He tried to perceive a remnant of the last carefree moment he had had a few minutes ago, but the feeling was gone. He understood with melancholy that spring was over for him.

The three riders followed each other. Lissandro led the way, Selen rode at the rear. Lissandro had been right; it was not easy to go over the rocks and thick roots with the horses. He tried to get his bearings with the help of the river and landmarks in sight. Yet, they had to make detours where the vegetation was too dense. He could feel his horse stagger on dead branches. If they kept on like this, he would soon need to dismount and test the ground first. It would mean a big loss of time. Concentrating on the difficult terrain, Lissandro had been disoriented and the river had vanished from his sight. He had already lost his way two times, but, afraid to worry his companions, he had not mentioned it. Now, Lissandro was growing anxious. He rode straight to the east in hopes of finding the stream. Fortunately, the river had grown into a torrent, and the noise had been easy to track.

They followed the water downstream for a while. Large, slippery stones that were covered with moss stood on each side. It only made the current stronger.

"Do we have to find a ford to cross the stream?" Louis asked.

"I don't think it is necessary right now," Lissandro said. "We won't reach the stone before tomorrow. I was thinking we could find a place near the water to spend the night, unless you prefer to camp on the other side in the middle of the forest."

"No, we can just as well stay near the stream. We can take advantage of the rest of the day to find some food and build a fire," Louis said.

A little further down, they found a nice place that was not wet or damp. There was even a large, flat stone where they could build a fire safely.

"This place looks perfect," Lissandro said.

They dismounted, took the saddles off their horses, unlaced their bags, and formed a circle with their belongings.

"I can search for wood," Louis proposed.

"If you let me borrow your bow, Lilo, I will try to find us some rabbits. These woods are full of life," Selen said.

"Well, it's yours." Lissandro gave the bow to Selen. "I will see if I can find something in the river."

Selen and Louis went on their way into the forest while Lissandro took one of his arrows and checked the stream. The water was crystal clear. He could see small fishes and snails but nothing edible. The time passed and, empty-handed, he made it to the reeds where a swamp stood.

Once he had found some food, Lissandro walked back to their bags. Louis was the first to come back to the bivouac. His arms were full of dry wood. He placed the heap to the side and put fire to some twigs with a fire steel.

"Did you find us some food?" Louis asked him.

"I have," Lissandro answered, "but it's a bit, um, hopping and slimy. Let's hope Selen had better luck than me." He patted his wet bag and sat closer to the fire. Selen came out of the forest, holding two fat rabbits on his back.

"I knew you would come back with something juicy," Lissandro said, taking the rabbits from his companion.

"I'm sorry I didn't find a third," Selen said. "I am exhausted. I think I will go for a dip in the river." He searched for something in his bags.

"The water is ice-cold," Lissandro said, raising an eyebrow.

"And I stink of sweat like a skunk," Selen carried on, laughing. "I'm from the Frozen Mountains. The water can't be colder here."

"Well, I don't really smell better," Lissandro said. "I will come with you. As long as I don't need to bathe my whole body in it."

"Go first, I will rub the horses down and prepare the meat in the meanwhile," Louis said.

Lissandro and Selen headed to the water.

"What have you got in your hand?" Lissandro asked.

"Soap," Selen answered, cheerfully. "I used to make it myself with my ewes' milk, some herbs, and honey. You want to share it?"

"I'd love to," Lissandro said, smiling back.

They found a nice place where the water was deep enough and the current not too strong. Selen took his clothes off. Lissandro watched him and turned around briskly.

"I think I will bathe over there," he said, trying to hide his uneasiness.

A few yards away, he undressed. He put one foot into the water and felt like he'd been hit by thousands of spears. Gathering his courage, he walked into the water until it reached to his waist. He had not bathed since the last inn he had visited, and he couldn't even remember how many days ago that was. Small fishes swam around him. Their scales glittered. It made him think of his boat. He knew he had made the best decision. Still, it had been four years of his life, and he had liked his work. He missed the sea, but it was wrong. If he wanted to complete this quest, he could not allow himself to be nostalgic.

He felt a light tap on his shoulder. Selen knelt beside him with his clothes on and his hair soaking wet.

"You still stink," he said, smiling. "Here, take my soap. I will go back to the fire. Don't be too long."

Lissandro thanked him and watched him go. He found it hard to understand how someone could be so joyful in times like these. Maybe it was a hell to live in the Frozen Mountains.

Clean and still wet, Lissandro came back to the bivouac. The fire gleamed orange, bright in the twilight. It warmed him and dried his clothes. The meat smelled delicious, making his belly rumble. He sat down between his companions.

"Do you want to try some of your frogs?" Louis proposed. He handed him what looked like frog legs. "They are excellent. Selen had some herbs to season them." Lissandro took the legs and chewed the meat off the bones.

"You said that when you crossed the Ebony Forest, you felt watched. Do you know what it was?" Selen asked him, gnawing at a rabbit leg.

"I saw nothing, but I felt as if a dark and evil presence was there. I can't explain it well. People of the Windy Isles used to tell tales about the Ebony Forest. That it was once a place filled with magic and beautiful creatures. Some kind of humans who had adapted to their environment, who could live in harmony with nature. They had built their houses in the trees, using wood, leaves, and moss. Some parts were even carved in the stone. Legends say that you can see ruins of it, if you're lucky."

"It sounds enchanting," Selen said, dreamily.

"But it was a long time ago," Lissandro carried on. "The people of the forest have disappeared, but I thought that the woods would look dead and monotonous, not …evil."

"The Ebony Forest is not far from here. Let's hope that what lurks inside does not creep into these parts," Louis said.

"We should set watch," Lissandro suggested. "Louis, you can start. Then Selen. I'll take the last shift."

Lissandro took his blanket and, followed by Selen, found a place between the fire and the river where they could lie down. Lissandro stretched on his blanket and prepared himself to sleep.

He wanted to scream but he could not. The shadow grew nearer. He heard the wicked laughs come out of it. A pale, bony hand stretched from the darkness and tried to grab his arm.

"Wake up, Lilo. It's your turn."

He turned around abruptly. Selen stood over him. "Did you have a nightmare?" Selen asked softly.

"Yes. Thank you for waking me up," Lissandro responded.

Lissandro got up and sat near the glowing embers while Selen prepared himself to go to sleep. He lay down on his resting place near Louis, and after a while, Lissandro heard him snore faintly, indicating he was asleep.

The fire had died out, but the warmth was still there. The dream had left Lissandro with a bad taste in his mouth. He shivered. Sometimes, he wished that these visions didn't mean anything. Now that some had proven to be true, he feared the worst. His companions looked brave, but they had not seen what he had. The dragon was only the tip of the iceberg. What lay beneath was even more frightening.

To clear his head, he checked for the horses. All three were under the trees. He heard them snore. They slept so peacefully. He kept on walking, first along the border of the forest, listening to the owls, then up the river side. The air was moist but not too cold, and the moon was shining. A regular night during spring. He passed in front of his companions, trying not to wake them up. He stopped. They lay near each other, wrapped up in their blankets, but a side of the cloth had slipped down. Lissandro smiled at their entwined hands. For the first time in four years, he felt less lonely. He went back to the dead fire and warmed his hands above the embers. Over him, the dark blue sky was streaked with gold. Dawn was coming.

The birds were chanting. The three men saddled their horses, rolled up their blankets, and packed their bags.

"If we ride fast, it shouldn't take the whole day to get there," Lissandro said.

They found a ford a bit lower down the stream. They crossed the river and headed through the forest. That side of the river was easier for the horses. The trees grew strong and broad, their foliage letting the sunbeams pass through. Yet, no sign of a stone.

"I don't want to alarm you, but shouldn't we be heading south?" Selen asked. "I have had the sun on my back for some time now."

"I know. I said south this morning, but I can feel we are going in the right direction. It shouldn't be long now," Lissandro answered.

The large trees spaced out, giving more place for sunlight to warm the earth. The air, which in the moisture of the morning had smelled of humus and decomposing leaves, felt lighter. Here and there stood carved stones with symbols emerging from the ground. He only discerned the top of the sculptures through the vegetation, but he knew that they approached a spiritual ground.

It appeared in front of them. It was more than the big rock Lissandro had seen in his visions. In the middle of a glade, many stones stood together, forming what could be a vault or a gigantic table. He could not say if it had been built by men or if it was a result of nature. The grass had grown wild around the base, and moss covered most of the structure. Earth had piled up against the north side and formed a slope to the top.

"It's a dolmen," Louis exclaimed.

"It's beautiful," Selen said. "I have never seen anything like this. Did people build it?"

"A long time ago, the people living on this land used to worship gods connected to nature. They used these stones as an altar to perpetrate rituals or celebrate rites. They would offer food or sacrifice animals to their gods," Louis explained.

"Did they also sacrifice people?" Selen asked.

"It wasn't the norm, but I guess, yes," Louis said.

"Let's have a look at it," Lissandro said. He dismounted and approached the stone. The others did the same. They spread out and explored the stone in search of some symbols that could prove helpful.

"There were writings on the plates on this side, but it has faded with time," Lissandro noticed. He scratched the moss off the rock with his nails, revealing the shape of old runes.

"Do you know what we are supposed to do?" Louis asked. He was scraping with his dagger in an interstice between the plates. "It seems to be solid stone."

"Come over here!" Selen shouted from the top of the structure.

Lissandro and Louis climbed the slope and joined him.

"This is a drain. It stretches on the whole length of the stone. And here, look, it looks like stains of blood," Selen said, pointing at a gutter covered with brown marks.

They followed the drain up to a rectangular stone, standing on the highest point of the structure. They brushed the leaves, scraped the moss, and pulled out the weeds to clear it. The top was curved, like a recipient.

"It was probably made to contain the blood of the victims," Lissandro said.

"And I think it's precisely what we should do," Louis said.

"Kill an animal?" Selen asked.

"Give our blood," Louis answered. "Let's make a fire."

They gathered some dead branches and made a fire on top of the structure. Lissandro drew out his knife and passed it through the flames. They moved to the altar and sat in a circle around it. With the blade of the knife, Lissandro cut through the palm of his hand. Blood flowed out of the open flesh. He held his hand over the stone and gave the knife to Selen, who did the same. Then, it was Louis's turn. The drops of their blood blended in the shallow recipient. Once it was full, the blood overflowed and ran down the drains on the side, onto the stone.

The edifice quaked. Lissandro heard the noise of a heavy stone door opening. They looked at each other.

"Did that come from under us?" Lissandro asked.

They got up and ran down the slope. Where one of the plates had been, now stood a deep, dark hole. The air coming from it smelled putrid. Lissandro tried to see something gleam, but the hole was pitch black.

"We should probably take a torch…and mend our wounds first," Selen said. "I'm still pouring blood everywhere."

They put some clean cloth around their cuts and a rag around a stick that they lit in the fire. Lissandro was first to go through the gaping hole. He ran one of his hands against the wall, while the other hand held the torch. Water dripped down the slimy wall. Its texture gave Lissandro the impression that he was running his fingers through a sea of slugs. The way was going down. He felt a slippery stair under his boots. The tunnel was narrow and warm.

"Maybe someone should have stayed outside in case the door closes itself again," Selen said.

"It's a bit late for that, don't you think, Selen?" Lissandro groused. "We already can be happy if nothing comes rushing at us the other way. It's narrower than a cellar stair. Wait! I see something."

Lissandro saw a glimpse of light in front of him. He stumbled on the bottom step of the staircase. "Stop. There is something," he said. His hand felt a crook with a torch on it. He lit it.

The walls opened on to a round cave without apertures. Right in front of them stood three pedestals, each supporting an armour. Lissandro passed the torch in front of them. "They are splendid," he whispered. Selen approached and stretched out his arm. Delicately, he laid his fingers on the massive armour standing in the middle, tracing the shapes of the minutely carved decorations.

"Wait… This one is…mine," he whispered.

"We haven't discussed it yet, but you can have it if you want," Louis responded, checking the wall on the other side of the cave. "It's too shiny for me anyway, too much gilt."

"No, I mean," Selen pursued, "I know this armour. It's mine. At least, it was. When I was…" He paused. "I remember!" Selen screamed. "I was a knight. A knight of the royal guard. Louis, I remember!" He cried out in joy. Lissandro ran to him, soon joined by Louis.

"What do you remember, Selen? Tell us," they both said, full of hope.

"I was a knight of the guard," Selen said. "There were fights, soldiers fighting, everywhere. I can't see well… I see fire. The palace was under attack. I see blood, people dying around me. I…died." He stopped, shocked. "I am dead." Selen looked at Lissandro in disbelief and then at Louis. "I am dead," he repeated.

7

"I am dead," Selen murmured. Tears ran down his cheeks. He remembered now. Flashes of memories rushed to his mind. After days of siege, the enemies had finally invaded the palace. They had massacred the king. As a member of the royal guard, it had been his duty to protect the queen, but they had been outnumbered, and he had been killed. Everyone had been slaughtered. He had failed, and he thought he remembered why. But that was too much to endure for now.

Selen felt his legs weaken. He thought he would fall when he felt a hand grab him gently by the wrist.

"I can assure you that you're not dead," Louis whispered. "Not one of us is. We bleed, we feel."

"I know what I saw. It happened," Selen said. He turned his tearful face to Louis, who gave him a hug.

"If what you saw was for real, it would mean that you survived, or that it happened in another life," Lissandro suggested. "With all that has happened to us, I am ready to believe in anything. Maybe we will get answers, somehow."

"We should have found some here," Louis said. "But now we are left with even more questions."

"Well, we needed equipment. Here it is." Lissandro gestured towards the armours.

Selen felt that Lissandro tried to stay positive, but he detected fear in his voice.

If he was dead, or had been killed, probably his companions had been too. Yet, he had no right to drag them down with him. He needed to calm down. It was true enough that he still had a body of flesh and blood. He dried his tears with the back of his hand.

"We should try out the armours," Selen said. "Which one do you want?"

There were two other suits of armours beside his old one. One looked to be made of adamantine. The whole armour was finely decorated with arabesques, and a large tree was embossed on the breastplate. There were also two pairs of imbricated pauldrons, making the highest part of the armour look huge. The large tassets, completed with chain mail, unfolded like superposed scales.

"Take it, Louis," Lissandro said. "You two seem stronger and taller than me. You should take the heavy armours. I will gladly take that one," he added, turning to the third one.

It consisted of a chain mail of high-quality steel, with inlaid protections for the arms, encrusted pauldrons, and a short breastplate. It did not mismatch the other two and was definitely made for an archer.

The armours fitted their proportions perfectly. Selen searched for signs of damage that could have occurred during what he now called his *previous life*. Strangely, there was nothing to be seen, not a single spot. Once clad, they got out of the cave. The rays of sunshine reflected on the armours like on a mirror. There was no sign of rust or even dust on them. It was like they had been placed there right before their arrival.

"We have no helmets. We will have to be careful during close fights," Louis said.

"Which way should we take now, Lilo?" Selen asked.

Lissandro turned to him. "I have no idea. I only saw this place. I guess that now that we are ready for battle, if I dare say, we could head east."

"East? I thought the war was down south?" Louis said.

"I want to avoid the Ebony Forest. We will go east and then turn south," Lissandro said.

"It sounds fine," Selen said.

"For me too," Louis added.

They put their cloaks in their bags and got on their horses. Selen noticed that the sky had turned a heavy grey with ragged, black clouds. The wind was blowing colder. He hoped it would not rain.

"Look up!" Louis shouted. Selen looked at the sky again. There was smoke rising from afar, too much smoke for a campfire.

"What do you think it is?" he asked.

"I don't know, but I don't like it. Something is burning," Louis answered.

"We should hurry," Lissandro said. "There may be people injured."

"Stop!" Louis called out. "Listen to me. This is exactly what we shouldn't do—run towards danger like it was a game or sport. It's not because we have armour that we are indestructible. Whatever we do, we plan it. We will go that way, analyze the situation, and act accordingly, because the last thing we want is to be hurt because of foolish actions. Agreed?"

Selen nodded. Though he agreed entirely with Louis, Selen was taken aback. It was the first time he had heard Louis speak that way. His voice had been clear and firm, as if he had talked to a troop and not to his two companions. Selen wondered if Louis had been aware of it, or if it had come as a reflex.

They followed Louis's recommendations and approached the place quietly. Two houses located at the border of the village were burning. They heard men and women scream, but no children. They were too far away to hear what was being said. Nasty looking men in leather outfits ran in every direction, some with swords in their hands, some with goods that they packed in bags. They saw a few villagers being harassed by the looters but no dead bodies.

"How many armed men do you count, Selen?" Louis asked him.

"I can see five. But there may be more somewhere else, or inside the houses. What should we do?" Selen whispered.

"You take the three on your left, and I'll take the two on the right—these ones look nastier. Lilo, you cover us with your arrows in case there are more. There are no bodies. It means the outlaws are mainly here to steal and not to raze the village. They may run away, or not," Louis told them. "Let's move, now."

They came out of the forest unnoticed. Everyone in the village was too preoccupied to look in their direction. Selen watched Louis go to his two who were busy loading a cart near a house. Louis surprised one of the bandits and cut through his chest with his blade. As he headed to the second one, a man waving an axe rushed out of the house. He was hit in the throat by one of Lissandro's arrows. Louis turned around again and ran his sword through the other man's belly as the bandit reached for a dagger. The men's agonizing screams had drawn the attention of more outlaws, who now advanced towards them. Without a sign of fear or hesitation, Louis faced the small group and attacked the first man with a thrust towards the legs. Blood gushed out of his thighs. Shrieking with pain, the outlaw stumbled and threw his sword forward in a desperate attempt. Louis sidestepped and cut the bandit's head neat. He paused. The next man engaged. Louis blocked the blow, flipped his sword, and pushed it through the second man. He looked around. The last two outlaws had been hit by arrows.

Selen, who had watched, petrified, decided to move. He headed left to the three men scavenging in the backyard of a house. They were busy plucking cabbages. He sneaked behind the nearest one and knocked him out with the pommel of his sword. As he was ready to attack the next one, the man knelt down.

"Please. Have pity, my lord," the man begged.

Selen held his blow. The third bandit took advantage of the situation to slip away. Selen did not know what to do with the man in front of him. He definitely could not kill an unarmed man, especially if the latter begged for his life.

"Spare my wretched life and the one of my friend. Look! He is unconscious. I can drag him on my back and disappear," the man said. "I swear you will never see me again."

Selen sighed and gave up. He made a sign to the man that he could fetch his friend and flee with him. The bandit did not hesitate. He picked up the unconscious man and ran away through the bushes.

Relieved that he had not needed to spill blood, Selen went back to the main road. Louis stood over the corpses, examining them.

"Selen, are you all right? Did you take care of your men?" Louis asked. He fumbled in a bag and took out a purse of coins. He threw it in again and let the bag fall to the ground.

"I did. I let them go," Selen said. He was sure that he had made the best decision.

Louis froze and looked at him with an ice-cold gaze. "You did what?" Louis's voice was more than threatening. It sounded deadly.

For the first time since his journey had begun, Selen felt fear. "I... I just..." he stuttered.

He saw Louis's expression change. "I am sorry, Selen. I didn't want to sound like that. Forgive me," Louis said, confused. "I know you are full of compassion, and I do admire you for that, but this is war. We can't let enemies flee if we don't want them to come back later in a larger number. These men had burned houses and would not have hesitated to kill villagers," he explained.

Selen saw that Louis tried hard to keep calm. If he was mad at him, at least he struggled to hide it. Selen realized that he had probably been wrong in letting the men go, but what pained him more was to have disappointed his friend. He felt ashamed and looked away.

"It's all right, Selen," Louis insisted, a hand on his shoulder. This time, Selen saw that his companion meant it. He smiled timidly.

Lissandro was joining them when they heard men come from the other side of the village. They discerned cries of joy and laughter. The villagers moved towards them.

"Thank you, my dear lords!" the big man leading the group burst out cheerfully. "You have saved our village!"

Selen could not avoid noticing that the man was one head taller than all of them and probably twice the weight of Lissandro. Yet, he congratulated them as if they were heroes.

"We only killed a few bandits," Lissandro said.

"Those few bandits, as you said, had ransomed the village for days. Today, they had decided to come for a raid. Thanks to you, no one got killed," the big man added. He turned to the villagers behind him and shouted, "I think these pretty lords deserve some drinks on the house! What do you think, guys?"

His proposition was welcomed by a cheerful roar from the crowd.

"Our horses are still in the forest," Selen managed to say.

"We will take care of them, my lord. Patrick, fetch the horses!" the man yelled.

Selen and his companions were dragged into the local tavern. The place was surprisingly big, like a barn, and even more astonishingly, clean. Tables and benches were arranged in rows, and a plain, wooden bar stood on one side. Massive wagon-wheel chandeliers hung from the ceiling, spreading a bright, yellow light in the room. The place rapidly packed with what looked like the whole population of the village. The atmosphere became bawdy, and songs were sung. The crowd forgot about them eventually, and they enjoyed some moments of peace.

"There is a room there, down the hall. We can have it for the night," Lissandro told them. He was back from the bar with beer mugs in each hand, and he placed one in front of each of them. Selen looked at his mug with suspicion. "You can drink it, it's just beer." Lissandro laughed.

"I don't usually... Well, I've never sat in a tavern like this," Selen said. Neither did he recall the last time he had drunk alcohol. He regretted he had no cloak to hide under. He felt too visible in his shiny armour. It was not even spotted with blood like Louis's.

"Then let's celebrate it," Lissandro said. Louis looked at Selen and smiled, but he stayed silent.

They enjoyed a few drinks and listened to the music. Selen felt the alcohol warm his body. He could still appreciate carefree moments, after all.

"I think I will check the horses," Lissandro said, "before I get drunk." He grinned. He rose and pushed his way through the crowd.

Louis turned to Selen. "Come," he said with a look that made Selen blush.

Selen followed him through the hall, to the room that the owner had left for them. It looked more like a warehouse than a room, but there were beds and it was warm. Selen felt an arm around his waist and was pushed against the door. Louis kissed him passionately, pinning him against the wood.

"I've missed your touch," Louis sighed. Selen felt a warmth spread from his cheeks to his loins.

"Me too," Selen said, overwhelmed by feelings he still could not explain. He hugged Louis and ran his fingers through his long, wild hair. The smell of his friend's skin reminded Selen of the scent of wood violet blended with a light odor of sweat. "Take me," Selen whispered into Louis's ear, his face beaming.

They struggled to remove their armours. It was a meticulous task, and haste did not make it easier. The metal plates fell down on the floor with a clunk. Selen's febrile hands were slow at unlacing the straps. Louis was more conscientious and was the first out of his armour. He came to Selen and helped him to undress. His friend's hands slipped under his clothes, rubbed his chest, and pulled the tunic over his head. Louis's hands cupped Selen's hips, his blue eyes staring at him. Shame invaded Selen's body when Louis tugged at the laces of his pants. Afraid that his friend saw his arousal, Selen pushed back Louis's hands clumsily.

"Oh, I'm sorry," Louis said, taking a step back. "I'm so rude." His friend removed his own clothes instead.

Selen gazed at him. At the inn, Selen had seen Louis in the light of the moon. The shadows had hidden most of his body from Selen's sight. Now that he saw him in the last rays of daylight, Selen realized how gorgeous he was. His skin was smooth and pale, except for the dark hair on his groin. He was slim, with barely shadows of muscles, thus accentuating his marked hips and sharp collarbones. Selen looked down at Louis's loins and thought that he probably should not have felt ashamed of his own state. He even felt a bit thrilled to be the cause of such turmoil in Louis. He was lost in the contemplation of his friend until he realized that he was the one being rude. Selen removed his pants. He did not try to hide himself anymore.

Louis took his hand and led him onto the bed, where he knelt, inviting Selen to sit in front of him. The grip on his hand made Selen understand that his friend, though calm, was eager. Selen sat and stretched his legs on each side of Louis's waist. The tips of Selen's fingers brushed Louis's chest. The light touch turned into caresses. Selen felt highly aroused and dizzy at the same time and dared to touch Louis in ways he usually would blush from. He thought that it was probably thanks to the alcohol. Selen looked at Louis's mouth. He had wanted to kiss it so many times during the day. Now, it was all his. He grabbed Louis's soft, plump lips with his. Louis kissed him back, keeping Selen's mouth open. His heart beat fast. Selen was about to suffocate, yet he would not break the kiss, and allowed Louis's tongue to plunge deeper. Louis's short nails scratched his back.

"You're so beautiful," his friend whispered. Selen did not realize at once that Louis talked of him. According to everyone, he was but a freak with pale skin.

Louis's mouth grasped his neck, biting gently at it. He lowered his head and reached for Selen's left nipple, playing with it with his tongue until it turned hard. Selen quivered and moaned softly. His friend's luscious mouth could awaken sensations in his flesh that he would never have fancied. The last time must have been his first. Selen knew how to release such tension from his body, but he had never imagined it could feel that way. Should he had ever experienced such pleasure, he guessed he would have remembered it. Selen arched backwards as Louis's hands ran down his back to his bottom. This part had been painful, however, and he was apprehensive to live it again. Selen's fingers clenched on the sheets. The feeling of Louis's fingers pushing their way in was still odd, nearly invasive. Still, though he needed time to adapt, he liked it, and the effects of alcohol on his mind helped. As Louis twitched his fingers, something exploded in Selen. His hips jerked, and he melted with pleasure. He looked down but he was still excited.

"What was that?" he whispered, gaping.

Louis only smiled at him. Selen held his breath as Louis grabbed Selen's cheeks and carefully pulled Selen onto him. This time, Selen felt a little less pain. He tried to relax. Louis buried his face against his chest. His friend, too, needed to calm down. The pain did not last. Selen let himself fall slowly backwards on the bed. His lilac hair spread out on the covers in long arabesques. Closing his eyes in ecstasy, he let his body move as if thrust by waves on water. Under his feeble moans, he heard Louis breathe hard. Selen barely noticed the door open behind them.

"Are you out of your mind?" Lissandro exclaimed. Selen awoke to reality in an instant. His naked body was covered by a blanket that Louis threw at him.

"The door was unlocked," Lissandro hissed through his teeth. He bolted the door behind him. "Beyond that door, there is not a single person who wouldn't kill you for this," Lissandro said, pointing at the door. "In their eyes, such inclination makes us even more disgusting than orcs." Selen and Louis looked down. The sad, angry look on their faces showed that they knew it too well. Lissandro calmed down. "Anyway, don't stop for me. I was going to sleep," Lissandro said, giving a faint smile. "The horses are fine."

Selen watched Lissandro sit down on the bed on the other side of the room, facing the wall. The blanket was pulled off his body. Louis's firm hands raised his hips up again. Selen bit his own lower lip as his friend took him ardently.

Selen woke up. A pale ray of moon lit the room. It was still night outside. The mattress of hay under him was soft, and Louis's touch was warm. He thought of getting back to sleep when he heard someone cry. He was certain that it came from Lissandro's bed. Delicately, he moved Louis's head and arm from his chest, trying not to wake him up. He pulled back the blankets and climbed out of the bed. Lissandro lay on the side under his blankets, facing the wall. Selen lay down beside him and hugged Lissandro's shoulder.

"Why do you cry?" he whispered gently.

"I want to remember," Lissandro muttered. "I need to. I know there is something important I should do. It came to my mind when I looked at you."

"Is it because of the *us*?" Selen asked. He had not missed Lissandro's choice of word. He felt selfish to have showed so little consideration for Lissandro's feelings. They had travelled with him, but they had not cared to know more about him. Selen thought that he probably was not the only one to have had a hard time for four years. He did not know how he could relieve his friend's sadness. Comforting words could also open fresh wounds.

"It may," Lissandro said. "And you were right. We died. But I didn't die alone. I can't remember more right now."

"Whatever comes back to your mind, tell us. We will help. I promise you," Selen said. "We should try to sleep now. Tomorrow is a long day." Selen got up.

"Selen?" Lissandro whispered.

"Yes?"

"Thank you."

Selen patted Lissandro's shoulder. He went back to his bed and curled up himself against Louis. He guessed that there would not be many taverns on the way after this one. He was determined to enjoy the warmth of his friend's body as long as he could.

"To go south you need to cross the Strelm River," the villager said. "But it would be folly to go there. Not even refugees come from there anymore. Even us here in Baybarrow think of leaving our village. They're coming, you know."

"Who is coming?" Louis asked. Selen saw the disapproval on his friend's face. Louis was irritated to see all these people flee, but Selen understood that they were scared and only wanted to protect themselves. Still, he would not dare to say anything and stayed silent.

"Bandits, monsters, the dark things from the south," the villager answered. Selen noticed the man's inclination to exaggerate. Yet, he was frightened. It meant that there was indeed something coming this way.

"And how do we cross the river?" Selen asked.

"There is a ferry two days south from here. Everything else has been destroyed or burned down to keep this side safe," the man said.

"And at the same time condemning many refugees to stay on the other side," Selen said reproachfully.

The man grunted and went back into his house.

"Should we head south?" Selen asked. His horse pawed the ground. They had been standing in the middle of the village, questioning the inhabitants, hoping to find out more about the situation. All they had heard were rumours. No one had seen anything with their own eyes.

"I don't like it," Lissandro said. "If we follow the river southwest as he said, we will ride straight towards the Ebony Forest."

"It's the only path, and we have to face danger at some point," Louis said. "Let's go." They turned their horses' reins and rode towards the woods.

"I could put a hand on some bread and cheese," Lissandro said. "These people are in short supply of everything. I wonder what the bandits can still find here."

"People," Louis said gloomily. "When there is no more food or gold, they take the people. There is never a short supply of slaves."

"How do you know that?" Selen asked, troubled.

"The smugglers make them pass through the Iron Marches to the east lands. They never come back," Louis answered.

They reached the Strelm River in the afternoon. The river was broad. Only large ferries could cross such a flood. They rode along the shore. The sandy banks were covered with high grass and dead trunks. Pools of water lay here and there.

"Look," Lissandro murmured, pointing at the river. Selen saw dead bodies float among scraps. Something brown and big hit a stone and turned around, revealing the rear legs of what could have been a cow. They watched in silence and kept on moving. Selen realized that the corpses had come from upstream. It meant that the war had reached the north.

Big, dark clouds were gathering above their heads. It would rain soon. "Should we search for some shelter?" Lissandro asked.

"It doesn't look like there is anything around here, neither a house nor a farm. Only marshes and swamps," Selen observed.

"If travellers used to take a ferry, there must be a road and some buildings nearby. We should search for it," Louis said.

A few miles ahead, they came across a small road. They concluded that, as it ran along the river, it should lead to the ferry. They followed the path.

Uphill on the right, they saw a ruin. It could have been a stable or a shack, only three walls and a sloping roof stood left. Still, it was enough to protect them from the storm. As they dismounted and drew the horses under the roof, they heard the first raindrops hit the ground. They gathered in a corner and waited until the rain stopped.

"We will stay here for the night," Lissandro said. "Louis and I will go search for some dry wood while you guard the horses," Lissandro told Selen.

While his companions went on their way, Selen explored the place. The fourth wall of the house was only a heap of stone on the side, but smaller walls could have been remnants of other rooms or sheds. He found some objects, mostly rusty junk, and some animal bones. He turned around towards the main ruin. A noise came from the forest. Still, nothing was to be seen in the nearest bushes.

He headed back. As he came closer to the north wall, something hit his forehead. The blow made him turn and fall backwards. His head hurt. He was bleeding. Selen saw muddy sabatons stamp near his head. Strong hands grabbed his arms and pulled him up violently, crushing his wrists together. He was face-to-face with the ugliest creature he had ever seen. It was huge, with broad shoulders covered by black plates and straps of leather. Its skin looked like dried mud. Teeth pointed out from the cracked lips. Its nose was flat and broken in many places. Shiny, nasty, black eyes looked at him from under a protruding arch of eyebrows.

"Bring that thing to Xruul," the creature grunted. Though it could speak, the creature could not be human, or maybe it was a degenerate race riddled with diseases. Selen had read about leprosy, but these things still had all their limbs, and it would not explain their teeth. However, as they were armed and dressed, they could not be animals.

Selen was brutally pushed along the wall to the other side of the ruin. There stood a company of six of those creatures, all uglier than the other, but Selen recognized warriors when he saw them. One of them stepped forward. He was hairier than the others and had scars on his arms. He held a long, jagged sword in his left hand.

"What do we have here?" he spat.

Selen guessed the creature was the one named Xruul and was obviously their chief. Xruul raised his sword against Selen's face. One of the creatures tied Selen's hands with a rope in front of him, but Selen kept his eyes on the cold blade on his cheek. He sensed the blood clot on his forehead where he had been hurt. Though he was scared, he tried to hide it.

"It was behind the ruins," a voice behind him said. "It probably came with the horses. It looks fresh. Maybe it's tasty."

Selen smelled the creature's foul breath. He wondered with fright in which way he could be tasty. Did they plan to roast him?

"Not now," Xruul mumbled. "This one doesn't look like the others. Maybe we should bring it back to the camp." He sniffed at Selen's face, as he winced in disgust. "But indeed, it's fresh." Xruul slid a hand between Selen's legs, up against his crotch. Twisting his hips, Selen tried to free himself at once from the repulsive, obscene touch.

"Male," Xruul said, removing his hand. "Argh, it doesn't matter. It's ages since we have seen a village. This one will do. We can have some good time with it before we head back," the creature grinned. Selen heard the others cackle. He dreaded to understand their insinuations. It could not be true. It was not happening.

"Bend him over this dead trunk," he heard Xruul say.

No, it was happening. Selen was terrified. He searched everywhere for a glimpse of his companions. They must be around. He struggled under the grip of his captors, but the two creatures holding him were strong.

They dragged him to the log. One of the creatures pushed his back, and Selen fell on his knees. His hands were pulled hard forward from the other side of the tree, forcing him to stretch out on the trunk. Xruul bent over him, his weight crushing his back.

"Now, I'll enjoy this juicy creature. Then, it will be my men's turn," Xruul whispered in his ear. A long, stinking, wet tongue licked Selen's face, leaving drops of slime that dribbled on his cheek.

Selen wiggled to escape, but his hands and legs were held fast. Rage and hatred grew inside him. At that moment, he hated his own weakness. It was not him. He had been beaten up many times, but that could not be. Selen wanted to scream. Hands grabbed at his pants. He sensed something warm and sticky land on his face. He looked up.

The creature holding him had an arrow through his throat. Blood gushed from the wound. Selen could move his hands again. He threw himself forward, grabbed the dead creature's dagger, and cut his ties. He heard screams and shouts. Arrows flew over him. A severed head bounced against his feet. He looked up. Louis pulled his sword out of one of the creatures' thorax, pushing on the thing's belly with his foot.

Selen seized a sword from one of the corpses and made his way to Xruul. Some creatures tried to engage him, but he cleared them out with single, powerful counterstrikes. Xruul charged him recklessly, putting all his weight into his attack. Selen hopped to the right, parried his blow and the next one coming from the left. Xruul moved to the side and aimed for Selen's legs. Selen twisted backwards and jumped over the blade. He landed, a knee on the ground, and chopped Xruul's sword hand. The creature shrieked. Selen rose, looked into the eyes of Xruul with fury, and pushed his sword through his bowels. He pulled the sword out and hammered the creature's head with the pommel.

"I am not a victim!" Selen yelled, smashing Xruul's head into pulp.

"No, you're not!" Louis shouted at Selen angrily, seizing him by the shoulders. "You are a warrior, an excellent warrior. But you will be a victim if you don't start to fight back!"

"Let me go!" Selen yelled back and freed himself from Louis's grip. "I've seen what war does to men. I don't want to be full of hate!"

"You need hate to fight, but you must learn to canalise it," Louis said more calmly. "Not like that." He pointed at the mashed head. "You have to protect yourself. I need to know you will be all right." Selen felt the worry in his voice.

"Am I a burden?" Selen murmured, feeling sorry.

"Only if you don't react," Louis sighed. "Now, go see to the horses. We're leaving." He turned away and left.

Selen looked at the carnage around him. He had acted like a fool, not really aware that such things could happen. Once again, Louis was right. Selen was angry at himself. He had yelled at his friend, when Louis had only been worried about him. Without Louis and Lissandro, he would be seriously wounded by now.

He hurried to the ruins. His companions were saddling their horses. Selen touched Louis on the shoulder. His friend turned around.

"I'm sorry," Selen said, looking down. "Forgive me. I should not have yelled."

Louis put a hand against Selen's face. He smiled. "Come, we need to go."

"I've saddled your horse, Selen," Lissandro said with a friendly tone.

"Thank you." Selen got on his horse. They rode back to the road and trotted away.

"What were those things?" Selen asked.

"Orcs," Louis answered.

Selen shivered. So those creatures were orcs. If they were the same creatures that they saw in their dreams, then there were thousands of them waiting down south. "What were they doing so far up north?" he asked.

"The Ebony Forest. They are coming through it," Lissandro said. They all felt silent.

They arrived to where the ferry stood. They had departed from the ruin at dusk. It was pitch black now. They could only guess where they were by the shape of the cabin near the river.

"We better make no noise and no fire and wait until dawn. Let's hope they don't trace us here," Louis said. "Lilo, check the cabin," he demanded.

Lissandro opened the door of the shack and looked inside. "It's empty and large," he answered promptly.

"Good, put the horses in it. At least no one will hear them. We will sleep in front of the door and keep guard," Louis carried on.

Lissandro took the horses inside the cabin and closed the door. They gathered and sat in front of the door, swords in hand, ready to jump up and charge at the first suspicious sound. They barely slept at all that night.

Dawn came. The place where they had slept was half covered in the mist growing from the river. They still sat tucked against each other, their backs against the door of the cabin. Their swords had slipped out of their hands and lay on the ground between them.

Louis shook his companions. "Selen, Lilo, wake up." While his friends opened their eyes and stretched, Louis rose and looked around.

The ferry was a long platform of wood with strong metal rings attached on one side. It could be towed by a mechanism of pulleys and ropes passing through the metal rings and attached on the other bank of the river.

Louis gazed at the river. The trees on the shore on the other side were silhouetted through the thick, misty cloud. The distance seemed reasonable, but he was worried about the flood. The current looked strong. He hoped that the ferry would not shake too much during the crossing.

"Let's fetch the horses," he said, turning to his friends.

Lilo stood by the mechanism and controlled the ropes. He tugged at a rope, scratched a nail against it, and frowned. Louis did not like the look on Lissandro's face.

Selen still stood near the cabin and stared at the road. He turned, opened the door, and went in. He led the three horses out of the cabin and led two of them to the ferry with haste.

"Hurry!" Selen called out to them. He forced his horse to board the platform. "We need to go to the other side before more orcs find us."

"It won't work," Lissandro exclaimed. "We can't all go aboard the ferry with three horses. The rope won't hold."

"It must," Louis replied, walking towards Lissandro. "No one stays behind."

"I will," Lissandro said. He rose and looked at him. "Go first with Selen and your horses, then send the ferry back to me."

Louis hesitated, but he realized that Lissandro was right. The ferry was not strong or big enough to carry all of them. Selen's horse was heavy and large, and he barely managed to have both his and Louis's horse aboard. They had no choice. They needed the horses. Louis would have stayed behind, but he could not let Selen cross without him. He wanted to be there to protect him. His blood had run cold when he had seen his friend with the orcs last night. He would not let such a thing happen again. Selen had shown admirable capacities to fight, but he was still too imprudent. Yet, it pained Louis to leave Lissandro behind. He was his friend, too. Louis made up his mind. There was no time to ponder. They had to act now.

"All right," he sighed. "But you flee at the first sign of an orc. Don't let yourself get killed."

Lissandro nodded. Louis turned around and headed to the ferry.

"What is he doing?" Selen asked, checking the knots of the mounts' bridles to the stanchions. "Lilo!"

"He waits. We will send the ferry back once we are on the other side," Louis said, going aboard. Selen turned towards the shore.

"No, no... He is coming with us. We don't leave Lilo behind." Selen tried to go back to their friend, but Louis blocked him. "Louis, please." Selen's eyes were wide. Louis felt him tremble. "We can't. He is our friend."

"Selen. Look at the ferry. Look at the horses. There is no place." Selen looked around. The helplessness on his face showed that he understood. Selen shook his head in silence. "Help me pull the rope. We need to be quick," Louis insisted.

Lissandro stayed with his mount by the mechanism. They all heaved the ropes. The current was strong. The ferry shook in every direction. They held fast to not stumble or fall into the river. The horses were frightened and reared up. The crossing seemed to take ages, but finally, they made it to the other bank. They attached their horses to the nearest tree and ran back to send the platform back to Lissandro. They pulled with all their might on the rope. Under his gloves, Louis felt like his hands were on fire. Yet, the ferry was lighter and easier to move when it was empty.

Eventually, it hit the shore on the other side.

Lissandro took his horse by the bridle and got on board. Louis relaxed when he thought his friend was safe, and he slowed his efforts.

The platform had reached halfway through when a group of orcs appeared behind on the beach. Louis felt his heart beat faster, but he calmed down when he realized that nothing could happen now. Louis saw the orcs approach the shore and gesticulate to each other. He could not hear what they were saying. Though he believed the danger was over, Lissandro was still on the river. They needed him by their side. The orcs had bows, and their friend was still in the shooting range. He tried to pull harder at the rope, but his hands hurt. Even if he felt agony, he kept on trying. He saw the orcs move to the mechanism. Louis realized at once what was going to happen, but he refused to believe it. He opened his mouth to scream, but no sounds came out. One of the orcs drew his sword and cut the rope. Selen shouted next to him, and Louis joined his call.

"Grab the rope!" they both yelled to Lissandro. "Grab the rope!"

The rope snapped and jumped in the air like a giant snake. Lissandro plunged onto the deck, with the rope in his arms. The platform spun and shook. The horse, terrified, reared up. Lissandro tried to hold on the best he could, but the current was too strong, and he had to let go of the rope.

"No! Lilo!" Selen shouted.

Selen hurried down the bank into the water. As fast as he could, Louis ran after him and seized him hard against him.

"Don't jump into the water!" he yelled. "You will drown!"

Selen struggled, his arms still stretched out towards the ferry. With utter sadness, they watched their friend drift away with the river. Lissandro waved slowly at them as the mist closed around him.

Selen burst into tears. Louis pulled his friend up.

"Come. We can follow the bank," Louis said, dragging Selen by the arm.

The bank was a mix of old trunks, pools of water, and reeds. Louis saw that the horses would never make it, and they were forced to leave the mounts behind them. They ran through the high grass in loud splashes. Yet, the ground was so treacherous and boggy that they never managed to get close to the shore. Selen stumbled. Louis pulled him up and they kept on running. Louis's greaves turned heavier with each step in the mud. It was foolish. Besides, they could not see the river through the mist. Lissandro may as well be a long way downstream by now. If they kept on running forward, they would lose their way and may never find the horses again.

"Stop. It's useless," Louis said, short of breath and choking on his tears. He was angry at himself. It was his fault. He had left their friend behind, and now they had lost him.

Selen turned towards him. "We can't give up. We can't."

"We will find him. I promise you," Louis said with more anger in his voice than he would have wished. He should have listened to Selen. They should have left their friend's horse behind. It was too late now.

Slowly, Louis turned back to where they came. Selen pulled at his hand.

"You won't leave me, will you? Please, say you won't leave me." Selen looked at him with his swollen eyes. His cheeks were wet from tears.

Louis stared at Selen with disbelief. How could his friend think such a thing? He took Selen's face in his hands, his thumbs caressing his cheeks delicately. "I will never leave you. Ever. I swear it," he said, insisting on each word. Raising his head, he kissed Selen's forehead and hugged him fast until his friend had calmed down.

With cautious steps, they walked back through the bog towards their horses. They mounted and turned away from the Strelm River. The road called them.

Selen's tears had dried, but he still felt a knot in his throat. "How will we find Lilo? Should we follow the river with a detour?" Selen asked. Once again, he relied on Louis to find a rational solution to their problems. If he had been alone, he would probably be among the corpses floating in the river. He admired Louis for his survival reflexes. He wondered what kind of life his friend had had before this one. "I don't think it would help. We can't wander erratically through swamps in a land at war. We need at least a map or more information," Louis said.

His friend had not said a word since the river. If the land swarmed with orcs, Lissandro's chances were thin. Yet, Selen refused to give up. After all, Lissandro had made the whole way from the Windy Isles without them.

"So, should we find a road or should we stroll around?" Selen asked. He wondered if their quest was still of any worth now that their group had been broken.

"Let's make it to the first hamlet. Then we will see," Louis answered.

The landscape on the south bank was a blend of copses and green fields of high grass, patched with wild flowers. Selen gazed at the poppies, the daisies, and the tall, blue linens growing among the wheat. The plants reminded him of his shack in the Frozen Mountains. Up there, he would have needed to wait at least two more months to see these flowers appear on the prairies. This place used to be a field once, but it had not been reaped for many years, and the vegetation had grown wild. The nature was flourishing. It was hard for him to believe that this land had suffered so much. At least, it was what he thought until they came to the oak.

The tree stood at the corner of a forest. It was broad and its branches overhung a dirt road. The first spring leaves were not completely unfolded, leaving plenty of space for the sight. Selen counted seven ropes. On each rope hung a corpse. It was hard to say if they were men or women. The clothes were rags. The decomposition was already advanced, and the crows had eaten their eyes and most of the flesh on the cheeks and noses. Pieces of bones and teeth shone white among the rotten pulp. The bodies' bellies had been opened, leaving the intestines to hang out. The stench was obnoxious. Yet, what pierced Selen's heart was even worse. Two corpses were a lot smaller than the others.

"Children. They did that to children."

He wanted to puke. The feeling of anger he had had when facing the orcs awakened within him again.

Louis looked at him with commiseration. "I'm sorry you have to face that. Unfortunately, this is what war looks like. I suppose it was the orcs."

"Then we will kill the orcs. All of them," Selen said. He kicked his horse and passed under the tree. Louis followed him.

A few miles ahead stood what had been a farm. "I suppose that it was where they lived," Selen said. "Let's have a look around. Maybe we can find some food."

They dismounted and attached their horses to a fence. Louis came to him. "Be careful. There may be more bodies or scavengers." He took Selen's hand. The touch was gentle and comforting. "Selen, remember what I said: use the hate, don't let it destroy you."

The concern in Louis's eyes was so sincere that Selen felt the need to reassure him. "Don't worry about me. I know who I am. I just need time to get over what happened."

They inspected the farm. It was big with two floors and dependencies. It was made of stone and had a porch opening to the courtyard. Unfortunately, the whole place had burned. The walls still stood, but the roof had collapsed. The windows' frames had been blackened by the flames. Half-destroyed carts and furniture stood in front of the main door. The barn still stored stacks of straw, but it was empty overall. There were no bodies or animal corpses to be seen. Whoever had done that had taken all living creatures. Selen approached the main door and tried to look inside the house. "I can see cupboards. Not everything has burned."

"Don't go in there," Louis said. "The floors may collapse on you."

"It's all right. The upper floor already lays on the ground."

Selen crawled under the shards of the broken door and climbed over the crumbs. The debris moved under his feet. He stepped carefully on a broken beam and tiptoed to the cupboards he had noticed. He opened the first one. Empty. Selen turned to the other one. There were broken plates and papers in it, but no food. He looked around. Another door stood on his left. He pushed it but in vain. It was stuck. Something blocked the door on the other side. He took some steps backwards and threw his weight against the door. It moved a bit. Selen heard something break in the room. He repeated the operation. This time, the door flung open. Selen fell forward and landed on the floor. Pain grew in his right arm. He noticed that he had landed in something wet. The smell was unmistakable. He turned his head down.

He lay in a pool of wine. Broken bottles were scattered on the floor. He realized that he had found the kitchen. He rose. On the table in front of him lay a block of cheese and a half-eaten piece of bread. Whether the inhabitants had been surprised at lunchtime, or someone had been standing right here a few seconds ago, he did not know. There were no dust or traces of mold on the food, so he inclined towards his second option. Selen reached for his sword and looked around. There was an opening through the wall where a window had been. He looked outside from a distance. Nothing. He packed the cheese and the bread and searched for more food. Two wine bottles were still intact. In the bottom of a trunk, he found a pot of jam and lactic-acid fermented cabbage. He considered that it was better than nothing. The other rooms were inaccessible or too dangerous to enter. He went out through the window. There was still no sign of life. He wondered if it had been a bandit or a survivor of the massacre.

Behind the farm grew an orchard. The first flower buds had appeared on the branches. Some of the last summer's apples were decaying on the ground. This place must have been prosperous once.

"Did you find something?" Louis walked towards him. He had a bag on his shoulder.

"Not something, someone. You didn't see him?"

"I was in the barn, and nothing came my way." He put the bag down. "They had buried that in the hay. It's only some vegetables and fruits but still good to eat. What did you see?"

"Nothing. But there was someone, and he ran away." Selen gazed around. "We should leave in case he or it comes back with a group."

"There is a path leading south from here. We could follow it." Louis picked up the bag again, and they headed to their horses.

The road south led to a forest. There were no more traces of habitations, but they found a road sign with names they did not know. They halted near the side of the road for the night, using bushes as shelter. They shared the bread, some wine, and apples. Selen was convinced that eyes were watching them. "I don't think I can sleep," he said.

Louis packed the food. "Take the first shift of watch then. We keep our armours on in case someone attacks us."

Selen stayed awake all night and dozed off only when the first birds sang. When he woke up, the horses were packed and ready. "What was the name that stood on the road sign again?" he mumbled.

"Grimewallow," Louis said, stretching out his hand to help him up. "According to the number of miles on the sign, we should reach the place today."

Selen took Louis's hand and rose laboriously. Louis kept his hand in his.

"Can you stand up?" His friend smiled.

"I'm sore all over. I'd forgotten how uncomfortable it is to sleep with an armour on," he chuckled.

"Wait until it rains." Louis laughed.

Grimewallow stood in a valley. It could have been a charming little village with its cherry trees, its little white and blue houses, and the shrubbery in front of them, if the place had not been smoking ruins. Selen and Louis came down the main road from the north. The bandits, or the orcs, had probably been there a few days ago, maybe yesterday. Smoke still rose here and there. The acrid smell burned Selen's nose. There was blood on some of the walls. Louis stopped.

"You don't need to look. Keep on riding straight ahead," his friend said, but Selen turned his head.

The orcs had piled the bloody, naked bodies in the yard in front of the temple. The faces he saw bore a mask of torment. "Oh, hell…" he said and felt like he would throw up. Selen saw something move behind a wall. He kicked his horse and galloped after it.

"Wait!" Louis yelled.

Selen halted where the shadow had been. He dismounted and drew his sword. A door creaked in the house on the right. He reached the threshold and looked inside. The roof had collapsed on what had been a bed. In a corner stood a broken table and a trunk. Selen moved slowly closer to the trunk, holding his sword towards it. With one foot, he pushed the lock up, ready to run his blade through whatever was hidden inside.

"Don't kill me!" a high-pitched, scared voice shrieked.

Inside the trunk hid a young boy with terrified eyes.

"Get out of the trunk slowly and show us your hands," Louis commanded behind him.

The young boy rose. His dirty clothes were torn everywhere. Selen noted with bitter sadness that he was a bag of bones. Judging by the freckles on his face and his feeble build, Selen doubted that he was a survivor of Grimewallow. The boy was too young to be a bandit. The poor child was frightened and probably hungry. Furthermore, if it was him he had sensed all along, Selen had even taken his cheese and bread. He noticed that he was still pointing his sword at him and put the blade away hastily. Louis did the same.

"What's your name, boy?" Louis asked.

"I… I'm… My name is Folc, my lords."

"We're no lords," Selen said. "What are you doing here, Folc? Is this your village?"

"No." He looked at them with misery. "Please, do you have food?"

"Of course," Selen said. "Follow us."

They left the house and took the boy with them, far from the macabre heap. They found a place to sit in the shade of a tree outside the village. Selen offered Folc bread, jam, and wine. The boy wolfed down the bread like a ravenous beast. Selen and Louis waited in silence while the boy ate.

"Who are you if you're not from this village?" Selen asked him.

"I'm a page. At least, I was. I got lost." Folc gazed at them with wary eyes.

"You can't be a page. You're too old for that," Louis said. "You're at least a squire. If what you say is true."

"It is true," Folc insisted. "I am a page. I used to follow Lord Unfray, but he died during the battle." Folc looked down. "He was a good man. He treated me fairly."

"And how long ago was that?" Louis asked.

"Four winters ago."

Selen and Louis looked at each other amazed. "The first battle against Agroln," Selen whispered. "You have lived in the wild since then?"

"Yes. I was afraid to be abused by the villagers or to be enslaved. Then, I was afraid to be found by the orcs. I did some scavenging…but I'm not a bandit! I didn't hurt anyone." Folc was shaking. Selen was pretty sure that he was not a bandit. "You are the first to find me," Folc added.

"You must be good at hiding," Louis said.

"I've followed you since the farm. You don't look like the others. I thought you may be nice people, especially you," he said, pointing at Selen. "I'm also bored of being lonely. Can I come with you?"

Louis and Selen were taken aback. "Well, we are going south and…you're only a young boy."

"I'm not a child anymore. And I can steal," Folc said with pride in his eyes. "I could also be your page. You are knights. You need a page."

"Can you defend yourself? A page should," Louis said, dubious.

Folc blushed. "I can throw rocks," he mumbled shamefully.

"I can teach you how to fight," Selen suggested.

Selen saw Louis turn towards him, trying to find the words to complain, but his friend realized that it was too late. The problem was settled. Selen smiled brightly at him and laughed. "I take the whole responsibility," he said.

Folc jumped for joy and ran to the horses.

Selen put a hand on Louis's arm. His friend still looked confused. "He would have died alone at some point anyway," Selen murmured.

10

As the platform drifted downstream with the currents and the mist engulfed him, his friends had progressively disappeared from his sight. Lissandro was now stuck on the uncontrollable ferry. His experience as a trained sailor was useless. There was not even a long enough plank on board that he could use to maneuver with. He could swim, but it would be madness to jump into the water with such strong currents. Moreover, he had his horse with him. The poor beast was terrified and reared in every direction. Lissandro wanted to calm it, but he did not dare to go near his mount. The last thing he wanted was to be thrown into the water with internal injuries caused by a kick to the chest. He held to the rail, hoping the currents would slow down. They did not. They became stronger instead. Water poured on top of the platform. If it hadn't been flat, they would have sunk already. Yet, they could still overturn. The platform hit a rock. Lissandro heard the wood crack. *It can't be*, he thought. *I can't die that way, not now.* He felt a metallic taste in his mouth. His vision blurred with white spots. Lissandro felt warm and sweaty. His body turned numb. As a last reflex, he unrolled the rope around his arm before losing consciousness. The dream state took him.

He opened his eyes. Lissandro lay on the ground. He felt sand against his cheek. His vision was blurry, but he knew that right in front of him, behind the heather, the waves crashed on the beach. The pain in his chest was overwhelming. He felt something in his mouth. He spat. It was blood. His father had had him beaten again by his brutes. Only, this time, it was worse. His father had burned down Lissandro's office and his ship. The whaler had been such a beauty with her white sails. No man had been injured, but all he had achieved over the years had been destroyed in the flames in a few hours. He got up and turned around. The family house stood there, a traditional New England manor. It looked as gloomy and cold as the monster living in it. Lissandro moved towards the porch and climbed the steps, slowly, holding the railing. His ribs hurt like hell. The front door was open. He entered the lounge. The classy furniture shone. All was tidy and clean. A fire was burning in the hearth. Lissandro moved closer to it.

"Here you are, scum." He heard a voice behind him, filled with disdain and anger.

"Hello, Father," Lissandro responded.

"How dare you come back here? I thought I was rid of you." His father came closer.

"You burned my home, my ship, my life…" Lissandro murmured slowly with sadness and despair.

"And? You think you can come back here?"

"I only wanted to see my mother." Lissandro felt tired, so tired.

"You have no mother…and you have no father. No one here gave birth to a sod." It sounded like his father had spat the last word at his face. "Now, disappear from this place and leave the country."

Lissandro realized what his father had said. He turned around. "Where is my mother?" he asked firmly.

"I told you to—" His father's face was filled with hatred.

"Where is my mother?" Lissandro yelled.

"You deserve this one." His father rolled his sleeves up and raised his fist high.

Lissandro grabbed one of the pokers hanging on a hook near the fire and ran it through his father's chest. The man gazed at him in disbelief. He grasped the metal bar and fell down on the Asian carpet with a thud. Lissandro gazed at him with relief and disgust. He took a burning log from the hearth and set fire to the carpet. The flames spread fast on the fabric.

Lissandro ran upstairs to the bedroom. His mother lay on the floor in a string of blood. Her face had marks of bruises, and her skull had been crushed. Lissandro fell on his knees. He held her and cried. Around him, the flames crawled inside the house, up into the bedroom.

Curled up next to his mother, Lissandro looked at the orange glow spinning and growing. Soon, he would not be able to leave. Maybe it was better that way. His heart was heavy as a stone. He did not want to live anymore.

"But why should you die?"

He heard a voice crawl inside his head. Calling at him, giving him hope. He rose. The flames were all around him, licking the walls and the curtains.

"Come. Follow me."

He heard the comforting voice again. He had to live. He looked at his mother with affection and gave her a last kiss. Lissandro rose. He closed his eyes, ran into the fire, and threw himself through the window. The glass exploded into a thousand pieces against his body, and the cold, night air rushed inside the room. He fell. Arms caught him. Hair brushed against his face.

"I will take care of you now," a deep, warm voice said above him.

Lissandro woke up, lost grip for a second, and screamed. The platform bumped into another stone. This time, the board whirled around. His hand found a rope to hold on to. He heard a noise. Was there a storm coming? The thunder grew louder. The mist cleared on the river. The platform's speed increased. More rocks pointed out of the water. Lissandro understood what was ahead. Yet, he closed his eyes and smiled. He remembered now. "I know who I am." Furthermore, a comforting feeling lingered in him. It warmed his heart and made him feel good. For a few seconds, the platform was suspended in the air. Then it dived, falling straight downwards. Lissandro disappeared into the waterfall.

II

As his friend's horse was stronger, Folc rode in front of Selen. The poor boy didn't weigh a lot anyway. Folc hummed a song while braiding the mare's mane.

"If you were a page, it should mean that you come from a rich or noble family, right?" Louis asked.

The boy felt silent and lowered his face. "They were noble, indeed. My father was Lord of Tyntagiel. They are dead."

"I'm sorry to hear it, Folc," Louis said, feeling more compassion for him, "but you must have relatives alive somewhere?"

"I have an aunt in Millhaven, but I don't know if she is still alive. I heard the city was taken by the orcs."

"I read about Millhaven in books. It stands at a strategic crossroad on the way to the Iron Marches. The city is big with strong walls. I would be surprised if the orcs have destroyed it. Millhaven is a major source of revenue for Trevalden." Louis hoped that he wasn't giving Folc false hope. Yet, the destruction of the second city of the realm seemed improbable.

"How well do you know what happened to the realm since you got lost?" Selen asked.

"I haven't talked to people since then, but I heard that the new king sent his armies north. I saw villagers flee from everywhere. Some of them spoke of what happened in Millhaven. Others told about burned towns and bandits. I scavenged in the gardens and the fields and slept in abandoned barns. I stood away from towns and inhabited villages. What you saw in Grimewallow happens everywhere. It's the big, green monsters, the ones you call orcs. They come and kill nearly everyone."

"Nearly?" Louis asked.

"They take some with them."

"I suppose they want slaves, too," Selen said.

His friend's face darkened. Louis thought that Selen remembered what had happened that night near the ruins. The thought of Selen being taken away and used as a slave made his blood boil. His hate for orcs grew stronger.

"So, Folc, what did you use to do as a page?" Selen asked.

The boy leaned his head against Selen's breastplate and looked up. "Oh, the usual page things: cleaning armours, running messages, cleaning clothes, dressing my lord, more cleaning… Is there something you want me to clean?"

Louis and Selen laughed.

"No, don't worry, boy. We have no goods to clean, and we can dress ourselves," Selen said, brushing Folc's hair with his hand. "But it's about time you learn how to handle something sharper than a broom. Maybe we can find you a sword on the way."

"Which way?" Folc asked.

"That, we will see," Louis answered.

The sun was high in the sky when they decided to halt for a break. The horses needed some rest, and they all had become hungry. By mutual agreement, they rationed their provisions to the strict minimum they needed to hold a day. Without a bow or a rope, they could not hunt game, and they did not put high hopes on scavenging either. They had not seen more habitations since Grimewallow, only woods and more fields. Most of the time, the path had wended its way at the bottom of a gully, preventing them from getting an overview of their location. They were lost and still had no idea which road to follow.

Louis sat on a stone in the sun, a short distance from the horses. He tried to calculate how many days they would be able to survive with only a dozen apples, some jam, and two loaves of bread as hard as stone. Maybe if he took a leather strap from one of their bags, Selen would be able to weave a snare and fetch them some rabbit. They also had a bottle of wine left. Yet, Louis was reluctant to propose too much strong alcohol to Folc. However, the water of the streams and rivers, polluted by the corpses, surely carried deadly diseases by now. Wine would have to go until they found beer.

"Bend your legs. Up with your left arm. And block!"

Selen and Folc trained on the grass right in front of him. Selen had found two branches that he had cleaned, and taught Folc the basics of sword fighting. Louis's calculations were continuously interrupted by the incessant knocking of their sticks. Still, he did not mind it for anything in the world. After all they had seen, blithe moments were more than welcome.

He saw that Folc learned fast. The boy hopped, blocked, sidestepped, slashed in the air, and stepped backwards. Selen swayed and dodged like a snake, making it impossible for Folc to hit him. Every time he raised his eyes, Louis was lost in the elegant moves of his friend and how his hair swirled around him. Selen's thrusts were short and precise but slow enough for Folc to see them. Though he still could not block most of Selen's blows, the boy memorized the positions well, which Louis thought was Selen's objective.

"Keep your balance. You're doing well. Don't stop moving. Left. Right. Bend your head." Selen hit Folc's stick with a twist and sent the branch flying. It landed a few feet away. "Your grip is too tight. If you squeeze your sword, this is what happens. Your weapon must be a part of your arm. Whatever happens, never hesitate to kill, because it's you or him."

"I can't feel my arms or my legs anymore," Folc laughed. He held his hands on his thighs, panting. "I think I need a break."

Louis rose. "I think we need to keep moving. Let's find a safe place before night comes."

They all got up on the horses and rode back to the road.

The sky was getting dark when they saw the house at the turn of the road. It was a little thatched cottage with white walls and blue window frames. The door, which had not been repainted for many years, was green. A plum tree stood amidst tulips in a lovely shrubbery of camellia, enclosed by a white fence. A cat lay on the bench near the door and warmed its fur on the last rays of sunshine. Louis discerned a small barn at the rear of the house. Smoke rose from the chimney. It was the first untouched house he had seen in a long time. The curtains moved behind the window to the left of the door. A short, old woman walked out of the house and came towards the gate. She wore a long black dress with an overcoat and an embroidered black shawl over her head.

"What do you want?" she quavered.

Louis heard anxiety in her voice. He kicked his horse and approached her. "Excuse me, madame. I know we are strangers, but would you mind if we stayed in your house for the night? We have our own food."

The elderly woman cackled. "Would you mind… madame… You come from another time, my dear lad. No one addresses himself that way these days. Are you lords?"

"No, we are no lords, but we are no bandits either," Louis continued.

"I may be turning blind, but I can see that quite well." She stared at him and scrutinized Selen and Folc, who stood at a distance.

"All right," she said, "you can come in. There is a small stable behind the house that you can use for your horses."

They thanked her and led their horses to the back of the house. There were some chickens lying on the hay in the stable, but no horse or cow. It was narrow but nothing two horses could not endure for a night. They untied their bags, unsaddled their horses, and rubbed them down. When they were done, they followed the decrepit stone path back to the front of the house and opened the door.

There were only two rooms inside the house; one that looked like a bedroom was hidden behind an ajar door, and the other one, the main room, was where the hearth stood. A table and three chairs took most of the space. A giant carved cupboard covered half the left wall, and an oak trunk served as a second table in the right corner. Needlework decorated the walls. A spinning wheel had been placed under the narrow window, and a huge rocking chair covered with wool cushions and a blanket stood near the fire. The room was welcoming and pleasantly warm.

"Come inside and close the door. It's getting late and the nights are cold," she mumbled.

"Is there any fresh water we could use?" Selen asked. "If it is not too much trouble."

The old lady pointed at a bucket. "All you can pump, you can use. The pump is outside in the yard. There is a basin in the bedroom if you need one."

While Selen was busy fetching water, Folc stirred the fire. The old woman sat in her rocking chair and covered herself with the blanket. Louis removed his armour and put it on the side against a wall. It felt good to move without the heavy weight on his shoulders. Selen came back inside and gave the water to Folc to boil it. A few minutes later, Folc filled the basin with warm water. They repeated their actions until the basin was entirely filled. While Selen took off his armour, Louis stepped into the basin. After so many days in the wild, it felt wonderful to bathe again. He washed his hair and rubbed himself with the soap. Once he was done, Selen took his place. Louis put his clothes on and stepped into the main room. He took some food out of their bag and offered an apple to the old woman.

"You're very kind, my lad, but I don't have the teeth anymore for that. If you are hungry, I may have some cheese and eggs left in the trunk."

"But, you need food for yourself," Louis replied. He considered that it must already be complicated enough for her to get food than to have three men eat her provisions.

"At my age, I don't eat so much, and the cheese will become moldy if you don't take it." Louis doubted. "Will you go against an old woman?" she added.

Louis took the cheese and the eggs out of the trunk and fried it all in a pan.

"How is it you are still here and alone?" he asked.

The old woman looked at him with sunken, moist eyes. "I wasn't always alone. They killed my husband and took my son. It happened last year. They came during winter—bandits. They wanted gold, they said. They tortured my good man and killed him. They took our son as a reward. I was too old and useless for them." She looked down with grief. Tears ran down her cheeks. "Now I wait until my final day comes."

The old woman's story filled Louis's heart with sorrow. "Is there really no one you can count on in this land? Why don't villagers fight back?" He tried to conceal his anger in his voice, but he failed.

"My poor boy, no one can face these cruel monsters, and the bandits are too many. Driven crazy by hunger and sorrow, villagers have turned on each other. One day a simple peasant, the next day a ravenous outlaw. The only hope had lain for a while on the Rebellion, but today…"

"Which rebellion?" Selen asked, coming from the bedroom. He had left his place to Folc. The boy had been so dirty that he could only go last in the water. Selen sat down at the table near Louis, took a piece of bread, and plunged it in the fried eggs. Water dropped from his hair onto the floor behind his chair.

"When the war was lost, some of the survivors, knights and footmen, formed an eclectic group in the north to resist a wider invasion," the old woman said. "It worked for a while, as we could live in peace for two years. Then, the monsters came, and we heard no more word of victory from the Rebellion."

"Could they still be alive somewhere?" Louis asked.

"Well, last autumn, they were preparing for winter a few miles from here. They may still be there," she sighed. "Do you want to join them?" she inquired.

"From what I've heard, it's more an army of good-for-nothings and scoundrels! Not handsome lords like you." The anger made her cough.

Louis got up and held a mug of wine for her. "I'm sorry, but we must see for ourselves. We will remember your wise words, though."

"You remind me of my boy," she said with melancholy, "brave and foolish." She nodded to the bedroom. "You can take the beds tonight. I'm used to sleeping in my chair near the fire."

The bedroom's furniture was basic. There was a large bed and a smaller one, both of plain wood. A bridal chest decorated with blue paint stood in the corner at the end of the room, and a chair stood on the other side of it.

Folc had removed and cleaned the basin. The boy lay on the smaller bed, already asleep. Selen took one of the blankets that stood at the bottom of the bed and wrapped it around Folc.

"It's probably the first time in four years that he can sleep," Selen whispered.

Louis put his arms around Selen's waist. "And we should do the same," he murmured.

Louis and Selen half undressed and lay down in the other bed. The cold, rough sheets smelled of lavender and olive soap. No one had slept in this bed for a long time, but it had been kept fresh. "I know we are in a house with only a nice, old lady on the other side of the door, but I would like to stand watch. We don't know what can come during the night," Louis said, laying an arm around Selen's waist. Though he was weary, he would not take the risk to get his throat slit during his sleep. This place could as well have been kept intact for a reason.

"All right," Selen answered, curling closer. "Will you take the first shift?"

"I will. You can sleep." Louis smiled at Selen.

"Will we ride towards this Rebellion tomorrow?" Selen yawned.

"Yes. It may be our only hope. We can't roam around forever."

"Did you hear what she said about what they are?" Selen sounded worried.

"There is what they can be and what they are. We will observe them from a distance and make our own opinions about them. She did think we were lords." Louis grinned.

"You look like a lord." Selen smiled, teasing him. His eyes closed.

"Sleep now." Louis gave him a tender kiss.

Louis sat straight up in the bed, looking at the half moon through the window. He thought of the rebellion. He, too, was worried about what they would find. Would there be a hundred men? Or maybe a thousand? Did they have a chief? Did they still want to fight? So many questions that would probably stay unanswered until they found themselves in the lion's den. Was this even what their quest was about? After all he had seen and heard, he was more than willing to fight the orcs, but what of his friends? Lissandro was still missing. And Selen? Louis looked at him. His friend had an arm around Louis's hips and his head lay against his waist. The warmth radiating from Selen's body stirred him up. It was wrong; he should stay focused. He pulled the blanket higher to cover Selen's bare shoulder. He caressed Selen's hair. What would happen to Selen if he did not stop with his foolish pacifism? Louis grew fonder of him with each day. He had been seduced instantly by Selen's ingenuousness and his natural, pristine beauty. To have him at his side was a gift, but also a source of worry. Yet, there was no way he would abandon him. He would have to deal with it. "I will protect you," he whispered. He caressed Selen's forehead. It was covered in sweat. Was his friend having a nightmare again? He shook him to wake him up.

Selen opened his eyes with a choked shriek. He sat up, shaken.

"Are you all right?" Louis asked, putting his hands on Selen's shoulders.

Selen looked at Louis. His eyes were wild.

"I saw a huge, hideous orc with an axe. He was followed by an army. I think… they were invading a city…at the bottom of a hill. There were heads on spikes. Long lines of heads. I saw fire coming from the sky and heard the hammering of their steps on the ground. They're coming north." Selen's fear was palpable.

"No," Louis said, holding him tight, "because we will stop them."

Selen rested against Louis's chest, getting his breath back. "I think I have slept enough for tonight. I can take my shift," Selen said.

"Wake me up if you feel unwell," Louis muttered. He slipped an arm around Selen's hips and fell asleep on his stomach.

12

Louis woke up. Rays of light blinded his eyes. It was already day. He had slept deeply through the rest of the night. He looked up. Selen sat on the bed beside him, his shoulders bent forward. His eyes were closed, and his mouth was half open, letting a thin dribble of saliva run down his chin. Louis heard him snore faintly. *Someone has had a tiresome watch*, Louis thought with amusement. He sat up.

"Good morning," he whispered, kissing Selen's cheek.

Selen woke up with a jerk. "I was just resting my eyes," he said with a moan. He rubbed his chin and looked out through the window. "It's day already."

Louis looked at Folc, who still slept. "At least, we are not the last ones."

"But we are probably not the first. We should get ready," Selen said.

They rose, got dressed, and went into the main room. The front door stood open. The old lady was trimming her rose bushes in the garden. She still wore the same black dress, but she had tightened a yellow apron around her waist.

"You woke up at last," she exclaimed. "You lads needed a good night sleep. There is some water and fresh eggs on the table. Help yourselves."

They ate breakfast sitting on the bench in the garden. The sky was clear blue with no clouds in sight. The day promised to be warm. Folc came out of the house.

"I have slept like a baby," he said, stretching himself. He picked an apple and took a bite.

On Louis's left side, Selen took a brush out of his bag and brushed his hair. The cat, which trotted nearby, grabbed at the flowing tips.

Louis turned to the old woman. "Is there something we can do for you before we leave? You have been so kind to us."

She looked at him with tenderness. "It's I who should thank you for giving me a little hope that there is still a world with decent people out there. You, young boy—" she hailed at Folc "—I have something for you." She vanished inside the house and came back with folded clothes in her hands. "These belonged to my dear son. He was taller than you, but they will surely fit. You can't walk around in these rags anymore."

"Thank you so much," Folc said with a short bow as he took the clothes.

He took off his tattered clothes and put the new ones on. They consisted of brown pants, a faded green tunic with a white shirt, a short, black belt, and leather boots. Once he had rolled the sleeves and the bottom of the pants, the clothes fit him perfectly.

"Now, I'm ready for the journey!" Folc raised his arms and grinned. It was as if he had received the most wonderful of all gifts. They all laughed at his childish and sweet reaction.

Louis and Selen went back inside the house, prepared themselves, and put their armours on again. They packed their belongings and fetched their horses from the stable. They were soon ready to depart. The group gathered in front of the house where the old woman waited for them.

"The army should be some miles down south. Follow the path, and at the creek, turn right." She put her wrinkled, dry palm on Louis's hand and clutched it. "You all take care of yourselves."

Louis nodded. They kicked their horses and rode south. Folc, who still sat in front of Selen, turned back and waved to the old lady.

The way south after the cottage wended its way through a forest of chestnut trees with large boulders and steep slopes on the side. Once again, the track line they followed kept them hidden from view, but it also made it difficult for them to see anything. Chaffinches sang in the canopy. Louis heard flaps of wings coming from the bushes from the side of the path. A fluffy red squirrel crossed the road in front of them. The breeze was fresh and smelled of spring flowers. The sun warmed his face. After a good night of sleep and a bath, Louis felt invigorated and brisk.

The creek wandered down from a crack in the boulders on the left to a swamp among pine trees on the right. Louis reined in.

"This is where we leave the path," he said. "Let's dismount and find a way through the bog. We can walk and pull the horses by the bridle."

The swamp was broad. Thick copses of pine and beech stood along the south side. Boughs and tall reeds poked out here and there. A stone's throw from them, herons were fishing frogs. The right side was less covered with peat moss, but brambles grew on the bank. Selen picked up a dry wooden stick and tested the ground in front of him. The clay made sucking noises against the stick. After a few steps, Louis's greaves were clogged in the mud.

"I don't think I can move forward," Louis said. "I must go back before I can't move at all. We must try through the brambles. We have our armours to protect us. Folc can stand with the horses while we open a way with our swords."

Louis and Selen hacked their way through the bushes. They spun their swords around with broad movements, crushing the leftover brindles with their feet. It was a fastidious task. Louis was already sweating in his stifling armour, and he got irritated that the sun shone so bright. They emerged on the other side, Folc and the horses on their heels. They progressed under the pines until they heard clashes of steel and faint shouts. They halted.

"We should leave the horses here and sneak forward," Louis said.

"I can stay with the horses," Folc proposed.

"All right. Don't go anywhere," Selen said, handing him his horse's bridle.

Louis and Selen stepped towards the sound. The pines cleared to a lawn. They stood at the top of a slope with a large valley stretching downwards in front of them. They threw themselves on the ground. The bottom of the valley was covered with white military tents. Standards of different colors, raised on poles at crossroads, clacked in the wind. Men dressed in plate armours, others in leather garments, moved to their occupations. A grey smoke rose from what could be the smithy, smaller ones rose from braziers. Bangs of hammers were heard in every direction, but the sound was largely covered by the barking of the dogs in the kennel and the whinnying of the several hundred horses stomping in the corrals right under them.

"How many do you think they are?" Selen asked.

"I would say between seven hundred and a thousand, judging by the tents," Louis answered. He looked for the biggest tent, which should normally be occupied by the headquarters or the infirmary. He found the pavilion in the middle of the camp. The central pole was higher than the others, and a blue flag was fastened to it. A pair of guards stood lazily in front of the entrance.

"How can such an army stay here doing nothing?" Selen asked with irritation.

"I don't know. We have no idea how it looks down there. Maybe they are less than what they seem," Louis answered.

"Want to have a closer look?" a voice said behind them.

Louis felt the cold flat of a blade touch his neck. They turned around slowly. Five men faced them. One had a battered, full-plate armour, and he threatened them with his sword. His visor was shut. Another one, also holding a sword, bore a mix of plates and harnesses, as if he had lost parts of his armour during battles. His face was a mess of pimples and unshaved beard. The other three were archers with crossbows and were simply dressed in brigandines and muddy, soiled pants. Their sneers revealed their brownish teeth. Only by looking at them, Louis could tell a lot about the hygiene in the camp. He hoped that they were an exception.

The one in the armour raised his visor, revealing a more civilized face under a bushy red beard. "What are you doing here?"

Before Louis answered, a soldier came from the forest with Folc under his arm. "Look what I've found," he bawled to his comrades. Folc gesticulated, kicking the man in the legs.

"Let him go," Louis commanded loud and clear.

The knight turned to him with a stern look. "No. You all come down with us."

The soldiers tied their hands behind their backs. Folc was still struggling. Louis thought that Folc should calm down. These men were all brutes and would not hesitate to hit the boy. "Let me talk to him," Louis requested. The knight agreed. Louis went to Folc. "We came here to talk to them. If you struggle, you could jeopardize our situation or get us hurt. I want you to follow their orders. Do it for me, or at least for Selen."

Folc grimaced yet calmed down. Selen stood quiet, but Louis saw his approval.

"Now, move," one of the soldiers said. Louis, Selen, and Folc stood in the middle, a guard marching at each corner, and one following at the tail with the horses. The knight led the way. They went down the slope by a trail Louis had not spotted before.

The camp was not as white as it looked from above. The tents were stained. Broken crates lay in the narrow alleys. The ground was spongy and sprinkled with dung, not to mention the stench that emanated from it. The place was a clutter of rusted material and rotten food. The men did not show a better picture. Many were sick, drunk, or both. They looked bitter and exhausted. All of them were unshaved and filthy. Most men they encountered on their way stared at them scornfully. Louis glanced at the interior of the tents. Inside, soldiers slept, played cards, or drank. As they progressed through the camp, Louis felt disgust grow inside him. He did not try to hide the reproachful look on his face. This place was a shame. Never would he fight in such conditions. They were indeed a group of good-for-nothing scoundrels. A giggling, shirtless harlot rushed out of a tent right in front of him. She was soon followed by a staggering drunkard. "What the…" Louis exclaimed, aghast, before getting a rough push on his back.

"Move along!" the soldier shouted. Louis was infuriated. How could this army dare to call itself the Rebellion? He could not wait to have a word with their so-called commander. If there even was someone to rule this dreg. At the same time, he knew that his friends would never make it in such a place and probably would be the first to pay should he mess things up.

They arrived at the headquarters. The soldiers made them halt in front of the entrance. The knight disappeared inside the pavilion. "Answer only when you're asked to," Louis whispered to his friends. What was going to happen now would seal their fate, for the better or for the worse.

13

Lissandro's body was cold. His fingers dug deep into the dirt. Tiny stones pelted his skin. The touch was moist on his hands. He felt them on his face too, and in his nose. He sneezed and raised his head. His long, brown hair was filled with sand. Strands of hair hung down like rattails, dripping water on his shoulders. It did not matter. He was soaking wet all over. His clothes stuck uncomfortably on his skin. Lissandro shivered. He tried to rise but stumbled, one knee in the mud. His head whirled as he turned around.

The waterfall was right in front of him. He could hear it. It only increased the buzzing in his ears. The foam coming from the cascade blew in his face. Lissandro sat down and took long, deep respirations. He remembered what had happened. He looked around but found no trace of the platform—or of his horse. He felt sorry for the poor beast. It had always been kind and willing. With horror, he realized that all his provisions and goods were in the bags tied to the saddle. Lissandro felt miserable. He was lost, alone, and frozen to death. He put his hands in his pockets. Maybe there was something useful on him.

From one pocket, he took out the rest of the ropes and Louis's fire steel he had kept on him. He felt lucky in his misfortune. That was useful. At least, he could make a fire. At the same time, it meant that Louis and Selen could not. Unless Selen could use two sticks together, which would not be impossible considering his survival skills. Lissandro checked the other pocket. Empty. He half smiled. *Well, that's all*, he thought. At least, he had his dagger still in his sheath. The arrows had fallen from his quiver, and the bow probably rested at the bottom of the pool under the cascade by now. Luckily, he did not wear heavy armour like his friends.

Lissandro looked around. He had washed up on a small beach on the north bank. There were big stones emerging from the water. *It has been a close one*, he thought. Boulders lay on the side on each bank. The river continued flowing straight forward into the forest. The currents were less strong, but the water whirled and splashed. The slopes downstream were covered with grass on the north side and with reeds on the south. The river bent after a hundred yards and disappeared from sight. On both sides of the river grew huge, dark trees. *Oaks*, Lissandro thought, *ancient oaks*. "I am in the Ebony Forest," he whispered. Fright grew in him like fire in the wind.

He knew that the river ran west to the shore, a hundred miles from here. If he wanted to leave the woods, he must either climb the ravine or head south. If he climbed, he would need to make a detour and try to find a path up to the top of the falls. It could take days before he reached the place where they had crossed. Besides, his friends would not have camped there. They probably rode south right now, which was the best solution for them. Lissandro wondered if his friends considered him dead. He shook his head in denial. *No*, he thought, *Louis looks like an honorable man, faithful to his friends, and Selen has far too much love in his heart to give up so easily*. Still, Lissandro knew that his friends were powerless to find him. He would have to fend for himself and join them in one way or another. He only had one option. To walk south until he reached the border of the forest.

The first thing to do was to cross the river, as he had landed on the wrong side. Besides, he was still wet. Of course, there was no place to cross over. His mail was heavy, and he was not strong enough to cross in a straight line. Maybe if he tried to swim from one stone to another. There were enough rocks to grab, and only the middle of the river looked deep. He walked into the water, tramping into shallow spots and searched for the first stone. He reached it. Now, he had water to his shoulders. Soon, he would lose his footing. He jumped to the next stone on his right and held his arms around it. The third stone was a bit further away downstream. He let go of his rock and paddled like a dog, aiming for it. He missed at first, but his left hand found a grip. He hung to it, turned to the next one, and gathered his energy. He jumped and caught it. He stretched his legs down. He felt the bottom of the river with the tip of his feet. He fought against the stream to the last stone. He missed it and hit another one further down. Now, he had water only to the waist. He paddled and crawled onto the bank. Lissandro collapsed, short of breath. He needed to move before he froze to death. He rose laboriously. *There should not be too much of a problem to find dry wood here*, he thought.

He entered the forest and searched for branches. It did not take him long to gather an armful of it. He got back to the river and found a flat stone where he could start a fire safely. He took out the fire steel and hit the two parts over dry sticks. The flames licked at the straws and sticks. He pushed branches under it. Lissandro undressed, laid his clothes and mail flat on one side of the fire, and warmed his body on the other side.

It took a while before he got dry, but it was only noon. He decided to walk. He put his clothes on and his mail over them. Lissandro entered the forest. There were no paths to follow, not even trails dug by the hooves of animals. Actually, there were no animals to spot, no singing birds, no noise in the bushes. The forest was silent. The trees were darker now. Lissandro looked up. He did not see the sky through the canopy, not even a ray of light. The oaks were large, tall, the bark covered with thick grooves. The branches growing in all directions were distorted and twisted like the arms of agonizing men consumed by fire. On most of the trees grew beard lichen. Usually, the fungus was a sign of healthy air in a forest. But here, the air was heavy and rancid. The lichen looked like decaying pieces of flesh, hanging from burned bodies. The ground was covered with worm-eaten trunks, mossy boulders, and ferns. Their colors went from dark green to purple. The humus was moist under his feet. There was something malevolent in these woods, a darkness that had been growing for years. Lissandro hated it. After a while, Lissandro noticed that he had walked with his dagger in his hand. He needed to calm down, or he would cut himself by inadvertence.

He advanced that way for many hours until he got hungry. There were no animals to see, and he did not even have his bow. He was resigned to eat some roots when he spotted a patch of wood sorrel. The leaves tasted sour under his tongue, but it was still better than chewing on earth covered roots.

Twilight came. Lissandro pondered on where to pass the night. There were boulders a little further ahead. Maybe he could slip between stones and crawl into a cavity. He found a hole his size, laid a litter of fern at the bottom, and lay down on it, curled like a ball. He would freeze, but at least he would not get the night moisture on him.

As he tried to sleep, he heard the first calls of tawny owls, followed by the croaking of toads, and darkest sounds he had never heard before. *There is life in this forest*, he thought. His blood froze in his veins. He knew he would not get much sleep this night.

14

"Sir Bertrant... Commander?" a voice called him.

He woke up with a terrible headache. His mouth felt dry and pasty. Bertrant had fallen asleep in his chair once again. He grumbled. His doublet felt too tight. He had moved during his sleep, and now his clothes were all twisted. He wiggled and drew on the fabric to put them back in place. It still felt wrong on his belly. *Too short*, he thought, *or too fat*. His doublet felt damp. He bent his head and sniffed at his armpit. When was the last time he had changed clothes? Or was it the tent? Everything stank in that darn camp anyway. He sat himself straight and accidentally hit the flagon of wine with the back of his hand. This would not improve the look of his board. Papers, maps, quills, and remainders of food on platters lay astray on the large oak table. While sponging up the wine with a pellet of paper, Bertrant tried to remember what he had done last before he drowsed. Yes, something about the furniture for the infirmary. That bloody monk turned him mad with his solicitations. He looked up. Only now, he noticed that Faremanne stood by the opening of the tent.

"My lord, Commander?" Faremanne repeated.

"Yes, what is it?" Bertrant grouched. It had better not be the monk again. The smell around him made his head ache.

"We have captured spies, Commander."

"What, orcs? Bandits? I already told you to kill those scum on sight." The woods crawled with these things by now.

"No orcs, Commander. I don't think they are bandits either…but they were spying on us from the outskirts of the camp," Faremanne said, confused.

"No bandits, you say? Bring them in." Bertrant was curious. Were there villagers still alive around here? Without his flagon of wine, he would never hold through the boredom of the days. He would not mind some distraction.

Faremanne left the tent and came back a few seconds later, pushing two men and a boy in front of him. Bertrant leaned forward and opened his eyes widely. What kind of peculiar company was that? The man standing on the left had long brown hair waving down to his shoulders, with short sideburns along the length of his ears. In comparison, Faremanne's long, red, curly hair looked like the fur of a shaggy dog. Yet, the most interesting was his refined features. He had a straight, thin nose and large cheekbones. His generous, feminine mouth was compensated by a sharp, steel-cold look under the prominent arch of his eyebrows. If he had not been sitting, Bertrant would have stepped back. He had seen nasty looks on murderers and butchers, but these eyes bore no mark of such filth. The hate they spread was cold and implacable. As if he had read Bertrant's thoughts, the man lowered his head. When he raised it again, his dark blue eyes had lost their bite. The man even looked confused. Bertrant's eyes turned on the man on the right. There was no trace of biting in this one. Despite being a grown man like his friend, his face reminded Bertrant of a young maiden. His huge, green eyes, over his large cheekbones and his small, upturned nose, reflected the innocence of newborn lambs dragged to the butcher's block. To make things worse, his hair, which reached the back of his thighs, was dyed lavender. Bertrant did not want to know if the sinuous drawings on the man's forehead were makeup or tattoos. Who on earth would inflict such a thing on himself? And moreover, stroll through a war zone with such a look? However, despite their supple physique, both men could carry heavy armour with ease. Bertrant noted to never misjudge their strength. Besides, their armours were magnificent. Only rich lords or Highnesses could afford such piece of art unless the men had stolen them or knew a blacksmith. The young boy, with his freckles and messy auburn hair, looked ordinary. Of all the three of them, only the child had his eyes riveted down by fear. Bertrant turned back to the man on the left. If someone would speak, it would be him.

"Who are you? And why were you spying on my camp?" Bertrant asked.

"My name is Louis, Sir. My companion and I are the personal guards of his lordship Folc of the House Tyntagiel," Louis said, bowing. The man knew his courtesies, but his salute seemed forced.

"And where is his lordship?" Bertrant asked, perplexed.

"Right here." The young boy stepped forward.

Bertrant wondered for a second if they made fun of him. He looked closely at the boy.

"And what is his lordship doing here?" he asked with sarcasm.

"My name is Folc of Tyntagiel, Sir. I was a page to Lord Hunfray of Berridan. Since his and my parents' deaths, my guards have protected me."

"And who were your parents?" Bertrant knew Lord Hunfray, and he did die during the war. Besides, the lad knew how to show his respect. The boy's story made sense.

"Raymond and Isabel, Sir." The boy looked genuinely sad. Raymond and Isabel of Tyntagiel. Bertrant remembered them now, a barony on the Crysas Peninsula. So many nobles had died during the war.

"I remember your mother, a beautiful red-haired woman. You've got her freckles. I'm sorry for your loss, lad. Faremanne, untie them." Bertrant got up and moved towards the group. "Why are you here?"

"We had heard of the Rebellion and hoped to join your ranks, Sir," Louis responded.

"Oh, so you want to join our army."

"No." Louis looked right at him. "This place…" He paused. "…is a mess."

It felt like a slap in Bertrant's face. The man had chosen his words, which made the insult even greater. Furthermore, Bertrant had seen a glimpse of contempt in his eyes, and it had not been for the place. The man clearly suggested that Bertrant too was a mess.

"I suppose that His Highness would do much better," mocked one of Bertrant's men standing on the side. He had watched the scene in silence, caressing his pointy goatee.

"And you are?" Louis snapped at the man.

"Captain Segar Mills. I guess that my men made a bad impression on you." Segar smirked.

"They are untrained. We could win against any of your men in a duel," Louis said, this time with open scorn. Bertrant realized that only his title as commander had spared him from this insolent attitude.

Bertrant watched the two men bite at each other. The insult was hard to swallow. Yet, he had to admit that Louis was right. That camp was a mess and he should be ashamed of his own appearance, except that no one would have dared to tell him that. The man had sass. However, Bertrant could only tolerate such an attitude if it was justified by actions.

"Well, we will see if you can be true to your words," Bertrant intervened. "Let's make a duel." If the man was a fraud, he would die. Should he win, he may well be of some worth.

"Not with me," Louis said and turned to his friend, "with him. Selen, against one of your men."

"Me?" Selen asked, astonished.

"If he loses, you can kill both of us," Louis added, holding Bertrant's gaze.

Bertrant wondered why the man would send his delicate companion to face one of Segar's brutes, condemning himself to death at the same time when he certainly had a better chance to save his skin himself. Something was fishy. He felt like a pawn on a board, and he did not like that at all. He remembered his own previous note, never judge a book by its cover. Bertrant gave a slight smile.

Segar stared at Selen and sneered. "You're in a hurry to die." He turned to Selen with a mocking bow. "If my lady can follow me out, we will find you a good match." Bertrant observed that the green eyes had lost their ingenuousness.

At the call of Segar, the men gathered in a circle in front of the pavilion. A long line of scruffy faces pressed on each other in search of some action.

"I need a volunteer," Segar yelled, "to give *that* a good thrashing!" Segar pointed at Selen. The men roared, many laughed. Soon, a forest of hands rose in the air. *Fools*, Bertrant thought, *all a bunch of fools*. Though he still had incomprehension marked on his face, Selen showed no sign of fear. Bertrant saw by the way he stared at the ground, the sun, and the crowd that he prepared himself. He might look like a maiden, but he was a soldier. The fight promised to be interesting.

"You remember the orcs," Bertrant heard Louis murmur to his friend. "These men are a thousand."

"Thank you. I'll get even with you for that," Selen responded, half smiling.

Segar had made his choice. A mountain of a man smashed his way through the crowd. Bertrant gulped. He knew the brute. The Mountain had made as many victims in the camp and in the villages as on the battlefield. The chances of Louis's friend winning the fight were thin. Selen stepped forward. The circle re-formed around the two men.

"When I'm done with you, can I keep your head? I like to decorate my tent with pretty things," The Mountain chuckled.

"You would probably make good use of a brain, indeed." Selen sidestepped, keeping his eyes on his adversary.

The big man grunted and engaged. He swirled his long sword. Selen rolled down and avoided the mighty blow. He rose and kept on sidestepping. The soldier threw another strike. Selen backstepped and kept on moving around. Selen hopped and dodged, avoiding all the blows. He only used his sword to deflect the closest strikes on the flat of his blade. The soldier gesticulated, sweeping his sword like a scythe. By luck, he hit Selen with the back of his wrong hand. Selen's body flew and smashed on the ground. He jumped up like a cat and cast himself on the side. The long sword cleft the dust behind him. The soldier growled. He turned around and cut downwards. Selen blocked the blow but hit the ground again. He twisted. Rose. Sidestepped. The Mountain panted. He snorted. The soldier rotated his sword low. Selen backflipped over the blade. He landed on the tip of his feet and plunged under the soldier. Selen cleaved the man's belly, rotated behind him and kicked his ass. The Mountain knelt as his guts spilled out. Selen jumped, weapon first, and landed on him. Selen's sword ran through the man's back. The chest exploded in gushes of blood.

The crowd was speechless. So was Bertrant. When Selen pulled out his sword, more blood spurted upwards. The young man hopped from the corpse and, in the heavy silence, walked back towards them. Bertrant saw Selen look at his friend and beam like a fluttered maiden. For a second, he saw the relief on Louis's face and a hint of joy. Standing one step behind Louis, Selen turned around and faced the crowd. The soldiers cheered. The men got what they wanted. They got blood. Bertrant glimpsed at Segar disappearing into the crowd. And Louis got an enemy.

"Well, it seems that you are accepted in the camp," Bertrand said, looking directly at Louis. He finally understood what the latter had planned all along. If the soldiers had seen Selen as Bertrant had seen the man himself, his chances of existing in the camp were nonexistent. Louis had known it. He had not sacrificed his friend. He had saved his life, unafraid to use his own to tip the scales. Bertrant could only admire the gesture, and he needed clever men. "A tent will be prepared for his lordship of Tyntagiel, according to his rank of course. Our champion will stand by his side, and you, you will share the tent of Faremanne." As pleased as he was to have new, talented recruits in the army, Bertrant was not foolish enough to let them form their own clan.

"Thank you, Commander," Louis said. The man was grateful, but his mouth twitched. Bertrant's decision to separate them had not pleased him.

"Faremanne will show you to your quarters. As for me, I would be pleased to have you at my table tonight." This was a dinner Bertrant looked forward to.

15

Bertrant turned away from them. Louis could breathe again. His plan had worked. He had given the boy a status and had secured Selen's safety in the camp. He had risked all on a throw of a dice. He still felt dizzy after the fight. He hoped that no one had seen the sweat on his brow or the terror in his eyes when Selen had fallen. They would have probably believed that he was afraid for his own life. Yet, he could not have cared less about the sword over his head. He had been a hairbreadth away from running into the arena to protect his friend. Still, he had trusted Selen to the very end. The way his friend had fought had filled him with admiration. Never had he seen such a beautiful warrior, in all senses of the term.

Faremanne led them to their quarters. The tent was not big but could be compartmented with curtains for privacy. It was much cleaner than the ones of the common footmen and had a litter of straw. Louis counted two beds covered with furs, four racks for swords and armours, and three massive trunks.

"I will let you install yourself. Call me if you need anything," Faremanne said. "That was a splendid fight," he added. The knight turned around and left the tent.

Louis grabbed Selen's hands. "Are you all right?" He had been eager to ask since the fight had ended. "Your forehead is bleeding. Let me see to it. Sit down. Folc, bring me some water!" He pulled Selen to a bed and forced him to sit.

"It's all right," Selen said with his usual, gentle smile. He sounded exhausted. "I feel a bit groggy, but I'm not injured. It was close still. Yet, I could not lose, not with your life in my hands."

The words went straight to Louis's heart. The remorse overwhelmed him. "I'm sorry I asked you to do that. I wanted the soldiers to respect you as a knight so that you could be safe here. I would not have let you die."

"I know. I understood it when I saw them cheer me." Selen flushed. "That was the first time I was cheered." Selen looked down at Louis's hands on his. "Your hands. They're bleeding."

"I may have hurt myself. I was a bit stressed." Louis smiled. He had pressed his fists so hard that he had cut his palms, opening the wounds and blisters he had made at the river. After the rope, his thin gloves had been in shreds, and he had thrown them away. Only now did he notice the pain in his hands.

"But you still sent me to fight," Selen said, surprised.

Without considering it, the truth crossed his lips. "I trust you." Louis stared at Selen.

"Here is the water!" Folc shouted. The boy put the jar on a trunk and filled a bowl. He handed the water and a clean cloth to Louis.

Louis dipped the cloth and wiped gently at Selen's brow. The cut was superficial. "You won't need stitches, but you should disinfect it. If you don't have something antiseptic with you in your bag, I suggest you visit the infirmary." Louis gave the water bowl back to Folc.

"I will," Selen answered. He took Louis's hands in his and observed the cuts. "You should clean your hands. Between the rope at the river and today, your hands are so damaged that they really need a balm. I will fix it for you."

"Should I fetch your soap, Selen?" Folc asked.

"Yes, do. Thank you."

The boy searched inside Selen's bag, took out the soap, and handed it to Selen with the bowl of water. Selen washed his forehead first, then proceeded in cleaning Louis's hands. The blood and the dust left his skin and blended in the soapy water.

"Will you accompany me to Bertrant's dinner tonight? The man seems disabused but clever. We may learn a lot," Louis asked.

"Are you sure he didn't want to talk to you in private?" Selen put the water on the side. Louis's hands were cleaned and felt fresh.

"Maybe, but he will have to deal with it. You have the right to know about our future in this camp. Besides, he didn't specify that he would be alone. I don't want to face an inquisition." Furthermore, Selen was the hero of the day, he should get the honors.

Selen rose and removed his armour. The blood on it was drying. Folc jumped to help him with the straps. Louis saw that it surprised Selen and put his friend ill-at-ease. They mounted the armour on the rack. Folc assembled the parts with dexterity. Selen frowned. He took a wet rag and filled a bowl with water.

"I can do it," Selen scolded towards Folc when the boy took hold of the rag.

"The kid is just doing his job," Louis pointed out. He did not remember if he had seen Selen angry at someone until now, considering the orcs were not people. He guessed his friend did not like to be served.

"I know. I'm sorry, Folc, but you don't have to. I'm no lord, not even a knight," Selen said.

But you are today's champion, Louis thought. Selen washed the blood from his breastplate. "I will come with you. You should check where your tent is while I clean my armour. Talk with Faremanne. Find out what kind of knight he is. If we are to stay here, we need allies."

Louis got up and made for the tent opening.

"Louis," Selen called out to him. "Watch out for this Segar." Louis saw that his friend was worried about him.

"I will."

Louis got out and went in search of his tent. Logically, it should not be too far from the headquarters and be of the same size as the one he had left. He wandered around among the tents. Once again he had to face the same scenes of debauchery and laxity. All this was beyond all comprehension. He could not wait to talk to Bertrant. He soon got tired of walking in circles and asked a soldier.

Faremanne's tent stood only a few yards away from the headquarters. It had a green flag on the top, tied to the main pole. Two guards stood on both sides of the entrance. Louis got in. Faremanne sat by the only table, reading papers. "Do you need two guards?" Louis asked.

"One I use for my errands, the other one is for dissuasion," Faremanne answered, his eyes still fixed on his papers.

"Dissuasion? Against your own men?" Louis hoped he had heard wrong.

"We have had some…incidents, with some drunkards. Nothing serious," Faremanne said placidly.

"In your own tent?" Louis nearly shouted. This place was a nightmare. "And you don't mind?"

Faremanne put down his papers. He turned his face to Louis. The man looked exhausted and desperate. "Of course I do," he said. He rose and walked towards

Louis. Standing in the opening of the tent, Faremanne gazed at the camp. "Do you know how many captains there are in this army? Four. Do you know how many care to win the war? One. Me."

Louis felt pity for the man. He sounded sincere. "And what of Bertrant? He seems to be a good man," Louis asked.

"He is. But the commander has been through a lot. We have lost many battles, sometimes against ourselves." Faremanne looked at him with dismay. "If you are willing to help us, please stay."

"If Bertrant lets me stay, we will be two who care." Louis hoped that he sounded comforting. He turned towards his bed. "But this will mean changes," he added. Louis lay down on the furs. He needed some rest before the dinner.

Louis woke up. He felt pain in his back. *Why on earth do I need to sleep with my armour on?* he thought. Faremanne stood on the side of the bed.

"Your friend is there," he said. Louis remembered their dinner with Bertrant. He got up and walked out.

Selen waited for him outside. His armour shone. "Nice work," Louis complimented him.

"It took time. That fat man had a lot of blood in him," Selen said with a wry smile. "I will go to the infirmary tomorrow. Did you manage to talk to Faremanne?"

"Only a few words. The man is on our side. However, if I understood well, we have to face three captains who are not. It won't be easy." They headed to the headquarters. The camp on this side was quiet. They heard clamours come from the south. "I can't wait to clean this pigsty." Louis's eyes narrowed.

Selen touched his arm. "I know you want things to change, but be careful. They don't know you, and Bertrant may take it wrong. You already have an enemy, soon it will be two more."

Louis saw that Selen was scared. They had slept in the wild in the fear of orcs, and now that they could finally sleep in tents, the threat had been replaced by men.

"I will be careful. In fact, it feels as if I have done these things before. I know what I have to do." He smiled. He had had a weird feeling of déjà vu at the sight of some scenes around him. However, in the last four years, he had never put a foot in an army camp. "Just promise me you will be careful too. Stay away from these captains. And, one more thing—" Louis paused, trying to get over the swelling in his chest "—I know it's very hard to ask, but stay away from me unless it's something crucial. We must not draw their attention to…what we are." He had tried to find the best words, but Louis could see the pain in his friend's eyes. It was as if his soul had shattered like glass. It echoed with his own sorrow. Selen should not misinterpret it. Louis needed to reassure him. "I'm not pushing you away." He stressed his words. "I will try to have enough errands for you to keep you in my way from time to time."

"I understand. It's all right," Selen said, but his eyes could not fool Louis. "Let's get inside now. This promises to be entertaining."

Bertrant sat at a large table, waiting for them. He was alone. He had changed his stained, creased doublet for a mustard-colored one with open sleeves and had a white shirt under it. Louis was pleased to see that the commander had rectified his outfit. He may even have taken a bath. The smell in the tent had not completely disappeared, but Louis could breathe without hurting his sinuses. The table had been set. The mugs and tin platters shone in the light of the candles.

"Here you are," Bertrant said. "I wasn't awaiting you dressed in your armour, but I guess that you may be short of fancy clothes. We will rectify that. Please, take a seat."

Louis and Selen approached the table and sat on both sides of Bertrant.

"I have to apologize. It has been a long winter, and we are short of supplies. The dinner will be frugal."

As Bertrant spoke, his orderly placed a large platter of roasted pheasants on the table. Louis felt his stomach rumble. It promised to be the best frugal dinner since they had eaten their last apples and cheese loaf. The orderly filled their mugs with red wine.

"It comes from the last cask I had spared from before the war. We should savor it," Bertrant said, studying his mug in the feeble candlelight. He turned to Selen. "I suggest we raise our mugs to the champion of the day. He offered us a good fight and rid me of a troublesome soldier."

Louis saw Selen disappear into his armour as a snail into his shell. "We only did what was necessary to save our lives," Louis said.

"And cleverly done. Now, I want to hear the truth. I know the boy is a Tyntagiel, but I can hardly believe you two are his bodyguards." Bertrant's tone was clear and slightly threatening. Louis opted for the truth.

"We found the boy on our way, scavenging in the remnants of a village, and decided to take him with us. What I said about our motivation to come here was true. We have seen enough horrors. We want to fight against Agroln's armies."

"Where are you from?" Bertrant asked.

"I am from the Iron Marches, Neolerim."

"And you?" Bertrant turned to Selen.

"I am from the Frozen Mountains."

Bertrant looked shocked. "You are from the land of the ferocious Northmen? What are those…?" As he stared at Selen's brow and hair, Bertrant's hand gestured around his head. "Is that part of a ritual? Are you a witch?" Bertrant leaned towards Selen with nasty eyes.

"No! I…" Selen said. Under the table, Louis kicked him in the leg. "Yes, it's part of a ritual. It is forbidden for the soldiers of the kingdom to cut their hair. Long hair is a sign of strength and virility. At the age of twenty-five, the king's most valuable warriors must dye their hair and tattoo their faces. I liked the color."

Louis believed the last part. Bertrant swallowed the whole as his features softened.

"Well, valuable you are, indeed," the commander said, turning amiable again, "but this country is not your home. Why would you fight for it?"

"Homeland is not the ground, it's the community of affections. Each man who fights for salvation, or for the freedom of what he holds dear, defends the homeland. On my way to Trevalden, I crossed refugees fleeing the country. By fighting at your side, I am a greater patriot than they will ever be. Should every single man in Trevalden leave his house with his sword in his hand, the land would soon be saved. One can only fight for what he loves. To fight for the greater good is only the consequence."

Bertrant stayed silent. "What do you want from me?" he said.

"I want the total control of the camp, under your supervision. Selen and I will answer directly to you and to no one else. I want Faremanne at my side. And I want to start now." Louis looked directly into Bertrant's eyes. "These are my terms."

Bertrant put a hand to his chin, caressing his goatee. It felt like forever to Louis before Bertrant gave his answer. "So it's all or nothing," the man said. Louis kept his eyes riveted on him. "Then you two should hear the whole story. When King Wymar Lambelin died four years ago, a civil war was trigged by the rival families of the realm," Bertrant said.

The orderly brought more plates on the table. One was pikes roasted in butter, the other one contained honey cakes and poached pears. Louis reached for a pheasant leg.

"Many died by treason or on the battlefield," Bertrant carried on. "However, their petty quarrels were hopeless. They were all soon wiped out by the king's counselor, Agroln, who took over the throne with the help of his army of orcs and his newborn dragon."

At the mention of the dragon, Louis and Selen exchanged looks. The beast was real.

"Some of the rich lords submitted themselves and joined Agroln. Others, like me, gathered on the battlefield. We paid for it dearly." Bertrant looked down and took a sip of wine. He sat silent for a while, lost in his thoughts.

"How did it turn out?" Selen asked eventually, gnawing at a pheasant bone.

"Agroln unleashed his dragon. The beast flew at us and burned all who stood in its way. The orcs finished the work. It was a bloodbath. I tried to gather the survivors, whoever they were, men who still wanted to fight and formed the Rebellion. We managed to hold the north two winters until the orcs came to us in larger numbers. The Rebellion was defeated. We are what is left of it—and not the best part. You have seen my men. I don't need to explain further."

No, you don't, Louis thought. If that was the story, then what he had seen was the result of despair more than of incompetence. Louis knew what to do. Yet, before that, he had a friend to find. "Do you have maps?" Louis asked.

"Of course, come." Bertrant rose, took the flask of wine in one hand, and went into the next compartment. Louis and Selen followed him.

Maps representing Trevalden were spread out on a giant board. Wood figurines and flags symbolized strategic points. Louis discerned the Strelm River they had crossed. It ran directly into the Ebony Forest. He wondered how he would be able to find Lissandro in there. As he could not leave the camp, he hoped his friend would manage by himself for a while.

"We are here," Bertrant pointed on the map, south of a black dot representing Grimewallow. "Troops of orcs roam everywhere, but their headquarters is based there, at Millhaven, a hundred and fifty miles from here. All the east of the country to the south is under their control. They haven't reached the west now, but companies of outlaws make the roads there unsafe."

"What is this place?" Louis asked, pointing at a city named Embermire. This place stood right south of the Ebony Forest and was the closest city to their position. "Who controls it?"

"This is Embermire, the city of Lord Pembroke. The man is a lost cause. We should focus ourselves on the east." Louis detected annoyance in Bertrant's voice.

"When was the last time you asked him for help?" Selen asked Bertrant.

"Four years ago. But you shouldn't—"

"I think you should write to him. We can't allow ourselves to be picky right now," Louis insisted.

Bertrant grunted. "All right, I'll send a crow. But I warn you, this man won't listen."

"I wouldn't either if I knew what the Rebellion looks like. Soon things will be different," Louis said.

"I'd like to see that," Bertrant sneered. "These men barely move to take a shit."

"You said that they volunteered to join the Rebellion, am I right? So what they need is motivation. They need hope." Louis turned to Bertrant. He was their commander. He had no right to abandon his men.

"I'm tired. I'm old. And I'm drunk. Do what you want, we will see if it works… or if they kill you," Bertrant said with a sullen look on his face. He grabbed the flask, drank the rest of the wine, and disappeared into the other side of the tent. Louis watched him leave with surprise and disapproval.

"He will get over it." Selen put a hand on Louis's shoulder. "It's not easy for a man to accept failure." Selen stepped back and made for the tent opening. "You got what you wanted. Now, show them." Selen had a tired smile on his face. He went out. Louis had gotten what he wanted, indeed, but it was not without a price.

Louis went back to his tent. Faremanne, who had been sleeping on his bed, woke up. "How was the dinner?"

"Get up. Go to the smithy and ask for as many shovels as the man can do in one night. If he complains, have him arrested and replaced." Louis passed in front of Faremanne and sat at the table, grabbing the papers. "Change starts now."

16

Selen felt a hand on his forehead. He wanted it to be Louis's. He opened his eyes and saw Folc standing beside the bed. Sorrow tugged at Selen's heartstrings. His friend's words yesterday had splintered his heart. Selen was glad that Louis could put his plans for the camp into practice, but Selen knew this was not the place for him. As the new champion, he may not be killed by the soldiers. Yet, the way they looked at him was clear—even Bertrant had given him the eyes. What would be his role in such a place? He would watch over Folc. They would stay out of the way and see how things turn out.

Besides, his health had worsened after the fight. He had felt exhausted for several days now, but yesterday, a bad, acrid taste had lingered in his mouth and his head had throbbed. Now, light hurt his eyes and he had cramps in his chest as if he needed to throw up.

"How do you feel?" Folc asked.

"As if I have been trampled by horses while crossing the desert." Folc stared at him with worry. Selen found that sweet and forced himself to smile.

"You screamed in your sleep, and your head is warm. Maybe you should rest."

"I probably had a nightmare again. I plan to go to the infirmary today. Could you bring me some water, please?" He rose and sat on the bed. He wore his tunic. He did not even remember having removed his armour last night. He had been so tired. Selen frowned as he felt a sharp pain go through his head. He put a hand to his forehead. It was warm, indeed. He did not know if it was because of the cut, or because he had exhausted himself these last weeks. Folc handed him a bowl of water. Selen washed his face. He noticed that men shouted outside. "How long have I slept?" he asked Folc.

"Most of the morning," the boy answered. "It's almost noon."

So long. And the screams. Had something happened? Selen's heart beat faster. He rose in a hurry, and his vision blurred. "Louis… I must…"

Folc caught his hand. "It's all right." The boy smiled. "Look." Folc opened a flap of the tent.

Soldiers ran in every direction. Yet, instead of carrying swords or bows, they all carried a shovel. "What is going on?" Selen asked, dumbfounded.

"He makes them dig." Folc laughed.

Selen stepped outside. He still had a terrible headache, but thanks to the fresh air, he was not dizzy anymore. He walked around in the camp. All around, men dug the mud, moving barrows of it. Some men gathered old twisted pieces of metal half buried in the ground, while others carried away old, rotten crates. The soldiers looked frightened, stressed, but no one looked gloomy anymore. He heard men shout ahead. He moved forward with curiosity.

"And someone move that cow out of the way!"

Selen saw Louis wade about in the mud. His black riding boots were filthy to the knees. He had the sleeves of his shirt rolled up his arms, and he was trying to dig a log out of the earth. Four men were around him to help, and a fifth one pushed back a cow. The soldier slid, fell on his rump, and the cow went to brush its muzzle against one of the soldiers next to Louis. Selen tried to hold back an irresistible wish to laugh.

"Here you are!" He heard a voice call behind him. Selen turned around. Faremanne came his way. He was gleaming.

"What is happening here?" Selen asked.

"Well, they're trying to fix the fence of the cattle corral," Faremanne answered.

"No, I mean the whole camp."

"Oh, that. The men clean the alleys, dig a drain, and lay out latrines. I could not have believed it if someone had told me yesterday that this would happen. You should have heard Louis talk to the men this morning. He was so mad at first that I thought he would create a riot, but once he talked about what they had been through and what they could still achieve, they really listened to him. That and the fact that it was a shovel or the rope. Still, the men did appreciate that he grabbed one himself as well."

"And what of Segar?" Selen knew that changes were rarely carried by consensus.

"We haven't seen him today. I think he and his men will be a real challenge for Louis. They are not done yet." The tall knight waved at some soldiers further away. "I have to go now. If you look for the infirmary, it's that way," he said, pointing right.

Selen followed Faremanne's directions. The infirmary's tent was as large as the headquarters. Inside were rows of rudimentary beds covered with brownish bedsheets. Many beds were empty. That was a relief. At least they had no epidemic raging in the camp. The men lying there were not injured either. By what Selen saw, most suffered from malnutrition, cough, and diarrhea. Soldiers wearing long, brown cloaks acted as nurses. Selen turned to one of them. "Excuse me, I need to get some ingredients for a medicine."

"Brother Benedict over there can help you with that," the man answered, pointing further away.

Selen looked in that direction. He saw an old man in a frock sitting on one of the beds. Selen could not say if the man was bald or if he had a tonsure. As he moved closer, he saw that the man had a book open on his lap. "Brother Benedict?" he called.

The monk turned to him. He had a jovial, round face and twinkling eyes. "What can I do for you, young man?" he said.

"I need some ingredients for a balm and for my headache. Would you by any chance have some calendula, thyme, and white willow bark left?" Selen asked.

The man smiled. "I see that you have some knowledge of plants. May I know your name?"

"My name is Selen. My friend Louis and I came with Lord Tyntagiel yesterday. And yes, I used to be a physician in my village." Selen felt a little proud.

"A knight physician? This is the first time I've heard that," the man chuckled. "I remember you now. You are the champion. I don't like to see men die, but I have to admit that that one deserved it. The idiot had sent me too many of his victims in the past." Brother Benedict closed his book and got up. "Well, I surely have some of the plants you ask for. I suppose you need beeswax and oil as well. I think that it is easier if you use my office. You can take exactly what you need and prepare it there."

"That would be perfect! Thank you." Selen could not have asked for anything better. "Do you run this place alone?"

"I have soldiers to help me in my tasks, but I am the only physician." Brother Benedict seemed sorry about it. "And I am always short of materials. I keep on asking Sir Bertrant, but he never listens. Maybe I could go and search for them if someone was willing to replace me here for a while."

So that is the price for using the office, Selen thought. Well, he did not have anything better to do in the camp right now, and he had been asked to step aside for a little while. He could certainly be helpful here. "I would gladly help you, but not today. I've got a terrible headache, and I would like to rest once I have made my balms."

"Of course, of course. Go make your things, young man, and come back to me once you feel better."

The office was bigger than Selen's old shack. The shelves sagged under the weight of the jars. Unfortunately, not all were filled with herbs. Selen saw that the monk needed more ingredients. He picked a jar of calendula, took some lemon balm and ground the herbs with some chamomile flowers. He infused the blend in oil and cut the beeswax. While it simmered, he prepared the teas for his headache and the balms for his cut and Louis's hands. Two hours later, his balms and teas were ready.

Selen left the infirmary and headed towards his tent. The strong scents in the office had worsened his dizziness. He felt nauseous and needed to lie down. Folc was waiting for him. The boy wore new, fresh clothes.

"Sir Bertrant's orderly came by and brought us new garments. I really look like a lord now!" Folc turned around and showed him his new clothes.

"You do indeed. You are elegant," Selen said. Folc was proud of his green doublet. It was embroidered in gold thread. He had received red pants of the same fabric to wear under it. Selen saw that a pile of clothes lay on his own bed. He hoped there was no doublet or red pants in it.

He unfolded the clothes. The pants were dark green, nearly black. Under it was a brown tunic. He held it in front of him. The tunic looked like a long dress but was slit on both sides up to the hips. There was a white shirt to wear under it, and a long belt he could tie around his waist. It was perfect. He wondered who could have picked clothes so well for both of them. He turned to Folc. "I have an errand for you. Can you go and give this balm to Louis?"

"Sure!" Folc took the tin box and ran out of the tent.

Selen picked up a goblet and poured water on the herbs. His eyes narrowed due to the pain in his head. He made a few unsteady steps backwards and collapsed onto the side of the bed. Darkness claimed him.

It was warm, so warm. The flames rose high. The palace was burning. The enemies had come during the night, forcing their way through the iron doors. They had passed the population through the sword. Everyone had been taken by surprise, even the royal guard.

Standing next to the king, Selen fought hard, but he could not stand the assault. He heard one of the royal guards scream.

"The king is down! Retreat!"

Selen looked at his side. The king lay in a pool of blood. Selen threw a last blow at his assailants and followed his companions.

"To the queen's megaron! Protect the queen!" one man yelled.

The last guards fled to save the royal family. Selen looked around him. One of the guards was missing. *Not him*, Selen thought. *All can die, even me, but not him.*

Instead of retreating to the royal chambers, he ran to the pillar hall, where his friend's post had been. By making this choice, he knew he failed to obey his oath as a royal guard. Still, he did not want to fail to his heart. He needed to tell him. His friend must know, should they both die.

Selen ran through the marble halls. The flames licked at the colorful plaster and red curtains, turning the place into an oven. Some parts of the bulls fresco were already collapsing. He knew the enemies were on his heels. Still, he was nearly there. He pushed the giant oak door with all his strength and entered the balcony overhanging the hall. He saw him down there. His friend faced a horde of enemies. Even then, he fought bravely. His long hair flew around him as he whirled his sword with skill.

Selen was ready to jump over the rail when he felt agonizing pain in his throat. He searched for air, but could not take another breath. He put a hand on his throat and felt blood gush through his fingers. As he collapsed, half-naked men in golden and red ran past him. Selen's head hit the stone floor. The last thing his eyes saw was his friend die in front of him. His heart broke. "No... I..." he muttered, but the words never crossed his lips.

17

A stag's bell woke him up. The air was cold and damp. Lissandro raised his head. Ferns were stuck to his face and hair. Troubled by the nocturnal screams and the waving shadows of the trees, he had barely closed his eyes. His stomach rumbled. He knew there would be nothing to eat before long. He felt like crying but held back his tears. This was not a time to break down. He needed to move and get out of here. He dragged himself out of the hole he had been hunched in. His muscles were sore. He stretched. Lissandro walked south again.

He had wandered for a while when weird shapes silhouetted in front of him. There was something in the trees that wasn't made of wood. As he came closer, he noticed a stone structure covered in moss. It was shaped like small lozenges. He realized it was a window. Among the trees, a wall had been built. There had been windows opening on different floors. Some were still intact. Others stood partially, their broken mullions stretching up to the sky. Honeysuckle grew around the stiles, unfolding cascades of fragrant red-pink flowers. Lissandro walked around the edifice. He saw columns covered with ivy. The stone had cracked over time. The place had an overall agreeable atmosphere, which contrasted sharply with the forest around. Lissandro realized that these must be ruins that once belonged to the people of the forest. Maybe it was one of their palaces or a temple.

His way was blocked by a huge stone wall. Stairs ran up on the side of it. Lissandro put a foot on the first step. The stone shone under the moss. He bent down and scraped. The stairs were carved marble. He progressed to the first floor. From the top of the stairs stretched a garden. It had been abandoned for ages, and the vegetation had grown wild, but the species that had been planted here did not belong to these woods. Besides, he could discern the form of old statues in different places. Lissandro strolled around. There were roses of many colors, magnolia trees, patches of lilies of the valley under weeping willows. He did not remember ever having seen such splendor in this world. At the turn of the path, he faced what could have been the most enchanted place of the garden. A large pond with a stone rim stood under the long branches of blooming lilac trees. The color made him think of his friend. In the middle of the pond, on a small island, grew an old, crooked elm.

"I have been waiting for you," the tree said.

Lissandro jumped in alarm. The tree bent and twisted its bark in weird, impossible moves. An arm detached itself, then another on the opposite side. The limbs rose lightly into the air. They could have been branches if it hadn't been for the elongated fingers at the end. In the middle of the trunk, a face appeared. He could not explain it, but Lissandro was sure it was the features of a woman. Her eyes were gleaming gold.

"Are you scared?" the face asked him with an ethereal voice.

"I don't know if I should be," Lissandro answered. At least, he trembled. "Who are you?"

"I am the face of time. I am the spirit of the forest. I am one of the last hamadryads," the creature said.

"You said you were waiting for me?" Lissandro was intrigued.

"You came here full of questions, about your past, about your future, about your visions."

"What do you know of my visions?" Lissandro asked.

"I know what they are and why you have to carry this burden, but do you really want to know?"

"I know who I am. I am Lissandro Lorca. Yet, I don't know what I am doing here, and by here, I mean here in this world."

"You think you know who you are. Look into the water. It will reveal it to you."

Lissandro approached the rim carefully. He gazed into the pond. The water was crystal clear. He could see the stones at the bottom. *There must be more to it*, he thought. He stretched his hand and skimmed the surface of the water. The blow was as powerful as a lightning bolt. Lissandro was pushed violently backwards and fell on his back. His vision blurred in patches of dark green and purple, turning into darkness like clouds in a thunderstorm. The tree's voice was deafening.

"You are a child of darkness! Doomed to walk the earth!"

Lissandro felt a terrible pain on the side of his neck. He touched his skin. Thick blood poured out of two small holes. He convulsed. Visions submerged him.

He saw teeth, a bite, blood, voices calling his name, faces he had known, sharp eyes in the night, a big city with cars and neon lights, and a voice, powerful and comforting.

"I will take care of you now."

A warm light blinded his eyes and overwhelmed his body. Lissandro was back on the ground in the garden.

"But it seems you have reached salvation. You are very special," the tree said.

Lissandro regained consciousness. More memories had come back to his mind. As nostalgia took hold of his heart, a tear ran down his cheek. "You haven't answered my question," he said, painfully. "What am I doing here?"

"Three you were and three you will be, across the worlds to fulfill your destiny," the tree said. "You are not from this world, all three of you. To achieve his goals, Agroln once used blood magic to summon the orcs and the mighty Rylarth, Eater of Sheep. Dragons live in the abyss of darkness. To reach him, Agroln needed to open a portal to hell. Yet, blood magic is unstable. More portals were simultaneously opened on other worlds, or more precisely, time lapses. But as Agroln's portal tried to break the barrier of hell, the other portals collided with heaven. To counterbalance the coming of the demon, heaven rejected three souls. The souls of men whose life's purpose had been unfulfilled."

"What do you mean by time lapses?"

"All from the same world, but not from the same time period."

"So, we are all dead?" Lissandro felt shocked by the news.

"Dead? What is dead? You are not in heaven. You breathe. You feel. No, what you all got is…a second chance."

"And our mission is to kill the dragon?"

"Only you have the power to fight darkness, but not all of you carry the same light. Three souls, three different lights. Still, you are also men. You have your free will."

"But should we refuse, it would mean the end of the world?"

"Yes."

"What will happen to us if we succeed? Will we be sent back into our respective worlds? Will we die?" Lissandro had no wish to go back where he came from. He had roamed there too long.

"I'm afraid you will have to live in this world. Until your death comes."

"Will my visions help us or can you take this curse from me?" If the creature could help him get rid of the nightmares, he would not mind trying.

"Your fate is bound to the one of darkness. In your case, the call is stronger than for your friends. These visions do not need to be the future. If you use them wisely."

"I have a last question. Why are we all… We all like men."

"Only tormented souls, troubled by sorrow and despair could wriggle their way through the portals. Peaceful souls stay in heaven. Yours were the strongest ones."

Lissandro stayed silent. He pondered on what he had learned. There was hope to win the war. He needed to inform his friends. "I thank you for sharing your deep knowledge." Lissandro bowed.

"I still have two things for you," the tree carried on. One fingerlike branch searched through a patch of leaves. It stretched to Lissandro. "Take these." Lissandro opened his palm under the branch. Two seeds, round like beans, fell out of it. They shone like two emeralds. "These are seeds of a tree long dead. It used to grow on an island where your friend Selen was born. With the vanishing of these trees, we have lost our most beautiful hamadryads. Give these seeds to your friend. He will know what to do."

Lissandro packed the seeds with care in a piece of cloth and stored them on the inside of his tunic.

"As for you, we have an even more precious gift. Come. Look into the pond's water. You don't need to touch it this time."

Lissandro felt suspicious. Still, he stepped forward nonetheless. He put his hands flat on the stone rim and gazed down. Something appeared. The image of a face. Its features were stern and manly. The man had a strong, square jaw, a large nose, and deep-set narrow eyes. His irises were of a piercing light blue, tainted with flecks of gold. His long golden hair floating like a lion's mane around his head made him look like a powerful king.

Lissandro put a shaking hand to his mouth. "Grimmr," he murmured. "I've lost…Grimmr." His heart missed a beat. He could not breathe anymore. He broke down in tears in front of the pond. The pain in his heart was agonizing. He screamed and hit the stone floor with his fists. It could not be real. He could not have been sent in a world away from his true love. It was unfair. He hated all of them, Agroln and his magic, the omniscient trees, even heaven and hell. He felt like a pawn on a board. They were all the silly pawns of these higher forces. He curled into a ball and sobbed.

When all the tears in his body had turned dry, Lissandro pondered on his future in this land. There was no hope for him, not without Grimmr. Yet, his friends were together. They had a future and they needed him. Lissandro took the resolution to help them, whatever the cost. He could still die later.

He rose. The tree had turned back to its lifeless shape. There was no face to be seen anymore. The arms had turned to branches. He looked up. The sun was shining. He could see the sky again. He could head south.

18

Folc walked among the tents in search for Louis. A crowd had gathered in the east of the camp. He heard shouts. Folc slipped between the curious and bumped into a large soldier in mail and leather straps, wrapped in a grey, muddy cloak. The man turned around.

"What are you doing here, boy? Get lost. This is no place for a child." The strong man scowled at him, pushing him back with his hand.

Folc wanted to complain that he was not a child but a lord. Yet, he had no time to lose with the soldier. The warning had intrigued him. Ignoring the man's remark, he pushed his way on the right. As he left the crowd behind, he halted. He gasped with shock. In front of him, soldiers guarded a line of prisoners. A group sat on the ground. Their hands were tied with a rope. Their heads hung down in apathy or desperation. Another group stood up, waiting. These showed fear. Some wailed, others swore and cursed. One man had wet his pants. Folc noticed that most of the men had the metal badge of a lieutenant. Surprisingly, there were a few women among the prisoners. Folc counted three.

Behind the last group, gallows had been constructed. Soldiers untied corpses from the ropes. The bodies fell to the wooden floor with a thud and were thrown negligently into a cart. A soldier gave a quick brush on the boards where the corpses had been. Folc noticed the smell of piss in the air. The line of prisoners that had waited standing was pushed towards the steps. The condemned took their place under the ropes. As one soldier fastened the nooses around their necks, another soldier tied their feet together. Folc looked around and saw Louis and Faremanne watch the execution with gravity. Folc strode towards them.

"What is going on?" he asked.

Without turning his gaze away from the gallows, Louis answered him. "You should not be here, Folc. Leave." His tone was cold as ice.

"But what have they done? Who are these women?" Folc had never seen an execution in an army camp, not on the soldiers of the same army at least.

Louis's eyes turned slowly towards him. Folk took a step back. His heart missed a beat, and he felt a shiver run through his body.

"Go away," Louis hissed. He looked straight ahead again.

"Wait for us in our tent, boy. It won't be long," Faremanne said without turning his head.

Folc saw Louis nod. On the gallows, the traps opened. The fall of the bodies stopped sharply with a crushing sound that sent gooseflesh down Folc's spine.

"Move the bodies. Next!" Faremanne shouted. The second group of prisoners was compelled to rise.

"No! Please!" A man on the line screamed.

Folc had seen enough. He walked away to the center of the camp. As he had not fulfilled his errand, he entered Faremanne and Louis's tent. The place was tidy except for the table which disappeared under a sea of papers. Folc sat on one of the beds and waited.

A moment later, Louis and Faremanne entered the tent. As Louis approached him, Folc shrank into himself. His friend stopped, startled.

"You should not have come there," Louis sighed. "I'm sorry I was a bit rough."

Folc noticed his friend's face turn gentle again. He relaxed. "What happened over there?" he asked.

"We cleaned the camp of its worst elements: gamblers, rebels, thieves, brutes. Anyone who is a danger to the stability and order of this army. It is not an enjoyable sight, but it was necessary. It will also be a lesson for the cowards and the lazy," Louis answered. He untied his gauntlets.

"But what of the women?" Folc inquired.

"Prostitutes. I warned them this would happen if they stayed. I warned all of them yesterday, commanding them to give up their despicable behavior and to follow the rules. Yet, some did not listen. Today they endured the consequences."

"Prostitutes only do their job. Couldn't you have shown them mercy and expelled them?" Folc could understand that brutes like The Mountain had to be stopped, but he felt pity for the women.

Louis turned to him and gave a faint smile. "You are young and you have a good heart. Still, you are here among us. Therefore, you must face the truth. Mercy is a weakness in wartime. Should we show mercy, not only would we lose the control of the men, but our motivation to fight. There is no place for doubt. We must be resolute in our actions." He paused. "We expulsed most of the girls yesterday. The ones who stayed gave me no choice."

Folc lowered his head and pondered on the words. Neither Lord Hunfray nor any lord he knew had presented him things that way. Besides, gambling and prostitutes were common at the side of large armies. Louis's voice dragged him out of his thoughts.

"Why are you here, Folc?" Louis asked.

Folc remembered his errand. He took the tin box from his pocket. "Selen gave me this for you." He handed the box to Louis.

"Thank you." Louis took it. "How is he?" he asked with a whisper.

"He did not feel very well…" Folc saw Louis's eyes grow wider. "But he felt better when I left," he added in a hurry. His friend had better things to do than to worry about them. "I should go back to my tent. I promise not to mess again in your command," he said, looking at Louis and Faremanne. He stepped clumsily out of the tent and hurried back to his quarters. Folc did not like to lie and preferred to avoid further questions.

Folc entered his tent. Selen lay unconscious on the ground. "Selen!" Folc's chest tightened with anxiety. He rushed down to the side of his friend. He laid the back of his hand against his brow. It was hot and moist. Folc dragged Selen onto the bed. "Damn, you're heavier than you look." He put the shoulders first, then raised his friend's hips and pushed them up onto the furs. Selen moaned unintelligible words. Folc looked at the cut on Selen's brow. It had a nasty crimson color. Could the wound have been infected? Another tin box lay on the small table. He opened it. Folc plunged one finger into the balm and spread it over the cut. He frowned at Selen.

"I'm sure you have felt bad for long, but you did not dare to complain. If only you had let me do my job and rested."

Folc picked up the goblet at the side of the bed. The water had been spilled, but the herbs still stuck on the bottom. He could fill it with hot water and give the tea to Selen. There was a brazier outside near the tent. Folc went out and warmed water over it. Once the water boiled, he removed it from the fire and filled the goblet. He returned inside the tent.

"Fire...wait..." Selen mumbled in his sleep, delirious.

"Oh, shut up," Folc said. The anger in his heart was only motivated by the worry he felt for his friend. An infection could be nasty on a battlefield. In infirmaries, he had seen men die of gangrene. Fortunately, the wound was on the brow and did not seem to spread. Yet, Selen burned with fever.

Folc sat on the side of the bed with the infusion. He slipped a hand behind Selen's head and raised it gently as he brought the goblet to his lips. He managed to have his friend drink most of the tea.

"And me who just said you felt better," Folc mumbled.

He did not dare to alert Louis. The two men were so close that it could affect the camp's new organization. Folc decided to stay silent and to watch alone over his friend. He could still change his mind later if the situation got worse. He filled a bowl with cold water and moistened Selen's head and hands to cool him down.

"Please don't get worse," he whispered, holding Selen's hand.

Three days passed by. Folc was mending his old clothes when he saw Selen stir. "Are you awake?" he asked. Joy filled his heart.

"Yes. I feel fine." Selen opened his eyes. He looked relaxed. His face was smooth and serene again. Folc could also detect happiness. "I remember what happened now." For a while, his friend seemed lost in memories. "Did Louis come searching for me?"

"I preferred not to tell anyone you were ill. Are you hungry? I fed you honey, but I guessed you would want more once you woke up." Folc rose and fetched brown bread that he gave to his friend.

"Thank you so much, Folc," Selen said, taking the bread. "What did I miss?"

"You should see the camp. It has never been this clean and tidy. We even have jails now. And they are not empty. There are new rules applying, with a death sentence for half of them. Lieutenants have been hung. I don't need to tell you who is behind it all." Folc smiled.

"I never doubted him," Selen said, chewing on the bread. "How are the three other captains reacting?"

"Actually, Captain Jamys is on a mission in the Iron Marches, and Captain Vakeg protects a village ten miles from here. Segar is the only one left in the camp for the moment. He didn't dare to move against both Louis and Faremanne. Not yet, at least."

"Good. Maybe our two captains will win the men's favors. Still, I would not count on it too much. Not everyone likes order and discipline."

"If you feel good enough, maybe we could have a look at the situation at the headquarters." Folc was bored of staying inside the tent and doing household tasks. He wasn't a page anymore and he longed for some action.

"You don't need me for that, Folc. You are a lord. You can go wherever you like."

"Are you not slightly curious to know what's going on?" Folc insisted. Maybe he was a lord, but he knew where young lads were not welcomed when uninvited. Probably his friend perceived his deception.

"Let's go," Selen answered. He rose and buckled his belt with his sword.

They headed to the headquarters and slipped inside the pavilion. Several lieutenants were gathered from the entrance to the front of the large table around which stood Sir Bertrant, Faremanne, and Louis. The three men studied a map, pointing at different places. Folc could not distinguish what they said, but they frowned and their voices sounded grave. Louis looked up from the map and saw them. His eyes gleamed, and he tried to hide a smile. Louis looked back at the map again. Folc felt some remorse for not telling about Selen's health.

"Maybe they are all dead," Folc heard Faremanne say. "It's too long since we received news of them."

"We should prepare a party and search for them. They may still be at the village or on the way here, wounded," Louis said to Bertrant.

A soldier rushed inside the tent. "Commander! My lords!" The man reached the table and whispered something to Bertrant.

"He is here!" the latter exclaimed. "He has just arrived!" He turned to the panting soldier. "Fetch the man. I want to see him at once."

Louis and Faremanne exchanged words Folc could not hear. Faremanne made a sign to a guard who disappeared behind a curtain.

A few minutes later, the tent entrance opened wide, and a strong, bushy man in leather armour entered. He had a battered breastplate half covering his fat belly. The man stank of sweat and a rancid smell of beer. His black hair was greasy, and he had not shaved in ages. There was something unpleasant about his face. He had a carnivorous smile and piggy eyes. Folc thought that he was probably the kind of man ogre legends were based on. Two of his men followed behind. He stopped two yards in front of the table and crossed his muscular arms over his chest.

"So, I'm back," the man spat with contempt.

"What are you doing here, Vakeg?" Bertrant grunted. "Why are you not holding the village? Did the orcs take it?"

"Maybe. I left before they arrived," the captain said, unperturbed.

"Wrong answer," Folc heard Selen whisper behind him.

"You left?" Louis stressed the words. Folc saw his fierce eyes narrow.

"Villagers were getting on my nerves. They said they had no more food for me and my men. They complained night and day like crybabies. All a bunch of reeky pig filth anyway. Couldn't even make decent beer." While the captain talked, Louis had left his place near the table and had placed himself in front of the large man.

"Are you saying that you left this village because the beer tasted of piss?" Louis asked slowly.

"Yep, I did. You can send someone else 'cause..." The man did not finish his sentence. Louis punched him brutally in the face. Bones cracked. Folc hoped it was not Louis's hand. Vakeg's head now faced right, but his body still stood, unshaken. Blood dripped from his lips. Like a shot, he grasped Louis's throat with his right hand. Vakeg's pudgy, dirty fingers pressed on the white skin as he pulled Louis to him. Louis's cold eyes did not flinch once. In the corner of his eye, Folc saw Selen reach for his sword. Then, it all went fast.

Louis drew the man's dagger from its sheath. He pushed it into the man's belly and hacked deep from left to right. As his bowels fell out, the man loosened his grip. Vakeg knelt and tried to push his slimy intestines back into his body. Louis moved around him, stepped between Vakeg's legs, took the man's chin in his left hand, and cut his throat clean in a gush of blood. He turned around, holding the half-beheaded head by the hair.

"No one leaves his post! No one surrenders! Is that clear?" Louis yelled at the lieutenants around him. He pointed at Vakeg's lieutenants. "Guards, arrest these men. And all the ones who came back!"

"What should we do with them?" Faremanne asked.

Louis turned around. "Hang them." He dropped Vakeg's head and kicked at it with his foot. "And put that thing on a spike in the yard. It will teach them. We are here to protect the people. Nothing else." Louis left the tent.

Bertrant came towards Folc and Selen. "Is he mad?" he whispered to Selen. "This man came back with thirty soldiers."

"He is not mad, and you should do what he says," Selen responded gravely, in full support of his friend. "I'll go talk to him. He will probably want to send troops back to the village. You should have men ready." He left the tent. Folc followed him.

Louis was cleaning the blood off his hands when they arrived in his tent. "I know. It was messy, but…"

"No, you were right. Someone needs to do the dirty work, and such men should not be in the Rebellion," Selen said. Louis had not been the only one to feel disgust for the captain's behavior. Folc had read outrage on Bertrant and Faremanne's faces, but Louis had been the one to act. "Is there anything I can do to help?" Selen asked.

Louis softened and came to them. "I'm sorry I haven't checked on you these last few days. I was busy with the camp. How have things been going for both of you?"

Neither Folc nor Selen dared to talk about the illness. It did not matter anymore now. "I may start to work at the infirmary," Selen said. "Brother Benedict needs help, and I can be useful."

"That is a good thing. And it's a safe place," Louis said.

Folc observed Louis. When they had travelled together, Louis had displayed a reserved but pleasant mood. Now that they were in the camp, his friend's moves were sharp and his words had edges. Yet, Folc could not help but notice that the tone Louis used with Selen was different from the one he used with everyone in the camp. It was caring to the extreme, as if Selen was made of porcelain. The rest of his entourage, Folc included, never got such consideration. Folc wondered if it had to do with Selen's kindness, or if they shared some kind of secret. There was something intriguing between them, but Folc could not put a word on it.

"I will ride to the village with another troop," Louis said, talking to Selen. "Wait for me here. I will probably need your help at my return. There are things bothering me." Folc saw that Louis reached out his hand towards Selen, but he had changed his mind and drew his hand back. As his hand contracted into a fist, his eyes twitched.

Folc got back to the conversation. "Can I come with you?" he asked. They both looked at him astounded. Folc sighed and turned to Louis. "Please, I'm not a child anymore. I need to do my share."

"He is right," Louis said to Selen. He turned to Folc. "You can come, but find yourself some kind of armour first—and a weapon. We leave in an hour. I want to be back as soon as possible."

Folc left the tent and went to the smithy. The place was hot and smelled of smoke. The men did not glance up from their anvils as Folc sifted through the leftovers. The sword was easy to find, but there was no armour his size. He mixed pieces together and completed it with leather straps. He thought that he did not look very lordly, but at least he felt protected. Once dressed, Folc hurried back. Thirty men were already gathered in the yard of the headquarters when he arrived. A horse was waiting for him.

"We will take the main road to the village. There should not be enemies on it right now. I hope to reach Freyhorn at noon. We will act depending on what we will find there. Should the villagers be unharmed, a garrison will stay there." Louis explained to the men. "Now, let's go."

Louis turned his mount and took the lead. Folc kicked his horse and followed them. They trotted to the village. The road was free of any obstacles. Still, the atmosphere in the group was tense. All Folc could hear was the pounding of the hooves and the singing of the birds above them.

The troop reached Freyhorn an hour later. Fortunately, the place was untouched by orcs. However, the villagers fled to their houses when they saw them. Folc watched Louis swing down from his horse and approach a group of people who had had no time to flee. They trembled and pleaded for their lives.

"Please, my lord! Have mercy!"

"Why on earth are you scared of me?" Louis asked.

"You're here to kill us. The captain sent you!" one of the inhabitants shrieked.

"No, I won't. Now, would you tell me what happened here? What did the captain do?"

One of the villagers calmed down and approached Louis cautiously. "The captain ate our provisions and drank our beer, my lord. When we ran out of beer, he was angry."

"Is that all?" Louis asked, irritated. Folc considered that, for a villager, it meant already a lot.

"He also raped some of our women," the man murmured, his head low.

"Did you react?" Louis asked. Folc thought that if he had not already killed Vakeg, Louis would have had the man put to death for that.

"We did, my lord, but then he hung some of us." The man cried.

"Well, he won't hurt you anymore. He has been executed. He and all his men," Louis replied with a softer tone. The villagers looked joyful. "I'm here with new soldiers to protect the village. You may not wish to have more of our men in your town, but I can assure you that they won't behave the same way."

"We don't have much food for them, but if they help us to gather provisions, we welcome them gladly, my lord. Thank you." The men lost themselves in words of gratitude.

Louis came back to the troops and called the lieutenant to him. "You stay here with your men. If any of you hurt any of the villagers, he will end up like Vakeg." Louis's voice had been smooth but clear to everyone. "Folc. You're coming back with me."

They rode back to the camp in silence. Louis looked preoccupied. "What is wrong?" Folc asked.

"A crow from Embermire arrived this morning."

They were back at the camp in the afternoon. The soldiers made space in front of their trotting mounts. Louis jumped off his horse and headed to the headquarters. "Go fetch Selen!" he shouted.

Folc dismounted and strode to his tent where his friend rested on his bed, reading. "You are needed at the headquarters," Folc said. "I think it's important."

Selen jumped up, buckled on his sword and followed him to the commander's pavilion. Louis stood at the table with Bertrant and Faremanne. The captain had a piece of paper in his hands. He gave it to Selen.

"It's from Lord Pembroke in Embermire," Bertrant said.

"His motivations are unclear," Selen said after reading the missive. "He talks about things coming from the woods and bandits."

"Excuses," Louis grumbled. "The excuses of a coward!" He pounded the table with his fist.

"It may be more serious than that, Louis," Faremanne said to keep things in perspective. "Maybe the man faces difficulties we don't know about."

"Or maybe we lose the help of twelve thousand men because their commander hides under his bed." Louis snarled.

"What do you propose?" Selen inquired, calm as usual.

"I will ride to Embermire and ask him myself. Maybe he won't dare to refuse," Louis said, marking it as his final decision.

Faremanne, Selen, and Bertrant looked aghast. Folc understood why Louis had asked for Selen. He would need a backup. Still, Folc could not see his own part in that.

"Embermire is sixty-five miles from where we are. It would take two days to ride there. Besides, you would need an escort big enough to impress the old lord. He is a count and you have no titles. And you better not count on a change of mind from that coward," Bertrant complained.

"I will take a hundred men with me. It should be enough to scare away any bandits on the way, and it will not weaken your forces. We won't take equipment or tents, only the food we can carry." Louis said, resolute.

"You have made good decisions until now. I grant you these hundred men, but we await your return in four days. Don't lose your time with that old bricon."

Bertrant didn't seem to like the man at all. Folc wondered if there was not something more about it.

"Is there some other lord you can contact during my absence?" Louis asked.

Faremanne pointed at a dot named Mighthorn on the map. "There. Down south. These are the lands of Count Elye. He may help us." His finger circled a large band of territory in the west.

"Down south? Is he not allied with Agroln?" Selen inquired.

"Elye is powerful and cunning enough to do what pleases him. He may want to get rid of Agroln. I will send him a message," Bertrant said.

"I'll prepare myself and leave tomorrow." Louis sighed. "Selen, I want you to come with me."

"Of course," Selen answered.

Folc waited and realized that they all had forgotten about him. "And what will I do?"

"You can help me in my tasks," Faremanne said, as if addressing a child. "I can show you how things work for a squire inside a camp."

Well, that could be interesting, Folc thought. As long as it did not include too much cleaning.

19

Lissandro had walked for four days now. He was starving. The leaves and roots he foraged barely gave him the strength to stand up. His stomach was so twisted with cramps that all he could vomit was mucus. Fortunately, he headed in the right direction. The forest was less dense. He had been able to spot animals again, and rays of the sun shone above his head. He halted near a brook to drink. The water was refreshing. He heard a noise from the bushes on the other side. He gazed. Nothing. He lay down on the grass and closed his eyes, but he could not sleep. Lissandro had the queer impression that something watched him. He rose and kept on walking. His progression was laborious. The grass was thick, and the ground was uneven. Boulders and thickets stood in his way. The large oaks had left space for hornbeams and ashes. Green saplings grew among their roots. The wind whispered in the leaves.

Lissandro still felt like he was being watched. He heard the crowing of a crow and saw the bird take off into the air a few steps away from him. Something shone where it had stood. He advanced cautiously with a hand on his dagger. A silvery object lay among the leaves. As he went to pick it up, he felt pressure on his ankle.

"Ow!" His right foot flew into the air, dragging his body behind. Blood rushed to his head as he lost his balance. He now hung from a rope six feet over the ground. His mail flipped over, covering his face. He pushed it up. Lissandro swung and reached for his dagger. The sheath was empty. The blade lay on the dead leaves under his head.

"What a nice catch," a voice said, approaching.

A man came from behind him and picked up the dagger. With a nonchalant hand, he pushed Lissandro on the shoulders, sending him swinging. The man laughed. There was something perturbing in his voice. The rope was cut loose. Lissandro crashed onto the ground with a thud, landing on his twisted mail around his ribs. His chest hurt. He coughed and blew his hair and the leaves out of his dirty face.

"Now. Don't move," he heard.

"As you wish, my lady," Lissandro answered with a grin.

With a firm grip, she tied his hands behind his back and dragged him against a tree. "It's quite unusual to have folk go for a walk in this part of the woods," she said. "Who are you?"

Lissandro was not tall for a man, but she was huge. Her dark hair had been cut short, probably with a dagger, and gave her a shaggy look. Though she had a scar on her left cheek, running from her almond, black eyes to her thin lips, her features retained some charm.

"What are you looking at?" she snapped.

"It's quite unusual to meet a woman clad in heavy armour." Lissandro guessed he probably wasn't the first to make that remark. Because it must have been the worst introduction sentence he could have found, he added, "But it suits you well." He knew he was clumsy with women.

"At least, you don't seem disgusted," she grunted. "I asked you a question. Who are you?"

"My name is Lissandro, and I'm no one." *Sad but true*, he thought.

"Everyone has a price," she said. She had untied the rope from the tree and rolled it around her arm.

"Oh, bandits. It's my lucky day," Lissandro mumbled to himself. "And where will you sell me?"

"I won't, but I know people who will. For now, you're coming with me." She grabbed him like a potato bag and dragged him behind her. She strode fast, forcing Lissandro to jog. After a few hundred yards, he collapsed. "Come on," she exclaimed, irritated. "Can't you even hold the pace?"

Lissandro felt dizzy in the head. "I'm starving," he muttered. "Please, I can't hold on."

She grabbed him and threw him over her shoulders. "You don't weight much, I grant you that." Like an angler after a good catch, she brought him back to her base camp.

Lissandro was thrown to the side of a dead fire. She tossed him a piece of brown bread.

"Eat," she commanded him.

He picked up the bread and chewed on it. It was hard with a moldy taste. Still, it felt good. She sat near the fire, trying to put it ablaze again. "What's your name?" he asked.

She stayed silent, her back turned. "Kilda," she finally said. The shadows of the trees stretched long. Twilight crept around them.

"Why are you a bandit?" Lissandro asked. He waited, but she never answered.

They spent the rest of the evening in silence. Lissandro regretted he had no blanket. He crept a bit closer to the fire. When he found a soft spot, he dug a hole in the leaves and buried himself. *Not better than a wild boar in its nest*, he thought.

"Good night, Kilda," he whispered as he fell asleep. She could hold the watch. He was her prisoner after all.

Lissandro felt a boot tramp on his shoulder. "Get up."

"Good morning to you too," he mumbled. "I had a fantastic sleep." He grinned at her, but she did not seem to notice. She packed her bags and rolled her blankets. Lissandro spotted his dagger attached to her belt.

"I'm afraid you will have to free me," he called out.

"And why would I do that?" she sighed.

"I need to pee."

She turned around and looked at him. "You wouldn't be the most disgusting thing I have held in my life."

Lissandro did not know how to take that. "Maybe, but I'm not sure I could manage."

"Too long in the wild, I guess." She came forward, a grumpy look on her face. "Turn around." She untied his ropes. Lissandro massaged his burning wrists and relieved himself.

"All right, now, you're coming with me," she said, stretching the rope again.

In an instant, Lissandro pushed her with his elbow and tried to grasp his dagger. The blow he got on his face threw him onto the ground. He put his hand on his aching jaw.

"Sorry for your pretty face," she said, "but that's what you get for being a fool."

"Just trying," Lissandro coughed. His hands were tied again, and her grip raised him off the ground. He knew he would be blue on the cheek for some days. They left the cold ashes of the fire behind them and walked south.

"Do you know where we are going?" Lissandro inquired. To him, it seemed as if they went in circles in the woods, always passing over the same stones, the same roots, and the same creeks.

"We head south to Embermire. Our camp is in the southwest of the city." Kilda strode, her back straight. Lissandro trotted behind, like a dog on a leash.

"A camp of bandits," Lissandro grunted. He was worried. Only the worst could happen there.

"No. A camp of people fighting against those treacherous lords. We sack and ransom because they can pay for it. And they will pay." Kilda's voice had a nasty tone.

"Really?" he exclaimed. "Of all the enemies you could turn your strength against, you chose the lords? Don't you think the orcs are a slight bit more important?" Such ridiculous reactions exasperated him. Some people would lose their energy in petty social class quarrels until the giant foot of a dragon crushed them like insects.

"It's personal," she snapped.

There we are, he thought. "Is it because of the lords that you took up arms?"

"This is none of your business." This time, she sounded melancholic. "Get down!" She pulled down on the rope. Lissandro stumbled and fell headfirst on the muddy leaves.

Down the slope, a road wound in a glade. It ran from east to southwest. Further away, a wagon had pulled over. They could hear shouts of children. "Should we have a look?" Lissandro asked.

"This is none of our business," Kilda answered.

Lissandro felt that she hesitated. "Come on. There are children," he insisted.

She stared at him. "If you try anything, I will kill you."

Lissandro nodded. She untied him, and they progressed towards the wagon. Two children, a boy and a girl, cried over a woman.

"What happened here?" Kilda asked.

The children jumped under the vehicle and hid behind the wheels.

Lissandro grabbed the woman by the shoulders and turned her slowly on her back. She was unconscious but alive. He put his hand on her head. She had a fever. She was probably sick and had fallen from her seat. Why would a woman travel alone in a wagon with two children?

"Where is your father?" he asked the children.

"He is dead," answered the boy with a sad look on his face. "Killed by the bandits."

Lissandro looked reproachfully at Kilda. She noticed it. He could discern shame on her face. *So much for attacking the lords*, he thought.

"We have no food," the child carried on. "Mama is sick. We are going to Embermire." He and his sister crept from under the wagon, blotted on each other.

Lissandro felt pity for these people. He rose and talked to Kilda. "We could drive them there. It's on our way."

Kilda pulled him on the side. Her grip was strong on his arm. "Are you mad? Do you think I will let you drive among people, let alone enter a city? You are still my prisoner," she hissed.

"Are you ready to let them stay here? A woman and her children? With bandits around?" He had insisted on the thorny word.

She looked furious, but the choice was clear. "Get in the wagon, all of you."

Lissandro picked up the mother and laid her down in the wagon. Kilda sat on the bench and took the reins. The wheels spun and rasped on the stones. They departed in a heavy silence.

A few hours later, Embermire stood in front of them.

20

Louis and Selen rode side by side at the head of the hundred men. Louis had insisted that most soldiers be mounted. The men at the camp didn't need to move anywhere, and riders always gave a better impression. They had departed early, leaving Folc under the protection of Faremanne. Their cortege was all but discreet. The throbbing sound of the horses on the ground made the earth shake, and the clanking of the armours could probably be heard miles away. The day was hot, especially for men in mails. Louis's armour was sweltering.

"Thank you for letting me come with you," Selen told him with his soft voice. He looked at him sidelong. Sweat shone on his brow.

"I could not be away four days and leave you behind. Besides, it's always good I have someone wise like you at my side." Louis smiled at Selen. In the camp, Selen was silent most of the time, but his interventions were always pertinent. However, his competence was only an excuse to have him by his side.

"I will help you find the right words," Selen teased him. His eyes gleamed. Louis realized how much he had missed his friend these last days.

"Embermire is just south of the Ebony Forest. Maybe we could send villagers to search for Lilo if we put a high reward."

"That's an excellent idea!" Selen exclaimed. "If only we had time to search for him ourselves."

The city appeared in front of them. Embermire was in a valley, the slopes of which were covered with forests. On the north side, the Ebony Forest looked deep and dark, like an impassable border. Its trees were old and gnarled. Brown spotted leaves covered the branches, forming a heavy canopy. While the south side was colorful and resounded of birds songs, the north was silent. Louis could understand that Lissandro had considered it evil. There was something cursed emanating from these trees. Maybe it explained why the city had such strong ramparts. The only thing he saw above the white walls were the last floors of the count's castle.

The road was broad, but their retinue was even larger. Carts coming from the other side were forced to pull over and watch them pass. They heard a horn blow in a distance. Louis liked to think that they had come unannounced. He hoped that, caught off his guard, the count would show his true self. Whatever the issue of this meeting, he was resolute to get to the bottom of things. He only regretted that he was bearing Bertrant's colors. The Rebellion needed its own symbol. It was important to rally the men on something material as well, something that would represent their ideal, their land. He would need to talk with Faremanne about it. He thought that he had already asked too much from the old commander. And it was his colors he meant to change. It would not please him. Louis looked at the main gate. At least, they had not raised the bridge.

"Let me do the talking," Louis said to Selen. "If things go wrong, you can still save our skins with your kind words." He grinned. "The most important is that we agree on what to say. Who knows what Bertrant has told the count until now?"

A man in mail and silver tabard rode towards them. He reined a few yards from their horses. "Welcome to Embermire, my lords. I am Captain Raolin. Lord Pembroke has been waiting for you. I will lead you to him."

So much for the element of surprise, Louis thought. He made a sign to the man that they were ready to follow him.

They passed under the gate. The stench filled Louis's nose at once. The streets were jam-packed and narrow, the houses high. The captain had to shout and threaten to remove the wagons from their path. There were too many people, far too many. Though the life in the city did not look flourishing, they still had some merchandise to sell in the stalls, but the prices the merchants shouted were abusive. Surrounded by the crowd, the troop of riders advanced laboriously. Louis thought that he had acted like a fool. If the count wanted them dead, they would be dead already. This time, he would be careful with his words. He did not want to be responsible for the death of a hundred men under his command, not that way. They followed the captain to the castle gate.

They dismounted in the inner courtyard. On the high walls around them, narrow, unglazed windows gaped open from the second floor to the machicolation. A wooden staircase in the wall under a wooden shingle roof led to the first floor. The riders pressed inside the yard around the stone well. Half of their hundred mounts could barely fit in the place. The horses trumpeted and piaffed. Inwardly, Louis cursed himself.

"Your men will have to wait here. They will be taken care of and will receive food. We have stables outside the castle for the horses. You can follow me to his Lordship." The captain walked in front of them, showing the way.

"I hope you know what you are doing," Louis heard Selen whisper. "We are trapped."

Louis knew it too well. He would have liked to say something reassuring to his friend, but he did not feel much comfortable himself. He climbed the stairs with a lump in his throat. He needed to stay focused. He tried to remember the poor excuses the man had written. Anger often helped him to be brave. Or foolish. They entered the castle and went up flights of stairs.

The great hall's doors opened in front of them. The hall had two fireplaces with elaborate overmantels. The walls were richly decorated with heavy beams, trophies, and moldings. The lower part was painted orange with blue arabesques. At the end of the hall, the count sat on his chair. He was a robust man, bald with a black beard with white strands. His dark eyes gazed at them with gravity.

"Leave us!" he shouted at his captain. The heavy doors closed slowly behind them. "I thought I had been clear," the count grunted with a sigh. He scratched a spot on the armrest, before laying his chin on his hand.

Louis approached him. "Do you like pheasants, my lord?" he asked. "Juicy, roasted pheasants?" Louis did not wait for an answer. "I'm sure you do. Everyone likes to eat. Orcs too. Juicy, roasted men. Yet, men are scarce now in the east, no one to cultivate the fields. Soon, the orcs will take the center of Trevalden and crush the Rebellion. But who cares, it's just scum anyway. Juicy scum. Maybe the orcs won't come here in the west. You have been left in peace for long. Yet, I have never heard of an orc using a plow. The lands in the east will turn barren. Besides, there are others who like to eat. Like the outlaws in your woods. I guess they don't mind robbing you of the harvests from your fields. That's why your streets are jammed with starving villagers. Soon there won't be any provisions to feed them with. No bread from the east, no apples from your orchards, no pheasants from the woods. No food for the children. There will be riots. And what does a hungry mob always do? They turn on their juicy lord, especially when this one can't feed his soldiers. And what will Agroln do to reward you for your heroic neutrality? Nothing. Because to Agroln, you, me, your people, we are just juicy orc shit."

"I know we are condemned," Pembroke said sullenly.

"If you stay here, yes. It will happen soon. Maybe not this year, but soon." The last thing Louis wanted to do was to nag on the man as a dog on a bone. He was conscious that, because of his insignificance due to his lack of title, he was tiptoeing on a thin thread.

"They have a dragon. I was there four years ago. I saw the flames. I saw the men roast in front of my eyes. No one can beat that!" Pembroke exclaimed. He rose from his chair and paced, his black velvet robes swirling around his legs, and stared through a mullioned window.

"Don't underestimate the fury of dead children's mothers, my lord. You would regret your dragon. Besides, dragons can die. We can find a way."

"If I leave my city to its fate, it's my people who will die," Pembroke sighed. "Is it what you want?" He turned his dark eyes on Louis.

"If you drain your city from all your soldiers, your folk will have provisions for a year. Who knows what can happen by then? Your walls are sound and high. Your people will defend themselves. Bandits won't take such a place, and orcs are far."

"Have you ever seen a battlefield once in your life, young man?" The count puffed with anger.

"I have." For a reason he could not explain, Louis knew that he had, and his words were filled with sincerity. "I know we may all die in horrible pains, but is the survival of our people not worth it?"

Lord Pembroke stayed silent. "How many men do you have?" he inquired.

Louis knew it was their biggest weakness. "A thousand."

The count chuckled. "It's suicide."

"No. It's courage." Louis stared at Pembroke. He thought of Bertrant, Faremanne, and how hard the men had worked these last days. There was hope. "We don't fight for Bertrant. We fight for Trevalden, for the people. We want to live. But we need to be united to win back our land," Louis said.

Pembroke turned to Louis and gazed at him. "Give me until tomorrow. You will have my final answer in the morning."

"Thank you, my lord." Louis and Selen bowed and took their leave.

The captain came back and showed them to their rooms. Selen's room was situated right under the solar and Louis's room was a floor under.

"You really don't trust us," Louis said when he saw that two guards stood on each side of his door. Selen had not had that privilege. "Should we consider ourselves your prisoners?"

"Not at all," the captain said. "You are free to walk inside the castle and through the city. It is only a precaution we take with all our guests, for their own safety."

Louis did not detect a threat in the man's voice, but he did not believe him either. He entered his room. It was comfortably furnished with a heavy bed covered with wool blankets, a table near a wall, and a small fireplace on the other side. Faded tapestries hung at the windows.

Louis removed his armour and opened his black jerkin. He stretched his arms. His muscles were sore. He reached for a carafe, filled a bowl with water, and washed his face and neck. Drops of cold water dribbled under his shirt. He looked through the window at the city down under. *It hasn't turned out that badly*, he thought. They were still alive. The man had not been the coward he had imagined. He reminded him of Bertrant. Same age, same delusion in the eyes. They probably had fought together and chosen different paths. It would be such a waste if the man should come with a negative answer tomorrow. They desperately needed seasoned knights that they could trust.

Louis heard the door open behind him. He turned and saw Selen enter the room. He had removed his armour and wore a plain, lace-up tunic. Silently, his friend locked the door behind him and came forth.

"I admire you. It was very brave to face that man as you did. I hope he will be as convinced as I was."

Louis smiled. "That we will see tomorrow when…"

Selen pressed his lips on his. "You can't imagine how many times I wanted to do that," his friend whispered. His arms around Louis's neck, Selen covered his face with kisses. Louis knew too well how much he had missed him and held him tight.

"I'm sorry I have to act so cold," Louis murmured. He kissed Selen. His friend's tongue tasted of cinnamon. Selen's hand firmly grasped his crotch and kneaded it. Louis gasped. He felt his member stir. A bolt of desire invaded his body, but he remembered the guards. "We can't. There are guards," he breathed.

"I don't care," Selen responded, nibbling at his ear. "We will have to be quick. I won't wait more weeks." If Selen did not stop at once, Louis was not sure he could hold back either.

Selen knelt down and pressed his mouth against the bulge in Louis's crotch, grabbing at him through the cloth. As Selen's tongue searched between the laces, one of his hands rubbed between Louis's legs. Louis put a hand against Selen's head to stop him, but he pulled him closer instead, running his fingers through the long hair. He gasped for air, and his hips twitched. He had never seen his friend so lustful, Selen, who had been so shy, so lovely. He pushed Selen back slightly to look at him.

"What happened to you?" he asked, confused.

Selen blushed and Louis was relieved to see again the man he knew. "I missed you," Selen cooed.

Louis smiled. Now, he lusted for him. "All right, but quick," he breathed.

With haste, Selen unlaced Louis's pants and threw his mouth on him. Louis's heart hastened as his friend pleasured him with enthusiasm, his long fingers rubbing him. Selen's mouth was warm and wet, his tongue quite skilled, though it was his first time. It felt wonderful. Louis saw Selen move his hand from Louis's thighs and caress his own crotch. The vision turned him on, but Louis did not want it that way. He wanted to be with Selen, to please him.

He pulled Selen up, plunged his tongue into his mouth before he turned him around. He tugged at his friend's tunic and undressed him with impatient hands. Selen pressed himself against him.

"Caress me," Selen whispered.

He took Louis's hands and rubbed them on his chest and down his abs to his crotch. Louis tugged on the ropes and slipped a hand inside Selen's pants. Selen was stone hard. Louis wrapped his hand around him and stroked him. His teeth nibbled at Selen's earlobe through his hair and grazed down to bite smoothly at Selen's warm neck. His friend had refreshed his face, but his body smelled of sweat from the trip. Small, sticky beads trickled on Louis's fingers. Selen stifled a moan. It only intensified Louis's own urge.

He bent Selen gently over on the table and pulled down Selen's pants. Kneading his firm buttocks, he gazed at his friend's slightly muscular shoulders, his stretched and supple, pale back with his long, beautiful hair falling loosely on it. Louis's heart fluttered. Selen raised his hips, waiting, craving. Louis put one hand on his mouth, then slipped it between Selen's cheeks. Selen gasped as the fingers plunged into him to the last knuckle. As Louis shifted them, he watched the features on Selen's face contract with delight. When he knew he would not hurt his friend, Louis stopped his thrusts and removed his hand. He placed his erection between Selen's cheeks and bit his lip at the sight.

"Don't moan," Louis whispered as he pushed himself slowly inside Selen. He pressed his hips against Selen's and sipped the air as his loins combusted. Selen clenched his jaws and frowned. The table shook when Louis took him. Selen panted, gasping for air. His nails scraped at the wood. Sweat pearled on his tensed face. Louis held Selen's cheeks harder, increasing the pace of his pounding. It was selfish, but he could not help it. He too had waited long for this moment, and the feeling of Selen clamped on to him was rapturous. He heard the frantic beating of his heart under the clapping noise of their flesh.

Louis could not hold it any longer. He pulled at Selen's arms. Selen's spine arched as he rose to meet him. Louis pressed his mouth to his left shoulder to stifle his moans when he felt his body climax. As the fire in his loins left his body, he collapsed with Selen on the table. He turned Selen around and knelt between his open legs, one arm wrapped around one of Selen's thighs. Louis had yearned for the occasion to make his friend feel good. He knew he could do better and would make this part mind-blowing. Selen brushed Louis's hair back from over his face. As Louis finished him off with his mouth, Selen's fingers contracted on his head like claws. Louis knew Selen did not attempt to control him but only needed the grip. His hold was gauche and instinctive. Louis felt Selen's blood throb. Soon, his friend's body was overwhelmed with spasms. Louis closed his eyes and received him. His throat tightened. Above him, he heard the stifled moans turn into heavy breathing as Selen calmed down. Licking his salty, reddened lips, Louis got up. He hugged Selen dearly against him, his face buried in his friend's neck and hair. "Don't leave," Louis whispered.

"You know I have to, but keep holding me tight," Selen answered, his fingers clenched on Louis's back.

Louis would have liked to hold him forever. Inside the camp, they could barely be seen talking. Louis did not allow himself any physical contact with his friend in case it would betray them. He could not let his feelings get in the way of his engagements. He fought for freedom, for their lives. He needed to stay concentrated, but above all, he needed the respect of his men, of everyone. His command must be unquestionable, should they admire him or fear him. No one must know. Therefore, he imposed severe rules on himself and wore his coldness as a mask, as a defense, and he was good at it. That was why he preferred the battlefield. Coldness was strength. In Neolerim, his aloof behavior to protect his privacy had been interpreted as puritanism, and criticism had flown. However, Louis had been alone in the Iron Marches. Now things were different. There were feelings under the mask, and sometimes, he would bear it as an iron maiden.

Despite the long journey they had made, Selen's hair smelled of honeysuckle.

Louis let his mind flow. He did not know how long it would be before they could hold each other again. A week? A month? Maybe never, should they die in battle. It was not about lust. Of course, Selen's perfect body aroused him, and many nights he had caressed himself fantasizing about Selen on his bed of furs. No, it was stronger than that, and he knew that Selen waited for a sign. Still, he could not acknowledge his feelings as long as he did not remember who he had been. He needed to feel whole first. The last thing he wanted was to deceive his friend.

"I had a dream again," Selen murmured. "I remember more about me. I had feelings for someone, but...I was a virgin."

Louis kissed the side of his head. *Don't make things even harder, Selen*, he thought. "I think you should get dressed. It has been too long already," he whispered. Selen looked at him with his puppy, emerald eyes. He got off the table, used one of the towels on the board, and put his clothes on. They had a last kiss. Louis's fingers caressed Selen's face. "However cold I may be in public, never forget these moments."

Selen smiled. "I will be strong, for you. We will win this war," Selen said before he left. The oaken door closed behind him.

Selen's gentle smile lingered in front of Louis's eyes. As they fluttered, his lashes turned heavy with beads of tears.

In the morning, they entered the great hall again. The count was in a vivid discussion with his captain. He sent him away at their arrival. He took an eternity to walk to his chair, rectifying a decoration, poking into the fire. Louis's anxiety grew as his patience ran low. At last, Pembroke turned to them.

"I have considered your request. Leaving my city. It is a big sacrifice you ask of me." He paused, scratching his beard. "It will take me a few weeks to gather all my troops."

Louis closed his eyes with relief. It had worked. "Thank you, my lord," he and Selen exclaimed.

"But I have terms," Pembroke went on. "First, I won't fight under Bertrant's orders, but as his equal. Secondly, while I call the banners, you will free Millhaven."

Louis was aghast. "Free Millhaven?" He could not have heard right.

"I don't doubt you are brave. Show me the power of your convictions." The count was resolute.

Louis had been caught in a trap forged by his own eloquence. Should he refuse, his words would lose all their worth. However, the man's tone showed no mischief. He meant to test them. If that was the price for his alliance, they would pay it.

"In the name of the Rebellion, I agree to your terms, my lord." He hoped Bertrant would not kill him for that.

"Then I hope we will meet again on the south road in a few weeks."

The count made a sign with his hand to mark the end of their discussion. Louis and Selen took their leave and left the great hall. Captain Raolin waited for them outside the room.

"I will show you out. Your men have been informed of your departure and should be waiting in the yard," the captain told them, leading the way.

"Before we leave Embermire, there is a favour I would like to ask you," Louis said.

"Yes?" Raolin halted and turned towards him.

"Our friend has been missing for some days now, and we have every reason to believe that he may be lost in the Ebony Forest. We would greatly appreciate if you could spread flyers through the city," Louis said.

"I understand. Yet, between the bandits and the fact that the Ebony Forest is a cursed place, I would not put my hopes too high if I were you. Still, we can spread the word and a description through the taverns. Come with me."

Louis and Selen followed Raolin to the guardroom. Halberds and crossbows hung on racks. Soldiers dressed in mails ground their weapons while others sitting on benches played cards over a stained table. Raolin went to a desk and drew a quill, ink, and paper.

"How does your friend look like?"

"I can write down his description," Louis proposed. Raolin handed him the quill. Louis wrote what he hoped to be a faithful description of Lissandro. He did not forget to mention his armour. Every detail could help. "You can offer the reward you judge sufficient. We will pay." Once he was done, he held back the paper. Raolin hailed one of his men.

"Have this paper copied and spread through the city at once," the captain said to his soldier. The man took the paper and left the room. Raolin turned to them again. "May I know how a man of the Rebellion ended in the Ebony Forest? It is not exactly near your camp."

"One of our missions took a wrong turn, and Lissandro drifted on the Strelm River," Louis replied. Actually, it was the truth.

"Well, let's hope your friend can make it out of there alive. I have heard that some groups of orcs wander through the forest now. However, in a few hours, many people will go in search of him in hopes of a reward, including the multitude of bandits prowling around."

"We thank you for your help." Louis nodded with gratitude.

They left the guardroom and followed Raolin to the yard. The soldiers of the Rebellion waited for them. Their horses were brought forth progressively in the courtyard. It took around an hour until every man stood on his mount. Louis could not wait to leave Embermire. The journey back to the camp was long, and they would soon have to make all the preparations for the army to journey south. The doors of the castle opened. They kicked their horses forward into the city.

Slowly, they rode down the crowded main street to the city gates, Pembroke's guards opening the way.

"Do you think he sent us to our deaths on purpose?" Selen had been morose all morning. Louis did not think his friend would have approved his decision on those terms.

"I can understand that a lord of such a rank needs more than words from young knights like us. Theoretically, we are not even knights."

"He could have asked for the leadership, a promise of reward, not sending a thousand men against a stronghold held by orcs." The irritation in Selen's voice was tainted with fear. Louis searched for words to bring his friend some comfort.

"I do believe in miracles. Such improbable victories have happened before. I read it in books." He tried to smile, but his heart failed him.

"Louis," Selen muttered. They looked at each other. "I am scared to death, I won't deny it, but I trust you. If you say we can do it, then we will."

Louis did not speak, but he hoped that Selen could at least read his words in his eyes.

21

The city gates surroundings were crowded with folk. The flow of refugees coming from the countryside mixed with the mass of Embermire's inhabitants returning home. Everyone wanted to go in, while only a few pushed their way to leave the city. The guards shouted orders to keep the newcomers in a line and did not hesitate to drive back the more insistent travellers. There was no panic on the people's faces, but dismay and confusion floated in the air. If they had not sat in the wagon, Lissandro was sure that the children and their mother would have been trampled. Kilda made a place for the wagon. She sat beside him on the bench. She had thrown an ample cloak over herself and had the hood hanging over half of her face. Her womanly features could lure the guards. Lissandro had been forced to remove his mail. His dirty clothes made him look miserable enough to pass unnoticed.

The streets of Embermire were as populous as the gates. With the high houses on both sides, it felt like maneuvering down a bottleneck. Though the colorful walls were relatively clean, the stench of so many people jammed together was strong. Lissandro wondered how they did not already have had an epidemic. He wanted to be out of the city as soon as possible.

Kilda reined in. They halted near a tavern. "I will ask if there's an infirmary somewhere. Don't move," she said.

Lissandro knew she was still angry with him and that the place made her feel unsafe. He could have run. Kilda had made him swear to follow her orders, but he would probably die if he kept on moving south with her. Yet, he thought that his life was not less at risk in this city. He had no idea where Embermire was, and he had no money. It was not good to be a beggar in a place like this. In a time of crisis, justice tended to be expeditious. He had no wish to play the scapegoat.

He looked around him. The street stretched forward in a semicircle following the ramparts on the right. This side was a line of shops and taverns. A larger street opened on his left. He saw the flow of people walking to and from the main street. He heard shouts ahead over the hurly-burly of the city life. Orders. The population was pushed aside on the main street. More people surged in his direction. Soon it would be easier to walk on people's heads than on the pavement.

He heard a wave of horse's hooves clapping on the cobbles. An army of mounted soldiers rode down the main street. Some men carried blue standards. Lissandro's eyes opened wide. He knew the man riding in the distance. There could only be one person in the whole of Trevalden with that hair color.

"Selen," he whispered, aghast.

Lissandro let go of the reins and rose. He had to reach him. He jumped into the crowd and pushed his way through. The army moved slowly. Lissandro hurried, throwing himself over heads, treading on feet. He was nearly there. Selen's armour shone white and golden in the sun. Lissandro wanted to shout, but the noise around was too loud. He reached the corner of the street. He climbed on a wooden box. Selen was only a few yards away, Louis riding by his side. Lissandro beamed. He was filling his lungs to scream when he felt a hand over his mouth, holding him fast. As he saw his friends ride away, tears of rage and despair misted his eyes. A blow hit his head.

When he regained consciousness, Lissandro lay in the wagon, his hands and feet bound fast. The wood shook as if they drove on a deteriorated road. He rose, pushing on his legs. They were back in the forest.

"Why did you do that?" he shouted. His heart was full of rage, and tears pearled in his eyes. "Why?"

Kilda pulled on the reins. The wagon stopped. She turned around, holding a piece of paper. She unfolded it in front of his eyes and threw it onto his lap. "This is why."

The paper was a bounty offer promising a high reward. The particulars fitted his description perfectly. His friends were not only near; they were also looking for him. Lissandro closed his eyes. There may be hope left. "Why didn't you hand me to the guards when we were in Embermire?"

"To be arrested?" She smirked. "If the people you waved at were your friends, my head would be on a spike by now." She whipped the horses, which walked again. "But don't worry. With friends like these, nothing will happen to you in the camp. You are a hostage of great price."

"And what about them?" Lissandro inquired, nodding at the children and their mother. The little boy cradled his sister in his arms and gazed at Lissandro with wild, red eyes. "I thought they wanted to stay in Embermire."

"There was no place for them. So I will take them to the camp."

"Children and a lonely, sick woman in a bandit camp? How cruel are you?" Lissandro asked.

"We have had some already. When we free villages. Colten Three Fingers sent them away to a better place. He will find a way for these."

She did believe what she said. "I'm sorry. I was wrong. You're not cruel. You're stupid."

Kilda turned her head and looked at him with heinous eyes. "What did you say?"

"That you're stupid," Lissandro insisted. "I came all the way from the Windy Isles. There is no better place. These children and their parents are sent as slaves. This Colten has fooled you."

"Don't say that," she snapped. "I'm sure you're some kind of lord anyway."

"If only I were," Lissandro snarled. "Your hate for the nobles is so strong that you have lost all notion of reality. What did they do to you? Abused you? Killed your family?" he exclaimed in anger.

Kilda stayed silent. Lissandro realized he had touched the truth. "I'm sorry," he said, "but if you want revenge, there are other ways. You don't need to turn into a monster."

They arrived at the camp in the evening. The sun plunged behind the pines in the horizon. A village of tents stood in a glade. Braziers colored the white cloth with yellow gleams. The wagon rolled and slowed on the side of the path. Kilda hailed one of the men walking nearby.

"I bring two children and their mother. She is sick. Have someone check on them." She turned to Lissandro. "We are going to Colten's pavilion." She grabbed his arm and pulled him down.

They headed to a large tent. Lissandro heard music come from it. They entered.

The room was warm and noisy. Trestle tables stood on both sides of the entrance. Men sat on the benches, and some had wenches on their laps. Beer flowed like water. Lissandro thought that the atmosphere was a mix between a tavern and a brothel. He wondered where Kilda had imagined her valiant heroes, sworn enemies of the noble class. She pushed him towards a slender man sitting on a high, wooden chair, made comfortable with furs. Colten Three Fingers looked like an old knight who would have lost all his goods and titles at a poker table. He had leather armour strapped around his muscular body. He was unshaved. Half of his hair was braided, and he had a scar on one eye.

"You should have been called Colten One Eye." Lissandro smirked.

"I still have two fingers on that hand to cut your tongue," the man replied with a larger smile. One of his teeth was black. All in his attitude screamed that he was a rogue. And a nasty one, moreover.

"I have found this man in the forest, Captain," Kilda said. "There is a large reward on his head. Alive, unfortunately."

"Interesting. Is he a friend of Pembroke?" Colten inquired.

"I don't know that name," Lissandro answered.

"He knows the captains of the army that left the city this morning," Kilda said.

"A friend of the Rebellion?" Colten made a face. "It's useless for us. Yet, still worth the money. We will contact them and ask for a ransom."

"We came here with a woman and her two children," Lissandro told Colten. "What do you plan to do with them?"

"Are they hostages too?" the bandit asked. He took a large gulp of his mug. A trickle of beer ran on his unkempt chin.

"No. They are villagers," Kilda said.

"Well, then they will be taken care of and placed with the others." Colten turned to one of his guards and pointed at Lissandro. "Find a secure place for this one. We will solve his case during the following days."

Lissandro was carried out of the tent to the side of the camp. The guard opened a cage and threw him into it. "Good night, my lord," he laughed.

Lissandro looked back at Colten's pavilion. He saw Kilda come out of it. She looked in his direction before disappearing into the night.

22

The cobalt blue sky was streaked with gold. The sun was setting under the tree line, bathing the entire camp in an orange light. It had been a good day. Faremanne had supervised the training of the men. It had been hard to restore discipline in the camp, especially to enforce the restriction on the beer. But since alcohol had been rationed to a reasonable amount between the men, fights and accidents had drastically reduced. The men's productivity had increased, and they had been able to rebuild the corral. They had fixed the last bolts on the gates this afternoon.

A cloud of dust rose far away. It grew up in the air. Faremanne smiled. Folc appeared between two tents, running in his direction. The boy waved his arms with joy. Louis and his troop were back. The sunlight glistened on the metal pieces of the armours. The blue standards floated in the wind. In a moment, they would walk across the camp, straight to the headquarters' pavilion. Faremanne wanted to be there. He belted his sword around his waist, picked up his helmet, and headed to the main tent.

Bertrant was already waiting outside his tent, his arms crossed over his chest. Faremanne detected anxiety on his face. He knew Bertrant did not like Pembroke. It was highly probable that the commander did not expect good news. Faremanne spotted Segar Mills's presence. The captain stood lurking near the pavilion, on the other side of Bertrant. The rivets on his brown gambeson sparkled in the twilight. Louis and Selen appeared among the tents and rode into the yard. Faremanne could not say that they looked satisfied, but they were not alarmed either. Their inscrutable faces stirred his curiosity. They dismounted and moved towards them.

"We go inside. You have much to tell us," Bertrant commanded.

They all entered the tent. Faremanne fetched a map in the other room, came back, and joined them around the huge table, taking his place at Bertrant's side. Segar stood at the right of the commander. Louis and Selen stopped on the other side of the table, ready to report. The board had been cleared for the occasion. The dim light of the lanterns revealed stains of wine and brown flecks on the wood. Faremanne unfolded the map. A large drawing of Trevalden lay unrolled in front of his eyes.

"You can start," Bertrant said, his fingers tapping the edge of the table.

"We met Lord Pembroke," Louis said. "Embermire is overpopulated, partly of refugees. Bandits roam in the forests all around but no sign of the orcs. In a few months, the city will run out of provisions. There are already risks of disease due to…"

"You are not here to talk of Embermire," Bertrant interrupted him harshly. "What did Pembroke say?"

Louis's face grew taut. "He will help us. He will summon the banners."

It was obvious that Louis did not want to jump to conclusion. There was more to it. "But?" Faremanne inquired.

"He wants us to prove our loyalty to the cause," Selen muttered.

"He wants us to free Millhaven," Louis said.

"What?" Bertrant shouted. "That coward wants us to prove our loyalty? When we have been fighting for four years now, our feet in the mud… I…" Bertrant spluttered over the table. The commander flushed red with anger. His chest puffed out like a rooster's.

"My lord, please," Faremanne tried to calm him down. "Let's hear what Louis has to say." He handed a goblet of wine to the commander. Faremanne turned to Louis, who stood silent, cold as marble, with an exasperated look on his face.

"Lord Pembroke doesn't know much about the Rebellion," Louis carried on, his words razor-sharp. "He doesn't know how hard our men have worked or how strong our will is. He has only heard of our failures. The man needs proof."

"Tell me you refused," Bertrant fumed. Faremanne could nearly see smoke blow out of his nose.

"I agreed," Louis answered with a challenging look.

The two men stared at each other. Bertrant's right hand turned into a clenched fist on the board. For a short instant, Faremanne wondered if the commander would punch Louis. Faremanne did not want to see how Louis would react to such a humiliation. He prayed that Louis had not glimpsed the rictus on Segar's face. The situation was a hairbreadth from a bloodbath.

"If I had said no, we would have faced the orcs for nothing," Louis continued with what seemed a superhuman effort to keep calm. "Now, if we win, we have an alliance. The confrontation with the orcs is inevitable anyway."

"Do you really believe that we would have faced the orcs with only a thousand men?" Segar sneered, placing himself on Bertrant's side.

Louis's sapphire eyes narrowed. He gazed at Segar like a war dog on a taut leash, ready to jump. The nerves in his throat pulsed. "And what do you think we're doing here?" He bit the words out slowly, his lower teeth shining.

Faremanne looked at Selen. The man had his hands spread on his hips. His eyes were riveted on the table, and his brow shone with sweat. Yet it wasn't fear but concentration. One of his fingers grazed the hilt. Selen was ready to draw his sword in a split second. It would be one side of the table against the other. Only Bertrant could put out the fire. Faremanne turned to him with a pleading look.

"My lord?"

Bertrant looked at him. Slowly, his face relaxed. He turned back to Louis. "What is done, is done."

Louis seemed to calm down. Segar shut up. Everyone breathed again.

"How will Pembroke proceed?" Bertrant asked.

"He will gather his troops, prepare his city for the eventuality of a siege, and march south. He hopes to meet us on the main road in a few weeks," Louis explained.

"What do you think we should do?" Faremanne asked Louis. He guessed the man had a plan, but he was not sure that Bertrant was ready to ask his opinion, brilliant as it would be. He had decided to ask the question himself. They should not let the Rebellion be destroyed by a conflict of egos.

Louis looked at him with gratitude. "I know we are outnumbered. Yet, we don't need to attack the orcs frontally. We can find another way."

"You mean a trick?" Faremanne asked.

"Yes. The city is conquered but has not fallen. The population is still trapped inside," Louis said.

"I see," Bertrant said. "We could use the population against them. Do you have a plan?"

"Not yet. But the road is long. We can figure something out," Louis answered.

"We should prepare ourselves for the road, draw up an inventory of our stocks, and check the materiel and the horses. I can take care of it. We should also send a word to the villages nearby; there may be volunteers. Every willing man is needed."

"I can do the inventory and the letters," Faremanne said. "You have something more important to do. I want you to motivate the men. Supervise their training while I do the chores."

"You will do both together," Bertrant said. "I want everything to be ready in four days. We will leave by the end of the week."

"I can inform the infirmary," Selen said. "I will make sure Brother Benedict has all that he needs."

Bertrant nodded in approval. "Well, that's settled then."

Not for everyone, Faremanne thought. Segar had stayed silent. If he meant to take part in the preparations, he had not mentioned it. Faremanne wondered if Mills felt like an outsider now that Louis and he collaborated. With Vakeg's death, the captain had lost one of his allies. He would probably keep a low profile for a while. Faremanne had no time to lose with him right now anyway.

"That will be all for tonight, Captains," Bertrant said.

Everyone was tired and running on nerves. When Louis, Selen, and Segar had left the pavilion, Faremanne turned to Bertrant. "Should I make my daily report tomorrow morning, as usual, my lord?"

"Don't lose your time with it. Start right away with the preparations. Report to me once the inventories are done," Bertrant said.

Faremanne took his leave. He saw Louis talk with Selen outside the tent. Selen departed before he could join them. Faremanne walked side by side with Louis to their tent. "You hate him," Faremanne said, "Segar."

"I have penetrated his soul," Louis answered. "I abhor corrupted cowards."

They walked the rest of the way in silence.

Once in the tent, Faremanne removed his armour. After all the tension during the evening, it felt good to breathe again. He unfastened his red gambeson, unlaced his shirt, and refreshed his chest with a wet cloth.

"Why are you here, Faremanne?" Louis asked. "Why do you care so much?"

Faremanne turned around. Louis had removed his armour and his shirt and used a bowl to wash himself. The man had a personal obsession with body hygiene. Every day, Faremanne saw him wash, shave, clean his teeth, and wash his clothes. Every two days, Louis hid behind a curtain and soaped down his entire body. His nails and eyebrows were trimmed. At that level, it was unhealthy and pathological.

At least, he did not shave his armpits. Faremanne could not see his face, but there had been sadness in Louis's voice.

"I haven't been in the Rebellion since the beginning," Faremanne answered. "I'm not actually from Trevalden, but from the Windy Isles. I used to live in Kilcairn with my family. I left three years ago when I heard of Bertrant and his men."

"Do you mean that you left your family behind, wife and children, to fight voluntarily in the Rebellion?" Louis asked, putting a white shirt on.

"Yes, that sounds foolish, I know," Faremanne sighed.

"No. Not at all. That's impressive."

"Thank you. I thought that someone had to do something. That if I wanted to protect my family, I should not wait until the orcs reached the Windy Isles. I had to stop them before, in Trevalden. So I rode south. As I was a knight, I got to be a captain. At that time, things didn't look as desperate as when you arrived."

"You should be glad that we are finally moving." Louis lay down on his bed. "The following days promise to be all but dull."

"Yes. There is much to do. I wonder if the men will react positively when they learn about our departure. They…" Faremanne stopped. Louis was asleep.

23

The flagon was empty. Bertrant grunted and rose from his bed.

"Prove their loyalty."

He had gone through it over and over again in his head. And the fool had agreed. It wasn't so much the fact that they were doomed to free Millhaven that stayed stuck in his throat. It was that Louis had knelt, in his name, in front of this coward. A man who had fled the battlefield and now spoke of loyalty. When the dragon had spilled his fire, Bertrant had seen Pembroke turn his troops around, leaving him and his man at the mercy of the beast. They could not have won that day, with or without Pembroke, but they had been abandoned. His own men had been sacrificed so that Pembroke's troops could live. And that, he would never forget, nor forgive.

Bertrant dragged himself to the table. He filled the bowl and splashed cold water on his face. He had wanted to punch Louis, but deep inside he knew that the man had had no choice. They could not stay indefinitely in this camp. To free Millhaven was madness. Yet, they must head south.

Bertrant was tired. These last four years had been tough on him. His appearance was far from glorious. He had put on so much weight that his body ached in his armour. His long, blond hair was scarcer. He was as pitiful as his camp. No, he rectified, as his camp had been. Now, he could not even hide behind that excuse anymore. He fastened his red doublet. It was time to inspect the preparations and to show his men that he still had a say in here. He grabbed the flagon. Empty. He grumbled and went out.

Two guards followed him as he sauntered through the camp. He had never seen the alleys that clean. It had been a high price to pay. Everything in the life of his soldiers had been taken under control: their food, their materiel, their occupations, even where to shit. They could still do as they pleased, but they were now responsible for it. Should their equipment be unpolished or their tent dirty, they would pay the consequences, dearly. Louis had required an irreproachable attitude of the officers. This was why Bertrant had stayed in his pavilion all this time. Though he would not have been sent to the jails, he would have felt the disapproving looks on him. He was far from being a model. Until today. Should they die in battle, he wanted to die as a commander, not as a pathetic drunk.

Bertrant reached the south of the camp where a wide, green prairie stretched out to a shallow river. The soldiers had spread out on the plain in groups. All wore their armour. Some men repeated moves while others dueled. Bales of hay had been aligned for the archers on the slope of the hill in the west. The men looked tired but cheerful. They trained hard. Bertrant heard the encouraging shouts of the officers. It was a pleasant sight he could be proud of, though he knew someone else had probably taken the credit for it. Louis progressed from one group to another, shouting counsel, rectifying a man's movement, challenging a lieutenant to a duel with his long sword. His charisma among the men was beyond belief. All from his agile moves to his refined appearance screamed that Louis did not belong among them. Yet, his determination forced admiration. Louis had coerced the men to prove their worth, rekindling their will to fight, and the soldiers had learned to respect him.

"He may not win the war," Bertrant said to himself, "but he has won my army. And I was fool enough to give it to him on a silver plate." He moved forward. Louis saw him and bowed.

"Commander," Louis said. His long hair was disheveled, but his armour was impeccable as always.

"Do the men know our plans?" Bertrant inquired.

"Yes, Commander. We have informed them that we will be moving south by the end of the week."

"Only moving south?" Bertrant raised an eyebrow.

"One thing at a time," Louis whispered. "They will know more once we are better prepared ourselves."

"Good. Come to my tent this afternoon. Birds arrived this morning," Bertrant said. "Inform Faremanne."

Bertrant headed to the infirmary. He was not looking forward to seeing the monk again, but he wanted to be sure the infirmary was operational.

The large tent was open on the south side. The beds were bathed in the sunlight. He didn't count more than thirty men lying on the beds. Some had been injured for good and would have been sent home if there had been a home left to send them to. Bertrant spotted Louis's friend. Selen sat on a bed, wiping the head of a wounded soldier with a wet rag. The sleeves of his shirt underneath his woolen tunic were rolled up to the elbows. Bertrant observed the man's forearms and how wasted they were in such a place. He headed to Selen.

"What the hell are you doing here?" Bertrant asked with anger.

"I...I said I would be in the infirmary, helping to prepare our departure, my lord," Selen said, startled. His soft-spoken voice was barely audible. Bertrant was tired of straining to hear him every time the man opened his mouth.

"You said you would inform them," Bertrant insisted, raising his voice, "not that you would play the nurse!"

Selen lowered his eyes. Bertrant wasn't sure if the man realized that he was in a military camp. Louis had given his friend a golden opportunity to make his place, and Selen refused to grab it. What was wrong with him? He was neither a coward nor a chump. It was time Bertrant hammered the melted iron.

"Why are you not with the others?" Bertrant shouted. He did not need to, but he wanted the man to feel uneasy. "Join them at once!"

"I don't think Louis would want me at the training field, my lord," Selen muttered.

"Louder!" Bertrant yelled.

"I don't think Louis wants me on the field," Selen repeated louder. Bertrant was glad to see a spark of irritation in the man's eyes. A hammer and an anvil were what he needed, indeed.

"I don't care what that man wants!" Bertrant barked. "I am your commander, and I gave you an order! Having you here is a shameful waste of a good warrior. Now go fetch your armour and move your ass down the field!" Selen turned white and pressed his lips. *You hate that,* Bertrant thought, *good, I will shout louder next time.* Bertrant watched the man leave the place in a hurry. He tried not to laugh. At least, he could still be frightening.

"I don't suppose you will take his place," he heard a reproachful voice say behind him.

"You have no authority to requisition my men, Brother," Bertrant complained.

"One day you will have to explain to me how you want a fully operational infirmary with only one physician," Brother Benedict said.

"Instruct the cripples; don't take my best men," Bertrant grunted. "Did you manage to fill your stocks?"

"And when would I have the occasion to do that?" the monk replied.

Bertrant knew he should have avoided the place. The man was painful like a knife stuck in his bowels. "I will send you someone else. You have four days to be ready."

"What should I do with the sick? They are not in a condition to follow."

"We will send them to the nearest village. We can't delay our departure. Should they recover, they could still join us." Bertrant did not count too much on that, but it was the best he could do for these men.

He left the pavilion and walked towards the headquarters. On the way, he passed in front of the smithy. The hammerings echoed in his head. The blacksmith and his lads bustled on forging axe's blades.

"Don't the men have swords already?" Bertrant inquired.

"It's a special command, Commander," the sweaty blacksmith answered, short of breath, "as many axes as we can forge."

"Did the captains tell you why?" Once again, something was on, and he had not been informed.

The blacksmith shrugged, clueless.

The afternoon came without incident. Bertrant sat at his table, waiting for his captains. As usual, Faremanne was the first to come, soon followed by Louis. Segar entered the pavilion last.

"Before we start," Bertrant said, "I would like to make one thing clear. You, Louis, are now officially one of my captains, as is your friend, Selen."

"But, Commander!" Segar exclaimed, outraged.

"No, it's settled," Bertrant carried on. "Vakeg is dead, and we are short of leading officers. What I don't want is free electrons roaming around the camp, using and abusing their authority." Bertrant remembered the axes. He would have to bring light on this. Besides, he needed the two men. They could as well be recognized officially. "Louis, you will inform your friend. And I don't want him near my infirmary unless he is mortally wounded."

"Yes, Commander."

"Now, back to our problems. I have received two letters this morning. One is from Pembroke. The man says that he has sent words to his captains and that he will help us. The other letter is from Count Elye." All the captains looked surprised.

"Did he respond?" Faremanne asked.

"He says that he will consider our request, depending on our next actions. You can read it yourself." Bertrant handed the paper to Faremanne, who passed it around to his fellow captains.

"It seems like every support wants us to face the walls of Millhaven," Louis said.

"How are the preparations going?" Bertrant asked.

"I have sent parties to hunt game and fish the river. Others collect bark to make flour. The stocks of food will soon be well-furnished. The troops are training. Yet, I haven't seen much of Segar's men," Louis said with a reproachful glance at Segar.

"Maybe they have better things to do," Segar answered, making a face, "like patrolling the forest in search of orcs."

"It's useless," Louis replied with disdain without looking at Segar. "We already have guards, and we know there are orcs around. They won't attack us now. But I need more men to fix the carts."

"They are my men. I assign their tasks," Segar protested, a finger raised in the air.

"Actually, I do," Bertrant interrupted him. "We need these carts ready in three days. Call your men back." Bertrant did not believe for a second that Segar's men sauntered through the woods, waiting to get shot by an orc. The man had had his hand on the camp for too long. Beside the prostitutes and the occasional dogfights, Bertrant had heard of questionable deals and deeds he could never prove. He knew what that kind of scum was capable of. Yet, Segar had many men under his command. The captain may be appalling, but Bertrant needed him. The only thing he could do was to rob Segar of his authority. "To accelerate the task, your men will follow Louis's orders on this."

"I will make sure they also follow the camp's rules. They may have crawled in the wild a bit too long," Louis said. The twist of his mouth expressed his open disgust and scorn.

The man really pushes his luck, Bertrant thought. Making intentionally cutting remarks to a nasty man was a risky business.

"They will behave impeccably," Segar answered with sarcasm in his voice.

"And I don't doubt you will set the example. You can start by presenting yourself on the training field tomorrow. Shaved," Louis said without raising his eyes from the papers he was reading.

Segar turned white, then red again. Bertrant wondered if Louis took pleasure in humiliating the captain or if it was pure scorn. Segar wanted to say something, but Bertrant was tired of their squabbling. "That will be all for today. Thank you, Captains."

Segar Mills left the pavilion with long strides.

"Maybe you should be more diplomatic, Louis," Faremanne said.

"I don't care, I meant it," Louis replied evasively. He walked away with a bunch of reports.

"I wonder if we will make it to Millhaven with both of them alive," Faremanne sighed.

Bertrant looked at his captain with tired, exasperated eyes.

24

"I can't stand this arrogant, cocky bastard!" Segar exclaimed as he entered his tent. "To dare confront me with his swaggering gait and his imperious glare!" He stopped and looked around. "Viola," he called. He brushed a hand through his curly, black hair and unstrapped his gambeson.

A buxom woman appeared from behind a curtain. Her red hair was uncombed and her clothes were slovenly.

"Yes, my lord?"

"Come here!" he yelled, grabbing her wrist. The girl tottered towards him. Segar unlaced his pants and took out his flabby cock. "Suck it," he snapped. The girl went on her knees and complied.

He had wanted to spit on the bastard's lordly face. The newly promoted captain had not even deigned to look at him. Who did he think he was? The scene repeated itself in his mind over again. He thought of what he could have answered, something sharp and preferably humiliating. The brat had the lips of a top-earning harlot. Segar found insults by the dozen, but nothing he could use in front of a commander.

Segar pulled the girl up harshly, bent her over the table, and pulled up her dress to her waist cincher, revealing her round bottom. He gave it a slap and pushed his horny cock inside her.

"To give me orders as to a dog." He shagged the girl hard, fondling one of her bare breasts with one hand. He rolled the nipple between his fingers. "After only two weeks in the camp. Wench-looking whoreson," Segar spat. The table rocked. He groaned and twisted his grip on her nipple as he came. The girl let out a faint scream of pain. He gave a last thrust and pulled back. "Clean yourself."

Segar laced up his pants and moved onto his bed. One flacon stood on a trunk on the side. He filled himself a cup of wine. One of his lieutenants appeared at the entrance of the tent. "Darcy, here you are at last."

"Bad day?" The man grinned. His teeth were yellow, flecked with brown. Darcy had a pox-ridden face and filthy, long hair. Segar thought that a dog butt looked more amiable.

"One day I'll rip his eyes out," Segar mumbled. Viola approached him and sat on his lap. Nonchalantly, Segar opened her bodice, revealing her heavy bosom.

"Or maybe you can bribe him." Darcy smirked. The lieutenant came closer.

"What are you thinking of?" Segar asked, interested.

"The flesh is weak," Darcy said with his gravelly voice. He grasped Viola's chin. "Send him some cunt. Such men usually need a good fuck."

"You're talking about the same man who sent away all of my whores on penalty of death?" Segar looked at his lieutenant doubtfully. "Should I send him Viola, who is not only my best whore but my last one? I may get only her head back." Segar ran a finger around her left breast. "Besides, did you have a look at his dear friend? I wouldn't be surprised if he liked another kind of ass." Why would the bastard burden himself with someone who had the face of a bed slave and the appearance of a savage if there was not something more under. Besides, sometimes the freak stared at the whoreson as if he drooled.

"This is a serious accusation. Do you have proof?" Darcy made a face of disgust.

"Not a single one. But I will." The only idea to humiliate the man publicly in front of the whole army for the most repulsive of all crimes aroused him. That would be a lynching worth remembering. Segar stroke his goatee and grinned.

"He wants you to work on the carts from tomorrow on. Summon the guys."

"He can shove…"

"No joke," Segar interjected. "Bertrant backs him up. Let's do what he says for now and keep a low profile. I'll get him at the right time."

"You're the boss," Darcy said. "I'll get the men to work. Won't mind leaving me the girl for tonight?" the man asked with a lewd look at his whore.

"I'm not done with her for tonight," Segar said, placing her hand on his crotch.

Darcy grumbled and left the tent.

"Wake up, bawdy rascal," a cheerful voice said above him. Segar opened his eyes. He lay naked on his bed with the girl across him. Captain Jamys stood beside the bed, his arms crossed over his chest.

"You ill-bred goat dung!" Segar exclaimed. "I have been waiting for your return for weeks." He slapped the girl on her buttock. "Leave us." The girl got up and disappeared behind the curtain. Segar rose and got dressed. "I am pleased to see your pretty face."

Jamys was not exactly pretty. He had a square chin, blond, shaggy hair, and a broken nose. The man was popular in every brothel up to the Iron Marches. Segar liked that he did not mince his words. That and his muscular build. The man was strong as a bull.

"So, how was your journey in the Iron Marches?" Segar asked. "Fruitful, I hope."

"As always." Jamys smiled, slipping a round purse in Segar's hand. "When is the next convoy?" Jamys eased himself into a chair.

Segar grimaced. "I'm sorry to say that our business is over. There won't be another *special freight*. There have been some changes during your absence."

"What kind?" Jamys asked worriedly. "The kind that gets us hung?"

"Not yet. But Vakeg has been cut in parts."

"What?" Jamys shouted, rising from his chair.

"Sit down, I'll explain," Segar said. "Bertrant has two new captains. Two men who arrived at the camp two weeks ago. One is a hysterical general wannabe who thinks he can shove this remnant of army into Agroln's ass. This drunk Bertrant gave him absolute powers. Do you figure? Look at the camp now! I've lost my whores, lost my fighting pits, even lost my command yesterday. Two years of good work turned to ruins."

"But I promised our clients in the east that I would be back with fresh meat. They won't appreciate it. And think of the loss. The price of children and pretty maidens is higher than ever."

"Are you deaf?" Segar retorted. "I have no men left to raid the villages and farms, and these captains can make the difference between an orc attack and ours. We won't even stay here. They want us to march on Millhaven." Yet, the city was opulent, and he had business there as well. *There may be things to sack if we are careful*, Segar thought.

"March on Millhaven?" Jamys gaped. "And what of the other man? You mentioned two."

"A painted savage. Never opens his mouth, but hacked The Mountain's guts."

"Should we break their necks?" Jamys asked. He wrinkled his nose and wheezed with anger.

"No. With Faremanne, they are now three captains, and the commander is behind them. They would know at once that it's us. Besides, they killed The Mountain and Vakeg. They are more dangerous than they look. I suggest we do nothing. We follow them south. They may even free Millhaven if they are lucky. We stay in the tail, and when the time comes, we act." Segar had a nasty smile on his face.

"With luck, we won't even have to kill them ourselves. The orcs may do the job." Jamys smirked. He relaxed in his seat again.

"As long as they leave me the whoreson. This one is mine." Segar's imagination ran wild again.

25

"What should I do with the woman and the children?" Kilda inquired.

"I already told you. Send them with the others. They will be taken care of. There should be a convoy leaving in two days. Just enough time for us to free another village," Colten said.

"Will we go on a raid again tomorrow?" Kilda asked, surprised. "I thought we would take over the tower controlling the bridge leading to the city. This is why I went alone in the Ebony Forest. To spy on them and take notes on the shifts of the guard," she said, upset. The tower was at a strategic crossroad to the city. The loss of the place could be a thorn in Pembroke's foot. Besides, they had enough provisions and saved enough villagers for the next convoy.

"There is a farm with a watermill four miles from here," Colten explained. "It's under the control of a small party of the count's men, but we will take it over easily."

"And what of the tower?" Kilda insisted. "You told me that after the farms, we would turn on the outposts. We have to get at Pembroke."

"Oh, but we will, my dear. One thing at a time." Colten rose and served himself a beer. He offered her one, but she refused. "You see. These people are forced to work under the control of Pembroke's soldiers. So why do we attack the farms?"

"To free the people," she answered, like a child reciting his lesson.

"And where do we send them?" Colten asked with his honeyed voice.

"To a better place in the north to form a community."

"Voilà," Colten exclaimed. "So when we have freed all the farms, we will turn to the outposts. Now, get yourself ready for tomorrow."

Kilda left the tent with a feeling of deception. She had worked hard to get information on the tower. Yet, she understood that saving the people was necessary. The villagers and farmers could not live with soldiers on their back. The idea of a community in the north, far from Pembroke's lands, was the best solution.

The air outside the tent was cold and damp. It was night now. She looked at the cages. The prisoner would not enjoy his night. She felt pity for him. The man had cried for his friends and had shown compassion for the children. She could make his detention less tough. Kilda went to the catering tent. She picked a loaf of bread and some cheese before she headed back to the cages. Lissandro stood in a corner, his head against the bars.

"I brought you some food," she said. "They don't feed the prisoners every day."

"A charming company you have there," Lissandro retorted, "but thank you for the bread." He took the food she was holding. "Will they contact my friends?"

"I suppose so. Colten wants a ransom."

Lissandro chuckled. "More money and nothing to buy."

"What do you mean?" Kilda grumbled.

"Well, what does he want to do with my ransom? Buy a farm he has already sacked? Or maybe buy himself a castle," Lissandro sneered. He bit the bread and chewed.

"Are you always so mean? I told you that he gives it to the people," Kilda objected.

"I don't think you are someone stupid," Lissandro said. "So please, forget your hatred for Pembroke for a second and look at Colten, look at the camp. Does all this look honorable to you? Do you think that a man called Colten Three Fingers can be trusted? He is luring you. If you don't trust me, and I can understand that, just investigate by yourself. See to the woman and her children. Learn what he does with the money."

The man sounded sincere. However, what he said was hard to conceive. The men here really hated the count. Why would they turn on the people? Yet, it cost nothing to check on the family she had brought here. She rose. "Good night."

"Kilda," Lissandro hailed her. "Don't get yourself caught."

She went to the pavilion where they sheltered the refugees. A guard stood at the entrance.

"You can't go in there," he said, scowling at her.

"I brought refugees today. I want to speak to them," Kilda insisted. The men did not reply and kept blocking the way. "Listen, it's really important…"

"No one can enter this tent without Colten's authorization," the guard said.

"And why is that? It's just a tent with some refugees." Kilda did not understand what could be so special about a tent that would only contain a few beds, blankets, and some nurses.

"It's related to the security of the camp." The man stood imperturbable.

Kilda gave up. It was useless. She would find another way or ask Colten directly. She headed to her tent and went to sleep.

The horses' whinnies woke her up. Kilda rose and got dressed. She pushed the flap of her tent. It was already morning. Yet, the sun was still low behind the top of the trees. She saw a group of riders leave further away at the camp's border.

"What on earth…?" she exclaimed, astounded. She could not believe that Colten and the group had left without her. She was always with them during the raids. Had she done something to upset him? Kilda had a bad feeling. She went to the cages in a hurry. She sighed with relief. He was still there. Lissandro slept on the ground, curled up on himself. Her footsteps seemed to have woken him up. He turned around, looked at her, and stretched.

"Good morning," he yawned. "Time for breakfast?"

"Don't be a fool," she grunted. "Why did they leave? Did they talk to you?"

"I have no idea what you are talking about. Did your dear friends go to the ball without you?" Lissandro sneered and stood up. "Good that I am not taller," he said when his hair stopped a few inches from the top of the cage.

"I really wonder why some people would pay to have you back," she muttered and went away.

So their departure had nothing to do with her prisoner. Maybe it had nothing to do with her after all. Maybe they had forgotten to wake her up. She was the only female soldier in the camp, after all.

She was pondering all the possibilities while walking through the camp when she stopped dead. The guard in front of the refugees' pavilion was gone. She moved closer slowly and gazed around. There was no one to be seen. She sneaked inside the tent. Kilda strangled a scream.

There were cages inside the tent. The same kind of cages where Lissandro was trapped, but these did not have a single man in them. They were full of women and children. Their hands were tied and they had gags on their mouths. Worse, there was blood on the ground. Some cages were open and empty. Only by the filth in it, she understood that people had been trapped in them. The prisoners looked at her with pleading eyes. There were no guards inside the tent, but no keys either. Kilda spotted a table in a corner. She rushed to it. It was covered with papers and writing objects. No key. She found a piece of metal and thought of picking the lock. She had never done it, but she could try. She ran to a cage and tried to force the bolt. The women inside the cage pressed against the bars. While she worked on the lock, Kilda realized that she had no idea what to do if the door of the cage opened. She could not save them from the camp. She panicked. She took the dagger she had on her belt and pulled at the nearest woman's wrists. The woman struggled, frightened, but Kilda was stronger. She cut the rope with her dagger and gave the knife and the piece of metal to the woman. "Save yourself and the others," Kilda told her, her voice full of grief. "I'm sorry." She looked around. "I'm sorry!" She ran out of the tent.

They would notice. They would soon know. Kilda ran through the camp. She stopped, her hands on her thighs. "Think," she muttered, "think."

Kilda went to the cage where Lissandro sat. She took a deep breath to stay calm. "You there," she hailed the guard. "Open that cage," she commanded him. "I have the order to bring him to the main tent to be interrogated."

The guard did not question her. He muttered some unintelligible words and opened the gate.

"And now comes the torture," Lissandro grumbled.

"Shut up!" She dragged him out by the arm and pushed him in front of her, holding him tight. "Keep walking."

"Did your friend change his mind?" Lissandro asked with a hint of worry in his voice.

"Don't talk," she whispered. "We're fleeing out of here."

26

The bucket of water was heavy. It was his fifth one this morning, and carrying it to the tent made his arm ache.

"Do you want some help, my lord?" a soldier coming the other way suggested.

"No, thank you. I can manage," Folc answered.

He insisted on doing his chores. Louis had asked the officers to be a good example for the soldiers. Folc was not an officer, but he wanted to be a solicitous squire to the captains. It was his way of being helpful. He would not be a lazy lord with an orderly around him. Faremanne had appreciated his services. The man had shown him around the camp, explaining in detail the resupplying. In exchange, Folc had had clothes to wash, boots to clean, and easy tasks like replacing the candles or boiling water. It was mostly page tasks, but he did not mind.

Things were a lot more difficult with Selen. His friend did not like to delegate work. The best Folc could do was fetching water and doing some washing when Selen was away, but he knew better not to make his bed, empty the pots, or touch the armour.

Folc entered the tent and poured the water from the bucket into a basin. He took the goblets and did the dishes.

"What are you doing?" Selen mumbled. He sat on his bed, sharpening his sword. Selen picked up the whetstone out of the water at his feet. The rasping noises of the stone on the steel were short. Selen was angry. His sweet friend had always been calm and complaisant, except these last two days. Selen had stood silent and had brooded on his own. It made the atmosphere in their tent unbearable. Folc could not hold it anymore.

"Washing the cups," Folc muttered. His fingers turned on the inside of the goblet. The water spun and spurted.

"I can see that," Selen said, irritated. "None is yours. I already told you. You're not my servant. We need to be on the field in half an hour. Get dressed."

"I need to feel useful," Folc complained. He let the goblet fall into the bucket. It disappeared with a plop.

Selen got up and strode towards him. He grabbed Folc's sword from the rack and removed it from the scabbard. Folc gulped and shrank his shoulders. Selen sat down next to him and placed the sword onto his lap.

"You see that?" Selen asked harshly, pointing at brown flecks on the blade. "That's rust. If you didn't lose all your precious time with things both of us don't care about, you would have taken care of your materiel." Selen looked directly at Folc. "I don't care if there are stains on the mugs or if my clothes need sewing; we are in an army camp. What I want is that you can watch my back during battles with a sword that won't fall into pieces. Now, take that stone and remove the flecks."

Folc took the whetstone from Selen's hand and complied. Selen went to his armour and got dressed. "What is wrong with you?" Folc asked.

Selen did not answer at first but kept strapping his armour on his legs. He stopped and lowered his head. "I don't want to be a captain," he muttered.

So there lay the problem. Selen had mentioned his promotion before without enthusiasm. Folc wondered how Bertrant had seen a captain in his friend. He must have been drunk. "Did you try to refuse?" Folc asked, knowing the answer. Selen never complained about what was asked of him.

"I said to Louis that I felt uneasy about it."

"That's not a refusal." Folc knew as well that Louis could not have changed the commander's decision. Besides, Bertrant would never have accepted a refusal. Folc tried to cheer him up. "But why don't you want to be a captain? You are certainly the best warrior in all the camp."

"There is a difference between fighting well and leading men. I'm not a leader. Definitely not to two hundred men." Selen fixed his breastplate.

"You won't have much to do. Shout here and there. Show the good example." Folc turned the blade down and polished the other side.

"What if they don't obey?" Selen stopped and looked at him, anxious.

"Because of what you are?" Folc looked straight at Selen. His friend's face turned pallid. Folc wondered if Selen thought of his appearance or something more specific Folc had suspicions about. *There are other reasons why you felt embarrassed to join the men on the training field*, Folc thought. "Because I see you as the man who killed The Mountain. They all do here," Folc said. "Besides, it would impress Louis to see you leading men." The blush on Selen's cheeks turned Folc's suspicions into certitude. Could that be their secret? He had heard of such men in dirty jokes, but they had nothing in common with either of his friends.

Selen smiled. He finished attaching his gauntlets. "Maybe you're right. Only a few orders here and there, you said?"

Folc was glad to see Selen happy again. "Yep!" he exclaimed with enthusiasm, though he had a hard time imagining his soft-spoken friend shouting orders in a melee. Folc got up and put his protections and plates on. "Leave the motivation stuff to Louis. Just be brave and fight like a hero." He smiled. They went out of their tent and headed to the south of the camp.

Many soldiers stood already dispersed on the field. Folc and Selen moved towards a group of men waiting their turn for a duel with Faremanne. The captain was covered in sweat. He had probably parried for a few hours now.

"Want something more challenging than a weary, old captain?" Selen asked the men.

"Give this blustering captain a good lesson," Faremanne said to his men, laughing. Two soldiers drew their swords and engaged on Selen. Folc encouraged the two captains.

"Want to train with me, boy?" a lieutenant asked Folc.

"Sure," Folc said. He spread his legs apart and ensured his balance, holding his sword straight, but not too tight. While taking his bases, he tried to remember his previous training with Selen. As a boy, he had a much shorter reach. Folc watched the man circle and moved around in the opposite direction. He and the lieutenant launched and parried strikes.

"You're good," the lieutenant said.

Folc kept the blade close to him. He did not forget to bend his knees. All was in the balance, Selen had insisted. The lieutenant leapt forward. Folc sidestepped and avoided him.

"You move like the purple mongoose over there. Did he teach you?" the lieutenant exclaimed.

Folc only grinned. He would not let himself be disturbed. He kept on blocking the strikes, waiting for an opening. Progressively, he found the flow. The lieutenant threw his sword. Folc saw an overture and rushed in, but his arm was too short. The man blocked and hit Folc on the wrist with the flat of the blade, disarming him.

"Ouch!" Folc cried out.

"Did I hurt you?" the lieutenant asked with concern.

"It's only a scratch," Folc answered. Blood ran from the cut. "I should go to the infirmary and put some antiseptic on it."

He looked in Selen's direction. His friend was engaged in a fight against two soldiers. *It's not a good time to distract him,* Folc thought. He left the field and headed to the infirmary. The pavilion was silent and almost all the beds were empty.

Brother Benedict was in his workshop. He was carving a wooden stick into the shape of a miniature spoon. His hand movements were precise, and the knife cut the splinters clean.

"Hello? Excuse me," Folc hailed the monk.

"Oh." Brother Benedict raised his head. "Come here, boy! What can I do for you?" he asked amiably, holding out a hand towards Folc.

"It happens that I cut myself on the field," Folc explained. He showed his cut to the monk.

"It's not as bad as it looks," the man reassured him. He put a clean cloth on the wound to stop the bleeding. "Hold it while I fetch some thyme tincture." The monk disappeared behind a shelf and came back with a flask and a cloth. "I had hoped to see you today, Folc."

"You know my name?" Folc asked, intrigued.

"Your friend told me about you." Brother Benedict smiled. He removed the cloth and applied the lotion. "I have a mission for you, but you will have to keep it to yourself and do it at once."

"Why should I stay silent?" Folc didn't know if he could even trust the man.

"Because it may be dangerous, and your friends won't approve." Brother Benedict lectured him as if he should not have asked the question. The monk put a clean bandage around Folc's hand.

"So why would I do it?" Folc insisted.

"Because it may be the key to all our problems." Brother Benedict leaned towards him.

Folc stayed silent and listened to the monk attentively.

"I was in the forest the other day, wildcrafting ingredients for the infirmary. Though I knew that part of the wood, I wandered further away than usual. I found myself in a darker part of the forest. This is where I found the shack." The monk stared at him. "There is more in this world than the mind can conceive. Men don't believe in these things anymore, but you are young and full of hopes. Do you believe in magic?"

"I believe in dragons. Everything is possible in this world. What was in the shack, Brother?" Folc asked curiously.

"A seer," the monk whispered with excitement.

"And? What is a seer?"

"The seers live in communion with nature. They know things, things from the future sometimes. Maybe this one could help us against the dragon."

"Did you ask him?" Folc inquired.

"Me? No!" the man exclaimed. "I'm a monk! I can't talk to seers. But you can. You are pure and your heart is true."

"I still don't understand. Why me? Why not Selen? I can't hardly have a purer heart than his."

"In your heart and body," Brother Benedict insisted. "It's the only way to enter in communication with a seer."

Folc pondered the information and understood. Still, he wondered how the monk could know such things about him and his friend. "Where will I find it?" he sighed. The monk explained the way for him.

Folc had left the camp unnoticed. Once in the forest, he followed Brother Benedict's instructions. The path was not too complicated to find. He only needed to follow the river upstream and head west at the first falls.

He had walked for two hours when he noticed the first changes in the forest around him. It was more difficult to step through the fens. The moss hid deep holes. Sometimes, what looked like moss was duckweed, and his foot would pass through it with a loud splash. The air was rancid. It stank of decay. The ground turned into a bog. Folc sloshed through it and hoped that the leeches would not feast on his legs. The chirping of the birds had stopped. Folc had heard tales about the Ebony Forest and thought that the forest may be similar to these woods. The bark on the trees looming over him was black and mossy. No wind blew through the greenish beard lichens hanging from the branches. Though it was only the middle of the day, there was mist in the air. Folc heard the bubble of the gas rising from the water to the surface. He wondered which kind of creature would want to live here.

He saw the shack at a distance and squelched towards it. The house was built of stone on an islet. The roof was rotten thatch. He knocked on the door. If the owner was a witch, he could end up as her supper. He thought of Selen. "I should have left a note," he whispered. The door opened with a creak.

"Come in, boy," someone croaked.

"How do you know I'm a boy?" Folc asked with a wobbly voice. An old woman stood inside the shack with her back turned. She was clad in threadbare brown robes. Her grey hair was long and entwined with wooden branches. The green leaves on them waved in the air.

"I'm a seer—" she gave a snigger "—my eyes are everywhere." She turned around. Her eye sockets were empty. "Come inside and sit."

The room was a mess of junk hanging from the walls and the ceiling. Stuffed animals looked at him with their charcoal eyes. The shelves had more pots than Brother Benedict's workshop. Some glass bottles were filled with floating dead animals, like lizards and frogs which had swollen in the liquid beyond recognition. A table stood in the middle of the room. Folc did not know if what lay on it could be called food or if it was ingredients for mystical experiments. Candles had blown out and had dripped their red wax on the board in large rings. The place was dark, dusty, and smelled like cat piss. Folc coughed. He spotted a stool and sat down on it.

"What can I do for you?" the seer asked.

"I thought you would already know."

"I know. I want to hear you say it." The seer coughed.

"My friends are worried about the dragon," Folc said.

"And who wouldn't? Dragons are not from this world. They are from hell!" she shrieked the last word. "Yet, everything dies in this world, including dragons."

"Can you kill the dragon?" Folc asked, full of hope.

The seer laughed and nearly choked herself. She spat. "I can't kill dragons, young fool, but I know how to extinguish his fire."

"How?" Folc hung on the edge of his stool.

"There is an artifact on the island on the Sihr Loch. It has been hidden there for an eternity. You and your friends could give it new life."

"So it's just that. Finding an artifact?" Folc was nearly deceived.

"Just that?" she repeated. "Maybe, maybe."

Folc did not like her nasty smile. "And what should we do with the artifact?"

"That is the most exciting part, my boy. The dragon has to eat it." She sniggered.

"And what would be the price for this information?" Folc inquired.

"Bring your friends to the island, and we will discuss it. Now, if you'll excuse me…" The seer's body blurred.

"No, wait!" Folc screamed, grasping after her.

The seer turned into a flock of crows and flew through the door.

Folc stood on the floor with black feathers in his hands. "Damn! How will I explain that to my friends? Unless…" He looked around and found what he needed.

27

Selen looked at the shiny, blue eyes. "It is as disgusting as it's fascinating," he whispered, rolling the two eyeballs in the palm of his hand.

"But why did you take them?" Louis asked. He stood at the entrance of the tent, making sure no one entered.

Folc sat on his bed, looking away. "I wasn't sure you would believe my story. I thought this could make it a bit more…convincing."

"I'm convinced that an angry seer will be looking for us in search of her eyes," Selen said, folding the cloth over the eyes and placing them on the table.

"Yeah, I got that," Folc grunted.

"Too bad it wasn't obvious when you decided to take them," Louis added. "So, what exactly did you learn about the artifact?"

"She said that it was hidden on an island on the Sihr Loch. If the dragon eats the artifact, it will extinguish the fire," Folc resumed. "Will you tell the others?"

"No. The incredulous ones will laugh in our faces, and the believers will deliver us to the seer," Louis answered. "I will find an excuse to get the army near the lake. It's on our way."

Selen turned to Louis. "Do you believe it can work?"

His friend shrugged. "How would I know? But it's definitely worth a try."

"How do we make a dragon eat an artifact?" Folc inquired.

"I guess you feed him with the bearer. Preferably a juicy, young boy." Selen grinned.

"I have a hard time thinking that it can work. It sounds too easy," Louis said.

"Those are exactly my thoughts," Folc added. "But Brother Benedict was sure it would help us."

"We will check the place. Maybe the seer doesn't believe we can find it. Maybe there are traps of some sort," Louis said.

"Lissandro could have had a vision about it," Selen murmured. They still had not received news about their friend. Worry grew in him with each passing day.

They all stayed silent. Louis sat down near him and stared at him. "Visions may help him right now. Maybe he has already learned the truth about all this."

Selen tilted his head sideways. If not for the boy, he would have closed the distance between their mouths. He thought about Lissandro again.

"But we leave tomorrow even further east. I can't stop thinking that we didn't do enough." Selen gnawed at his hand and turned his eyes on the lantern behind Folc's bed.

"I know. We didn't." Louis wrapped an arm around Selen's back. Selen closed his eyes. The touch of his friend felt so good, so comforting. His left arm curled around Louis's waist. Selen surprised himself by laying his head on Louis's shoulder but raised it quickly.

"No. You did all you could!" Folc exclaimed. "You had no choice. You did more for this army in three weeks than anyone could have conceived. You have no right to give up."

Selen and Louis looked at Folc in astonishment.

"I am only a young boy. I would probably be dead by now if you hadn't rescued me. You give hope to people. You give us the will to fight. I admire you," Folc said with a thick, brittle voice.

Deeply moved by his words, Selen smiled heartily at Folc and stretched out his right arm. The boy rushed to them for a hug. When Selen heard the sobbing between their chests, he realized it was the first time Folc had cried in their presence. Selen and Louis put an arm behind Folc's back and stayed silent for a while.

Selen heard the men outside dismantle the tents and put the materiel on the carts. They would leave tomorrow morning. Nothing but large poles of wood would be left behind. The stocks were full and ready. Even Brother Benedict had been satisfied. From the villages around, a hundred men had volunteered to join the new Rebellion. Surprisingly, the soldiers were motivated to depart. Maybe they too felt it was time to act. The decisive battle for the reconquest of Trevalden could start. Many would die, but many would regret to have stayed at home. From tomorrow, they would write history. Though he still had no idea what to do and how, Selen was proud to be a captain in this army. Proud to walk alongside his friends. He was scared to death to lose them, yet he knew it would not happen. Not this time. This time, he would win. Selen smiled and laid his head on Louis's shoulder.

28

The apple was juicy. Kraalh took another powerful bite between his huge tusks and ground the piece with his strong molars. Bits fell from his mouth onto his hairy chest. "Get him out of here!" he yelled, spitting slimy morsels in the air. "Put him on a spike!" Two guards dragged the pleading man out of the room. Kraalh took another mouthful. *Boring buffoons, all of them*, he thought. "I should have impaled more," he spat.

Millhaven had been hard to conquer. Sound, strong walls, only three gates, the east side backed by a high cliff. He had lost many soldiers, expendable scum and good officers. The sack had been a treat. The nobles here were filthy rich, and the women beautiful. His orcs had thrown trunks of gold through the windows onto the streets when he had walked by. As for the women, five chains were fixed to his seat. Kraalh tugged at one. A blond girl rose from the floor in front of him. She only had veils around her. Kraalh saw the bruises on her body. *I shouldn't have hit that one*, he thought, *it's not pretty*. He looked at her breasts instead. That was better. The girl was shaking, terrified, but already tame. He pulled another chain. Another girl rose from the other side. This one was better looking. He pushed his loincloth to the side and pulled on both chains. The girls knew what they had to do. The heads of previous slaves stood on the hearth's overmantel in different stages of decomposition as a delicate reminder.

Over his long stay in the city, Kraalh had learned that not all the comely girls of Millhaven could be tamed. Some had had a tragic end, usually by his own hand. It was even more pleasurable for him to know that he had taken over the city from the hand of a woman. The old nag was locked away in the prison tower. He may use her later, once he was done with all these, just to observe the fear and disgust in her eyes. He looked at the two girls having their way with him. He grimaced. They could at least try to put some little enthusiasm in it. He was the orcs' general after all and, in his opinion, among the most handsome of his kind. His eyes were sharp and deep-set in his skull. His nose could be compared to a pig's snout, in shape as well as in dirtiness. His protruding tusks were large and of shiny ivory. Kraalh's long, black, braided hair contrasted with his green-greyish skin which he liked to grease to make his huge muscles gleam. Of his armour, he only bore the pauldrons. The plates were adorned with short, sharp spikes. Kraalh's girth made the massive wooden chair look tiny. "This great hall will need a new decoration," he mumbled, looking at the dull mouldings and carvings. Who could want flowers and horses on his walls?

Kraalh was bogged in boredom. He pulled on a third chain. Maybe this one would make the difference, or maybe he should try something new. By what he had heard, his son, Xruul, had been killed by a peculiar creature, a she-knight painted in weird colors. Kraalh would not mind adding a sixth chain with something more exotic. He straightened in his seat. That last one was at least more skilled than the others. As the girl finished him, the apple exploded in his hand.

The door opened. "One of your chieftains, General!" the guard barked.

"Let him in," Kraalh grunted. That would be a change for him from all these human solicitors. Always pleading for food or justice. As if he had not been accommodating enough. He had only asked for four hundred heads, after all. On a big city like Millhaven, it was nothing. He could have killed them all, but Agroln would not have appreciated. The king wanted to keep the place running. Too much gold at stake, he had said. Kraalh sniggered. The man already had a dragon and most of the country; why bother about gold? The king did not even have to pay him. Pillaging and eating on the land was a lot more exciting. What an orc wants, he takes, as simple as that.

The Chieftain entered the room and knelt in front of him. "General."

"Speak!" Kraalh shouted. He picked up an apple from the large silver plate on his side and aimed at the orc. The fruit missed him.

"An army is heading south towards us, General. My soldiers say it's the Rebellion."

"It's impossible," Kraalh grunted. "I have crushed that coward. His army was in ruin." The Rebellion had been challenging at first, but with time, it had reduced to nothing. The men left were drunken beggars wading in their shit in what they called a camp. He had even heard rumours that they had burned villages in his name.

"But there is an army coming, General," the Chieftain said.

"How many?" Kraalh asked, chewing noisily on an apple.

"Around a thousand," the orc said.

Kraalh guffawed. "That is not an army! I will crush them in a blow. Where are they?"

"Near the Sihr Loch, General."

Kraalh swallowed the piece of fruit he had in his mouth. "What?"

"They are near the Sihr Loch," the Chieftain repeated.

"I heard you, son of a troll!" Kraalh yelled. "What are they doing by the lake?" They could not have heard about the artifact. It was impossible. No human had that knowledge.

"We don't know, General."

Kraalh pondered the situation. He could not leave the city. With his soldiers roaming the whole country, he only had three thousand orcs in garrison in Millhaven. He had been too confident of his strength. Should he meet the Rebellion on an open ground, he would lose his advantage. Still, he could not let them find the artifact either.

"Send a party of our best orcs. Let them spy on the Rebellion. Whatever the humans find on that lake, make our orcs steal it," Kraalh ordered. It was all he could do for now. Should they march towards the city, he could still destroy them. The artifact was useless against orcs.

"Yes, General," the Chieftain said. He knelt and took his leave.

Kraalh got up. It was time he paid a visit to the landlady.

The cells were crowded. The orcs had so many prisoners that they had requisitioned rooms in the keep, but that was not where Kraalh was heading. These poorly lit corridors were at the top of the old tower, the most insalubrious part of the prison. It was murky and humid to a point that he was forced to tramp in pools of water. It stank. Some prisoners had been voluntarily forgotten in their cells. The rats had made a feast on the most delectable morsels. Kraalh thought that they would have to clean one day to prevent any disease. The guard sitting on a chair in front of the door snored in his sleep. Kraalh kicked him with his foot. The orc fell heavily to the floor.

"Open the door!" Kraalh bawled. The guard rose hastily and obeyed. The hinges grated when the large oak door opened.

He had locked her in one of the cells facing west so that she could admire the misfortunes happening to her dear city. The windows offered a good view of the execution yard and on the ramparts where he had had the four hundred men impaled. Kraalh had seen the rage in her eyes, but she had never uttered a word. The countess had endured all his vile persecutions, from the rotten food to the most despicable filth, without a single twist of her mouth. Now, she still stood proudly at her window.

"Still waiting for a sign?" Kraalh scoffed.

"What is the object of your visit?" she inquired in a croaky yet plummy voice.

Still too noble to cry, Kraalh thought. Some women were harder to tame, indeed. "What do you know of the Rebellion?"

"I thought you had eradicated them," she said. Kraalh noted the faint, sarcastic smile hidden in her words. "Unfortunately, I don't know much about their last moves. I have some complications with following the latest news."

"But what can you tell me about them?" Kraalh insisted. She had better not test his patience.

"That the Rebellion is commanded by Sir Bertrant Heymon, a valiant knight and a brave lord, once."

"What more? What of his captains? Of his men?"

"Are you expecting me to reveal useful information? That I betray their cause?" She sounded offended.

"I could squeeze the words out of your brittle body," Kraalh hissed, approaching the countess's face.

She lowered her eyelids with disdain. "Well, I suppose that death could only improve my present situation."

"I won't kill you now." Kraalh swayed slowly around her shoulders, hissing from one ear to the other. "First, you will admire your precious Rebellion being crushed against your high walls in waves of blood. Then, maybe I'll give you the honour of raising your head next to Bertrant's skull."

"I can't wait to see that," she whispered coldly.

Kraalh stayed silent, burning with rage. His curled lips trembled on his sharp fangs. He left the cell with a tremendous roar.

29

They had ridden for a week now. The army was comprised of approximatively a thousand soldiers, and most of them were mounted. The Rebellion had lost so many men in the past that it was more lacking riders than horses. Behind the cavalry, a long cortege of chariots and carts followed with the materiel and provisions. Because of the supply train, they could not cover over fifteen miles per day. The pace felt horribly slow for Louis. They had not met orcs on their way, but he knew they were being watched. He considered that the orcs in Millhaven would be warned of their coming long enough to build a proper defense. Louis could only hope that the enemy would not take the threat seriously and consequently drop its guard.

Faremanne rode by his side. The tall, redhead captain had been in a bright mood since their departure. Louis thought that action, even in the shadow of the scythe, was better than tedious procrastination.

"When was the last time you had news of your family?" Louis asked the captain.

"Three years ago," Faremanne answered, "a few months before we lost contact with the north. I miss them every day, but I know I made the right choice. If I die…"

"You won't," Louis interjected. "You may die, but you won't."

"I still don't get why you are so passionate about fighting at our side," Faremanne inquired. "You are well-read, clever, and handsome. You should be working with the city council in Neolerim and get a family of your own, not risking your life with unshaved churls like us."

Louis laughed. "Did it occur to you that I like it here?" His face turned solemn again. "There are only two reasons to fight and die in life. Justice and love. I've seen enough injustice in this land to lead this army to Nysa Serin."

"And love?" Faremanne joked, lighthearted.

Louis did not answer but looked dreamily at the group in front of them. He turned to Faremanne. "And I see no churls here. Every man ready to fight for justice is a brother to me," he said with a smile. "But it's true you are unshaved." Both men laughed.

A sentinel galloped the other way, right towards them. "My lords! Captains!"

"What is it?" Faremanne exclaimed.

The soldier's horse reared when he pulled on the reins. "The lake, Captain! The Sihr Loch is beyond that hill!"

Louis and Faremanne moved their horses from the column and trotted forward. Louis made a sign to Folc and Selen, riding at the front, to urge them to follow. The four riders galloped to the top of the hill.

Downhill, the lake stretched on for miles. Its waters of cobalt blue reflected the sunlight in thousands of sparks. The banks, covered in high grass and speckled with flowers, were emerald green. Down in the valley, near the shore, a flock of cranes took flight. Their white wings flapped slowly in splashes of water.

"And here lies the island," Selen said, pointing at a long rock on their side of the lake.

"The island?" Faremanne turned to him, disconcerted. Louis noticed he had forgotten about Faremanne.

Selen shrank. "We may have something to do on that rock," he muttered.

"The boy has learned about an artifact that may help against the dragon. The object should be on the island," Louis resumed. "It was on our way."

"And you planned this expedition behind my back all these days? I'm very disappointed in you all," Faremanne scolded.

"Behind your back and behind Bertrant's," Louis added.

"Damn, Louis! Maybe he really will hit you this time," Faremanne still fumed.

"He can't. I'm his captain," Louis retorted, "and there are rules. No one hits a soldier or a superior."

"Your rules, his army," Faremanne objected. "And you know the man, short fuse."

"He doesn't need to know. No one needs to until we find something. While the army camps along the shore for the night, we sail to the island, check the place, and come back as if nothing happened," Louis insisted.

"As if nothing happened?"

"We don't even know if this artifact exists. We don't want to spread false hope. What do you say?" Louis asked with an appealing look.

"All right, but I'm coming with you." Louis grasped by Faremanne's look that it was his final word.

They trotted back to the column of soldiers. Louis and Faremanne hailed the lieutenants. Louis rode to the ones at the head of the column.

"Settle camp on the prairie to the west of the lake. Make sure food is distributed to everyone and that they dig the trench," Louis commanded. Louis had insisted that they dig latrines wherever they stayed. He had been so upset by the terrible hygiene in the camp that one of his first rules had been related to the sanitation. He still thought that he would kill on sight the first man he saw defecate near someone else's sleeping place.

The army reached the prairie, and everyone bustled about his tasks, whether it was to gather wood or to groom the horses. Because of the fine weather, they had never lost time building the tents, except the headquarters. The men slept wrapped in their blankets, and campfires were lit among the groups.

Louis left his horse with the others and walked through the camp. The men relaxed on the grass, massaging their sore legs or backs. The captains had made sure not to exhaust the men with long walks on the hot, dusty roads. Louis could see that, as a result, no one complained about their conditions. The men shared jokes, played, or polished their weapons. A light soup of nettles and ramsons with a loaf of bread was served. Louis spotted Selen by one of the huge cauldrons. His friend, with the help of an orderly, filled the soldiers' bowls. This was a task way below his status. Louis headed towards Selen to stop him, but the look of gratitude on the soldiers' faces made him change his mind. Louis watched Selen exchange a word or a smile with the soldiers. He would have a word with his friend, but he would not scold him or ruin his efforts to mingle with the men. Selen had probably acted spontaneously. The status of captain had fallen like a burden on Selen's shoulders. To ease his task, Louis had not entrusted him responsibilities others than to walk at the front of a company or give a few orders here and there. If Selen wanted to help out at the camp, as long as it was not degrading activities, he would let him. Louis approached the group of men waiting for their meal around the cauldron.

"Do you have a bowl for me, Captain?" Louis asked, half smiling. Selen's lips turned white as he bit on them.

"Of course," Selen whispered.

"You should take one for yourself as well and follow me. We have a mission to do, if you remember," Louis said. The orderly handed him bread and a bowl. Louis felt the warmth through his gloves. The smell of garlic made his nose twitch, but the promise of food made his stomach rumble. In front of him, Selen filled himself a bowl and handed the orderly the ladle.

"Have you seen Folc?" Selen asked, walking towards him while blowing on his soup.

"He went with Faremanne. I suppose they are waiting for us near the lake." Louis and Selen crossed the camp. The soup was a bit acrid, but it was fresh. "Why did you serve the soup?" he asked.

"Someone had to do it. I stood nearby," Selen answered. "Was it wrong?"

"No. As long as you remember you are their captain. But it was not wrong." Louis looked at Selen to make him see that he meant it. Selen smiled back.

They finished their soup before joining Folc and Faremanne. Their friends waited on the shore.

"We still have a few hours before the sun disappears on the horizon," Faremanne said.

Louis, Faremanne, Selen, and Folc walked along the shore in search of a boat. Among the reeds, they found an old fishing boat that still floated.

"Four men in armour on that?" Selen interjected.

"Well, we are all coming," Faremanne protested.

"I'm not suggesting something else," Selen carried on, "just that I don't want to drown halfway."

"We don't really need our armour, not all of us. I can take mine off," Folc suggested.

"Exactly. The island is small, and as I can see, there is hardly something bigger than lizards living on it," Selen said. He removed his armour and only kept his sword attached to his belt. Folc did the same.

Louis hoped that the boat would hold the crossing because there was no way he would remove his armour. An artifact so powerful would not be left unguarded. Just because they didn't see a threat didn't mean there wasn't one. Faremanne seemed to share his thoughts since he kept his armour on too.

They got on board. Faremanne and Selen rowed while Folc stood at the bow. Louis observed the island. It was a line of sandy earth covered with gigantic boulders and stones. No grass grew on it. The vegetation consisted only of thorny bushes and dead, gnarled trees, mostly buckthorn. There were stones shining white here and there.

"Those are no stones," Louis muttered, his eyes scrutinizing the land.

"It's bones," Folc whispered with a tremulous voice.

The boat hit the shore.

Folc was the first to leave the boat. "I see nothing," he said. "There are no houses, no constructions, nothing."

"Stay behind us," Louis said, "you have no armour."

They pulled the boat onto the shore and walked around carefully. The ground was a mix of stones, sand, and bones of all sizes. Some were those of small animals, some were clearly human.

"What could have killed them?" Selen inquired. He picked up a skull and inspected it.

They progressed among the rocks, searching for a door or an engraved stone behind the brambles. Louis looked up. A crow was perched on one of the branches. Louis could swear it stared at them.

"I have found something!" Folc shouted. His call was followed by a scream of distress.

The three men ran to where the boy had been. A black hole gaped in the ground. Roots grew around it, and large stones blocked the way.

"Folc!" Selen shouted. "Folc, do you hear us?"

There was no answer.

"It's too tight for any of us to pass through," Faremanne said.

"We need to fetch him, one way or another," Louis said, trying to stay calm.

"It's not vertical. He may have slipped into a tunnel. There may be another opening somewhere. We should search for it," Selen proposed.

Louis heard a croaking coming from above their heads. He looked up and saw that they were surrounded by crows.

"What mischief is this?" Faremanne cried out. He drew out his sword.

The crows croaked with a deafening noise. They flew and whirled together. A blurred shape appeared. The seer materialized in front of their eyes. Louis thought that the old hag looked even more dreadful than Folc had described her. Her empty eye sockets, veined with dark blood, were repulsive. One of the crows flew down and perched on her shoulder.

"You finally came," she cackled. Her voice was as raucous as a croaking.

"Did you take the boy?" Louis asked warily.

"The boy?" she asked. "You mean the thief, the nasty, little thief," she hissed, wrinkling her nose. "If I find him…" She made a fist with her hand and shook it as if strangling the air. "I thought you were here for the artifact," she sniggered.

"Well, that too," Faremanne said. "Where is it? Tell us!" he ordered.

"I could…but to get the artifact, I need pure, pristine flesh," she said, licking her dry, cracked lips. "I could make good use of some gorgeous, innocent young man."

"What is she insinuating?" Selen asked, worried.

"Something that doesn't concern you anymore," Louis whispered to his friend.

"That is revolting!" Faremanne interjected.

"I was only talking about eating you! But you, you have something I want," she said, turning to Selen.

"You mean, this is what you want," Selen said, taking a cloth out of his pocket. He unfolded the corners, revealing two shiny, white eyeballs.

"Give it back," the seer growled heinously. She rose a scrawny, clawlike arm in Selen's direction and jumped onto him like a bobcat.

"Don't touch him!" Louis shouted, hitting the old nag in the face with the back of his left gauntlet.

Her shriek was strident. A faint, white flash appeared, and the seer was projected backwards onto the ground. She rose laboriously. Half of her face looked like it had been scorched by a white-hot iron bar.

"Hell! How did you do that?" Faremanne shouted.

"I don't know," Louis answered, startled.

Selen came forward, holding the two eyes up in his palm, and crushed them. Mucus, slimy as egg white, ran down his hand and dripped to the ground.

The hag howled and trampled. Behind her, someone crept through the bushes. Louis recognized Folc but stayed silent. The seer was ready to attack again when the boy rushed forward. Her head flew into the air, chopped clean from her body. Behind the decapitated corpse stood Folc, his sword raised. He had mud on his shirt, and leaves hung from his hair.

"I've found the artifact!" he exclaimed, beaming. "What did I miss?"

They all stood struck by surprise. "Folc! Where have you been?" Selen exclaimed. They strode towards the boy.

"I fell through a tunnel," he told them. "It was pitch black, so I crawled on the ground and held on to roots. The artifact glowed faintly on a pedestal in the middle of a chamber hidden inside the island."

"How did you come out?" Faremanne asked.

"I followed a draught and another tunnel. I think only a child could have ventured through these tunnels. Maybe that's what the seer meant by an innocent boy," Folc told them.

"Can we see it?" Louis asked. He had listened until Folc had finished his story, but he could not wait to observe the magical object.

"Of course." Folc took the artifact from his pocket. It was shaped as two folded wings that were made of silver. In the center was a flask with some kind of watery, transparent liquid.

"This is what we have to use against the dragon?" Faremanne asked. "How can we know it's the right object or that it will work?"

"We can't," Louis answered.

"Therefore, I suggest we don't talk about it to Bertrant. We can find out by ourselves when the time comes," Faremanne proposed.

"Now, we need to find a way to get it inside the dragon. A creature we only have heard of," Selen said.

"I have seen it in my dreams," Louis objected.

"Well, everyone makes nightmares of orcs and dragons these days," Faremanne retorted.

Louis did not see the point in explaining to the captain about his dreams and the visions. He stayed silent. He was more concerned about what he had done to the seer. He had not felt heat on his gauntlet. Yet, her face had been badly burned. Was his armour protected against magic? Had the seer done it to herself with her own powers? Selen touched his shoulder. "Hmm?"

"Shall we go?" Selen had washed his sticky hand in the lake. The feeling must have been repugnant. Louis wondered if he would have dared to do it on his own bare palm.

"Yes. Let's move." They still didn't know what had caused all those bones around the island, but it was information he could live without.

They went on board and rowed back to the nearest bank. They dragged the boat onto the shore. Selen and Folc put their armours on again.

"I would like to keep the artifact on me if it's all right with everyone?" Louis asked his friends. He was not especially interested in the artifact itself, but he was afraid that something was bound to it. He did not want Selen or Folc to suffer from some kind of spell or to have a creature searching for them in the middle of the night.

"What do you plan to do with it?" Faremanne questioned, raising an eyebrow.

Louis sighed. Someone had to ask that stupid question. He had crude words coming to his mind, but he gave up. "Keep it safe," he said. "It's not that I don't trust you with it, Folc. On the contrary. I don't trust anyone around you. This is silver." At least, Louis wanted to justify himself to the boy.

Folc handed him the bag containing the artifact. They walked back together to the camp where everyone took his leave and went his own way.

Like every night, Louis would sleep at the headquarters. Sleeping on the ground in Bertrant's tent was most unpleasant. The commander got drunk every night and snored like a bear. But should he sleep under the stars among the others, Louis would never close an eyelid all night. In an open camp, Louis was far too scared to have his throat cut during his sleep by one of Segar's men. Bertrant had given him tacit approval the first time Louis had entered the tent with his blanket. Louis had appreciated the commander's silence. He would have hated to ask.

He entered the tent. Bertrant sat on his bed with a book in his hands. The man tried hard to give a better image of himself every day. Louis felt remorse for not telling Bertrant about the artifact. He did not like to lie, especially to good men. Yet, the greater good was always more important in his eyes. He would have to deal with it. "Do you like reading?" he asked.

"I am a bad reader, but my wife liked reading," Bertrant answered.

"Are you married?" Louis inquired. He had never imagined the commander with a family.

"I was," Bertrant said. He raised his eyes from his book. "She died."

"I'm truly sorry," Louis said, sincere. "May I ask how?"

"It was during the war of the lords, right after the dead of King Lambelin. A family, the Harpers, wanted to get rid of me because I had sided with their enemies. They rode to our castle one day. They killed everyone. My household, the cooks, the lads…my children, and my wife." Tears gathered in his eyes. "They dishonored my wife and killed her." Bertrant's voice was thick with grief and rage. He rubbed the palm of his hand over his eyes. "I was away that day. My lord had called on me in the morning to settle a conflict in a village. When I came back in the evening…" Bertrant's voice died out.

Louis did not know what to say. His feelings were a mix of sorrow and compassion for the man who had fought bravely, despite such a terrible loss. "We will avenge their deaths, my lord."

Bertrant gave a slight smile. "It's what I have done for four years now. I have fought every day, carrying my family in my heart. I'm tired. I know what I look like. I see it in your eyes. Some men need to drink. Some men need something to hold them together during the days. And the nights." Bertrant made a gesture. "No, don't talk. You are right. I used to be like you once. Always wanted things to be perfect. Filled with ideals. I know you want to win the war. But never forget that we all want it. For all we have lost. For all we are afraid to lose." Bertrant turned around and lay down.

"Thank you, my lord," Louis whispered.

He went to the other side of the tent, removed his armour, stretched out his blanket, and lay down on it. He took the artifact out of his pocket and pulled it out of the bag. The wings were nicely carved. They did not look like demon wings. They were more birdlike. As he touched the flask with a finger, the water radiated a feeble light. Frightened to have done something wrong, Louis dropped the artifact. The light died out. He looked at the flask, startled, and reached towards it again with his finger. The white glow came back. It shone like the light which had appeared on his gauntlet when he had hit the seer. It did not hurt or burn. It only glimmered like a diamond. Why did it happen now? Why not when Folc had held it? He knew he had no answer to all his questions. He pushed the artifact back inside the bag. He did not know what to do with it, but he had sworn to protect it. He put it back in his pocket, hoping it would not burn him to death while he slept. Behind him, Bertrant snored already. Louis laid his arm on his head and fell asleep.

Screams and shrieks woke him up. Louis flew up on his feet. "What happened?" he shouted. He searched for his sword and saw that Bertrant stood up next to him. Dark slime stained his clothes. At his feet lay the bodies of two orcs.

"I caught them sniffing at you. You can be lucky that I was feeling thirsty," Bertrant said. "Now, would you please tell me why, in the whole camp, they would sneak in here, searching especially for you?" Louis heard the threat in the words.

"You should call for Faremanne first. We can explain everything." Louis knew it was time to inform Bertrant.

30

Lissandro and Kilda had stolen two horses and had left the camp unnoticed. They had galloped through the forest for a while now.

"Stop!" Lissandro shouted. He reined in. His horse stopped in puffs of dust. In front of him, Kilda slowed down. "I'm not riding any further until you have told me what's going on." Lissandro was tired of her erratic behavior. "First you bring me to that camp, praising your friends, and now you make us flee?"

She rode back to him. "Are you not happy with it? Did you prefer your cage?"

"Well, if it meant I could see my friends again, yes!" Lissandro yelled. He would have cursed and called her names if she had not been a woman. Her bad mood got on his nerves, and his spirits were on the verge of breaking down again.

"I saw what they are doing!" she yelled back at him. Tears came to her eyes. "I saw the truth! Are you happy now?"

She was as upset as he was. Lissandro lowered his tone. "What did you see?"

"The cages. They park them in cages. The villagers." She got down from her mount and paced back and forth. "I was a fool." Kilda sat down and put her hands to her face.

Lissandro heard her sob. He could not help but feel sorry for her. He dismounted and tied the horses' bridles to a branch. Silently, he approached her and waited.

"I thought I was doing something good. How stupid," she muttered from under her hands.

"We all make mistakes. Why did you trust someone like that?" Lissandro sat behind her.

"He did not mind that I was a woman. He did not laugh at me. He gave me a chance." She sniffled.

That, Lissandro could understand. It was a feeling he had encountered many times. Lonely, rejected people like himself craved attention and, as he had seen in Selen, were often gullible. Through years of torment, Lissandro had learned the painful lesson not to take the wrong helping hand. "I don't mind either. You are a good warrior," he said. "Why did you free me?"

"When I saw the cages and the blood and what they could do to children, I thought they would never hesitate to hurt you. So I took you with me. I'm sorry I messed up. You are free now. Go," she said with a low, thick voice.

Lissandro was moved by her gesture. He had done nothing to deserve her compassion. Instead, considering he had nothing to lose, he had been mean and rude. "Thank you."

"You're still here?" she mumbled, angry.

Lissandro rose and walked in front of her. He held out his hand. "Shall we carry on?"

She looked up. "Your friends are searching for you."

"I know, but I have no idea where they are, and you are alone. We both need company." He smiled. "I promise not to be mean."

She took his hand and rose. They got back on their mounts and kept on riding east.

"You said that my friends were in the Rebellion. What is it exactly?" Lissandro asked. Under him, his horse stumbled and blew. He patted his mount on the neck.

"The Rebellion is the army fighting against the orc legions of King Agroln. Suicidal fools, for the most. I have heard that their camp was two days ride to the east. Is it where you want to go?"

"If it's where my friends are, yes." So, they had joined an army and fought to free the country. *That happened fast*, Lissandro thought. It also meant that they could not search for him themselves. That's why they had put a ransom on his head.

"I don't think I can come with you," Kilda said.

"Well, it's your choice, but I don't understand why. You are a warrior."

"A woman warrior. The Rebellion doesn't want me in its ranks. I tried a few years ago," she said, bitter.

"But, the Rebellion and Colten… It's two different fights." Lissandro was confused. "Well, at least what Colten pretended to fight for."

"I know, but I needed to see Pembroke dead," she said with resentment.

They came into view of a tower. "Hush," Kilda said.

"What is it?" Lissandro reined in.

The tower was of grey stones and rose high in the sky. It had a slate roof on top and a defensive wall at the bottom. Light shone through one of the windows. They could not see the door from where they stood.

"This is an outpost," she whispered. "It's controlled by Pembroke's men."

"Can't we ride past it?" Lissandro asked.

"You could. But I am a bandit. They will want to arrest me," she sighed.

"Well, let's try through the woods instead."

"We need to cross the river, and it's the only path."

Not a river again, Lissandro thought. "Are there no other bridges or a ford downstream we could try?"

"There is a rope bridge, but I'm not sure the horses will make it."

"Let's have a try," he said and spun his horse to the right.

It only took them a moment to come into sight of the bridge. It stretched from one bank to the other a few yards above the river. The ropes looked solid, but the planks had a nasty green color.

"I'm not sure…" Kilda said.

"Then I will go first," Lissandro said. "Hold my horse." He dismounted and handed her the reins.

Slowly, Lissandro stepped on the first plank. It seemed safe. He progressed step by step, taking his time. The wood squeaked a little, but nothing alarming. Under his weight, the ropes swung gently. He felt the cold air of the river blow on his face. He had walked a few yards now. The water ran under him in gurgles. It was not the Strelm River, but there were currents. Holding on to the ropes, he stomped, then hopped a little. The wood held fast. Feeling a bit more secured, he continued. Soon, Lissandro reached the other bank. Nothing had happened. He ran back to Kilda. "I think it's secu—" he said when the planks gave way under him, breaking in a loud creak. He desperately tried to grab a rope or the edge of a board but missed. "Kilda!" The cold water engulfed him.

Lissandro felt pain in his chest. Lips touched his mouth. He wanted to puke and turned his head to the side. Water gushed from his throat. He lay on the shore, soaking wet.

"You idiot!" Kilda yelled.

Lissandro sat down. "Did you rescue me?"

"Yeah, and it cost us our horses. It was tying the bridles or running down the shore. And trust me, you're not worth more than a horse," she lectured him, frowning with one finger pointed up as if he had been a disobedient child. She backed and sat down. "You scared me."

"What are we going to do now?" he asked, worried. "Do you know where we are?"

"I don't know. We can't go up to the tower; we can't go west to the camp. We're stuck here without food. We should make a fire. You need to dry." She got up and gathered dead wood.

Lissandro raged against himself. He was useless, just good to put other people's lives in danger. She was right, he was worthless. He had been lost, captured, imprisoned. He felt disoriented, hungry, wet, and terribly alone. How could he even consider helping his friends? They had succeeded so well without him. She should have let him drown. He felt tears run down his cheeks. He squirmed. Kilda was coming back, and the last thing he wanted was her pity. He turned away to hide his face.

"I was not always a warrior, you know," she said while lighting the fire. "I used to be a wife, a mother. I can feel when someone is crying."

Lissandro turned around. "What happened?"

"I was the lady of Lord Hewald. He was a good husband and a good lord." Her voice was thick with sorrow. "I loved him." With a stick, she poked at the fire. Lissandro drew closer. "We had moved together before the war began. I was carrying his child."

"Did he die during the war?" Lissandro asked softly.

"On the battlefield. He was fighting with the Rebellion when Pembroke abandoned them," she muttered, filled with rage. "All the lords, our friends, turned their backs on me. Without him, I lost our castle, our lands, and…I lost the baby."

"I'm so sorry." He came to her and put an arm around her shoulders. She leaned against him.

"This armour is all I have left of my beloved." Kilda broke down in tears. "I swore I would avenge his death."

"It is not the lords you should fight," Lissandro whispered, cradling her. "It's Agroln. We must join the Rebellion. If my friends have a little power in the army, you will be welcome."

He heard wood creak behind them. Kilda rose bolt upright and reached for her sword.

A group of men came out of the forest. Some had bows drawn, some held massive hounds on the leash. The dogs barked. Slobber spurted out of their waggling chops. A man in a plate armour came forward.

"What do we have here?" he sneered.

31

The city of Millhaven was majestic. Only the most beautiful cities of his previous life's kingdom could be compared to the city. It had been a long time since Selen had seen something so gigantic. The citadel gleamed sandy white. The ramparts stretched around the city in a semicircle, from north to south. The whole city faced west. Millhaven had been built from the rock of the mountain, and its walls had been whitewashed. Behind it rose a red cliff with a high plateau on the top. Selen counted five large towers and seven smaller ones on the ramparts. The city had one main gate with a gatehouse, facing west, and two gates of less importance, one in the north and one in the south. In the background, the imposing keep and its outbuildings overhung the city houses. He saw the green patches of the trees in the rich villa's gardens. The city could have been an exquisite painting if it had not been disfigured by the most shocking ornament.

"Please, tell me they are dead," Selen begged his friend.

"No one can survive that," Louis answered. His voice was low.

The whole length of the rampart was covered with spikes with impaled men on them. The several hundred corpses stood rigid in their last pose. Only their clothes flapped in the wind. The ones with their arms and head stretched towards the sun, as if imploring the gods, made a lasting impression on Selen.

"Don't look at it," Faremanne said to Selen. "It's exactly what they want: to impress you with their viciousness."

"I don't know if I can turn my eyes away from it. This vision will haunt me," Selen responded.

"Thank the gods it's a moat and not a glacis!" Bertrant exclaimed.

"Well, that's a positive attitude," Faremanne noted towards Selen.

"Should we pitch the camp? I would like to start at once with the preparations," Louis suggested.

The captains and Bertrant stood at the top of the last mound before the plain which separated the citadel from the forest. The soldiers were gathered behind them, waiting for orders.

"Let's do that," Bertrant said. He turned to one of his lieutenants. "Install the camp. Start with the headquarters. It must be ready as soon as possible. Call for all my captains. I want Segar and Jamys here in an hour."

Selen saw Louis turn to Faremanne. "Once they are done with the main tents, distribute the axes to the men and explain to them what to do. They must start at once."

"What have you planned?" Selen asked.

"You will see," they answered with a smile.

The headquarters were ready on time. All the five captains and their commander were gathered around the large, oak table. A map of the city lay displayed in front of them.

"I have been in Millhaven many times," Bertrant said, "and I know its strength. The ramparts are broad and sound. The towers cover every corner. We won't be able to approach near enough for undermining. The moat is not deep, but the drawbridge is heavy and reinforced with bands of steel. We can't force it from the outside."

"This is an impregnable stronghold. How did the orcs get into it?" Segar exclaimed.

"The city had been under siege for months. Half of the army had made a desperate sortie to clear the orcs. They were outnumbered. The city never got time to raise the bridge again," Bertrant explained.

"We have no time for a siege," Faremanne said. "We have to act before they summon their forces."

"This is precisely what I'd hoped. They have so many orcs dispersed into the realm that only a handful is left in the city," Louis said.

"A handful of at least three thousand. We are only one thousand—and on the wrong side of the wall," Jamys sneered.

"We have between forty and fifty thousand men trapped inside the city," Louis objected.

"Civilians! You can be sure that the orcs didn't leave any soldier alive," Segar exclaimed.

"Do you really think civilians can't fight?" Louis sounded offended by the captain's comment.

"Don't they have some kind of sewers?" Jamys asked Bertrant.

"They do. But we don't have the power to tear off the steel gates blocking the tunnels," Bertrant answered with a pessimistic sigh.

"Excuse me," Selen said with his soft voice. He had stayed silent the whole time, listening carefully to Bertrant and analyzing the map. "If I am right, the city is rich and powerful because of its gold mine."

"It is, indeed," Bertrant confirmed.

"Then, all this is a mine," Selen said, passing his long fingers on the map, underlining the east side of Millhaven. "The entrances are in the city, here and there." He tapped on two tiny black crosses.

"Yes?" Bertrant sounded intrigued.

"It is a large mine," Selen continued. "They need plenty of air exhausts and intakes, and in this case, these must only go straight up. They are scattered on the plateau."

"Go on," Bertrant urged him.

"If we crawl into the air intakes there, we can go out here. Into the city," Selen suggested.

"This is brilliant," Bertrant acknowledged. "But we can't ask a thousand men to crawl into tunnels."

"No, no! Not a thousand men," Selen objected. "Only a party. They could sneak into the city and lower the drawbridge."

Selen saw Louis's face turn radiant. "This could work."

"But what if they get caught?" Segar grunted.

"This is why we will do the diversion," Louis suggested. "We will prepare ourselves to battle and draw the orcs' attention to us."

"And who will be the fool leading the expedition in the tunnels?" Segar asked.

"Me," Selen said, raising his hand.

Everyone turned to him, aghast. "We can send a lieutenant," Bertrant retorted.

"No. It's my idea. I will take the risk," Selen insisted. He desperately craved to do something helpful of his own. He was bored of following the captains without having his own word to say. "I will gather a party of quick, nimble men. We will run to the plateau following the north path. It's mostly out of sight from the towers. Once we are inside the city, we will send you a sign."

"The birds," Faremanne said. "Take the birds with you. Release the whole flock once you are out of the mine."

"There is something more you can do," Louis said. "Commander, it's time you see what Faremanne and I have been planning."

Bertrant opened his mouth to scold the two captains, but Louis stopped him and made a sign for him to follow him outside. They all went out.

"What on earth is that?" Bertrant said amazed, his eyes scanning the men transporting the long wooden beams.

"These are our trebuchets," Louis answered with a hint of pride in his voice.

"How did you manage to have so many so quickly?" Bertrant inquired.

"I knew there would be enough wood, and we had all the hinges from the corrals. We distributed an axe to every man. They have worked like ants." Louis smiled. "That should work as a diversion."

Louis turned to Faremanne. "Once they are done with the cutting, gather the axes. Selen, how many weapons can you and your men carry?"

Selen understood now how he could improve his plan.

Selen went back to his and Folc's quarters. He had walked around the camp the rest of the day, choosing the men for his party. He knew he could have asked a lieutenant to do the task, but he wanted to know exactly with whom he would risk his life. He did not know if the risks were higher to crawl into the tunnels or to charge against the city walls. As dusk fell, he had felt more and more insecure about the result of his initiative. Neither did he have a map of the mine, nor did he know if the openings were large enough. The eventuality of getting lost or stuck somewhere in a narrow passageway under the earth frightened him, and he decided to stop thinking about it. They would see when they got there.

Selen entered the tent and sat on his bed, his arms on his thighs. Folc stood near a rack, greasing his own armour. "I guess I can't come with you?" the boy asked.

"Not this time, Folc," Selen answered. "You stay in the camp. You should stand near the trebuchets tomorrow. It's a safe place, out of range." Selen knew that the boy would do as he pleased, but he insisted anyway.

"Are you scared?" Folc asked.

"Yes, I'm scared," Selen answered. "We have a long run, and we don't know if there will be patrols on the way. There are so many probabilities that I have stopped to count." Selen gave a faint smile.

"But you will be back?" Folc pleaded.

Selen did not know what to say. He did not want to lie to the boy. "I want to."

"Did you talk about it with Louis?" Folc asked.

"I said I would talk with him about the last details tomorrow at dawn," Selen said. Sorrow gripped his heart. The lie still burned in his throat like poison, filling his chest with queasiness.

"But?" Folc inquired. He had a reproachful look. The boy was not easily fooled.

"But I told the men we will leave during the night," Selen whispered.

"You can't do that to him!" Folc shouted.

"I must," Selen objected. "We are here to fight. We must stay focused on the battle. Everyone's future depends on me in this. I can't bear any more weight on my shoulders!" He already hated himself. He did not need the boy to turn the knife in the wound.

Folc looked at him with disapproval but did not insist. He carried on polishing his armour with rough moves.

"Please, don't be angry at me before I leave," Selen sighed.

"I'm angry because I care. I've lost my parents. If you go and die somewhere…" The boy shook his head. "And if you think I'm upset, think of what will happen tomorrow morning," Folc responded. "But you know I can't be mad at you. Just promise you'll be back. Even if you can't," the boy said with a brittle voice.

"I promise," Selen said with a sad smile. "I will."

The flap of the tent was open. Selen lay on his bed, looking at the moon rise in the sky. It was a full moon. At least they would see something on their way. The camp had turned silent. Folc slept in his bed, breathing deeply. Selen rose and put his armour on. He approached the boy and caressed his hair. "I will try to be back. I promise." He went out.

The braziers glowed in the night. He saw sentinels standing guard. Nothing moved in the camp. He wondered if the men could sleep the night before the battle, or if they lay awake, thinking of their dear ones. Selen walked towards Louis's tent. He stopped before the entrance. A single lantern in a corner threw a faint light. The candle was dying out. Faremanne snored in his bed in a corner. Louis sat at the table, his head lying on a pile of papers. He had fallen asleep while working. Selen walked nearer. Bertrant may be the commander, but Louis took all the work on his shoulders. Selen knew that it was not for the pride. Louis wanted to win, and he only trusted himself. Selen looked at his friend's comely features, maybe for the last time.

"I'm sorry I have to go. I hope you can forgive me," he whispered. Selen grabbed his hair from behind his back and untied the ribbon that fastened it. He folded the ribbon and placed it near Louis's hand. "Win this battle for me," he whispered. He needed to go before his heart imploded. In the silence of the night, Selen left the tent, his cheeks bathed with tears.

32

They ran in the shadows of the forest, the moon as their guide. The city lights glowed in the distance. They halted here and there to catch their breath. They would have to hold through the night and the following day. Yet, they could not stop to rest. Once in the tunnels, they would lose all notion of time. They had to send the signal in the morning. Every instant counted.

The bag on Selen's shoulder was heavy. Each of the forty men of his party had gathered as many axes as they could carry. They had to make it to the hill before dawn. If there were patrols, the orcs would stay on the plain. There was no point for them to venture into the hills with the Rebellion standing in the west. Selen looked back. The men followed him in a line. He spotted the soldier carrying the bird cage wrapped in cloth on his back. Faremanne's idea was good, if the animals survived the trip. The sky's color was changing. They had to hasten.

The first rays of the sun shone on the horizon as they climbed the last levels of the hill. Selen's pulse was high and his legs hurt. When he stepped onto the plateau, Selen fell on his knees. His hair stuck with sweat to his neck and brow. At his side, the soldiers staggered and fell on their backs.

"We'll take a short break," Selen said, trying to catch his breath, "then we search for the tunnels." He stared at the blue sky and concentrated on his breathing. At this altitude, the air was fresh and cold. After a few minutes, his lungs responded again.

He rose. "Everyone up! Find me these intakes!"

The plateau was mostly rock, dust, and short grass. The men scattered on the surface, their eyes scrutinizing the ground. It was not hard to find the air intakes. They located three of them. Selen checked the three and opted for the largest one. One soldier tied to a rope was lowered down the hole. Once he touched the ground, they secured the rope and went down after him.

The tunnel allowed only one man at a time, but at least they did not need to crawl. A draft blew on their faces. The ground sloped gently. Two times, they were forced to use the rope to change levels, always progressing deeper into the heart of the mountain. After a while, they heard the first sounds.

"I think it's picks," one of the soldiers said.

They followed the noise. The sound grew clearer and louder.

"It's just here in the hole under us," a soldier whispered. "I can see light."

"I can go first," Selen said. He drew his sword out of its sheath. It may as well be orcs down there. He removed the bag from his shoulders. Selen could see the ground of the next level through the hole. He sat, leaned on the edge, and let himself fall down. In front of him, a dirty, brown man looked at him with terror. "Don't scream," Selen whispered. Above his head, the soldiers climbed down.

The miner raised his pick in protection. "What are you? Demons?"

"We are soldiers of the Rebellion, idiot," one of the soldiers said, irritated. "We are here to free the city."

"Free the city?" the miner repeated.

"Unless you enjoy the company of the orcs," Selen said.

The miner realized. "No, no! Help us, please! Guys, over here!" the man called to his coworkers before turning back to them. "What are you doing here?"

"The Rebellion army is waiting outside your walls. We need to reach the bridge and open the gate."

"How can we help?" the men asked.

"We want you to create a diversion in the city and help us take over the gatehouse. How many men can you gather?" Selen inquired.

"We are several hundred in that part of the mine, but not all of us have picks."

A soldier stepped forward and emptied his bag on the ground. Axes fell with loud chinks. "Does this change the game?"

"Come with us," the miners said, picking up the axes.

Selen and his soldiers followed the miners to a great hall. The news of their presence spread fast through the galleries. Soon, several hundred men stood in the hall. The soldiers emptied the bags and distributed the axes between the miners.

The soldiers looked at Selen, waiting for him to speak. Though he was jittery, Selen concentrated on his mission. It was orcs they wanted to kill, not him. He stepped forward.

"We are here to free the city," he said a bit louder than usual. "What we need is the gatehouse. Once out of the mine, we will free the birds." Fortunately, the animals were alive. He pointed at the cage. "This is our signal. Once the birds are in the air, we have to be quick." Selen pointed at a group of men he judged strong and resolute. "You will guide us to the gate. The rest of you will spread chaos throughout the city as a diversion. Is it clear for everyone?"

"Yeah." The men nodded and held their weapons fast in front of them.

They sneaked up towards the entrance of the mine. A line of orcs guarded the way, facing out. Selen breathed deeply. At this moment, Louis would be waiting outside on the field, counting on him. He could not fail. Should he crawl in his blood, he would open that gate and see him again. "At my move," he whispered. He spotted the orc he considered to be the leader. The creature had two feathers tied on his helmet. Selen raised his sword, approached silently, and cleft the orc's shoulders in two pieces. The alarm was raised.

33

The sun was rising behind the plateau when the army appeared on the top of the mound and rode down on the plain. The thousand riders were aligned on five lines, stretched to cover as much field as possible. They needed to display a mass effect. Behind the soldiers, the oxen pulled the five trebuchets. They had used most of their materiel and deconstructed their carts to build the wheels. The wind whipped from the south. The blue standards and banners flapped against their poles. The armours and plates shone white in the sun. They would not impress the orcs, but at least they would catch their attention. When the trebuchets reached their shooting range, they halted. The army was still many yards away from the ramparts. The four captains rode in a front line, at a long distance from each other. Louis stood on the left of Bertrant. He did not wear a helmet, but he had fixed a large, triangular shield on the side of his saddle.

He scrutinized the sky in search of the birds. They were ready. They could only wait for the signal. Louis felt the pressure of the ribbon he had tied on his wrist. He had been surprised by Selen's decision to lead the expedition, but it had been an honorable and brave choice. He would not have stopped him. At this point, all of them could be dead by the end of the day. However, though he could understand his motivation, he still could not believe that Selen had left without a word. Devastated by his friend's secret departure, Louis had forced himself to invest his last energy in the organization of the troops. Now, only victory mattered. If only he could see the birds. In the distance, Bertrant shouted the orders to load the trebuchets.

The waiting felt like an eternity. Trails of smoke rose from the city's roofs. Clouds crossed the sky. The tension among their ranks was palpable. A silence of death hovered over the field. Louis burned his eyes on the white walls of the city and begged God for a sign. He saw it. A flock of crows rose in the air among the houses. The iron vise around his heart broke loose. He breathed deeply with relief. The soldiers roared behind him. Louis saw black dots move with haste on the ramparts. It was their time to act. Louis turned to Bertrant. The commander did not move. Louis urged him with his eyes, but the man did not react. Anger filled Louis, and he clenched his jaws. He pulled on the right rein.

"Loose!" Louis yelled, turning his horse. "Loose!"

The trebuchets revolved, throwing boulders high in the air. The huge stones crashed and exploded on the ramparts. "Load!" he shouted. The other captains repeated his orders. Louis glanced at Bertrant. His commander gazed at him with infuriated eyes. "I'm sorry," Louis muttered. He kicked his horse and left his post.

Louis galloped up and down the line, haranguing the men.

"Four years of defeat, four years of shame! There is no turning back! We will take back Millhaven! We will put their heads on these spikes! If we flee, we die! Today, you fight for yourselves! For honour! For revenge!"

The soldiers broke out in wild cries. Arms clashed against shields. Louis whirled his pawing horse towards the citadel. The mount reared up and charged. The riders drew behind him and about him. In the distance, the drawbridge was still closed. On the ramparts, the orcs turned around, taking their posts again. Some grabbed bows. Boulders whizzed above the riders' heads. One of the small tower's merlons exploded. The gates drew near at high speed. Louis could not slow down his mount. He wrapped the reins around the pommel and drew out his sword. With his left hand, he grabbed his shield and raised it above his head. The first arrows flew on them. The riders stretched on a column. "Open that damn door, Selen," he whispered like a prayer. The bridge shook and fell, dragging its black, heavy chains behind. The huge oaken board slammed on the stone edge as Louis's horse was reaching the moat. The riders rushed through the gatehouse to the citadel.

34

The Rebellion had gathered their pitiful forces on the field at dawn. Certainly, they had trebuchets, but Millhaven's walls were strong. All they would manage to take down would be the edges of the ramparts and the houses on the other side. And Kraalh did not care for the houses. He wondered if he should let them exhaust themselves on his walls or if he should gather a party to clean the field. He remembered how they had conquered the city in the first place. It was best to let them use their strength and pick up the pieces afterwards, once the reinforcements would have arrived. Kraalh did not panic when he heard the alarm. He was persuaded that it was the jesters on the plain using a new trick. He walked onto his balcony with one apple in his hand to admire the show. He looked down and saw the dead orcs lying on the streets. His stupefaction made place for wrath. Kraalh cursed the people of Millhaven and his own mansuetude.

"I should have burned them all!" he yelled, smashing the apple with rage.

Kraalh grabbed his axe and rushed outside to the galleries leading to the allure. He heard the clatter of blades and screams rise from everywhere in the city. However, what worried him most was that the riders on the field maneuvered.

"Where are they going?" he raged. He had a horrible feeling. "With me! To the gate!" the general summoned his orcs.

They ran down the city, killing all and everyone standing in their way. Kraalh and his orcs were attacked by civilians holding the first weapon they had found.

Others brandished axes. The rats were still no match for Kraalh and his soldiers. One man ran in his direction, screaming. Kraalh slid his axe through his skull. The next one, he chopped the legs off. Kraalh neared the yard in front of the gate. Bodies lay scattered all around. He heard shouts and a low, steadily growing hum. Men fought on the ramparts. An orc fell and cracked his skull open on the cobbles. The enemy had taken over the gatehouse. The ground quaked.

"Form a line!" Kraalh cried out. "Spears forward!"

His soldiers aligned in a semicircle, their lances blocked on a wall of shields. The drawbridge moved and fell. Kraalh raised his axe. "Hold!"

The first wave of riders rushed inside the yard. Some of the mounts crashed against the shields and rammed onto the spears in agonizing shrieks. Others jumped over the improvised wall, pulverizing orcs' faces with their hooves, and galloped forward into the city. More orcs dashed down the main street and clashed swords with the breakaway. Meanwhile, a second wave of riders forced its way through the gate and spun into the alleys on both sides. Soon the yard would turn into mayhem, and Kraalh did not want to be trapped in the middle. Heads of soldiers from both camps already rolled in the gutter. Men screamed in agony, mashed under wiggling horses with broken legs. Spurts of blood gushed in the air.

"Kill those riders!" Kraalh yelled.

The general knew that he could not hold the city with the bridge down and the population against him. He climbed the nearest stair that led to the gatehouse. From there, the path would take him straight to the stables on the other side. He spun his axe at the men in front of him and threw blows on the ones following him. In the yard, his soldiers retreated into the main street and the alleys. The Rebellion was hewing and slaying the orcs into pieces. It was a bloodbath. The flow of horses still poured in, the beasts stumbling and trampling on the bodies of men, orcs, and mounts. Kraalh was heading to the gatehouse when the door opened wide.

"What...?" he uttered.

He barely had time to realize what was happening when the creature in front of him flung itself off the ramparts onto the yard and disappeared. He saw it again further away, pushing its way into an alley, its purple hair flowing on its back.

"The she-knight," Kraalh muttered.

Fire and smoke rose from different parts of the city. Kraalh heard the banging of the swords against the shields, the orders yelled, and the screams of pain and terror. Kraalh continued on his way through the gatehouse and to the stables. He swore that he would get his revenge. At any cost.

35

His horse bolted and continued galloping through the main street until it crashed against a second wall of orcs. Louis flew over his mount and the orcs as if he did not weight more than a ball of straw. He rose at once. Fortunately, he was unharmed and still had his sword in his hand. The orcs were on him in an instant, launching themselves at him. He only had time to raise his sword to counter the first blows. The fight was hard, but at the end he stood alone, exhausted, in a pool of dark, slimy blood.

More riders came his way. Louis ran to a terrace overhanging the streets. The cavalry wandered in the alleys as in a maze, mowing all enemy standing in front of it. The battle was chaotic. There were no chiefs shouting orders, only men and orcs rushing against each other in wild screams. He smelled smoke. Some parts of the city were probably in flames.

Orcs came down from stairs above him. He raised his sword and prepared himself for the fight. The first orc engaged him frontally. Louis sidestepped and aimed for the beast's hips. As his sword passed through the flesh, he ducked his head and avoided the clumsy blow of the second orc. He whirled, blocked, and hacked. The head rolled to his feet. The third orc stepped back and wanted to run, but Louis threw his sword which ran through the beast's chest as into butter. The creature fell with a shrill cry of pain. Louis fetched his weapon and stopped to catch his breath again. A rider trotted from down the street.

"We won, Captain! It's a great victory!" the man shouted with joy.

The screams around Louis grew quiet. The clashes of swords became scarcer, then fell silent. They had won. Louis headed to the castle.

As he neared the yard in front of the castle's gate, Louis saw Selen stand near Faremanne. His chest filled with joy. He smiled and walked towards his friend. Bertrant appeared in his way, his hand raised. Louis barely saw the blow. The brutal slap on his face was as humiliating as painful.

"You had it coming!" Bertrant shouted in anger. "But we won. So this will have to do. Just remember who commands here!"

Louis placed his hand on his cheek and knew he deserved it. He was not even sure if he would have been so magnanimous should he had been in Bertrant's place. This time, he did not care about the wound to his pride. They were alive, and they had won. Behind Bertrant, Selen looked at him with a broad smile on his face. Louis smiled back at him, still holding his cheek.

"Should we inspect the keep?" Faremanne suggested.

"Before we do, tell all the lieutenants to spread the word that if one soldier is caught plundering or abusing of the population, I will kill him myself. Millhaven is a free city and these are our people, not a reward," Louis said.

"I will," Faremanne said. Bertrant nodded in approval.

Louis and the other four captains entered the castle. They stayed on their guard, ready to face the last resistance. They climbed the stairs to the great hall. The place was a mess, but it looked as if someone had already tried to put some order to it. The overmantel was covered with gore. Apples had rolled everywhere. But the most shocking was the high chair. It had been hacked to pieces with an axe, and heavy chains lay in front of the wretched piece of furniture.

"Welcome to my castle, if I may present it that way," a clear, charming voice said.

A woman in rich, exuberant clothes appeared in the hall. She was tall and blond with a gracious bearing. She was of a certain age but still comely.

"Lady Hegora Khorkina!" Bertrant exclaimed, aghast. The commander knelt at once, followed by all the captains. "My lady, we didn't know…" Bertrant stuttered.

"That I was still alive?" she interrupted him. She gave a faint smile. "I forgive you, Bertrant. I still have a hard time believing it myself after so many years." She turned to all of them. "My lords and captains, let me thank you deeply for your heroic battle. You saved my city and its people. Millhaven will always be in your debt. I gladly offer you my hospitality. Unfortunately, these creatures have damaged a part of the keep and of the outbuildings. You will have to share the rooms that are left," she told them. "Is there something more we can do for you?"

"Yes," Selen said spontaneously. Louis gazed at him, surprised. "A bath," his friend added with a blush on his cheeks.

36

With the penury of clean rooms, Selen and Louis got to share one. Maybe the countess had placed them together because of their affinities or because of their appearances. All that mattered to Selen now is that they would have a few days of rest together with the possibility of enjoying a warm bath.

The room was of a higher standing than the one they had had in Embermire. The furniture was of chestnut and the orange curtains were finely embroidered with gold threads. Red carpets covered the floor, and silver candelabras lighted the chamber. Selen removed his bloodstained armour while housemaids filled two large copper tubs in the center of the room. Blood had clotted in his hair, and his clothes reeked. He removed them and let them fall onto the floor. Once naked, Selen moved towards the nearest tub. He glanced at the housemaids. He was not used to having servants around him, especially women. He could swear that one of the maids gazed with concupiscence at his anatomy. It felt weird and awkward. Selen stepped inside the tub and sat down in the water. Louis sat in the tub on his right and washed the blood off his face. Though the tubs were filled, the maids still stood at their side. One leaned over the rim of his tub. Selen wondered if the girl waited for a coin or if he had orders to say.

"Louis," Selen whispered. "Shouldn't they leave?"

Selen saw Louis raise his head and watch the three housemaids. The girls gazed at them in a way Selen thought that proper housemaids would never dare to. "You can leave now, thank you," Louis said evasively.

The girls did not move. Instead, they undressed. Selen stared at them in utter shock. Was this what the lords meant by *a bath*? One opened her bodice, revealing her firm, round breasts. When she untied her waist cincher, her dress fell to the floor. The girl was naked and half-shaved. She exposed her tanned skin through lascivious moves. As a guard of the palace, Selen had already seen naked women. Yet, this time, he could not lose himself in thoughts or shift his gaze. They were here for him. The woman behind the naked maid put her fingers on one of the girl's pink nipples and caressed it sensually. The third girl approached Selen's tub. She put her bare foot on the edge of the tub and bunched up her skirts to the waist. Selen turned his head away before he could see anything. He squirmed with disgust and backed against the cold metal. He repressed the need to call for help or to make his uneasiness more obvious by covering his eyes. He wondered how an honorable, married man would get himself out of such a situation. Could a polite and firm refusal be enough?

"What on earth do you think you're doing?" Louis exclaimed, outraged. "This is the castle of Lady Khorkina, not a brothel."

Selen was relieved that Louis disapproved. It meant that all this should not happen. Only then did Selen realize that Louis would not have welcomed such a thing either.

"We are used to entertaining the guests, and we are very talented," the first girl said with a smoky voice. She walked towards Louis, pushing her breasts together with one hand. Selen was glad he could not see the other hand. "We can't wait to start with both of you. Does my lord want a taste?" As she reached his friend, Selen's eyes narrowed, and his mouth turned dry as he sucked on his teeth.

Louis's voice turned to ice. "Make a step closer, and I will have you all executed for depravation in an honorable house."

Selen did not know if the crime existed, but it sounded less humiliating than *attempted rape*. The girls stepped backwards, frightened by the threat. They grabbed their clothes and made for the door.

"Wait!" Selen shouted. He had a hunch all this was not fortuitous. "Who sent you?"

"We don't know the man's name, my lord, but he had a narrow face, an unkempt beard, and dark hair like a sheep fur."

Segar on all points, Selen thought. The housemaids went out and closed the door.

"Do you think he suspects us?" Selen asked, worried.

"I don't know. The man is a weasel, but I don't want to think about him right now," Louis sighed.

The water was warm and relaxing. Selen had never bathed in a tub, not in this life at least. At home, he used to bathe in the river during summer, and he kept a wooden basin stored for the winter. Selen washed his hair with soap. It was made with milk and olive oil and was perfumed with lavender. The flecks of blood on his hair and skin were soon gone. He had scrubbed so hard that his arms and hands had turned pink. He wanted to remove that putrid orc smell. He did not know how many he had killed today, but between the run, the mine, and the orcs, he felt as if he had bathed in a sewer. Now, with soap all over, his body felt alive again.

He noticed Louis get up, go to the door, and move in his direction. His friend knelt at the side of the tub. Delicately, he took Selen's face in his hands and kissed him. Selen's heart bloomed like a lotus under the warm rays of the sun. All the nerves in his body quivered. He put his hands on both sides of Louis's head. His lips parted.

"I thought I had lost you," Louis whispered with infinite softness. His words were tinged with dolor. Selen felt the warm breath skim his lips.

Their foreheads touched. For a second, the world around him stood still and floated in the golden light of the candles. Selen kissed Louis back, burying the words he wanted to say deep inside his heart. Louis let go of him and took a jar. Selen closed his eyes, tilted his head, and let the cold water wash the soap away from his lilac hair. He stood up in the tub. Droplets trickled down his skin. Selen turned to Louis, who gazed at him, his mouth half open, and his hair drying in a disheveled way. Selen's hands reached for his friend's shoulders. At the same time, he felt Louis's arms close around his back.

"I'm sorry I left. I won't do it again," Selen whispered, pressing his chest against Louis's. As he felt the arms crush his ribs, Selen nuzzled up his face against Louis's neck. Louis slipped an arm down Selen's back to his knees and lifted him up in the air. Selen laughed. "Don't hurt yourself!"

"I can manage a few seconds," Louis replied, joining his laughter.

When Louis carried him to the bed, Selen shivered with expectation. "Wait," Selen said. "Here."

Louis put him down in front of the bed. Grabbing Louis's hair, Selen gave him a long kiss, twisting his tongue in Louis's mouth, savoring him. His lecherous eyes looked at Louis as he sat down on the edge of the bed. Selen's hands clasped firmly on Louis's bottom and pulled him closer. He kissed Louis's flat abdomen, trailed down a cheek on it, and breathed in the fragrance of his dark hair. There was no hurry, no threat this time. His pulse hastened. He breathed out. He tilted his shoulders backwards. While his right hand slipped between Louis's legs and massaged his perineum, his left hand folded tightly around his friend's length and stroked it. It reacted at once. Selen bent forward, wetted his full lips, and took the head of the aroused member in his mouth. His tongue pressed and swirled around it in eager moves. Considering he had only done it once before, he hoped he was not too clumsy. Selen realized he enjoyed it and sucked as on a juicy fruit. Saliva dribbled on his chin. As he proceeded, ardent fire spread between his legs, and he felt his member come to life. His thoughts wandered.

Only a few months before, Selen would have blushed just to think about doing such things. Now that he had recovered his memories, he remembered that what he had seen of sex in the palace had put him off. The animalistic orgies, the violence, and the size of the men called stud had scared him. It was not impossible in his world for men with inclinations like his to satisfy their needs, as long as they never bottomed. Most soldiers visited brothels, but Selen did not want it that way. As he was not sure there was another way, he had stayed a virgin, becoming the laughingstock of some fellow soldiers. Yet, now that he had met Louis, he knew roughness and pain were not natural. Louis gave him so much pleasure that his whole body craved the touch of his friend. Selen wanted to taste him, to please him, to feel one with him. His mind had never been so distressed. Sparks of desire had coursed through his body at the most awkward moments. Even during meetings at the headquarters, he had surprised himself looking at Louis's pulsing throat, his hands, and his fierce eyes with something more than admiration. One time, back in his tent, unable to wait for the night, he had lain down on his bed, both hands in his pants, and had rubbed himself hard where he had learned he was most sensitive. The furs on the bed had caressed his bare lower back as his hips had moved in rhythm until his clothes had turned into a mess. The opportunity of privacy they had now had been a long-awaited moment.

He felt Louis's hand against his head, pushing him back abruptly.

"Stop," his friend whispered, short of breath.

"Forgive me," Selen said. A blush came to his cheeks. "It has been too long."

"Exactly," Louis answered with a light smile.

Selen understood. He grabbed Louis by the hips and threw him onto the bed. Louis gazed at him, shocked. Selen knelt down and crawled over him. Cold water dropped from his hair, running over the sides of his hot body and down onto the bed. Selen kissed Louis passionately. He nibbled at his ear and bit his throat gently. It tasted of soap. He grazed his mouth over Louis's defined collarbones and moved down to his nipples, squeezing them between his lips. "I miss you every day…and night," Selen whispered.

"Kiss me," Louis murmured.

Slowly, Selen moved forward and approached his lips. While they kissed, Louis glided a hand through Selen's wet hair and slipped his other hand between Selen's spread legs, cupping his balls in his palm. Selen moaned as Louis's fingers sank inside him. His kiss became more passionate. Their mouths opened wide. With one hand, Selen reached down for Louis's erect member.

"I can't wait anymore," Selen whispered.

He sat astride Louis, grasping his own cheeks, and impaled himself gradually on him. He moaned. It hurt at first, but the pain was soon gone, turning into intense pleasure. His hips rocked, dancing in harmony with his friend's loud breathing, slowing down sometimes to make the feeling last. He looked at Louis's slender body, his chest as hairless as his own. His physique was more the one of a rider than of a warrior. With his fingers, Selen traced the shape of his friend's light muscles, pinching at his brown nipples and circling around his navel, down to the fuzz of hair on his groin. He saw Louis's hand reach for him and wrap around his stiff shaft. It caressed him, teased him. Heat grew from Selen's lower parts, taking over his brain.

"Does it feel good?" Louis whispered.

Selen nodded and rode faster, wilder in response. His hair floated around his waist. Selen tilted his head backwards and closed his eyes. As he sensed every bit of tingle in his lower back, he bobbed to guide Louis on the spot. His moans turned to squeaks, and his hands grasped Louis's thighs. Selen could hear by his friend's moans that Louis was getting close. He raised his head and kept eye contact with Louis, watching his tense face with delight. Louis's eyes were half opened, and he bit his lower lip while thrusting his hips upwards to meet Selen's moves, shoving himself as deep as he could.

"Oh, Selen… I'm going to come," Louis breathed.

"Don't…stop. I'm close."

A lock of hair fell over Selen's face. Louis's moist, soft hands ran nimbly up and down on him from shaft to tip. The blood in Selen's member pulsed. He clenched his fingers on Louis. Selen moaned Louis's name, squeezed his eyes shut, and cried out. His whole body throbbed and contracted around Louis, who screamed. Their climax was intense and simultaneous. Selen slowed down his moves, then sat still.

Panting, he looked down. Louis's palms and fingers were covered with his seed. It dripped along his wrists onto his abdomen.

"I'm sorry," Selen breathed, embarrassed.

Louis smiled and put one hand to his mouth, his blue eyes looking straight at him. It made Selen blush. Exhausted, he lay down on Louis's chest, his head on the top of his friend's shoulder.

They stayed silent for a while, embracing. Selen felt the beating of their hearts. A wave of feelings submerged him. He knew Louis was tormented. He had seen the melancholy in Louis's eyes when he was not absorbed by his command. If only Louis would confide to him. Selen had felt like a shadow these last weeks. Louis did not even allow him to act as a friend. He had warned him that he would be distant and cold, but this was beyond Selen's strength. Every day, Selen craved a look, a word, a kind gesture that would show him that he still existed. He knew Louis cared, but he could not live on ideas. Still, considering how unreachable Louis made himself to everyone, and how miserable he himself could be, Selen knew he was blessed. Now that he had seen his ribbon on his friend's wrist, he would endure the suffering in silence, no matter how many times his heart broke, should he never hear the words. He felt the arm around his back and wished Louis would not stop holding him.

"Will we stay here a few days?" Selen asked after a while. They gazed through the window. Outside, the blue sky was now streaked with amber clouds.

"I suppose so. The men need to rest. There are probably many wounded, and we need more materiel. We should stay a few days, three at least," Louis answered. "It also means a lot of work and preparations." Louis held his hand. Their fingers played. "But we will have the nights," Louis added with a sigh of bliss.

Only four nights, Selen thought, *but I will make them count*. There was nothing but wilderness after Millhaven. Only a long, tiresome road stretching south. He would be back in his tent or asleep under the stars. With Pembroke's forces, the army would grow in number. They would come across larger battalions, maybe the dragon. Finally, they may die somewhere on a battlefield.

"Our lives are absurd," Selen muttered, on the verge of crying. "These men fight for their land, for their family, for all they have lost. Why do we fight? What is left of us without our ideals? We have nothing. We are nothing."

"We can still build our own future. We can create something. If it is a second chance for us, I want to believe in it," Louis said. "I still can't remember my past." Selen noticed that his friend cried. "Should I lose my faith in our cause…? If it's only about survival in a meaningless world, how can I believe in life? Or in love? I am only dust. Worse, I am but a piece of myself. I need hope to hold on to."

"You will remember. It will come back. You are more than dust. So much more." Selen grazed his lips against Louis's wet cheek and held him tight. "We will share this hope," he whispered. His heart ached.

"Selen," Louis said. His friend gazed long into his eyes and smiled. "We should get dressed. I don't want us to be the last arriving at the dinner."

The great hall had been cleaned. The damaged furniture had been removed. There were still dark stains where the blood had been poured. At the end of the hall, down the steps leading to the dais, a large table stood. It was set sumptuously. Four candelabras stood prominently in a row. Their light, the only one in the whole hall, was reflected against large bowls, copiously filled with fruits. The glasses, the wine carafes, and the high cake stands shone like crystal. Faremanne and Bertrant had already made themselves comfortable on the red cushioned chairs. Bertrant was dressed in a carmine doublet with long, puffed out sleeves and golden buttons. Faremanne's doublet was similar but tawny. Selen and Louis had chosen less exuberant outfits. His friend wore a long, dark blue jerkin with a high collar over his white shirt. Selen had opted for a leaf green jacket with metal and leather buckles. It felt pleasant to walk around without his armour. His muscles relaxed from the loss of weight.

"Here you are. Join us!" Faremanne exclaimed, holding out his hand in a warm, welcoming gesture.

Selen hesitated to take a seat. Never in this life or the other had he sat at such a table. As a knight of the royal guard, he had assisted with dinners, but he had stood up by the door or on the side of the dais, at best. It was not his world. It felt to him as if he were trespassing. He drew a chair and sat down with his back straight, ready to stand up again. He took a quick glance at Louis. Though his friend looked a bit more comfortable, his confusion in front of the food was obvious. Louis stretched his hand to a bowl.

"What is this?" Louis asked him in a whisper.

"It's a pomegranate," Selen answered. "It's a fruit."

"All these things are fruits?" Louis inquired, puzzled.

"Yes, it's all…" Selen said. He pondered over the words. "How can they have such exotic fruits with a climate like this one?" he asked out loud.

"It is because our trunks are filled with gold. Or were," a honeyed voice answered. Lady Khorkina appeared near the table. They all rose in one move.

"My lady," Bertrant bowed.

"Please, please, sit down. Though I have to admit that I am filled with delight to be back in the civilization," she said with a hint of a smile. The countess approached in front of them. Bertrant drew her the chair next to his. She sat down right in front of Selen. "Well, my dear, maybe you could present your charming captains," she suggested to Bertrant.

"Of course," the commander replied. "Here on the right is Captain Faremanne. A brave knight from the Windy Isles who joined the Rebellion with enthusiasm. He has fought at my side for many years now. Always ready to do the best for his country and bring us victory."

Faremanne raised his glass respectfully and bowed. "My lady."

"Here in front of me is Louis, from Neolerim," Bertrant continued. Selen sensed that the commander searched his words with mixed feelings. "He is...a brave soldier," Bertrant said hastily as to get rid of it.

Selen saw Louis gape with disbelief and tried hard not to laugh.

"And in front of you, my lady," Bertrant pursued, "is the valiant captain who crawled through your mines and opened the gates of Millhaven to the Rebellion."

Selen squirmed. *A brave soldier* would have been enough.

"And what is your name, Captain?" Lady Khorkina asked. She looked at him with curiosity in her eyes while rolling her wine glass in one hand.

"Selen," he whispered. "From the Frozen Mountains," he added. He did not wish to sound as exotic as the fruits in the bowl.

"Well, let me thank you all three once again. You fought bravely today. I only regret that this beast— excuse me—the orc general escaped," she said with repressed anger. "We have lived in terror, my people and I. I saw everything from my cell. My poor city," she lamented but with such restraint that Selen wondered if she could actually cry.

Selen remembered the gigantic orc he had met on the ramparts. He had preferred to jump into the melee than to face such a monster. So this orc was the general. Selen was sure that they would hear from him soon. The creature would want his revenge.

While they conversed, the servants brought the plates. As usual, there would be food for a company though they were only five around the table. The game was declined in pâtés, roasted birds, smoked fillets, and venison in sauces. Selen searched everywhere for the salad, waited, and gave up. Most of the dishes were served in a sea of cold gravy. He had never understood why the nobles would fill themselves to death with such unhealthy food.

The cutlery and plates were made of silver and stamped with the arms of the countess. With his spoon, Selen picked some carrots and boiled onions, conscious that he filled his plate with the decoration. More food was served on the table. A large meatloaf, covered with candied cherries, was laid in front of him. Bertrant cut himself a big slice and ate it with appetite. The commander told of his battles with the Rebellion while the countess listened to him attentively with a charming smile. Discreetly, Louis placed an orange on Selen's plate. Selen took it and peeled it. The fruit was fresh and sweet. Though it had been a common fruit in his previous life, he had forgotten the taste.

The countess explained how they had lost the city and the humiliations she had had to endure in her cell. "It will take a long time for the city to heal its wounds," she said. "But we will do all that is possible to help you. I will call my soldiers and the officers who are still alive. We will need to make lists of our stocks before we can promise any food or materiel. It will leave you time to organize yourselves."

"Thank you, my lady," they all replied.

"I will see you all tomorrow," Bertrant said to his captains. "We have to plan the following operations. I guess that Agroln will take us seriously now. This victory will have a cost."

"Do you fear the return of the orcs?" Louis asked the countess.

"As you could see for yourself, the one who holds the bridge holds the city. We won't make the same mistake again. And thanks to your friend, now we know our weakness," she answered, smiling at Selen.

"You could train your people in the arts of war. If they were armed and ready to fight, no one would dare take that city again. And by training, I don't mean to throw a spear in their hands and a boiled leather helmet on their head. I mean to turn them into fighters," Louis suggested.

The countess and Bertrant looked at him with incomprehension. "Arm and train the populace?" she said. "What a peculiar idea. No. My only fear is Rylarth, the dragon. No one can face a dragon."

"What do you know about this dragon, my lady?" Louis inquired.

"There are no dragons in Trevalden. Agroln created it. The king controls it like a pet. This creature does not have its own will. I fear the beast is invincible." Selen noticed that she looked tired. Her years in captivity must have worn her out.

"Forgive me, my lady, but it may be more correct not to use the word *invincible* in front of the soldiers and the people," Louis noted.

"Yes, of course," she approved. "We need to keep their spirits up."

"It's not only for their spirits. It is the truth. Nothing and no one is invincible," Louis added.

Bertrant turned to them, with a black eye on Louis. "I think my captains and myself have had a long day, my lady. We will take our leave, if you will excuse us."

"I think we all had an animated day. I will retire as well to my apartments. Good night, my lord, Captains." They all rose as she got up and left the room. The countess walked away with the pride of a queen. She had faced that hideous general for three years and could still act as if nothing had happened. Selen admired her strength.

"You. I want to see you in my apartments tomorrow morning for a word," Bertrant said, pointing at Louis. Without waiting for an answer from Louis, the commander rose and left the hall with Faremanne.

When he saw the ire on Louis's face, Selen avoided his friend's gaze. It was preferable to let him brood than to aggravate the humiliation with words. They returned to their chamber in silence.

The room was dark. Selen lit candles on the bedside table. He untied the ribbon holding his hair and undressed.

"Is there something I…" he said, but Louis raised a hand to tell him he was not ready.

Louis stood near the window, his arms crossed. Sitting on the bed, Selen waited. He counted the arabesques on the canopy, gave up, and observed the tapestries instead. Standing in front of a tent, a woman in an elegant burgundy gown held a necklace in her hand. In spring vegetation, she was surrounded by watchful animals. There were rabbits, birds, dogs, a lion, and also an animal Selen had never seen. It looked a lot like a horse, but it was somehow different. "What is this?" he asked.

"What is what?" Louis asked out of his thoughts.

"This," Selen pointed at the tapestry.

Louis came closer. "It's a unicorn," he said. "Have you never seen one?"

Selen shook his head. "Are there unicorns in Neolerim?" Louis smiled at him as if he had said something stupid. "What?" Selen asked, slightly offended.

Louis sat down on the bed. "I'm sorry. That was just too cute. Unicorns don't exist. They are a fairy tale."

"Like dragons? But there is one dragon now."

"Well, a bit like dragons. Yet, they are different. The unicorns are pure and a symbol of innocence."

Selen crawled behind Louis and held his shoulders. "But you just said that they don't exist, so how can we know? Is it a fable?"

"Precisely. Like a fable. But maybe they exist somewhere. If there are dragons…" While he listened to Louis, Selen massaged his friend's shoulders. Maybe one day, he would see a unicorn. It must be beautiful in reality. "The unicorn is a common symbol in heraldry. It is a proud and noble animal." There was awe in Louis's voice.

"How do you know such things? Was it all in your books in the archives?" Selen asked. He did not consider himself as an idiot, but sometimes Louis's knowledge lifted him off the ground.

Louis rose and undressed. "The archives were actually pretty boring I must say. You can count thousands of papers on taxes, disputes, donations, and other administrative, tedious acts for one relevant document and precious information. No, I have not learned what I know in the archives. I guess that my previous self already knew all that." Once naked, Louis climbed onto the bed and sat next to him.

Selen realized. He moved in front of Louis and grabbed his friend's bent legs. "Are you aware of what it means?" he asked, joyful. "It means that we are not a blank page. We carry in us the knowledge we had before. It is more than just reflexes. This is why I can fight. This is why you can lead the men and talk about unicorns. You have souvenirs."

Louis looked at him, speechless. "What did you say? The word you used."

"Souvenirs?" Selen repeated without understanding the importance of it.

Louis was lost in his thoughts again. Selen sighed. He took one of Louis's legs on his lap and massaged it.

"It felt familiar," Louis said.

His friend stayed silent for a while. Selen continued his moves on both legs. His fingers searched for the pressure points on the muscles. Not a sound could be heard coming from outside. The silence in the room and the amber glow of the candlelight made the atmosphere peaceful.

"Do you think he hates me?" Louis asked, looking at the swaying candle.

Selen had no idea what Louis meant. "Considering your long list of friends, I feel obliged to ask whom you are talking about," Selen answered in a teasing tone. He now sat cross-legged with Louis's feet on his thighs.

"Bertrant," Louis said. "I know that I took liberties, that I should have followed his orders, but I was right."

Selen sighed. "You are always right, at least, most of the time. But you do it wrong." Selen stopped his massage. He leaned forward on Louis's bent knees and looked at him. "You're taking over his army under his eyes and considered yourself his equal when you only arrived in the camp a month ago. You can't show so little consideration for other people's feelings only because they are not ready to follow you blindly into the fire. Bertrant is a good, willing man. He likes you and will probably forgive you. Or you would be dead by now." Selen looked down. The simple idea frightened him. "You have to respect his authority. Be his counselor," Selen suggested. "He will listen to you. He has always done it."

Louis looked at him. "I find it hard to trust weary men in battle."

"You find it hard to trust men," Selen rectified. He smiled, crossed his bare arms under Louis's knees and rested his chin on them. "Yet, I have to admit that only a few can be trusted."

"You lived in the woods," Louis said. "Why? What did men do to you?" There was anger in his voice.

"Nothing." It was a half lie, but he did not want Louis to be angry again. "Precisely because I lived in the woods. I was lonely, but I was safe. The wilderness is cold and cruel, but still less than the men. I know what I look like. I know what I am. I would not have had a long life expectancy in a city." Selen smiled, but it was a sad one.

"This is so unfair. They will have to get used to your presence now. I won't let anyone look down on you." Louis's voice was firm.

"I'm not sure I want it. Not that I don't care about what they think, though I can't change who I am and I like how I look. But to change minds is a tiresome, useless fight."

"It is never useless if it is for the better. It is a duty for men to aim for the highest virtues of their hearts and spread them around." Louis stopped and pondered on his own words, frowning. He shook his head as if he brushed a feeling away. "How was it in your previous life? Were you…like the others?" Louis asked.

Selen laughed. "If you talk of my look, I was not the worst." He massaged Louis's legs again. "I was what this world would call a knight. We soldiers had a very harsh life which consisted only of training, learning, and fighting with spears and swords. The rules were severe, the food scarce, and the pay low. We had no right to talk if not addressed. We were not allowed to have a life of our own. I don't even remember having had parents. Soldiers began their training at an early age, and only the strong and tenacious survived. I became part of the elite. The tattoos I have on my forehead are the marks of the king's guard. An owner's brand, but the symbol of the highest rank in knighthood," he said with a hint of pride.

"Were you a slave?" Louis asked.

"No!" Selen exclaimed, outraged. "I was respected. The city was proud of its best warriors. No one could touch us. The slaves… I don't know how they could endure their life," Selen said. He remembered the abuses and rapes he had seen. He brushed the thought away and continued his description.

"We lived in a wonderful city with red walls. The terrace gardens were full of colors and heady perfumes. And the birds, you should have seen the birds. The streets filled with the chants of the voices of merchants and singers. We had magical, snowy winters and warm summers," Selen carried on with dreamy eyes. "Everything was a display of luxury. The nobles had beautiful clothes of precious fabric and eccentric haircuts. They waxed their hair to make it shine and dyed it. My color is extracted from sea snails. They also underlined their eyes with black kohl, even the men."

"Now you mention the aesthetic, I don't think I have ever seen you shave. Can't you have body hair higher than your hips?" Louis joked.

Selen laughed. "Warriors waxed off their hair on their face, chest, and armpits. Some waxed their whole body, but I didn't need to as I have fair hair. Though a beard could be a mark of prestige for the nobles who had reached manhood, hair on soldiers was considered unhygienic and disgraceful. That's why I can't grow a beard anymore, and I don't miss it." Selen answered. "Anyway. The city was rich in gold, metals, and gems. But as always, greed and corruption took over the hearts of the men." Selen's lips twitched. "A war began, first opposing factions and rival families, then the victorious factions fought against other realms. The land was destroyed. The beautiful nature, devastated. Poseidon punished us, drowning the kingdom in ashes and walls of waves. In the chaos, our enemies launched a strike. This was when I died."

Louis raised his back and sat in front of him, holding Selen's hands. "Do you miss your world?"

"Not a single instant," Selen answered, gazing at his friend. He stretched his lips and kissed Louis. He felt Louis's tongue and welcomed the intrusion. "What I did earlier today," he whispered with arousal, "let me try again."

Louis looked at him, intrigued. Realizing what Selen meant, his eyes narrowed, and he smiled naughtily. Louis let his back fall onto the bed. Selen stretched his hands and lowered his head.

37

Louis had to tell the truth. They had crawled to him in the darkness of the night, whispering lies and sweet promises in his ears. Their honeyed smiles could not disguise their sharp teeth. Treason, crookedness dwelled in their hearts. He could have saved his life for the price of his soul. It would have been a pact signed with the blood of his dreams, with the immolation of his love. The demons would have offered him favors, maybe glory. Still, it was not him. No, it was not him. And there he stood now, petrified. The air was warm, suffocating. His vision was coated in white. He could barely breathe under his layers of clothes. His ears buzzed. Slowly, his eyes focused. Louis saw all the faces turn upwards, looking at him. Faces of anger, faces of hate, and faces of fear. *Cowards and demons*, he thought. He grabbed the balustrade. His legs were giving way under him. He could not faint. Not now. He spoke, loud and clear as he used to, but his words sounded void, even to his ears. All hope had left his heart, leaving him empty as a shell. Yet, he must hold on. His friend, his love, counted on him. But their eyes. All those eyes. He raised his head and looked at the white wall on the other side of the hall. Louis forced himself to utter the words written on the pages in his hands. He noticed the change in their faces. They were deformed, elongated. Fangs grew from inside their mouth. *Dragons*, he thought, *dragon hatchlings*. They snapped their muzzles in his direction, crying out at him with rage.

"Say our names!" the hatchling shouted with hatred. "Say our names!"

The hundreds of dragons turned into a ring of fire. He closed his eyes. "I am here to tell the truth. I fight for my land and for justice," Louis whispered to himself. He opened his eyes and looked straight forward. "My fight is pure," he countered, resolute. From the circle of fire rose a gigantic dragon head. Its eyes blazed with the intensity of hell. The heat was unbearable. It drew closer to him, but he did not twitch. The dragon moved its massive jaws. "Say. My. Name," his guttural, stentorian voice clamoured.

Louis woke up with a start, panting. His eyes were wide open. He placed a hand on his chest and tried to calm down. He was covered in sweat. His nightmares had never been this intense. However, it had not been a dream this time, not all of it. This was a déjà vu. He put his head between his hands, trying to remember what he had seen, what he had felt. Scraps of memories came back to him, but he still wandered in the shadows. *There could not have been dragons*, he thought. What was the meaning of this? Why had he held the speech? At least, he had felt himself. Though he could not understand it, he was persuaded that what he had been doing in his previous life was good. He had followed his heart, and it was all that mattered for now. Louis hoped more dreams would reveal his past. At the same time, he did not want to live something similar again. It seemed as if the dragon focused on him. He remembered the artifact. Maybe the beast was his fate.

He turned his head to the left. Selen slept on his back. The moon's silver beams gave a white radiance to his willowy body, playing a game of shadows and light along his fine muscles. One of Selen's hands was delicately folded under his navel. His hair was pushed from behind his back and spread in waves across his chest. Louis looked at his face. His eyes were shut tight, his long lashes twitching. His mouth was slightly open, revealing the white edge of his teeth behind his curved lips. He looked tender and as innocent as a white dove. It only made him more desirable in Louis's eyes. Louis lay down on his side, facing Selen. He considered everything they had to prepare to be ready to leave in three days.

They were less than a thousand now, which meant that the Rebellion was theoretically destroyed. The countess could join her forces to their army, filling their ranks. They would probably meet Pembroke on the south road in a week. They needed men to counterbalance the lord's troops. Louis did not want to give the control of the Rebellion to a man who could not be trusted on the battlefield. He would have to support Bertrant as Chief Commander. The idea did not please him, but he remembered what Selen had said about giving the man a chance. Maybe he could work under Bertrant's authority for a while.

Louis listened to Selen's soft breathing. He grazed his fingers against Selen's face and reached his mouth delicately with his lips. Selen mumbled in his sleep and wrapped a lethargic arm around him. Tiredness won over Louis, and he fell asleep cuddled up against his friend.

38

The Rotten Duck was probably the best place in all Millhaven to get rid of your life, as well as your money. The cook attached great importance to suit his meals to the tavern's name. From the outside, the place looked dirty and of ill repute. That was only because it was nearly impossible to see through the small, greasy, stained-glass windows. The filth inside was beyond imagination. The air was so thick it stuck to the skin. It reeked of vomit and piss, an aroma which did not come necessarily from the floor. If you were lucky, you could even discern unknown scents, usually coming from the kitchen. The walls bore the marks of previous customers, in different shades of red and brown. Rounded, wooden beams supported the upper floor. The ceiling was too low to support the lights. Therefore, metallic lanterns hung on the sides of the doors and on the pillars. The long wooden benches around the tables were packed with soldiers. The enthusiastic noises from within propagated to the street outside. Sitting on a stool by a barrel in a corner, Segar contemplated his men, a whisky in his hand. The inn was much to his liking. First, it would be the last place where he would encounter his fellow captains. Secondly, there was good pussy, and cheap, by the way. From what he saw, the men made good use of it. The rooms upstairs had been requisitioned by the lieutenants. Therefore, the main room had slowly turned into a brothel.

"You did not join the commander for dinner?" Jamys smirked. He had a girl between his legs working on his cock.

"That countess is a bit too mature for me," Segar answered. "Neither was I tempted to hear the old man boast about his exploits. Besides, we have more important things to discuss."

"Let's talk business," Jamys grunted.

"Now that Captain Holier-than-thou got us inside Millhaven, we don't need orc intermediaries anymore," Segar said. He still had goose bumps of joy when remembering how the commander had slapped that cocky bitch's face. "We can post our own men at the loading of the convoys."

"I've got some guys that could do the job. There, near the bar," Jamys cocked his head in their direction.

Segar spotted a bunch of burly soldiers playing cards. One cleaned his black nails with his dagger. Another fondled a wench while emptying his mug. Segar would not even have handed them his horse's reins to hold while taking a piss. *They are perfect*, Segar thought.

"We can start tomorrow. We have to sort out the merchandise. After a day like this, there are certainly a lot of new orphans and isolated women to pick from the streets. Do you hear me?" The girl between his partner's legs finished her business.

"Yeah, I hear you," Jamys cried out, his chiselled face tensed.

"Have the infirmaries and temples checked. Have your men dressed as civilians, but don't be foolish. This is smuggling, not an exodus," Segar insisted. "Don't be too greedy."

"I know my job," Jamys grumbled. "Where do I find the chariots?"

This was the real difficulty. The control-freak brat would certainly make a list of all that went in and out of Millhaven, especially chariots. "Corrupt a shopkeeper and use his trade as a cover or use some religious pretext to send people north. Building a village, founding a community, I don't care." Segar had heard that this was the way Colten Three Fingers from Embermire used to run his trade.

"I've heard they want us back on the road in three days," Jamys said.

"Eager to have their throats cut by orcs or their asses roasted by a dragon." Segar cleared his throat and spat. "We have no choice but to follow them. Now I tell you, they won't have me on the front line." Segar was pretty sure they would not fetch him either. "I give them the men, they leave me alone. We'll see who'll turn out roasted in the end." Segar smirked.

"Three days of rest after four years of war. Curse them." Jamys snorted and spat.

Segar saw three young, busty wenches enter the tavern. "Eh! If it's not my gift!" he exclaimed.

The girls walked in his direction and stopped by his barrel. "My lord," the first one said with a curtsy.

"So. How did it go? Did they give you a good shag? I want all the details," Segar asked with a lubricious smile. When he had heard the man ask for a bath, Segar had jumped on the occasion to have his theory tested. He had run to the best brothel of Millhaven and had sent the most attractive harlots to the castle. Such girls knew their way in castles alcoves and would play their part brilliantly.

The girls lowered their heads and exchanged looks. "They didn't touch us, my lord."

"How can that be possible?" Segar yelled. "Did you do as I said? Did you show some cunt?"

The girls squirmed. "We did as you said, my lord. We poured the baths and undressed. The tattooed one didn't even look at us. The gorgeous one…he threatened to get us killed!" she shrieked faintly.

"That would be a waste," Jamys said. "Three beauties like you."

"And expensive," Segar interjected. Yet, the trap had worked. It was what he had suspected. If a man would not touch these girls, he would touch none. "And that tattooed one," he asked the girls, "you saw him naked? Is he a man?"

"Oh yes, my lord. He is," the girls sighed with disappointment.

Segar smirked. The noose was tightening. When the girls made a move to leave, Segar grabbed one. "I still have paid you for a job." At his side, Jamys had a coarse chuckle.

39

"My lord?" Louis called politely at the entrance of the commander's chambers. For once, he did not wear his armour. It had been so stained with blood that he would need to have it cleaned thoroughly. He was dressed in black, narrow pants, a white shirt with ample sleeves, and a long, simple, royal blue tunic slit from the waist and falling on both sides of his legs. His sword and a dagger were fastened to his belt. Louis did not fear that someone would attack him in Millhaven, but he would never go out unarmed. He had to admit that walking around in his riding boots was a lot more comfortable than the heavy greaves.

Bertrant sat at the table, studying the maps. The stay in Millhaven had drastically improved his appearance. He wore a new doublet made of red velvet. He was freshly shaved and his blond hair was combed. "Come in," Bertrant said.

Louis breathed deeply. He forced the words out. "I wanted to apologize for my behavior yesterday. What I did was…" *right*, he thought, "unforgivable. It won't happen again."

"Excuses rejected," Bertrant responded. "You don't believe a word of what you say." Louis was opening his mouth again to object when Bertrant turned to him. "No. Don't speak. I'm not done. Close the door."

Louis entered the room and moved to the other side of the table, facing Bertrant. He felt uneasy and upset.

"Now that we are just you and me, rested after what I assume a good night's sleep, let me make things clear to you," Bertrant said. "You are a stubborn, irritating, insubordinate man, following only your own rules and turning them into laws. One day, you will find someone with less patience than me, and it will turn ugly. Now, on the other side, you are brave and the best captain I have ever had or seen. The Rebellion needs you, and yesterday, the men showed that they would follow you to the death. As your commander, and according to your own rules, I should have had you executed. Yet, I would like to give you one more chance, if you would finally agree to work with me and respect my authority. I will not tolerate a second Millhaven. Besides, if you want to control Pembroke, and I know you do, you will need me."

"There won't be another Millhaven, my lord," Louis said. This time, he meant what he said. "I sincerely apologize. I despise my insubordination, and my behavior yesterday was unforgivable. Yet, I did what I thought was right. All that matters to me is our victory. I have no interest in glory or power. Our men deserve the glory more than us."

"This is why you still breathe. Do you agree to follow my orders and keep me informed of your moves and decisions *before* you make them?" Bertrant insisted. "In return, I will put you in charge of the organization of the men and the camp. You can carry on setting your rules, but I must have your report on it the day before."

"I do agree, my lord," Louis answered. He could never have hoped for more.

"And you will never contradict me again in front of my men," Bertrant added.

"I won't, my lord." Louis felt humiliated, but he swallowed his pride for the greater good.

"There is one last thing," Bertrant carried on. "You and your friend Selen are nothing but mere captains in the eyes of the lords. To establish your authority, I have to dub you. We will do it in two days in the great hall. I don't do it for your own sake. I do it to show them what the Rebellion is worth."

Louis was taken aback. People had called him *lord* and *knight* for weeks, but he had never believed that he could become one. He wanted to be someone, but he did not want to be a lord. If the knighthood Bertrant had mentioned was just a military title to acknowledge his actions, it already sounded better. On the other hand, he remembered how Selen had talked about his tattoos. To become a knight would certainly please his friend. "It would be an honour, my lord. Thank you."

"Then I think it's settled. Come here." Bertrant pointed at the map. "These fields here are where we will encounter Pembroke in six days. I have sent a bird to inform him of our victory. You have three days to prepare our army, find volunteers, and reorganize the stocks. Can you manage it?"

"Can I ask the help of Faremanne?" Louis asked.

"Of course. All the captains are at your disposition."

"On that subject… What of Segar and Jamys? It's not that I like to have them around, but I find their absence disconcerting. Do you trust these rascals?" Louis asked.

"Segar and Jamys are a plague in my army, but I desperately need their men. Keep them away if you have to. Just don't create a scandal, not here," Bertrant insisted.

"Yes, my lord. If you excuse me, I will start immediately." Louis gave a short bow and took his leave.

Selen was waiting for him in the castle's inner yard. He had changed his old clothes for a green hooded tunic and brown pants. "How did it go?" Selen asked.

"I think we came to an agreement," Louis answered, satisfied. "We have a lot to do. I…"

"My Captains!" Lady Khorkina interrupted them. She walked towards them with a young man in her path. The countess looked radiant. "Let me present you my nephew, Josselin of Langdon." The young man behind her was tall with long blond hair. He had a broad scar on the left side of his once comely face and had lost the use of his eye on that side.

Louis noticed that he stared at the man with commiseration. "I'm sorry."

"You do not need to apologize. I am used to the looks," Josselin said.

"I'm sorry to ask," Selen said, "but who did that to you?"

"I was commander of Millhaven's army three years ago. The orcs did that to me when I was imprisoned," Josselin answered.

"What can we do for you, my lord?" Louis inquired.

"It's more what I can do for you. I would like to join the Rebellion with the men that the orcs left me. I can also help you to recruit more soldiers among the city's inhabitants," Josselin said.

"We would be honored to have you on our side, my lord," Louis responded.

"I will go to the infirmary," Selen said. "We need to know how many men were injured or dead. I will also search for Folc. I haven't seen him since before the battle."

"Maybe Josselin can go with you," Louis proposed. "I need to check our stocks of food. I could find Folc over there. He stood with the attendance before the battle." The last thing Louis had wanted that morning was to see the boy on the first line. Thus, he had been clear with Folc that disobedience of a direct order would have consequences.

The men departed. Louis headed to the lower parts of the city where the materiel had been stored. He found the warehouses easily. Guards of the Rebellion stood on the sides of the open doors, and some of their men were busy unloading chariots. They bore casks inside the depot. Louis spotted Faremanne writing a list in a corner. He hailed the captain.

"You came here early," Louis said.

"I knew you would be busy with Bertrant. I was worried about our stocks. As you can see for yourself, I had some reasons."

"Is that really what we have left?" Louis asked Faremanne, contemplating the pieces of woods, bits of metal, and beams scattered in the warehouse.

"We have dismantled all the carts and chariots to build the trebuchets. The hinges won't endure another bend. It would take more than three days to forge all the parts again," Faremanne replied.

"But three days is all we have. We need chariots to transport the supplies. We must requisition the city's artisans. What of the food?"

"It depends on if we eat the cows or if we milk them, but we are short of meat," Faremanne sighed.

"Men don't need meat." They could well hold on wheat and chickpeas. A better diet would improve their constitution and intellect.

"They do," Faremanne objected. "You don't, but they do. Meat and wine. You won't have them walking without that."

Louis sighed. "And what of the latter?" Wine was important.

"With the restriction on alcohol, we have plenty enough of it. Same with the rest." Faremanne gestured in the direction of barrels and casks stored on the left of the warehouse.

"I will see what I can do for the meat. Send one of your men to me with a list of the details," Louis said. As they talked, he grew worried for Folc. The boy had not stayed with the supplies. Louis left the warehouse and went down the paved street to the part of the city where the cheapest taverns and inns stood. If he had not appeared at the castle, the boy had probably looked for a room somewhere.

The streets in this area were narrow. Hardwood planks and soiled sandstone pillars made up most of the shabby facades. Broken barrels leaned against the walls. A brown slime mixed with twigs of straw ran in the gutter. Horse dung was scattered on the pavement. Rusted, chipped signs squeaked in the wind above the thresholds. Louis heard the clinks of beer mugs and the jolly chanting of men. Heavily made-up harlots harangued the men on the streets. Their faded gowns opened up, revealing besmirched petticoats. Their dresses had square or V-necks which displayed their firm, generous tits. They showed legs and pouted with fleshy, red lips.

"By the gods, girls, look what's walking down there!" he heard one say, followed by whispers of awe. "I have not seen such a mouth since Katheryn left us."

Louis realized they talked of him. He hated when anyone who was not Selen commented on his lips.

"Want to try your mouth on my cunt, sweetheart?" the same voice said. He turned his head towards the girl with utter shock.

"You're scaring him, Rose. You see our prince's lost his way to the castle. You can have me any way you want, babe. I'll help you find the back door!" the redhead exclaimed, bunching up her skirts over her rear. The girls giggled with bawdy laughter. Louis looked at them with consternation and disgust.

"Don't make such a face, darling. We've been bad. Come. You can punish us all three with your cock. With such a sexy ass, we'll definitely make you a price," the young girl with the unlaced corsage said.

Louis scowled at such vulgarity and hastened his pace before their spectacle attracted the attention of his soldiers. He heard someone scream in the distance.

"My man has already paid you. So do as you're told!" a man shouted. Louis could not see him, but he read the fear on the woman's face as the man pressed on her shoulder, forcing her to her knees.

"Let go of her," Louis ordered with a calm, toneless voice.

The man turned around, revealing Segar's hatchet face. His angry, nasty eyes narrowed. "Oh, if it's not our brave captain! Acting all smug again?" Segar let go of the girl and turned to Louis.

"Watch your words, Segar," Louis said, his teeth clenched. He walked towards the man.

"Or what? You're going to arrest me, in front of my men?" Segar bawled. Soldiers poked their heads out of taverns doorframes. "You don't have the…"

Louis silenced him with a hard smack in the face. "I have authority over you, Segar," he said loud and clear. Only force would impress the men around. Louis felt a spark of pleasure from humiliating someone that vile. He would gladly have kicked him down and rid the world of this trash.

Segar stood on one knee, pressing on his cheek with one hand. "I see…" As he rose, Segar punched Louis rudely in the chest, then in the face.

Louis's face turned with the blow. He bent with his hands on his thighs. His ribs were in flames. He put his fingers to his lips. He was bleeding. The vermin had hurt him. Out of the corner of his eye, he saw Segar come forward, his right fist raised and clenched, ready to hit. Quick as a cat, Louis rose. He grabbed the captain's arm with his left hand and smashed his right fist into Segar's face. To free his right arm from Louis's iron grip, Segar bit his wrist. Louis yelled with pain yet did not let go. At the same time, the captain threw a knee to his crotch, but Louis turned and got the mighty blow on the hip instead. Mad with hatred, Louis unsheathed his dagger and sliced at Segar's left forearm. A trickle of blood appeared on the man's shirt. Twisting the man's right arm, Louis pushed Segar violently against a wall and pressed his dagger against the man's throat. Louis breathed hard. His eyes were filled with rage, his jaws clenched. His brain urged him not to kill the man. Segar's execrable smirk was still on his face. Louis could smell his foul, beer-taste breath. Segar had saliva dripping on his goatee. Louis was conscious that every man around had gathered in a semicircle around them, observing the scene.

"You may have seduced Bertrant, but you don't fool me," Segar sneered, wrinkling his nose. "You can stroll around puffed up with your self-importance, preaching about honour and rules, but I know what you are." The man's eyes gleamed with wicked malice. "I don't know which one of you, you or your tasty, purple slut, takes it deep, but I know the filth you do. You will pay for your swagger and the mess you made," he whispered with provocative repulsion.

Louis's eyes were piercing with cold fury. His right hand shook. He contracted it harder on the hilt. "I will have your head for that," Louis hissed in Segar's face, showing his lower teeth.

"Oh, you would love that, wouldn't you?" Segar murmured. "But I'm not like that fat Vakeg. I've got plenty of men behind me, and the last thing you want right now is a mutiny in *your* army."

"Do it," Louis snarled low with an appealing voice. "Just give me a single excuse to execute you and your scum."

"You would start a bloodbath just for my head?" Segar chuckled. "Does blood turn you on? You're sick."

Louis did not care how much blood he would need to shed to clean the army of its worst elements. Not only did they threaten their mission, but they had spat on his honour and insulted his friend. The only thing that prevented Louis from slicing the man's throat was the promise he had made to Bertrant a few hours ago. Yet, he could not let the man go so easily, and the men were watching him.

"Louis," a high-pitched voice said behind him.

He turned his eyes and saw Folc watching him with dread. It was the opportunity to let go. Louis relaxed his grip. "I won't do that in front of the boy," he said, trying to calm down. He backed up, his eyes and dagger still on Segar. "But I'll get you one day."

"Not if I get you first," Segar hissed. The threat was plain and clear.

"This is over. Now move along!" Louis yelled at the crowd. The men complied. "Follow me," he said to Folc. They left the street and strode back to the castle.

"Nice color," Selen commented when Louis entered their room. His friend was already back from the infirmary and sat near the window with a book in his hand. "Segar?"

"He doesn't look better," Louis replied. It was a meager consolation to the frightful show he had given the men and the terrible revelation he had heard. "He knows."

"I had figured that. But it doesn't matter."

"It does! What if he spreads the word?"

"I don't think he will do it now. He has no proof. To insult you would only be rebellion. He could be hanged for that." Selen came to him and touched his face. "The cheekbone is not broken, but the bruise will match my hair for a few days. Let me put water on it."

"Bertrant will surely say that I had it coming." His lips twitched. Yet, Louis knew that Bertrant did not show more consideration for Segar. He unbuckled his belt and put his sword on the table. "How was it at the infirmary? Tell me."

"We have lost around two hundred men and have as many wounded. However, most of them will be ready to ride in two days." With care, Selen applied cold water on his bruise. It soothed his cheek. At least, it had not been the eye. "Brother Benedict complains that he doesn't have enough assistants and that he needs more time to fill his stocks of oils."

"What do you think?" Louis asked.

"I think he is not the kind of man to be satisfied, should he even have his own dispensary and an army of nurses," Selen sighed. He saw the mark on his wrist. "Teeth?"

"I hope I did not get rabies." Louis went to the table and washed his wound with soap.

"I talked with Lord Josselin. The man is willing, but he wants revenge. I don't think you should let him take ascendance over Bertrant. He sounded…perturbed," Selen said, worried. They moved and sat on the bed. "Did you find Folc?"

"I have," Louis answered. He saw relief on Selen's face. "The boy had searched for his aunt. It happened that she died two years ago which makes him the last one of his line. I found him a room in the keep. Folc has made up his mind and wants to follow the Rebellion. It's an honorable choice, and you can keep an eye on him." Louis smiled. He knew Selen felt responsible for the boy. "I have more good news for you. Bertrant wants to dub us. You will be a knight again."

Selen laughed. "I am already a knight. Unlike you," he sneered. Selen looked so happy.

"You don't know what I am," Louis said with a sly smile. His cheek hurt.

"Show me," Selen said, taking his hand.

40

Folc watched himself in the mirror. His brown doublet embroidered with red flowers fitted him perfectly. To match his garment, he had black hose and small brown boots. On his head, he wore a hat adorned with a jay feather. He was not always concerned about his appearance, but he liked to give a good image of himself. Besides, today was a big day. His two friends would become knights. He had seen adoubement ceremonies before. It was always impressive, and everyone wanted to be seen at his best. Folc tied a sharp, thin dagger to his belt, had a last glance in the mirror, and left his chamber.

Louis had insisted that he have a room for himself so that he could have privacy and act as it pleased him during their stay in the city. Folc was grateful for that. He had felt sad to learn that his aunt was dead. Not that he knew her, but she had been his only kin alive. Now, he was the last of the Tyntagiel. He had sworn to himself that he would bear his name proudly and be a valiant lord. He would follow his friends in the Rebellion and fight at their side.

Folc entered the crowded great hall. An adoubement was an important ceremony in castle life. All the nobles and rich families of Millhaven wanted to assist. It was the first official event after four years of terror. The great hall had been restored. There were rows of benches. The floor had been scraped clean. The stained-glass windows shone in the sunlight, and a new great chair had been built. Folc stepped to the first row. The Countess Khorkina stood on the dais. She wore a splendid pastel green gown adorned with silver pearls. It was supported by a large crinoline. Around her neck was a white lace collar, stretched up to her bun. Folc had seen many kinds of women before but never any as graceful as the countess. She had the demeanor of a queen. Beside her stood Bertrant. He was richly dressed in a green doublet. They both looked solemn but kind.

The crowd fell silent and moved aside. Selen and Louis came along the main alley. Their armours gleamed. His friends did not have the massive appearance armored knights usually gave. They had a majestic bearing. As if their armours had grown on them. It was obvious on Selen whose cuisses and greaves coated his long legs as if the metal and the flesh were one. His armour was covered with embossed foliate scrolls and was heavily gilded. His heels made him slightly taller than Louis. An impression that Louis compensated for with his double pauldrons. Louis's armour was engraved with a tree pattern and blued. Folc had always wondered where his friends had found armours fitted to kings. The simplicity of their weapons showed that they could not have afforded their armours, but they must have received them somehow. Louis's light brown curls floated around his head and down his shoulders with the rhythm of his steps. Folc saw the pride and honour on their faces. They walked to the edge of the dais, stopped, and knelt low. Selen's long hair, fastened low with an amaranth ribbon, cascaded on his back to the floor.

Bertrant approached them. He unsheathed his sword and laid the blade on Louis's right shoulder. He raised the sword and placed it on the left shoulder. Bertrant renewed the ritual with Selen. The commander put his sword away and took the two men's hands in his. Loudly and clearly, Louis and Selen swore their oath.

"I solemnly swear by the gods, and of my own free will, to serve as a knight of the Kingdom of Trevalden. I swear to be true to my words and chivalric in my actions, to be brave in battle, and to give assistance to the unfortunate. These are my knightly obligations, and I will fulfill them."

Usually, this was where the lord used to hit the knight, as a symbol, so that he would remember the day. Folc wondered if Bertrant would hit the two men. The commander turned to Louis, but instead of hitting him, he took Louis by the shoulders and kissed him on the cheek. He turned to Selen and kissed him as well. The two men could rise as knights.

Louis and Selen got up and turned to the cheering crowd. Folc applauded and shouted his congratulations. Selen smiled heartily. Louis looked more reserved but smiled nonetheless. Folc saw Selen turn to Louis. The look they shared would have been imperceptible to a stranger, but it touched Folc deeply. He was glad that his friends had a few days together.

Folc grew uneasy among strangers. He left the great hall and went out into the yard to breathe the fresh air of the evening. He sat on a bench under a tree. A shaggy, grey dog scraped at a door on the other side of the yard. Folc whistled at it. The dog stared at him with caution before trotting in his direction. It had hair falling into his eyes, and his fur was clotted with mud. Folc caressed his head and clapped on his side. He could feel the floating ribs under his fingers.

"Poor thing," he muttered. Folc had an idea. He rose and ran into the great hall.

In the alleys, the guests chatted and socialized. Folc reached the buffet and filled his hands with cakes. No one seemed to notice him. He went out again with a smirk on his face. He had not completely forgotten his skills at stealing food. The dog had waited for him by the side of the bench.

"Here, take." He gave the pastries to the dog, one at a time. "Good boy."

"I saw you," he heard a soft, kind voice say behind his back.

"He was hungry," Folc objected.

"You know I don't mind," Selen said, sitting beside him on the bench.

"Why are you not inside? It is your day," Folc asked. The dog slobbered on his hand while licking the last morsels.

"You know I don't like to have so many people looking at me. I don't even know them. Besides, I wanted to see you," Selen said. "I am sorry for your loss. I don't know how it is to lose a family. I never had one myself, but I suppose it must be horrible."

"Thank you. I did not know her, but it was still a difficult time," Folc said, melancholic. The dog whirled and sat on his feet with a sigh. "I miss my parents." He was silent for a while. He turned to Selen. "Do you know what is hard? It's that I never told them how much I loved them." Folc had tears coming to his eyes. "One should always tell these things if he doesn't want to regret it all his life." He caressed the dog's head. Selen's long silence surprised him. "Selen?" Folc said, turning to his friend. Next to him, Selen wept.

"You are right," Selen whispered.

Folc considered that, after what he had said, his friend had only one reason to cry. "Do you mean that you have never told him?" Folc could hardly believe it.

"What are you talking about?" Selen muttered, drying his tears with the back of his hand.

"Louis, of course. I know you both try to be discreet, but I have lived with you.

I'm not blind…and I don't mind."

Selen turned to him and smiled. "I'm scared to tell. I have my reasons."

"Well, that's foolish. You are everything to him. Besides, one of you can get killed during that war. Think of the one doomed to stay alive," Folc said with reproach.

"You're a smart boy," Selen said. His voice was doleful. Folc understood he had caused his friend pain. "Sometimes, I wonder why I'm so scared for you," Selen added. He got up and went back inside the castle without a glance.

"Because you care," Folc whispered. He got up and walked away, the dog following close on his heels.

41

Louis left the ceremony as soon as he could. Without much surprise, Selen had already sneaked off. The adoubement and its preparation had taken more time than Louis had expected. They would leave tomorrow, and he had not received the reports on their supplies yet. At least, Selen had been happy. Louis hurried down the stairs. Outside, the last rays of sun disappeared on the horizon. He met Faremanne in the inner courtyard. The captain was back from the city.

"I'm sorry I could not assist during the ceremony, but I had to make the last checks," Faremanne said. The captain breathed as if he had run the whole way from the warehouses.

"Don't be sorry. I'm happy someone here still has a notion of priorities," Louis said, a bit nervous. "I was on my way to see you. How are our stocks?"

"Good. We have the carts and wagons. I received the meat this afternoon." Faremanne sounded satisfied. Louis nodded with approval.

"Do you have the lists and reports?" Louis believed Faremanne, but he needed to check through all this to make sure they had not missed anything. Tomorrow, it would be too late.

"Of course." Faremanne handed him the papers. "I also talked with Josselin. He has gathered impressive forces. Ten thousand men will join our ranks." Faremanne's eyes gleamed with joy.

"Ten thousand?" Louis froze, shocked. "Only?"

Faremanne was taken aback. "What do you mean *only*? Louis, it's much more than we could have dreamed of."

"But the population of Millhaven is over fifty thousand!" Anger filled him. He could not believe it. Faremanne looked at him with disbelief and opened his mouth, but Louis interrupted him. "I must talk to Bertrant." Louis turned around and headed towards the castle.

"Louis, no…" He heard Faremanne sigh.

Louis climbed the staircase leading to Bertrant's chambers. The door stood ajar. Louis pushed it open and knocked.

"I suppose I can't avoid this important conversation," Bertrant sighed. He adjusted his doublet. "What happened?"

"Only ten thousand?" Louis jumped to the point. He walked into the room. "Did they only choose soldiers?"

"First, you should be glad it is ten thousand and not fewer. Secondly, it is ten thousand volunteers," Bertrant said. The commander tugged on his sleeves.

Louis pinched his brow. This was what he had feared. "I understand you want motivated soldiers, Commander. I too prefer the company of courageous men who love their country, but we need the mass. We freed this city. We could apply conscription."

"Conscription could indeed bring us more men, but it would spread fear and hate against us among the people. The Rebellion needs popularity. We need to make people dream of victory."

"These cowards have had four years to make their hate useful!" Louis exclaimed. He approached Bertrant. "I don't want dreams of victory. I want victory."

Bertrant stared back at him. "The men here have suffered much. We can't ask more from them."

"On the contrary. They have seen what orcs can do. Their motivation should be greater," Louis insisted. "Besides, freedom has a price. Not to mention that it should be a duty for a man to defend his land." Louis frowned.

"Louis." Bertrant looked at him and sighed. "No." Louis wanted to object, but Bertrant raised a hand and left his own chambers. The commander halted, came back, and made a sign for Louis to leave.

Louis gave up and left the room. He had promised to collaborate with Bertrant; he would have to satisfy himself with the ten thousand soldiers. He walked through the halls to his own chamber.

The room was so dark when Louis opened the door that he first thought Selen was already asleep. Then, he saw the dim light of the candle on the bedtable. Selen lay on the bed with the sheets pulled over him, his long hair spread around his body. Selen's eyes looked at him.

Louis undressed. He went to the table, washed his face, and brushed his hair. He was not angry anymore. He was done being a captain or a knight for today. Even the reports laid on the corner of the table. He would have a look at them later. He climbed onto the bed and slipped under the sheets next to Selen.

"Did you wait for me?" Louis asked, wrapping an arm around his friend. Even in the pale light of the candle, Louis could see by Selen's expression that something was wrong.

"It is the last night," Selen whispered. "I could not fall asleep."

"I know," Louis sighed. He grazed one hand against Selen's cheek and kissed his lips. Selen laid one hand on his shoulder to stop him.

"Blow out the candle, please," Selen murmured, his eyes looking down.

Louis stared at Selen, surprised. He wanted to speak, but he saw Selen bite his lower lip. Louis put out the light. He noticed that the moon was shining brightly outside. He turned back towards Selen.

He had never felt Selen so melancholic. He caressed the side of his head. His hair shone white, and the moonlight reflected in his eyes. Selen wrapped an arm around his chest and crept closer. "You know, we don't need…" Louis murmured. He yearned for it, but if Selen did not feel good, he would not force him.

"No. No, I want it," Selen responded at once. "I want you." He took Louis's hand and put it around his waist. Louis felt Selen's desire when Selen's mouth assaulted his, but his kiss was rough and unusually clumsy.

Louis laid Selen down on his back and crept on top of him. As he felt the warmth of Selen's body against his, his thoughts flowed. The idea that this was their last moment sneaked into his mind, but he pushed it back and traced his mouth around Selen's face and neck as if it were their first night, back there in the inn. It felt to Louis like it had been a year ago. How carefree they had been. Louis wondered if Selen had chosen to follow him—or if he had dragged his friend into this chaos. Louis felt Selen's fingertips trail on his back and Selen's thigh rub against his hip. He took an eternity to graze down Selen's body with his lips, tasting his smooth skin and skimming his tongue on Selen's nipples and down his abdomen. Louis did not want the moment to end. He inhaled the lavender perfume of his fair curls before nestling his face between Selen's legs. Selen grabbed a lock of his hair and led Louis's mouth where his urge was the most earnest. Louis complied graciously and soothed Selen's ache with hunger. Something in Selen's grip was awkward, too firm, but Louis would pleasure him nonetheless. Louis noticed that Selen's little squeaks halted. When his sliding fingers felt that Selen was ready, he crawled up for a kiss.

"Are you sure you want me?"

"Please, I want you. Now," Selen whispered, lifting his hips.

As Louis sank into Selen, he felt Selen's nails scratch his back and Selen's arms squeeze his chest. His face tensed under the pain. "Stop, Selen," Louis whispered in his ear, "you're hurting me." Louis brushed his fingers through Selen's hair and kissed the side of his head. "Please." The vise on his ribs eased. He kissed Selen again. Maybe for Selen's sake, he should not try to make it last this time. Louis knew it was not Selen's body that suffered, but his shattered soul. Louis was torn between his lust and the wish to comfort Selen. At this moment, the second feeling only stirred the first one up, and as he could feel, Selen's lust was obvious. With one hand, he reached down for Selen and caressed him in teasing moves. As Selen's delicious little moans in his ear fired him, his hand's moves turned into ravishing strokes. He let his hips grind into Selen's, conscious it may be the last time. At that moment, unspoken words rushed to his head, where they faded like mist. Their mouths rubbed against each other as they screamed their pleasure. While the pressure in his loins decreased with each long throb, warm wet spilled on his chest. Louis stood still. Selen's hot, pulsing breath coated his mouth. Louis's lips slipped onto Selen's cheek and turned moist. He looked at his friend. Selen cried.

"No, Selen. What is wrong?" He kissed his tears. Louis knew what was wrong. He was not stupid. Selen only waited for one thing, and he refused to give it to him. A few times already, he had choked on the words in his throat and cursed himself for the pain in Selen's eyes. Though Louis abhorred his own coldness, he was resolute not to promise words he may not hold. Yet, days went by, and his past stayed sealed. The dreamless nights were his nightmare. Besides, at this point, should he confide in his friend and die, it would only make it worse. He did not want Selen to mourn. The despair in Selen's pleading eyes made his heart bleed. He pressed Selen's head against his. *Forgive me*, Louis thought. Selen had still not answered but sobbed and clenched him.

"I am here," Louis whispered. "You have to stay strong. Use this night. It is yours. You will carry these moments inside you through the following weeks." Louis had created memories from perfumes and tastes. Should he sleep in his tent or lay injured on the field, he would still remember these sensations, from the honeysuckle of his hair to the smoothness of his fair fuzz between his legs. Louis felt that he already missed him and was on the verge of crying when Selen spoke.

"I'm scared," Selen peeped. He sniffled and dried his tears with one hand. "I'm sorry, I'm weak."

"Don't be. I'm terrified." It was true, but Louis would barely recognize it, even to himself. Selen chuckled and sniffled again.

"Hold me," Selen whispered. Louis hugged Selen with his limbs entwined around his friend's body. He would do it all night long, even if his muscles got sore.

In the moonlight, they embraced, gazing at each other, sharing long kisses. Yet, as he would not say what Selen wanted to hear, he would not say any more words for the night, not to lose hope, not to lose courage. Louis refused to think that it could be their last days, though the feeling dwelt on them. Louis's emptiness had never been so profound. He did feel like dust.

42

Lissandro's wrists hurt. The soldiers had tied him and Kilda to a rope and dragged them behind their horses. He and his companion had not resisted and, therefore, were unharmed. The road had been terribly long. Lissandro had counted four days. The party had slept in the open, the two prisoners fastened to a tree a few yards from the dogs. Lissandro had been so scared to be eaten during his sleep that he had barely closed his eyes. He felt exhausted. At the end of the fifth day, they reached a stronghold. It stood alone at the top of a hill, circled by a ditch. The last rays of the sun shone on its black stones. Moss clung in the shade of the ancient walls. The keep was high and sinister. Three tall towers rose around it. Their windows stood dark and gaping. Cages hung in the air on heavy iron chains. They approached the thick battlements. Two guards stood on each side of the drawbridge.

"Bringing fresh meat?" they bawled.

Lissandro felt a shiver run down his spine. "Where are we?" he asked Kilda discreetly.

The woman's face was white. Lissandro read terror in her eyes. "Mighthorn Keep," she whispered.

The inside yard was as welcoming as the façade. The ground was muddy with pools of water and shit-stained straw. Remnants of broken casks and rusted shields leaning against the walls of decrepit shacks littered the sides of the yard. A group of nasty-looking soldiers were dismantling what could have been gibbets. There were crusts of blood on the cobbles under it. In front of Lissandro, a wide, stone staircase led up to a black, wooden door. Lissandro wondered if he would come out of the keep alive, should their captors make them pass the door. The gates opened. They were pushed inside, and the heavy doors closed behind them with a fatidic thud.

The group went through a poorly lit hall. Paintings of riders and ancestors' portraits hung on the walls. With ancient halberds and shields, it was the only decoration. They climbed stairs probably leading to the great hall. Guards in mails opened the doors. The hall was cold and silent. The end of the room faded into darkness. A long board stood in the middle of the room circled by threatening statues of warriors. Near the hearth, a man sat on a high, carved, wooden chair. He had a long, emaciated face, with seductive black eyes set deep in their sockets. The flames of the fire made his black hair shine. As they approached, he rose and moved forward, his dark purple robes swirling around his legs.

"Do you know who I am?" he inquired, sucking on his thin, dry lips.

"You are Count Elye, my lord," Kilda muttered. Lissandro noticed that she was trembling.

"Precisely," the count affirmed. "And I know who you are, Lady Hewald. But you," the count said, turning to Lissandro, "I have never seen your face before." He grabbed Lissandro's cheeks with one hand and looked into his eyes. His grip hurt like the claws of an eagle. The soldiers holding Lissandro's arms pushed him forward. "You have a noble face, maybe a knight?"

"He is a knight," Kilda said. Lissandro wondered if she was denouncing him or trying to protect him. "He is a knight of the Rebellion. A friend of Bertrant," she added.

"Hmm, interesting." Elye released his grip. Lissandro twisted his jaw. He could still feel the marks of the man's fingers on it. Elye turned to Kilda again. "But I know someone who isn't. What did I tell you the last time we met, Lady Hewald? Mourn your husband, join the Sisters. Yes, something like that."

"You took my lands!" she shouted. She was crying.

"Women should not rule on their own. As they shouldn't take to arms. Maybe I should show you what happens to a woman who wants to be on the battlefield?" The count turned to his men. "Take off her armour."

The soldiers complied. Kilda struggled and screamed.

"Leave her alone!" Lissandro shouted. "Disgusting bastards!"

"You better shut up and watch, because you could be next," Elye threatened. He moved towards Kilda and violently tore off her linen. She tried to hide herself with her hands, but Elye pushed her arms away. As he grabbed and squeezed one of her small breasts, she uttered a sharp squeak of pain.

"You can be lucky you look like a cow," he scoffed to her face. The count took a step back and punched her.

"No!" Lissandro yelled.

"Your turn," Elye said to his soldiers. The men sniggered and circled Kilda.

Powerless and outraged, Lissandro was forced to watch. Lying on the floor, Kilda neither screamed nor cried. She protected her naked body as best as she could and endured each blow. The blood in Lissandro's veins boiled with fury. Too often had he seen such abject scenes in his own home. He swore in his heart to avenge her honour, by himself or by unleashing the wrath of the Rebellion upon the count. The man would pay for his crime.

They had been thrown into large cages in a windowless cell in the prison tower. It was littered with straw, and there were pots in a corner. An iron grate separated them. Kilda lay curled in on herself in the corner of her cage. They had taken away her armour and dressed her up with rags of an old gown. Lissandro heard her sob. "Kilda," he whispered, "I'm sorry. I'm really sorry. They will pay for this, I swear." He paused. "You are still a warrior to me. You were very brave."

"I wish I were dead," she muttered.

"I wish I were dead too. But here we stand. You have sworn an oath to your husband. You can't give up now."

"I miss him. Maybe death is sweeter than this life. We could be together," she sobbed.

Lissandro thought about his own beloved and sneered. Death did not bring people back together. Nothing could. "I too have lost the one I love," he told her with sadness in his voice, "and I have no one in this world to blame for that."

"Did she die during the war?" Kilda asked. She turned to Lissandro.

He smiled. Tears ran down his face. He could not even remember how he had died, or if his love had died with him. "It was in another world. In another life." He tried hard to remember him. He only had scraps of memories; a smile, a word. He closed his eyes. "We are children of the night, bound by blood, bound by love. Please come back to me," he whispered and repeated the phrase like a mantra until he fell asleep.

First, there was nothing but darkness. Then, a light shone. The wind ripped against his face. Lissandro had climbed to the top of the skyscraper and stood on its roof.

In the horizon, the purple sky was streaked with gold. Dawn was rising on the City that Never Sleeps. His round, blue eyes looked at the light with amazement. "I haven't seen such beauty since…"

"Two hundred years," a low, husky voice said behind him. Strong arms curled gently around his waist. Lissandro leaned backwards, his head resting against the broad chest of his companion. His long, blond hair floated against Lissandro's face. "Are you ready?" Grimmr asked him.

"Are you sure we won't burn?" Lissandro asked with a hint of worry.

"We made the journey and passed the test. We won't. We could even survive it if we wanted to."

"Then I'm ready." Lissandro smiled, resolute. "I have seen so much. I have travelled around the earth. I have contemplated the most beautiful wonders and the worst creations of mankind. I have been through wars, including against myself. And most of all, I have been happy, with you." Lissandro turned around. He looked at the heavy-lidded, blue eyes of his companion. "You saved me that night. You gave me a chance to love and be loved. We've been through a lot. I have felt delightful joy and insufferable pain. I have lived. Now, I want to share eternity in the sky with you."

"Then we will be one among the stars," Grimmr whispered to him. He kissed him lovingly.

Lissandro turned around and faced the light again. The first sunbeams appeared on the horizon. His mind was at peace, his body light as a feather. Dust rose from around him and from his own self. It did not burn. It did not hurt. Soon, they would float to heaven.

Lissandro opened his eyes.

"Lissandro?" he heard Kilda whisper. "Are you all right?"

"As one among the stars…" he muttered as he rose and sat on the floor of his cell. "As one…" He felt the spark of hope set his heart ablaze. "I came back as two," he whispered, realizing. "This is why I have intense visions. It's unbalanced!" he exclaimed, full of joy. His entire face was radiant. "It means he is alive somewhere!"

"Lissandro! What is it?" Kilda shouted.

"My love, Grimmr. He is here somewhere. I will fight this war and we will win. Then, I will search the whole world if needed, but I will find him." Lissandro rose and grabbed the metal bars of his cage. "He saved me. He has never given up on me. I will never stop fighting for him!" Lissandro turned to Kilda. "Don't give up, Kilda.

You have suffered a lot, but there is hope. For you and for me. There is always hope in life. And we will get out of this cell. Together!"

Kilda looked at him with a mix of hope and surprise. "He?"

43

From the top of the stairs leading to the castle entrance, imperial as a goddess, the countess had given her blessing to the Rebellion. Louis and the other captains turned their horses down the main street and followed Bertrant out of the city.

The army leaving Millhaven was impressive. Louis knew they could have had more soldiers had Bertrant listened to him, but Louis had sworn to collaborate and he had not insisted. The other captains had nearly cried with joy at the sight of the considerable mass of men, clad in shiny mail and plate. Faremanne had told him that this was as many soldiers as the Rebellion had known in its glory days, at the beginning of the war, before Agroln unleashed his dragon. The two men knew that they would be wiped out as easily as before if they could not control the beast, but at least there was a glimpse of a chance. Josselin had agreed to give the whole command of his troops to Bertrant, satisfying himself with the title of Captain. As Selen had foreseen, the man was there for revenge, not for glory.

The population of Millhaven gathered in the streets cheered them with acclamations and flowers as if they were already victorious. The cavalry opened the way down the main street to the drawbridge. The horses' manes and colorful caparisons floated majestically in the wind. Their barding glittered in the sun.

They left the city by the south road, which meandered through golden fields and shallow rivers. Louis rode alongside Faremanne, leading the second battalion. It should have been a glorious day. Yet, his chest was heavy.

"I have never seen such a big army. And we are the captains. Isn't it marvelous?" Faremanne exclaimed, his chest swollen with pride and joy.

"Yes, of course," Louis answered, trying to sound as cheerful as possible to avoid embarrassing questions. He yawned. "How long do you think it will take before we reach the meeting place?"

"It depends on the weather, but I would say a week."

A week of chitchat and a sore bottom. In other words, an eternity.

Over the following days, the Rebellion crossed golden wheat fields and passed in front of abandoned windmills. They let their horses graze on green meadows covered with dandelions. Louis listened politely to Faremanne's monologues on the Windy Isles and the beauty of the sea, nodding here and there and pleasing his friend with a few questions. They had sunny days and days where it rained so hard that men needed to dismount to push the chariots out of the mud. The nights were warmer as summer was coming. During the evenings, Louis sat with the men around campfires, listening to tales about the past and songs about wenches. Later, lying on his blanket in the headquarters, he spent many hours watching the artifact that always glowed brighter in his hand. Though he wanted to show it to Selen, he did not dare to worry his friend about the dragon. Not now. Selen was progressively finding his place in the camp. Louis saw Selen help where he could, to fix wounds or to carry materiel. He would always be an outsider, but it seemed the soldiers did not see him as a freak anymore. After a week, they reached the swamps.

"Don't tell me we have to cross that," Louis said.

"I fear we do," Faremanne answered.

The wetlands stretched for miles on both sides in a multitude of brambles, reeds, and smoking ponds. An unpleasant wind hissed through the heather.

"Send scouts to search for solid ground. We can't lose too much time here," Louis said.

Faremanne turned his horse back to the army. Louis followed him. Bertrant trotted the other way to meet them.

"Are we blocked?" the commander asked.

"We need to find a path, but we shouldn't camp here. This is a foul place to stay. Men will be sick," Louis said. "I suggest we tell the men to share the weight from the wagons and carry all they can."

Around noon, the first scouts were back. One of them approached him. He was exhausted and half covered with mud.

"We have found a way to the other side, Captain," the man panted.

"Can we make it before the night?" Louis asked.

"I can't say, Captain. We did not test with wagons."

This was what Louis feared, but he would chance it nonetheless. "Show us the way."

The army regrouped and followed the scouts on the firm land. They were obliged to move in a line between bogs and pools of clay. The noxious air smelled of decaying vegetation and other kinds of gas with odors similar to that of boiled cabbage. The wagons' wheels spun in the mud. Louis stood on the side of the column and evaluated their progression. In the distance, one of the wagons leaned. When he heard men scream, Louis kicked his horse and rode to them.

The oxen mooed and pulled with all their strength. On the side of the wagon, soldiers pushed to bring it back in balance, their shoes sliding in the mud. Louis looked south and saw the column progress without them. He dismounted, tied his horse to the wagon, and stepped next to the men. His boots squelched. This side had left the firm ground. He grabbed the wooden edge.

"Now listen to me. One, two…three!"

Louis pushed as hard as he could. He felt his feet dig into the ground, but the wagon moved.

"Push!" one of the soldiers shouted.

The men groaned. The wagon rose and rolled forward. Losing his grip, Louis stumbled, but one soldier held him up.

"Thank you," Louis said before he strode to his horse and mounted.

Their forces had stretched so much that the first battalion seemed a mile away while the rest of the army pressed behind them. Louis rode on the side of the wagon. The smell made him so nauseous that he wondered if he could eat again.

The first stars shone in the sky when they reached the other side. The first battalion was busy setting camp on a grassy field. Fires had been lit and blows of hammers resounded.

Louis approached a lieutenant. "Don't let anyone drink water from that place. Spread the word."

The wagon passed him by and joined the rest of the supply train. Louis rode to the corral. Soldiers rubbed down horses. One man took his mount's bridle as he dismounted. Louis's head spun. He walked a few steps away and opened his mouth to retch. A hand grabbed his shoulder.

"That was a tough day," Faremanne said. "Care for a loaf of salted pork?"

The next morning, they arrived at the meeting point. Pembroke's army was larger than theirs. They had pitched their tents on the plain, turning the green meadow into a sea of white linen. A lot more banners than they carried floated above masts. Pembroke had summoned many of his barons. As they approached, their horses responded to the whinnies of the other army's mounts. Soon, the groups mixed, and men saluted and hailed to each other. The captains of the Rebellion proceeded to Pembroke's pavilion. Louis hoped that the count's meeting with Bertrant would not be too tumultuous.

"He could have stood outside his tent to welcome us," Bertrant grumbled as they dismounted. Louis sighed with apprehension. Soldiers came to take care of their horses.

Bertrant, Faremanne, Selen, Josselin, and Louis entered the tent. The headquarters were similar to Bertrant's. Dressed in a black doublet rimmed with gold, Pembroke stood behind his board with his captains and lieutenants around him. Louis noticed at once that the men of the Rebellion were largely outnumbered. He strode alongside Bertrant.

"We had hoped for a better welcome!" the commander exclaimed. The lieutenants cleared the way as they approached.

"Bertrant! We were not expecting you until tomorrow," Pembroke said.

Louis did not believe that they had surprised the count, yet if it actually was genuine confusion he read on the man's face, he would have a word with their sentinels. "Excuse us for arriving too early," Louis retorted. "We had a stronghold filled with orcs standing in our way. It's true it should have delayed us a bit."

"I hope you were positively impressed by the strength of our motivation," Bertrant said, adding a layer. He halted in front of the board and crossed his arms. Louis stood at his side, his arms behind his back.

Pembroke sighed. "I left my city unguarded. Don't make me regret my decision." He turned to his captains and lieutenants. "Leave us." The men went out.

"We came with eleven thousand men, mostly soldiers from Millhaven," Bertrant said, cocking his head backwards towards Josselin. In the corner of his eye, Louis saw the captain bow. "How many men do you bring?" Bertrant asked.

"Twenty thousand. It's the best I could do," Pembroke answered. His fingers tapped the table. "Now, before we start. I want to make things clear."

Louis saw anger rise in Bertrant. The commander was ready for the worst and would certainly make a scene about it. Pembroke closed his hand on the table into a fist.

"Bertrant, I'm sorry."

Bertrant was taken aback. Louis looked at Pembroke, startled. The man had his eyes downcast.

"I fled when I should have been brave. My cowardice condemned you and your men. You showed me with your victory in Millhaven that the Rebellion still stands. I was wrong. My men are yours. Don't make me repeat these words again."

Louis looked at his commander for a reaction. Bertrant stood gaping. Though Louis condemned Pembroke's cowardice, he respected his noble decision. "We thank you for your support, my lord," he said with a bow.

"Well, yes. That's a nice gesture," Bertrant mumbled. "Let me introduce my captains. You have already met Louis," the commander said, pointing at him. "Behind me are Faremanne, Selen, and Josselin." Each man bowed at the sound of his name.

"I still wonder how you plan to take care of the dragon. You don't intend to charge frontally against it, do you?" Pembroke inquired.

"We have found an artifact," Bertrant said. He turned to Louis. "Show him."

Louis took out the pouch from under his armour and emptied it on the table, careful not to touch the vial with his fingers. Pembroke reached for the artifact.

"What is this?" he asked, gazing at the object on all side.

"It may stop the dragon's fire. If it works," Bertrant said.

"May? If? Is it all you've got?" Pembroke stared at them, worried.

"It's all we've got," Faremanne said.

"And how does it work?" Pembroke asked.

"The dragon must eat it," Selen said.

Pembroke was silent for a while. "And who came up with this brilliant idea?" No one jumped to take the blame. "Does one of you even know where the dragon is?" Pembroke insisted.

"I do," Josselin said. "Last time we heard of it, it was south of Earthfell. The city is in the mountains. In legends, dragons are known to live in mountains. It makes sense."

"So someone will have to ride to Earthfell, find the dragon, and make it eat that thing?"

"I volunteer," Josselin said.

Everyone stared at him. "You don't need to volunteer. We can find a solution," Faremanne protested.

"There is no need for you to do that, boy," Bertrant said.

"Look at me," Josselin sighed. "Half of my face is missing. Let me take care of the dragon. Should I be remembered in this war, I don't want it to be as a monster."

"But you will probably die," Selen said.

"And better me than you." Josselin smiled.

The words struck Louis like a bolt. Despite the selfishness of this thought, Louis had to agree on that and jumped on the occasion. "We will plan everything to give you the best chances," he said, making things settled.

"We have much to do the following days. We need to coordinate our troops. We also need to contact Elye and check the road south," Bertrant said.

"Contact Elye?" Pembroke repeated. "Don't tell me you trust that adder."

"He wants to support our cause," Bertrant said.

"Elye support the cause of Elye. I won't put my men in his hands," Pembroke objected.

"We need all the strength we can get. Besides, it's best to have someone like him with us than against us," Bertrant insisted.

"What kind of man is this Elye?" Louis asked Pembroke.

"The nasty kind. He sided with the Rebellion but never got consequences from Agroln. The gods know what kind of deals the man made," Pembroke said, scratching his beard.

That sounded bad enough indeed. Louis turned to Bertrant. "I can send soldiers to the villages and towns around. With the prestige of our victory, we will get more men, better men," he proposed.

"Do it, but I'll still send the crows." Bertrant closed the discussion. He turned to his captains. "When the men are ready, we will move south. We are only a few miles from Breyburgh. The city is under the control of Agroln's troops, but we have to start somewhere. That will be all for today, Captains."

The four captains walked out of the headquarters, leaving Bertrant and Pembroke discuss other matters. The captains gathered in front of the pavilion.

"We have much to do in the camp," Louis said. "Pembroke's men must know that they are under our command from now on. We need coherent battalions. The same rules for everyone. Ours. We need to check their training and make a list of the stocks."

Faremanne grinned at Louis, his arms crossed over his chest. "He never stops, does he?" the captain whispered to Selen, who shifted from one foot to the other.

"My men are yours," Selen said with a broad smile. "We all heard it." He winked at Faremanne.

Louis smiled. "Let's work."

At the end of the day, the soldiers' tents had been built. Bertrant's pavilion stood beside Pembroke's. The two commanders had decided to raise a third tent to use as neutral headquarters. Pembroke's men had received new orders. They would follow the rules applying to the Rebellion's army. They were now under Bertrant's command which, in other words, meant that Louis had total control over the whole camp. Under Bertrant's supervision, he reminded himself. The captains had sauntered around the camp to show themselves to the soldiers and create bonds. Lists of the stocks would be made, and provisions would be gathered. Louis and Faremanne had returned to their tent, satisfied with the men's work.

Louis removed his armour and placed it on the rack. "I'm starting to believe that we may have a chance," Louis said.

"We will fight Agroln's army and save the day!" Faremanne exclaimed. They both laughed.

Louis liked the captain's enthusiasm. If Faremanne felt fear or doubts, he never let them show. Louis considered that this was how captains should be. An example of courage to their men, a rock where they could find strength. Louis stepped behind the curtain. He removed his clothes, filled a large bowl with water, and washed his body.

"I feel bad for Josselin," he heard Faremanne say.

"I know. Me too, but I understand the man." Who wanted to die in his bed when there was a world to save? Louis only hoped that the man would succeed. His mission was everything or nothing, and the future of the Rebellion depended on it. Louis dried himself, rubbed his teeth with bone powder, and brushed his hair. The grass was cold under his feet. Considering their lack of chariots, all that had been judged superfluous had been left behind. It included the rags for the tent's floor, some of the furniture, and unnecessary clothes. Only the commander's tent had kept most of its accommodations intact. Louis put his clothes on again. The shirt smelled of sweat and felt unpleasant, but one of the rules of the camp forbade him from sleeping naked, and his second shirt, encrusted with mud, needed to be washed. He took the dirty garment and plunged it into the soapy water bowl.

Faremanne already lay on his bed. Though he kept his beard trimmed, the man was not particular about his corporal hygiene. For most of the men in the camp, to wash meant to moisten their armpits and chest with a wet cloth. Yet, it was still a huge improvement since Louis and his friends had joined the camp. Louis glanced at the table. The board was bare. No rapport had come during the day. The lieutenants had until tomorrow. He lay down on his bed and thought of everything that still needed to be done. He thought of Selen and fell asleep, dreaming.

Soon it would be over. Around him, the crowd roared with hatred, shouted insults, laughed. Blurred faces grimaced, spat at him. He would not deign to look at them. People he had only wanted to protect, to save. Their ingratitude had withered his heart. The demons had won. As they always did. Because they were legion. He felt the fresh morning wind on his neck. They had cut his long curls with a knife. Locks fell on his face, over his eyes. He did not care. He was only dust. They could take his body, put it to death; they could never take away from him what he had achieved or the dreams burning inside him. To live or to die, his own existence didn't matter. The only precious thing they could have taken was his friend, and that was precisely what they had done. Therefore, he had chosen death. Only to stay at his side, to the end. Louis had always been there, to protect, to counsel, to hold him, as he had done the night before, pressing on his friend's bleeding wound until the guards grabbed him. Now, to die together was all that mattered. Proud and calm he sat. He welcomed death. He longed for it. He despised the world that had rejected him, a world of crimes and injustice. For two years, he had fought for his country, for justice. The soldiers had admired him. They had followed his last command and had won many battles. Yet, others had taken the glory. Now, the same men would cover his name with blood. They would charge him with their sins as a scapegoat. The abrupt halt of the horses snapped him out of his thoughts. The guards grabbed him and pulled him down from the cart. Louis stumbled. "Wait," he said. His voice was strong and clear again. He approached his wounded friend and kissed him. "Goodbye," he whispered. His heart was breaking, but he would not cry. He had cried during the night when watching over him, under the scornful gazes of their captors, but he would not give the crowd this pleasure. Firm hands pushed him forward onto the scaffold. His body rammed against the wooden plank. His chest hurt. Louis smiled at the irony. He looked up at the bloodstained blade of the guillotine. He should have felt fright. He felt only relief. "At least, I have lived," he whispered. Now, he belonged to the sky. As the board straps closed around his chest and legs, his sapphire eyes looked over the crowd, one last time, with a cold glare. They called him brave, he would show them that great men do not waver.

Louis rose with a start on his bed with a strangled scream. His hands grabbed his neck. His chest contracted. Louis turned around, fell on the ground, and puked. It could not be. He was dead. His fingers dug the earth. His heart was swollen with tears. *Why here? Why a second chance? Why alone?* "Why?" he shouted, throwing the table down.

44

"Selen!" Faremanne appeared in a panic at the entrance of the tent. "You better come. Quick!"

"What happened?" His heart contracted.

"It's Louis."

Selen rose, his chair falling behind him. In an instant, he was rushing through the camp as if his life depended on it. He nearly stumbled in front of Louis's tent. He took a deep breath and pulled at the flap, terrified of what he would see inside.

It was mayhem. The inside of the tent had been trashed. His heart beat again; there was no blood. Yet, he could not see his friend. "Louis?" he whispered. "It's me, only me."

"Please, leave, Selen," a thick, wobbly voice said behind the bed.

"What happened?" Selen asked softly while entering the tent. He approached with care and sat on the ground by the corner of the bed. "Please, tell me."

"I remember." The voice was ice cold.

Oh no, Selen thought, *not like that*. When he had learned that he had died, Selen had felt sadness at first, but his previous life had been austere and dull. He had never had a reason to live. Despite the war, this world had turned for the best for him. He had feared that it would be the contrary for Louis. Dread crept into his heart.

"Tell me, how did you die?" Selen asked.

"We fought for freedom, for a better world. We shared dreams. We killed the king. We won the war. Yet, sometimes there is more than one tyrant. There were factions, rebels, traitors… All those weak creatures, they hated us. They hated him. They wanted him dead. Unworthy of his words, all of them."

Selen barely understood what Louis talked about. Only one thing had struck him, and he wanted to know. "Did you care for him?" He hoped the fear in his voice was not too obvious.

"I gave him my life. I didn't want… I couldn't outlive him," Louis sobbed.

Louis's words hit Selen's heart like a bolt. He did not dare to speak, afraid to cry.

"I don't understand," Louis continued. "Why should I fight here? It's not my land. It's not even my world. They'll turn on me. They'll hate me."

"No, they like you." It was not exactly true, many did not, but Selen did not care. "Remember what you said, with the community of feelings. It was a beautiful thought." Selen's words only met silence. "They need you, Louis." He grew desperate. He repressed his tears. "I need you." His voice was a squeak.

"Please, leave me," Louis whispered, cold and distant.

Selen stretched out a trembling hand to the corner of the bed but changed his mind at the last second. He jumped up and rushed outside. He stumbled on Faremanne. "Leave him alone, please," he ordered, pushing the captain back. "Leave me alone!" Selen went away.

Once back in his tent, Selen broke down in tears to the ground, gasping and letting his heart explode in silent screams as his world shattered like broken glass.

The captains had been summoned to the headquarters. Everyone was there except Louis. Selen stood, empty and wrecked, nodding mechanically in approval. He had wept the whole night and day until his last tears had dried on his cheeks. Folc had stayed silent, patting his head from time to time, and hugging him. Selen looked paler than usual, but no one had commented on it. He listened to Faremanne with one ear. He could not care less.

"We have received crows from Elye," the captain said. "He wishes us to send a delegation."

"A delegation? I thought we had already reached an understanding," Bertrant said.

"Well, he says he has something for us. A gift of some kind," Faremanne explained.

"I don't understand. I thought you did not trust the man?" Josselin said.

"We don't really trust him," Faremanne said.

"Then, why send a delegation?" Josselin asked.

"Because we need to see what he wants. There must be a reason why he doesn't give more explanation in his message," Faremanne answered. "What do you think, Selen?"

"Hmm. I don't know. Send a lieutenant," he mumbled.

"You can't send a lieutenant to a count. It's insulting. Someone has to go. It may be important," Faremanne said.

"But what if it's a trap?" Josselin retorted.

"A trap against a delegation? It doesn't make any sense…" Faremanne replied.

"Oh, enough!" Bertrant exclaimed. "Can we come to a solution? And where the hell is Louis?"

"He doesn't feel well," Faremanne said in a low, worried tone. "I think he cracked up."

"Well, I had noticed for a long time that he didn't have both oars in the water," Bertrant grumbled.

"Thank you, Bertrant," Louis said, coming towards them, smiling.

"I spoke too fast," Bertrant mumbled.

"Louis! What a pleasant surprise!" Faremanne welcomed Louis with open arms.

Selen gaped. His heart tightened. Louis embraced Faremanne, but his gaze was set on Selen. His eyes were hollow, and he was still mourning, but Selen understood that his friend was sorry. Selen felt blood come back to his cheeks and beamed.

"Faremanne told us that you had a moment of…weakness," Bertrant said.

"I did. But if you want to get King Agroln's head, you better have me on the team." Louis smiled.

"Faremanne, could you explain the situation to your fellow captain?" Bertrant bid.

"Elye wants us to send a delegation. He claims he has something, a gift. One of us has to ride to Mighthorn with a party," Faremanne said. Selen hoped his friend would let it pass this time, but he knew him too well.

"I volunteer," Louis said.

"I was sure you would, but no, not you," Bertrant said. "We need someone who has the right qualifications to negotiate with the count." Selen presumed Bertrant meant someone with patience and diplomacy. "Faremanne for example."

"Yes, of course, I would volunteer," the captain said, surprised.

"Good. You ride as soon as you are ready. That is all for now. You can take your leave," Bertrant ordered.

Selen strode to Faremanne and took him to the side. "Could I have a word with

Louis in private? I would like to be sure that he feels better," he whispered.

"Of course," Faremanne answered. "Please, talk to him. We do need him with us."

Selen left the pavilion and hurried back to his tent. He grabbed a box and headed to Louis's tent. The inside had been cleaned up, as if nothing had happened. His friend sorted papers on the table. He saw Selen and squirmed.

"I made a mess of this place." He put the papers down. Louis kept his head low. "I'm sorry for…"

"Don't talk," Selen whispered, as kindly as he could. "I have something to show you." He presented the box. It was finely carved with arabesques and made of walnut. Selen went to a wooden trunk and knelt in front of it. He opened the box.

"Candles. They are beautiful," Louis whispered.

"I found them in Millhaven." Selen took a candle out of the box, fixed it on the trunk, and lit it. "In my land, when someone dear died, we used to offer libations and burn incense on an altar consecrated to the loved ones. I could not find incense, but I found these candles." The orange flame burned brightly in the dimness of the tent. The light was comforting. Louis knelt beside him. "I lost someone in my world," Selen carried on. "Someone I had never dared to confess to, but someone I cared about. I know he and I never received proper burials. So I pray for his soul to rest in peace. I know that what you felt was much deeper, and shared." Selen paused. It hurt him to think of it. "It is good to mourn. Immortality lays in the continued remembrance of the dead. These candles will help us remember our lost ones and find peace in our hearts. You can keep them. I don't need them anymore. My prayers will suffice." Selen felt Louis's hand reach for his and hold it tenderly.

"You have the same kindness in your heart," Louis whispered. He carried Selen's hand to his chest.

They heard alarming screams coming from outside. Louis rose, pulling him up. They went out. The sky on the horizon in the south burned red in the dusk of the day. Above it rose a gigantic cloud of black smoke. The air around them had the smell of wood and bacon.

"What is this?" Selen exclaimed in terror.

"A city burning," Louis answered. "Breyburgh."

"We have to do something. They may need help!" Selen shouted, looking at his friend.

"We don't know what is happening there. If it's the dragon, we are not ready. But we will help them. Come!" They hurried to the headquarters.

45

"Burn! Burn them all!" Kraalh yelled.

The general jogged through the main street of Breyburgh towards the temple. Bodies were scattered along his path, some lying in pools of blood. His orcs ran through the alleys, holding torches. Kraalh had ordered them to burn all that would provoke arson. As the city was made of wood, it was an easy task. He could see the glow behind the windows. The flames licked at the ceilings. Kraalh heard wood and glass explode. The dry thatch roofs spluttered. The dust particles of the grey smoke tickled his nose. Flames, fanned by a steady wind, spread to the adjacent houses. Kraalh knew that they would need to leave before the place turned into an inferno.

In the meanwhile, his orcs had all liberty to sack. Furniture was thrown on the streets. Trunks were carried out of the burning houses and torn open, sometimes revealing gold jewelry, sometimes silver cutlery.

Kraalh tasted his revenge. He had fled Millhaven by the back door, filled with shame and hatred. His first act had been to gather as many of his soldiers as he could summon and form a front here, down south. The Rebellion would come after them, but they would only find ashes. He had sent messengers to Agroln and still waited for the answer. Yet, the final fight was coming. It was time to prepare the ground. Kraalh promised them a back draft right from hell.

The temple stood tall at the end of the street. Its white walls had turned yellow in the light of the flames. In the yard, the orcs had parked the inhabitants that had not succeeded in fleeing the city. Around six hundred men, women, and children were pressed in front of the huge oak doors. Kraalh gazed at their terrified faces. Women cried, men wailed like women.

"A flock of sheep," Kraalh muttered. He picked an apple out of one of his pockets and took a bite. He paced around the prisoners, looking closer at their frightened eyes. He grimaced. "I have had enough. Take the children!"

The howls and squeals of the mothers were deafening. Hands held tight and arms clenched, but nothing resisted his soldiers. Blood was spilled, strident shrieks resounded, and eventually, two groups were formed.

"Take the children away and await my orders," Kraalh brawled. "As for these ones, push them inside." Kraalh savored his apple while the population of Breyburgh was crammed inside the temple. The doors were locked, and torches were thrown into the air. Soon, the sour taste of the apple juice in Kraalh's mouth blended with a smoke of charred meat. The howling was music to his ears.

A couple of hours later, Kraalh heard the horses of the cavalry arrive their way. The ground shook. "Time to leave!" Kraalh yelled. He did not want to engage in the fight with the Rebellion. It was neither the right time nor the right place. Besides, he had left them a gift to enjoy and a message. He sneered and chewed on a new apple bite. His revenge tasted sweet.

46

The captains, Bertrant, and Pembroke waited in the headquarters in a leaden atmosphere. They had sent troops to the city to help anyone who would flee in their direction and to report on the situation. Segar and Jamys were absent as usual. Josselin stood in a corner, arms crossed, observing the lords. Bertrant and Pembroke sat on their chairs, scratching their beards. In front of Faremanne, Selen sat livid and twitched his long fingers so hard his knuckles turned white. Louis paced between them in the center of the tent.

"Please, sit down, Louis. You're getting on my nerves," Faremanne said.

"I am stressed," Louis responded. Yet, he turned his heels and sat down on a trunk, his hands against his temples. "I should have ridden with them," he muttered.

"I said no," Bertrant grumbled. "We wait and see."

Faremanne thought the waiting would never end when a lieutenant rushed inside the tent. "I come for the report, my lords!"

"Speak!" Bertrant and Pembroke cried out. Everyone in the pavilion rose from his seat.

"We met many refugees on the way to the city," the man said. He was shaking, and his eyes were wide open, frantic. "We brought them back to the camp, in a separate section, near the infirmary. We rode to the city. There was no one to be saved. They…they had burned."

"Burned?" Louis exclaimed.

"Yes, Captain. But there is worse… No, I can't say. You must see for yourself."

How could anything be worse than that? Faremanne wondered. The lieutenant ran out and came back, pushing an orc in front of him. The creature held a large bag.

"We caught him and a few others. The rest had left the city. The bags, my lords, there are many." The lieutenant stepped back.

Louis approached the orc. "What is in that bag?" he asked. His face was tense.

The creature smirked. Even condemned, the orc was still nasty and foul. He did not answer but kept showing his rotten teeth to Louis. Irritated, Louis grabbed the bag from the orc's hands.

"Be careful," Faremanne exclaimed.

Louis untied the rope around the neck of the bag and peeked inside from a distance. Louis's eyes grew wide. His fingers dropped the bag, and he turned around to puke. Selen approached, picked the bottom corners of the bag, and pulled them up. What fell out contorted Faremanne's stomach as Louis's had. He felt bile come up in his mouth and threw up. In front of him, Selen's shriek was piercing. The captain fell to his knees, his shaking hands over his eyes.

"What madness!" Bertrant shouted, stepping back.

In the middle of the tent, the heads of children rolled in the dust, their eyes frozen wide forever.

They all gazed at the tortured little faces in silence. Faremanne's blood boiled in his veins. Selen stretched a trembling hand to one of the heads, picked it up, and cradled it.

"Why?" Selen sobbed.

"How many bags?" Louis asked, still sounding nauseous. The captain had tears in his eyes.

"A whole cart," the lieutenant muttered.

Faremanne closed his eyes. Tears ran down his cheeks. They would pay. On his honour, they would pay.

"I've got a message," the orc hissed with a grating voice. He sniggered. "Kraalh is not happy about Millhaven. He will kill and burn all. He will have your bodies on a spike. And he will have the she-knight."

"The she-knight?" Bertrant asked, confused.

The orc raised a scrawny, filthy finger and pointed it at Selen. His chuckles grew louder.

In an instant, Selen was on him, screaming and smashing the orc's head violently with his fist. He grabbed a stone and hit the orc's face repeatedly. First, Faremanne heard the bones break, then it was only the sucking noises of a pulp mixed with slime. No one moved to stop Selen.

"Selen. He is dead," Faremanne whispered.

Louis moved behind Selen and helped him get up. The captain whispered something in Selen's ear. Faremanne noticed how tenderly Louis held his friend's trembling arms. The men were a bit too close for his liking, but they were his companions. He would not judge.

"We will avenge these people," Selen said.

"We will kill every orc in Trevalden," Bertrant replied.

"I will ride to Elye's castle tomorrow morning," Faremanne said.

"While you are away, I suggest we take care of the refugees and check the ruins of the city for survivors," Louis said.

"Let's do that," Bertrant said. "Now, I suggest we all get some rest. If we can."

Faremanne got up early. On his bed, on the other side of the tent, Louis was still asleep. After such rough days, his companion was exhausted. Faremanne tried not to wake him up. He washed his face, put his armour on, and left the tent.

He would depart with a force of a hundred soldiers. In the cold morning mist, the men were already waiting for him. Their mounts pawed the ground. As Faremanne got on his horse, Bertrant walked towards him.

"It shouldn't take you longer than a day's ride. Don't be away too long, and send us a crow as soon as you know what the man wants."

"I will," Faremanne said.

"I don't feel comfortable with this," Bertrant muttered.

"We have no choice. Send for me if I'm not back in a few days." Faremanne kicked his horse. The riders turned their mounts and rode down the main alley to the border of the camp.

Faremanne had never met Elye. What Pembroke had said of the count made him feel uneasy. If the man was a weasel, they should not have sided with him, however powerful he might be. Maybe the man wanted to use the Rebellion for his own profit. Yet, they could not allow themselves to have several enemies. The orcs and the dragon were enough. Should Elye turn against them, the Rebellion would be trapped in a pincer movement, unable to move forward, unable to retreat, though Faremanne knew that his fellow captain did not tolerate the sound of this last word.

Faremanne wanted to fight, but he also wanted to live. He missed his family and children. He wondered if they would recognize him now, should he ever come back to the Windy Isles. He had looked like a lad when he had left, a foolish young knight ready to serve and protect his country. The three years had turned him into a man. He was sturdy, and his red hair was longer. He had grown a thick beard to mingle with the soldiers and assert his authority. *No*, Faremanne thought, *now that things are turning better for the Rebellion, we need to play it wisely*. They needed alliances, not cocky bravery. Running straight blindfolded would be madness. Yet, he did not hold the cards, and to have Louis change his mind was a lost cause. However, his companion would not be deaf to another tactic, should the result be the same.

They rode through forests and prairies at a steady pace. At the end of the day, Faremanne and his party were in sight of Mighthorn. In the distance, the city stood still in the shadow of the big stronghold on the hill. A troop of men rode their way, their mails glittering in the last rays of the sun. They were too numerous for a welcoming party. Something was amiss. The riders were on them in a moment. Their leader, a man, dressed in black robes with a cloak rimmed with grey fur, trotted towards him.

"I suppose you are Faremanne, Captain of the Rebellion," the man said. "Let me introduce myself. I am Count Elye."

The man had something queer in his bony face. Faremanne did not like his smile. It was more the premise of a rictus. He spotted an unpleasant light in the man's beady, dark eyes.

"I am Captain Faremanne, indeed," he said. "We have received your words, my lord. Yet, we do not understand them. You talk about a gift?"

"Hmm, straight to the point. I like resolute men." The count approached his horse. "A gift indeed, but a gift that needs spice. You see, to attract the enemy you need something he holds dear. Then, you light the fuse. You know, the little spark of tension to motivate the hunt." The man chuckled and wriggled on his saddle.

"Do you mean that you have something that belongs to Agroln?" Faremanne asked, confused.

"Well, not exactly…unless you are talking about his money. No, in this case, *you* are the enemy." The count grinned with the most vicious smile.

The pain in his abdomen was as sharp as it was sudden. Faremanne looked down. The quarrel had hit him between two plates of his fauld. His vision blurred and was speckled with white. He heard his men draw their swords. Faremanne collapsed onto his horse's collar.

"Arrest them!" Elye commanded. "If they resist, kill them. We don't need that many."

Faremanne grabbed his horse's mane, pulled the reins, and kicked the beast which jerked forward. It surprised Elye's mount, which reared. Faremanne rode through his men's line. While they charged and engaged the count's soldiers, Faremanne's horse galloped back east. With his last strength, he held fast to his horse's mane, letting his body bounce and jolt in the saddle.

97

"I promise to be careful," Josselin said, "but the only thing that matters is that I succeed with my mission."

Selen gave a faint smile. He felt sad for the young captain. It should not have been him. Actually, no one should undertake this mission. It was suicide and without the guarantee of success. Selen had doubts on the artifact. What did they have besides the false words of a vicious woman? They should have found another way.

"You make sure the beast eats it," Louis gave the pouch to Josselin. The captain opened it and contemplated the artifact.

"Such a little thing," Josselin whispered, "in such a giant monster." He looked at Louis. "I will. You have my word."

"And come back," Louis said, one hand on the captain's shoulder.

"If I don't, have a bard write songs about me," Josselin smiled. "The knight with the scar."

"Who defeated the dragon," Louis added seriously.

"Are you sure you don't want a company with you?" Selen asked.

"I will travel faster by myself. I don't think there is much danger in the east. The orcs are gathering south, and I don't want to draw attention," Josselin said.

"Good luck then." Selen and Louis embraced the captain before he got on his horse.

"Kill the orcs for me," Josselin told them. He kicked his horse and rode away east. Selen watched him disappear behind the tents.

"Men like him will be remembered," Selen heard Louis say.

"A dead hero?" Selen whispered.

"It's always better than a living coward," Louis said.

"I only want to be a living hero." Selen smiled, but it was only a façade.

Selen followed Louis to Bertrant's pavilion. Leaning above the maps, the commander was in a conversation with Pembroke.

"Here you are," Bertrant exclaimed. "Darn, I could count my captains on the hand of a leper."

"I thought you had at least two more?" Pembroke asked, puzzled.

"Boisterous elements. I gave them orders to control the camp's perimeter and the supply train," Bertrant replied.

"I still disapprove their implication in the supply train. There will be frauds," Louis complained.

"I don't doubt you will have an eye on it," Bertrant said. "Now, look here, both of you." He pointed at the map. "We are here, and here is Breyburgh, or what is left of it. The city has burned to the ground. Only charred walls and remnants of beams stand here and there and will collapse with the first heavy rains." Bertrant looked at Louis. "Did you speak with the survivors?"

"Hundreds of refugees are parked on the side of the camp. We talked with them this morning. They described how the orcs arrived in the city, massacring everyone. Many people fled, leaving all belongings behind. I proposed the men to join the Rebellion while their families would head to Millhaven." Louis stopped and frowned. Selen knew Louis had still not stomached their answer.

Selen continued the report in Louis's place. "A few accepted, but many chose to head north. I insisted that they get at least a one-day ration of food," Selen whispered the last part. It had been a source of tension between him and Louis. Hearing the refugees' refusal to his proposition, Louis had considered sending them away at once with nothing more than a kick in the rear. Selen had pleaded for mercy and reminded Louis that there were women and children as well. Louis had finally agreed, on the condition that they leave the camp at once. He had authorized a double ration of food to the women and children.

"Good. We can't afford to feed civilians." Bertrant pointed at the map again. "This is the way we have to follow if we want to reach Nysa Serin. South and down that plain, the Eryas Lowlands," Bertrant said.

"This is where the Rebellion was defeated by the dragon four years ago. It is barren lands. Only high, dry grass grows there. It was once a fertile plain, but not anymore since they built the Silverfall dam on the Falst River to irrigate the southern lands," Pembroke said.

"Where is the dam?" Selen asked.

"Here in the mountains." Bertrant pointed at a cross in the east of the plain where the mountains began.

"Oh no," Louis whispered.

"Do you see it too?" Bertrant asked. Selen feared he saw it as well.

"They will destroy the dam to inundate the plain. Preferably with us on it," Louis said.

"I did not understand first why no one attacked us," Bertrant said, "but I see it now. They don't need to attack. They only need to wait."

"Unless we take over the dam," Selen said.

"We can't. We are too big and slow to lead an attack in the mountains," Louis replied.

"We will have to divide our forces," Bertrant said. "A battalion will go to the mountains while the rest of the army will move south. Hopefully, Josselin is keeping the dragon away."

"I can lead the battalion," Louis proposed.

They heard screams come from outside.

Selen hurried outside the tent, followed by the others. A horse galloped towards the pavilion. The rider lay across the collar, his hands gripping the mane. Selen recognized Faremanne. He ran towards the horse and took down the captain. The man was covered in blood from the waist down. A crossbow bolt was set deep in his flank.

"Don't move," Selen said, holding the man still on the ground. "Someone give me water!"

Louis knelt on the other side. "What happened?" he cried out. Behind them, Bertrant shouted orders to bring the man to the infirmary.

A board was slipped under Faremanne, and four soldiers carried him to Brother Benedict's pavilion. Pembroke hurried to join them. Selen stood at Faremanne's side, washing the blood from his face and mouth. Louis strode on the other side, shouting to clear the way. At the infirmary, Faremanne was placed on a bed. His blood from the wound tainted the white sheets red.

"Remove his armour," the monk ordered.

"I need to cut the bolt first," Selen replied, looking behind him for help.

"Take this," Bertrant gave him tongs.

Selen took them and cut the bolt right above the armour. The metal snapped. Selen and Louis proceeded to remove the armour. Faremanne's gambeson and linen were soaking wet. "He has lost too much blood," Selen whispered. He took pincers to remove the bolt's head.

Faremanne opened his eyes. "Am I dying?" he asked with a feeble, croaky voice.

"Don't talk," Louis said, holding the man's hand. "You're not going to die."

Faremanne grinned. "You really can't lie," he coughed. The captain grabbed Louis's hand tighter and pulled it to him. "It was the count, Elye, he …"

"He betrayed us. We got it," Louis interrupted the captain.

"Shut up for once and listen," Faremanne snapped. "He's got my men as hostages and…he's got…something else." Faremanne coughed and spat blood clots. "Something precious. Louis, you need…to go there. Argh!"

The bolt went free. Selen cast it to the side and took clamps. "Hold the wound open," he said to Bertrant, who knelt at his side. Selen worked hard on the wound to block the bleeding. He pressed on the flesh where he thought the artery was, but the blood kept on spurting. Selen barely contained his anger enough to steady his hands. "I can't stop it. I can't clamp the artery. There is too much blood." He felt helpless. Tears came to his eyes. "Brother, you have to do it!"

"I won't do it better than you," Brother Benedict said, resigned. The monk looked at Faremanne with compassion.

"It's all right, Selen," Faremanne whispered. "Louis, you must free my men…"

"I will, I swear." Louis cried.

"Tell my family I love…" Faremanne sighed. He closed his eyes.

Heavy tears ran down Selen's cheeks. His throat choked with emotion. He laid his bloody left hand on the captain's right shoulder. On the other side of the bed, Louis clenched his fists on the man's hand and bedsheet. His jaws pulsed. Selen saw burning hate in his wet eyes.

"Blood will be shed," Bertrant said, hoarse. "Everyone, back to my tent."

Selen and Louis embraced their dead friend.

"We will give him a proper burial," Louis said to Brother Benedict with anger.

Selen, Louis, Bertrant, and Pembroke returned to the pavilion in mourning silence. Soon, they were back at the headquarters again. Their faces were red and their eyes swollen.

"I'm leaving at once with a battalion!" Louis exclaimed.

"Don't be a fool. It's exactly what the man wants," Pembroke replied.

"We need to act, but we need to plan it well. I don't want to lose more men to this," Bertrant said.

"I want to help," a silvery, appealing voice said. Folc walked towards them. The boy cried and his features were taut. They all looked at him, stunned.

"This is not the time for a young boy to take part in these matters, my lord," Bertrant objected.

"He was my friend as well as yours!" Folc shouted. "You will let me help. I too want revenge!"

"Folc…" Selen said. The boy was too young and inexperienced to be part of an expedition against the count. Selen did not want to lose another friend.

"No. That's enough with the coddling," Folc retorted towards him. "I'm not a child anymore. I am here to fight. Faremanne had always been good to me. He wanted me to be a knight. I will avenge him."

"The boy is right," Pembroke said. "Everyone has to do his part. He is ready enough for me."

"Then, that's settled," Bertrant said. "Folc will be part of the expedition."

Selen sighed. "What do we know about the castle? Has someone been there?" he inquired.

"It's a stronghold on a hill. The walls are ancient but thick. It's too uncovered to approach with riders without being seen from afar," Bertrant said. "I suppose the man will be expecting us."

"If he is waiting for a battalion, I could try to sneak inside with a small party of men," Louis suggested.

"I could help you with that," Folc said. "My parents and I stayed at Mighthorn a few times. I know of tunnels leading into the castle."

"Are they still in useful condition?" Louis asked.

"They were, some years ago."

"Then, we will use that way," Selen said. "It's a full moon. We could leave in an hour and take advantage of the night."

"No," Bertrant objected. "Not you."

"Not me?" Selen was puzzled. "But…"

"You will take a battalion and ride to the dam. We can't waste time with that. You need to attack simultaneously with Josselin while we progress south," Bertrant said.

"But…my lord." Selen gaped, searching for words. He gave an appealing look at Louis. His friend looked confused but did not dare to speak. There was nothing to say.

"It's an order," Bertrant insisted, inflexible. "You will lead the attack on the dam while Louis rescues our men. Louis, you leave in an hour." Bertrant's voice resounded in Selen's chest like the bang of a judge's gavel. The sentence was death. "Take your leave," Bertrant said.

Under shock, Selen gazed at the ground and walked outside the pavilion. He felt a hand on his wrist.

"Come," Folc said. "I'm sorry."

Once back in their tent, Selen sat on his bed, his eyes wide open. He could not grasp all that had happened. Faremanne first, then Bertrant's decision. It was a nightmare.

"We will make it," Folc said, confident. The boy put his armour on. "I know these tunnels well, and I promise to watch over Louis." Folc smiled.

"Maybe I won't make it," Selen said. He had no idea where he was heading. Every step he made in this land was a discovery, let alone to protect a structure he had never heard of.

"With a whole battalion? Of course you will."

Unless the orcs are waiting for us with a bigger army, Selen thought. He would have to send scouts ahead.

Louis entered the tent, looking overwhelmed. "I'm sorry, Selen. I could not object to his orders, not on that," his friend said. "Besides, he is right. We need to act now."

"I agree on the what. I am blocked on the how," Selen said, getting up.

"Don't be scared." Louis approached him. "I am sure you can make it." He smiled. Behind him, Folc tiptoed out of the tent.

"Me, leading a battalion?" It sounded awkward to his ears. He shook his head.

"You led that party brilliantly in Millhaven. I trust you." Louis put a hand on his shoulder.

Selen looked up. Louis was tired. His eyes were streaked with red. Even faint smiles could not hide his misery. "What about you?" Selen asked with concern.

"I have the boy to protect." A poor answer that his friend did not even try to enhance with a smile. Louis laid his hand on Selen's cheek. "I will avenge Faremanne," he said, resolute. Louis kissed him softly. His lips were full and warm. "I have to go," Louis whispered. The fingers left his cheek, but the sensation lingered.

Selen watched Louis walk away. His tormented heart hurt him as never before. It could not be, it would not be the last time. Then, he thought of Faremanne. He thought of Folc and his parents. His heart screamed. The words crossed his lips.

"Louis, wait!"

His friend halted.

"I see the sorrow that you hide deep in your soul. Fate has been hard on both of us, but you keep on fighting. I admire you. I have laid my heart in your hands from the start. You protect me. You hold my hands when I shiver with fear. The force I feel inside to carry on, I find it in you. Louis… I can be strong, but I can't live without you by my side. If we are to die…" Selen stopped. "I love you." He took a deep breath. "From the depths of my soul, I love you."

Louis turned around. "So many times I have lost hope. So many nights I have wanted to die. Then I look at you, my angel, my love…and I see a world worth fighting for. You keep your faith strong, even in the darkest hours, never asking for more than a smile. You are so pure, so kind, and yet so brave. We may lose the war. We may die on the field. Or we can survive and save this land. But it will be together. You and me." Tears ran down Louis's face. "Whatever tomorrow brings, I will love you, forever."

Chuckling and crying, Selen tottered to his friend and embraced him. Louis sobbed and chuckled. Grazing his trembling fingers on Selen's cheeks, he kissed him long and deeply. Selen's heart ignited with adoration. "I love you, Louis. I love you." He sniffled and pressed his forehead against Louis's.

"And I love you too. I always have." Louis hugged him tightly. "My Selen."

"It was about time," Folc said, looking at them with a broad smile.

98

For several days, Josselin rode east with haste through meadows and forests. Hoping to escape the notice of the enemy's eyes, he slept in hollow grounds or under thickets. As he did not dare to light a fire, he was perpetually cold. He had taken enough food with him to sustain himself during the journey. Alone with his thoughts, he had pondered his mission. Of course, it was suicide. He did not even hope to come back. But as he had said to his fellow captains, he wanted his death to be worth it. While he did not doubt the captains' bravery, he did not put much hope in the Rebellion, especially if no one could control the dragon. Josselin knew that his life was already ruined. With such a large scar on his face, he would never find someone, get married, or have children. Everyone looked at him with pity and commiseration, when not with disgust. Even his own aunt had asked him to return to his lands. Though she had insisted that he consider it as a reward for his services, he knew that the noble court of Millhaven could not bear his presence. Should he stay in the city, he would have to be confined to the army's barracks and fight until death called for him. Therefore, it might as well come now. Dying a hero was a beautiful way to leave this world.

The mountains were drawing nearer and bent southwards. He would reach Earthfell the next day. Josselin wondered which way would be the most effective to get the small artifact inside the dragon's belly. He could use an arrow and shoot into the beast's throat. However, this technique required perfect timing, and he wasn't skilled in archery. There was also the possibility of using bait. Earthfell would not lack sheep or cows to open and to fill with the artifact. Yet, it would have to be a living prey to attract the dragon, and to torture an animal was not his thing. Should he die, he would make it prestigious. He would be the bait.

"The bards will write songs about me," he whispered.

Earthfell stood at the foot of the mountains, dominating the grassy plains. It was perched high on the rocky, western slope. The city was circled by high, wooden walls. As opposed to Millhaven, Earthfell was entirely made of wood. The constructions denoted its archaic origins. The place, situated at a commercial crossroad, had been the center of horse breeding and trading for a long time. Now, goods coming from the Crysas Peninsula had replaced the horses. The trading was still flourishing, but no one had ever come up with the idea to modernize the battlements and the main buildings. Only the keep, rising high and proud into the sky, was made of grey stone. Josselin passed under the main gates. Despite its situation in the south of Trevalden, Earthfell retained the feel of a village of the Frozen Mountains. The city had been built in concentric circles, forming three distinct districts. The first district was the most populous and spread widely. It included most of the taverns as well as the shops and a broad marketplace. Josselin smelled the smoked meat and seasoned ham hanging on the hooks and felt tempted by the red apples displayed in the stall. He heard the banging of the smith's hammer coming from the smithy by the riverbank. On this bright day of late spring, the atmosphere was joyful, each conducting his daily business. The streets were tightly packed. Josselin focused on his mission and moved his mount towards the second district, where the residences of the rich families stood. From there, he headed to the last district. He crossed a bridge and passed in front of the temple. It was constructed in the style of the great Nordic longhouses, with carved patterns painted in red on the beams.

Josselin had not met a single orc during his progression through the city. Still, it did not mean that the inhabitants would welcome a captain of the Rebellion. Some cities like Embermire or Earthfell had chosen a relative neutrality. They would pay a heavy tribute in exchange for their preservation and the lives of their people. Occasionally, they would deliver traitors to the king to prove their good will. The tragic fate of Millhaven had proven to be an effective example to turbulent cities.

Between the temple and the keep, a stony path wound its way upwards to the mountains. Josselin followed it. There, between the cliffs and large boulders overhanging Earthfell, should lie the dragon's lair. He had reached the first level of the path when light glowed through his pocket. Josselin took out the bag containing the artifact. The amulet hummed and irradiated white. Something was peculiar with the humming. Josselin raised the object to his ear. He listened. It was no humming—the artifact sang.

"It's a call," he whispered. "The amulet is calling for the dragon."

He realized with horror what that meant. For a moment, he did not know if he should gallop higher on the path, away from Earthfell, or if he should hurry down and raise the alarm. From behind the first cliffs in the east came a steady flapping sound similar to giant sails unfolding in the wind, but Josselin knew that the sea was far. He raised his head and gazed at the sky as the buzzing grew. It was too late for the alarm.

The black shape passed over him, covering him with its shadow in a split second. Josselin's horse stumbled backwards as he pulled on the reins. The dragon whirled around over the city. The scales on its broad body shone with the color of amber. It had the wings of a bat and was at least the size of two longships. Rows of bony plates ran down its back.

In the first district, black dots hurried in every direction. The beast came back on them, searching the ground like a bird of prey. The guards on the battlements shot their first arrows. Josselin judged it useless and foolish. It only increased the aggressiveness of the beast. The lean neck glowed crimson. As the wide jaws opened, the flames gushed out, down to the wooden palisade. Josselin heard bells resound. As soon as they heard the bong of the tocsin, people rushed out of every house, including the keep and the temple. The dragon spat more flames. It looked up and saw him.

The dragon's massive head turned towards Josselin in a brisk move, its antennae extended straight up from its forehead. The dragon's ruby eyes glimmered wickedly within the creature's angular, hard skull. Even at such a distance, he felt the warm air blown through the giant nostrils. Frightened, Josselin's mount reared and headed down the path, wild. He fell from the saddle and rolled down on the slope, using his arms to protect his neck. The dragon flew and landed on the roof of the temple, crushing it under its weight. The beast gave out a strident, metallic shrill. It pierced his ears and froze his blood. Yet, Josselin did not feel cold. The flames had spread in the wind. The city burned like a torch. Around him rose columns of fire, twisting and swirling like tornadoes. Earthfell had turned into the pit of hell. He heard screams in the distance, covered by the thundering shrieks of collapsing metal and burning beams. The sky, which had been so bright an hour ago, was dark as night as the smoke rose higher and higher.

Josselin got up. The dragon uttered another roar, deeper and more threatening this time. It headed in his direction. Its ponderous limbs smashed the bridge and stone parapets. Josselin drew his sword from its scabbard and raised it in front of him in a pathetic attempt at defense. The dragon ran and snapped in the air. Josselin plunged and rolled on the side. The beast twirled and cracked its long tail like a whip, sweeping the house roofs that stood in the way. Josselin prepared himself for the second attack. As the beast charged, he ran on its side, revolving his sword against the front legs. The metal blade barely scratched the scales. Josselin knew it was hopeless. He stood straight and took the artifact in his hand. It glowed like a beacon in the night. He raised his left arm high above him. The dragon gazed at his hand with covetousness.

"This is what you want," Josselin muttered. "Then come and get it."

The knight ran straight forward with a long scream, ready to be eaten alive. The dragon rushed from the opposite side, quaking the earth, but instead of aiming for his body and swallowing him whole, the beast aimed for his hand. The huge jaws clasped violently around his gauntlet, projecting Josselin backwards and carrying him into the air as the beast took its flight. The pain was insufferable. With his last strength, Josselin raised his sword in his right hand and drove it in under the dragon's eye. The beast clenched its jaws, chopping off his arm and swallowing it. Josselin fell towards the ground, blood gushing in the air from where his left arm had been. He hoped the songs would mention that too.

49

Ominous clouds hurried overhead, dark and low. The long shadows of the evening fell on the fields. Louis journeyed west with a small party of trustworthy soldiers. Folc rode at his side. They had stayed off of the main road and had followed narrow paths among the growing wheat fields. Louis knew that their expedition was a perilous one. Should the tunnels be trapped or blocked, they would be unable to enter the stronghold. Besides, Elye had proved that he did not hesitate to kill men of the Rebellion, even captains.

However, Louis was lighthearted. The weight of years of torment had fallen from his shoulders. He felt one again proud of who he was and of who he had been. Furthermore, he had sworn to his love that he would come back. Love. He enjoyed the word, now fully assumed. Folc had promised to tell no one, and he knew he could trust the boy. For an instant, he had yearned to stay, Selen tucked in his arms. Yet, those were not virtuous thoughts, and he had swept them aside. He had sworn an oath to Faremanne.

They progressed under the cover of night. Eventually, they came in sight of Mighthorn.

"There stands the castle," Folc said, pointing at the gloomy stronghold. It stood out in the moonlight, overshadowing the city below. Beacons on the battlements glowed red. "The tunnel's entrance should be in the patch of woods up there." The boy moved his finger to the trees on the hill at their right.

They wound up the steep path leading to the woods. As they rode up the hill, Louis felt the first drops of water fall on him. Once they were under the trees, the rain poured down in buckets. His long hair was plastered to his neck and cheeks. In the darkness, it was not easy for Folc to find his landmarks. They searched the thickets for a while before finding the entrance.

"It's here!" Folc exclaimed.

The wind roared, and they could barely hear each other. Where his body was not covered by his armour, Louis was soaked to the bone. The tunnel's opening was too low for the horses to get in. Therefore, they tied their mounts' bridles to branches before taking shelter under the entrance.

"I hope you know the place well, Folc," Louis said, "because I don't think we can light a fire or find dry wood with this rain. We have no means to make torches. We will have to creep in utter darkness. It's not a maze, is it?"

"No, it's not a maze, but there are different rooms. We must walk straight ahead or we could stay lost for a long time," Folc answered. Louis did not feel reassured at all. "Follow me," the boy said.

They advanced with caution in the darkness, each following the man in front closely. They were all ears to any noise that could announce danger. A cool draft was blowing in their faces. Louis grazed the wall on his right with his gauntlet. He felt fissures and crusts of mud. The humidity of the moss growing on the wall pierced through his leather gloves. From the ceiling, unseen water dripped into pools where their sabatons tramped in loud splashes. Louis dragged his frozen feet slowly, afraid to fall into a hidden crack in the ground.

They soon lost all notion of time. For what seemed like hours, they met no danger, saw nothing, and heard nothing but their own breathing. The moist air grew hot and stifling, but it smelled of only earth and roots. The passage wound steadily upwards. Sometimes, Louis's hand lost contact with the wall. He remembered that the boy had talked about rooms opening on the side. He stretched his hand and laid it on Folc's shoulder instead. They kept moving on.

The boy slipped under his hand with a scream. Louis heard a loud splash.

"Folc!" he shouted. He knelt and stretched out his hand. It plunged into water. He swirled it around and met Folc's arm.

"I'm all right," Folc said. "This room is partially inundated now, but we can still cross to the other side. I can touch bottom."

"How can you find your way in that?" Louis muttered. He slipped into the ice-cold water with a gasp. The water level reached his chest, which meant that Folc had barely his head out. He followed the wash made by Folc. Behind him, the men cursed as they entered the water. Pieces of wood and rubbish floated around them. Louis felt something creep onto his hair. He struggled, horrified.

"Something climbed up on me!" he shouted. The thing had fallen into the water again. Louis's heart beat fast.

"Did you see what it was?" Folc asked.

"A rat maybe, or a mouse," Louis said. "I couldn't *see*. We have to get out of the water, fast."

On the other side of the room, they reached a stone stair. As Louis climbed the steps, water flew from under his plates. It turned into trickles. With the padding and his linen soaking wet, his armour felt like twice its weight. Furthermore, with his hair cold and wet on his neck, Louis was freezing.

"I think we are in the underground of the prison tower," Folc whispered.

"How can you know that?" Louis asked.

"I tramped on a human bone."

Louis thought that he glimpsed bars to his right. Something metallic shone. He saw a faint glow in the distance. They drew nearer silently. The group arrived in a poorly lit cellar. Casks had been stored on the side. A torch, hung to the stone wall, burned low. Faint whimpers could be heard in the distance. Louis looked at his men and communicated his plans by signs. While tiptoeing against the wall, he drew out his dagger. He glimpsed at the corner of the next opening.

A guard sat at a small table, his back turned towards him. Further away, jails were packed with men, their men. The wall turned at an angle. Louis did not see more guards, but he guessed that, considering the thickness of the bars, strict surveillance was not necessary. Without a sound, he moved to the guard on the chair, put his hand on the man's mouth, and slit his throat clean. The gushing of the blood attracted the attention of the prisoners. Louis put a finger on his lips and progressed into the room, following the wall. One of the prisoners lifted two fingers. Louis unsheathed his sword. He took a deep breath and turned the corner.

The two guards rose, startled. Louis's dagger reached the first one in the throat as he tried to flee. The other guard grabbed an axe, but he had not raised it high when Louis's sword severed his belly in two gaping red lips. Louis turned around, spun his sword, and chopped the man's head off. The jail's keys on the man's belt shone in the torchlight. He picked them up and ran to the jail's gate.

"Don't make any noise," Louis whispered. "How many of you are still alive?"

"We were around seventy when we were brought here, my captain. But the men are scattered in the whole tower," one soldier responded.

"We will have to take over the tower then," Louis said. "We are only a handful, so you will have to manage it yourself. Can you do that?"

"Yes, my captain," the man said, resolute.

Furtive as cats, and using ruses, the soldiers moved through the different rooms of the tower. They picked up weapons and freed their comrades. Louis had ordered them to take over the whole tower before stepping outside. He supervised the operation from the staircase. The more they grew in numbers, the better. Louis sent the soldiers clean each level one after the other. In the end, it was only Folc and him left. They climbed the snail stairs swiftly and reached the last level of the tower.

"This is the last door," Folc whispered.

"Good. Once we're done here, we rush inside the yard," Louis said, pushing the key into the keyhole. He opened the door.

Louis tried to adapt his eyes to the light, thinking he was hallucinating, but his vision was clear. "Lilo?"

The two prisoners in front of him rose. "Louis? Louis, is that you?" Lissandro exclaimed, incredulous. "Louis! You look terrible."

"Yes, I know. I am glad to see you too."

Folc opened the cage. Lissandro rushed into Louis's arms. The two men embraced each other warmly. "Did you go through the sewers?" Lissandro asked, looking at him and wrinkling his nose.

"I don't know what I went through, but I intend to leave this place by the main door. Come." Louis paused and stared at the other prisoner. The woman was approximatively their age. She had short, dark hair and doe eyes. Though she had a long scar on her cheek and some bruises, she was comely in her way. Yet, she looked miserable and was dressed in rags. "Who is she?" he asked Lissandro.

"Oh! I'm sorry. This is Kilda," Lissandro said. "Kilda, this is Louis."

"Is he your dear one?" the woman asked, confused.

"No, not him," Lissandro answered with a blush, "but he is a friend. He will get us out." Lissandro turned to Louis. "Kilda is a valiant knight, but they took her armour." He moved against him. "Elye mistreated her," he whispered in his ear.

Disgusting bastard, Louis thought. The man sickened him. He felt compassion for Kilda. "You think you can follow us?" he asked.

She nodded.

They went down the stairs. The soldiers had freed every prisoner, even people unknown to the Rebellion, and had taken the guards' weapons. They now gathered in the large room in front of the entrance door. A lieutenant came to talk to Louis in private.

"We found a room, my captain." The man was under shock. "A torture chamber. I have never seen anything like it in my whole life. There were corpses at different stages…and cages. We asked the guards what it was for before we killed them."

"And?" Louis pressed the lieutenant.

"They said it was…a command for the king."

"Did you free all who could be freed?"

"Yes, my captain."

"Good." Louis did not want to investigate deeper on that now. For some people, there were no limits in crime. Louis moved to the door and faced the men.

"We need to reach the keep before they seal it," Louis said. "How far is it from here?"

"It's only a few yards away, but we need to pass in front of the kennels. It won't be silent," a soldier answered.

"How do you evaluate their forces?" Louis inquired.

"I would say two hundred men, but we have already killed some here. Maybe a hundred and fifty. We need more weapons if we want to fight."

"More weapons won't help us if they block the keep. You will need to take whatever sharp object we find on the way. Those of you who already have a weapon can follow me on the front line," Louis told them. "Whatever we see out there, don't stop. Now, on my move." He took a deep breath and slammed the door open.

They rushed into the yard, slicing and chopping everyone they found on their way. On their right side, the dogs in the kennels barked wildly, raising the alarm. Louis and the soldiers hurried up the staircase leading to the keep's heavy oak gates.

"Watch out for archers!" Louis yelled as he pushed the left side of the door with all his strength.

Guards were waiting for them in the hall inside, but they were unprepared and were soon overrun. The soldiers of the Rebellion progressed inside the keep, picking up weapons as the enemy collapsed. They visited the rooms one after another—the chambers, the kitchen and the halls, killing men on sight. Blood jetted onto the walls. People caught in their beds in the middle of the night screamed of terror. No one was spared.

Louis ran upstairs, followed by a group of soldiers. "I want Elye alive, you hear me?" he shouted.

The great hall was empty, but a door at the end of the room stood ajar. He ran to it. Elye's soldiers hurried down the staircase. Louis threw his sword at them. His blood burned in his veins. He felt only the need to kill every living soul in this wretched place. Too many of his friends and innocent victims had suffered by the count's hands. The last guard stumbled in front of him. Louis drew his sword out of the man's chest. When he entered the room at the top of the stairs, Elye stood by the fire in the solar.

"You were more cunning than I thought," the man said, steadfast. Though he had lost, the count showed no sign of fear. "Now, I suppose you will kill me?"

"No," Louis said. He grasped the man by the shoulder and pushed him down the stairs, holding his arm fast.

When Louis appeared outside the keep, pushing the count in front of him, the soldiers had already gathered in the yard. With one harsh push, Elye fell down the stairs, then rose. He stood alone, facing his former captives.

Louis placed himself in front of Elye. He was half covered in dry mud, half covered in blood. His hair, shaggy and soiled, fell on his face. With one hand, Louis grabbed the man's jaw. With the other, he laid his dagger under the count's left eye.

"Faremanne is dead," he muttered with rage.

The count stared at him with contempt. He reminded Louis of Segar. More, he reminded Louis of all these dragons who had led to his and his previous love's downfall, vicious, corrupted men. His dagger trailed slowly down, cutting the flesh of the man's cheek.

"I would love to kill you," he whispered, "but you are not mine." Louis moved his dagger away and stepped back. He turned to the crowd and walked towards Kilda. "He is yours." He gave her his dagger. "Make him pay."

Still trembling, Kilda moved forward with insecure steps. She stopped in front of Elye. The tall, wretched woman rose straight, facing her torturer, looking him in the eyes. Elye shrieked when she stabbed him in the crotch with the dagger. She pulled out the blade and slit his throat. Elye's body fell on the pavement in a pool of his own blood. *That was tough*, Louis thought, impressed. Behind him, the crowd of soldiers roared in approval.

"What should we do with the prisoners?" one of the lieutenants asked Louis.

"Kill them. Kill them all and burn this place down. Send the villagers you rescued back home and take all the horses. We're leaving." He turned to Lissandro. "Help her retrieve her armour and join me in the stables."

Louis went to the stables with Folc and saddled horses for himself and his friends.

Lissandro joined them. At his side, the woman had put her armour on. Louis did not approve of women soldiers, yet, he had to admit that she did look like a knight. They mounted and led their horses into the courtyard.

As Louis rode through the gatehouse over the drawbridge, Lissandro, Folc, and Kilda by his sides, the flames of the braziers licked at the walls outside the windows, reaching for the roof. Soon, Mighthorn Keep would be ashes. Blood had been shed.

50

They had a long distance to cover. The dam was many miles further south, in the first hills of the mountains. Selen rode at the head of over a thousand soldiers. He did not know which title applied to him now, as he had four of Pembroke's captains under his command. He should have squirmed. He always had hated to be the center of attention. Yet, today, he was too happy to care. Love filled his heart. He was glad to ride at the front. No one could see him smile stupidly for hours. He barely considered that something could happen to him. He knew that of both of their missions, his was the most dangerous one. The orcs never took prisoners. Yet, the size of his battalion made him feel invincible.

Once again, the mission he had to accomplish was decisive for the Rebellion. He had asked for experienced riders with light armours. Normally, it would take two days for a company to make the journey, but Selen wanted the battalion to reach the dam at dawn. They would push their mounts to their limits, first heading south. Then, they would take advantage of the night and turn east, up the river. Promptness seemed the only way for Selen to take the enemy unprepared. Once the battle was over, they would have to ride back as soon as they could. The Rebellion already marched to the Eryas Lowlands and would wait north of the plain for their return.

The forests had made a place for golden fields and green prairies. They had probably been spotted, but it was not sure that the enemy would understand their motives. Selen hoped that no army rode on them from the south. He had sent scouts to explore the way ahead and waited impatiently for their return.

Nightfall came. Selen ordered a short break to let the horses rest a while. He wanted them to act quickly, but he did not want to kill the poor beasts. They had not bothered to carry tents or materials. Each man had the responsibility to tend to his needs. Selen had also forbidden them to light any fire. In such an open range, their moves would be spotted easily. In his previous life, Selen had heard of ferocious tribes of riders launching raids on cities and strategic points. It was exactly what he meant to do, apart from the fact that he was all but ferocious.

He heard noises in the night. The scouts were back. He headed to them.

"We have seen the dam, my captain!" one of the men exclaimed. "There is an army of orcs guarding it."

"What of their strength?" Selen inquired.

"We could not see the whole of them, but I would say inferior to us. Yet, the dam is high. They have the advantage."

"Is there anything we can use to hide our approach? Forest, bushes?" The worst would be to progress in the open, with the orcs archers aiming at them.

"There are woods in the valley and on the slopes of the hills."

"Good. Do you think you can make the way back in the middle of the night?" Selen asked.

"I can, my captain. It's right ahead along the river. The orcs are too confident. There are no sentinels."

"Give your horse a rest. We depart in a few hours," Selen said.

The gorges were narrow. The basin and the bottoms of the hills were covered with lobe-leaved trees, which, with the altitude, gave way to pine trees. The tops of the hills were bare and rocky. Patches of snow glittered on the summit.

It was an arch dam. The size of it was breathtaking. A long lake spread on the other side. Its deep blue water shimmered in the sunlight. The slopes rose steeply above the water's surface. Selen thought that the dam was probably used to irrigate the fields in the plains. It was also a perfect reservoir to supply water to Nysa Serin during the dry season.

"The horses would have never made it," Selen said, observing the site. He was glad to have left their mounts in the woods before the gorges. Only men on foot could climb such slopes.

Orcs bustled about everywhere on the dam like industrious ants. They had not pierced through yet. The foul creatures hung scaffoldings and ropes on the wall. They planned to weaken the structure at different places.

"If the dam explodes, everything along the river will be destroyed," Selen muttered. He turned to the captains. "I want you to divide your forces into three groups. Two to climb on each side and one to form a rear line, which will block the way in the basin and shoot at the orcs hanging on the ropes. The beasts may be expecting us, so walk warily and try to take them from above," Selen said, forming a semicircle with his hand. "And remember. No prisoners." After all they had done, none of these beasts deserved pity.

They all rose. The captains departed to take their positions. Selen knew he had a special task to undertake. This time, he would not let the monster escape.

Selen led the group on the eastern slope. He and his men jogged long through the woods, holding on to branches and roots, hopping on boulders like goats. The soldiers climbed as high as they could to the edge of the forest and the pines. When they reached the level of the lake, Selen raised his hand to give the signal to run down towards the dam. The slope was so abrupt that it was hard not to stumble forward. As he saw the first orcs, Selen drew out his sword. The men around him screamed wildly. The hunt began. For once, the predator was the prey.

The first line of orcs, taken by surprise, retreated in panic. Selen's soldiers crashed on them like a wave. Selen knew that on the other side of the dam, four hundred men blocked the only way out. He swirled his swords and hacked, pushing the enemy nearer to the lake or to the precipice. Orcs stampeded and jumped into the water, where they drowned.

"Force the orcs downhill!" Selen shouted. "Towards our lines!"

While the majority of the men rushed down in pursuit, Selen and a party halted by the dam's crest. From the bridge, orcs shot arrows at their men in the basin. In the middle of the line of filthy creatures stood Kraalh. Selen repressed the fright he felt having to face such a greenish monstrosity. He thought of all the dead bodies the orcs had left; he thought of the children. He was not used to feeling hate, but the hate he had awakened towards the orcs was beyond measure.

While his men engaged against the orcs, Selen climbed onto the rim of the bridge and brandished his sword towards the general, challenging him.

"Kraalh!" he yelled at the top of his lungs.

Kraalh gazed in his direction, wrinkling his nose. With a deafening roar, the beast raised his axe high. Selen jumped on the crest and raced forward, pushing aside the last enemies still standing. Kraalh rushed from the other side, his feet pounding on the ground.

The two opponents reached the middle of the crest. Kraalh spun his axe towards him in a killing arc. His black braids and loincloth flapped in the wind. Selen bent at the knees and dodged low. With the speed, his greaves grated against the stone. He grazed the ground with his back and saw the blade pass over him. He jumped up and moved right.

"Where are you going, little squirrel?" the general brawled. He rotated his axe and cleft the crest in a savage blow a few inches from Selen, who stumbled. The stone exploded into grit.

Selen got up and noticed that he was trapped. He could not circle the huge orc on such a narrow bridge. He would have to wait for an opening and enter the orc's reach, if he could wait that long. Compared to the axe, his sword looked like a toy in his hand. To try to block the blows would be madness. The axe crushed the stone again, this time on his left. Selen rolled in the dirt.

"You can't escape me, wench!" Kraalh shouted. "Soon you will be mine!"

Selen's eyes narrowed. "I will kill you! As I killed Xruul!" he shouted at the revolting thing towering over him.

"Xruul was my son!" Kraalh yelled and threw his axe.

Selen avoided the blow but hit the rim hard with his chest. "A stupid, ugly son," he replied, coughing.

"I will chain you as my bed slave, she-knight. We will then see how proud you will be," the general growled with fury. The axe swirled.

Selen saw the opening. He jumped towards Kraalh's legs with his sword high and cut the flesh on the left thigh.

Kraalh roared. "I will tame you." The orc turned around, limping. "And if you can't be tamed, I will impale you, like all the others," he groaned.

He is slow, Selen thought, *strong, but slow*. Selen felt his heart race. He was getting exhausted. He had to win, now. The blade of the axe fell behind him, blocking the way. Kraalh staggered. The general raised his muscular arms for another blow. Selen saw the move, jumped along Kraalh's arm, a foot on the heavy axe's blade, and stabbed the orc through the shoulder with his sword. Kraalh roared in pain but still stood up, with Selen hanging on his shoulder. Selen's gauntlet was fastened on the hilt. He tried to pull his sword out. His limbs, clenched around the orc's torso, kicked and punched. His face had never been so close to Kraalh's. He looked into his shiny, nasty, black eyes and gulped. The orc's strong jaws opened, the long fangs bending in his direction.

"Is it your dagger you want, pretty girl?" Kraalh asked. His breath had the strong odor of apple mixed with the acrid smell of sweat. The orc put his right hand on the hilt over Selen's hand.

"I will kill you," Selen whispered. Tears of rage blurred his vision.

Kraalh pulled the sword out of his shoulder and hurled Selen against the rim in gushes of slimy blood. Selen screamed in pain as his back hit the stone.

"Fool! No bitch will kill me!" the general yelled.

Ignoring the throbbing ache in his back, Selen squatted. "Good news, I'm a man." He stretched, dipped, and jumped. As his body flew in an aerial cartwheel, his foot hit Kraalh violently in the throat.

Kraalh raised his arms as he stumbled backwards, but he grabbed only thin air. The orc fell over the rim, down the precipice.

Selen landed back on the bridge, a few inches from falling into the lake on the other side. He got up and looked down. All he saw of Kraalh was a greenish-black heap. Selen cleared his throat and spat. He looked around. The men downhill raised their swords to him and shouted. He hailed them back. They had won.

"We can cross the plains, my love," he whispered. His hate was gone.

51

The smell of burning wood spread on for miles. As radical as it had sounded, Lissandro had approved Louis's decision. Lissandro was a child of darkness. In his world, fire was the only way of purification, and he knew too well how much this place had needed to be cleansed.

They had headed east along the main road. The first rays of sun shone a light on their condition. The men were shaggy and dirty, especially Louis and his party. Furthermore, they all looked exhausted. Lissandro rode alongside Louis.

"As soon as I see a brook or whatever running water, we take a break. I'm so grubby that it gives me a headache," Louis said. "Then, I want to hear all about your journey. I am so relieved to know you are all right." His friend smiled at him, half of his face mucked up with brownish bloodstains.

They stopped by a river a few miles ahead. The horses were brought together and wood was gathered for campfires. The dirtiest soldiers strolled to the river and washed in the cold, fresh water. Though he was their captain, Louis mingled with his men. Lissandro went with Kilda upstream where she could have some privacy, away from all those naked men.

They found a nice spot with grassy slopes and a small, stone beach. Lissandro sat on the green grass and faced the forest while Kilda undressed and bathed. She had stayed silent since their departure.

"Would you like to stay with us in the Rebellion? I can ask Louis if it's what you wish," Lissandro proposed.

"Do you think they will accept me?" she asked, worried.

"Considering the way you killed Elye, I would say that no man would dare to mess with you now," he laughed.

Kilda chuckled. "Was Louis the man you waved at in Embermire? I thought the man looked different."

"It wasn't Louis I saw in Embermire but my friend, Selen. There is no doubt Selen will stand in your favour to stay with us." Lissandro thought that if someone could understand Kilda, it would be Selen.

"You can take my place. I'm done bathing," she said. He heard the splashes of water as she walked towards the beach.

Lissandro undressed and went to the river while Kilda dried herself on the shore. Once they were clean and dressed, they headed back to the bivouac.

They sat by a fire at the edge of the group. Lissandro still felt like an outsider and did not dare to socialize with the soldiers.

Louis came to them. His skin was white again. His hair dried and fell wild about his shoulders. His half-open, wet shirt stuck to his skin, but Lissandro guessed that his friend did not want to present himself bare-chested in front of a lady. The sight made Lissandro blush, and he looked at Kilda instead. She had turned her face towards him and her cheeks were flushed. Kilda noticed his uneasiness and laughed heartily. Lissandro was glad to hear her laugh.

"I'm glad you both are in such a bright mood," Louis said. He sat down cross-legged in front of them. "Now, tell me what happened to you."

"To make it short, after I lost you, I wandered through the Ebony Forest for days until I found Kilda," Lissandro said, "or to be exact, until Kilda took me as her prisoner. She brought me to a bandit camp to exchange me for a ransom." Lissandro saw Louis's gaze turn hard. "But she is not a bad person!" Lissandro exclaimed. "She was fooled by the bandits. She thought they wanted to help the population. Once she learned the truth, she freed me and we ran away together. Unfortunately, we got captured by Elye." Lissandro leaned towards his friend. "There is something more of great importance, but I think I should develop it once we arrive at the camp. Selen must learn about it too." A shadow crossed over his friend's face. "What? Has something happened to Selen?"

"No!" Louis exclaimed. "I hope not. He went on a mission against the orcs in the east. This is why I want to be back as soon as possible."

"I understand," Lissandro said. He saw that his friend was anxious and changed the conversation. "How is it that you ended up commanding an army?"

"I do not command the army. I am only a captain. Bertrant is in charge of the Rebellion. We thought joining this army was the only solution to progress through the country. Now that we have seen what this land has been through, we have to win the war. We have already freed Millhaven. Now, the army marches on Nysa Serin. A decisive battle awaits." While Louis spoke, Folc came towards them and sat by the fire.

"I have missed so much," Lissandro said, overwhelmed by the events.

"You are safe and with us. That is the most important. You will fight by our side," Louis said, putting a hand on his shoulder.

"Louis, I must ask. Can my friend Kilda join us in the Rebellion?" Lissandro asked with an appealing look.

Louis was silent for a moment as if he pondered the idea. "I have forbidden women in the camp. Yet, it was mainly to prevent prostitution. Your friend is a warrior, if I can say so, and you owe her your life."

"I want to fight for our land. Besides, I have nowhere else to go," Kilda said in her favour.

"Your wish is legitimate. Maybe as long as you keep your armour on and stay in your tent most of the time," Louis said. Lissandro saw that he was still uneasy. "I don't want you to create trouble. The men may feel provoked."

"With what she did to Elye?" Lissandro intervened.

"Yes, I know. I had Selen do…" Louis interrupted himself. "But it's not only up to me. I will have to talk to Bertrant."

"Come on. You can nag him into having her in," Folc added. "Don't search for excuses."

Louis frowned. He did not appreciate the boy's tone, yet he did not reprimand Folc.

Louis sighed. "All right. She can come." Lissandro grinned at Kilda and felt Louis pull him up by the arm. "Now, I would have a word with you." His friend dragged him further away.

"Dear one?" Louis's narrow eyes were sharp as a blade. Lissandro had forgotten that detail. He squirmed.

"I may have had a light moment of weakness at the darkest hour…" Lissandro muttered, looking at the waving grass around his feet.

"How much does she know?" Louis asked, exasperated.

"All…about me. She does not know about our death, our quest or…" Lissandro looked at his friend. "But I think we can trust her," he hurried to say.

"How well do you know her?"

"I know her husband died fighting with the Rebellion, that she wants to avenge him, and that she hates Lord Pembroke of Embermire." Lissandro saw Louis's face fall.

"Pembroke is right here alongside Bertrant at the head of the Rebellion," Louis hissed, grabbing his arm. "What if I bring her there and she kills him? And what if I tell her I won't take her along, and she makes a scandal about what you are? Do you have any idea how hard I have worked here? You imbecile!"

Lissandro stayed silent. He knew how deeply he had screwed up. "I'm sorry," was all he could say.

Louis calmed down. "You could not have known. I will talk to her."

They went back to the fire where Folc and Kilda sat, chatting together. Louis knelt down. "Kilda. Pembroke is one of the commanders of the Rebellion. Whatever the grievance you have against him, if you kill him, you endanger all of us." Louis gestured with his hand. "The boy, my friends, and I. Not to mention the chaos it will create in the camp. Be sure I won't let that happen." Lissandro thought that she understood.

"I hate the count with all my strength, but I will be eternally grateful to Lissandro and to you for rescuing me. I can wait until the war takes him," she said, sounding sincere, "but I will not fight for him."

"No one fights for a lord here. We fight for our country," Louis replied. He got up and went back to his soldiers.

"Did I put you in trouble?" Kilda asked.

"I don't know, but it's not your fault," Lissandro said. "Come. Let's pack our horses."

The Rebellion had marched southwards and had set the camp north of the Eryas Lowlands. When Lissandro and his group arrived, the tents were already pitched, the flaps clapping in the sharp wind. Louis dismissed the men and rode to the headquarters with Lissandro, Kilda, and Folc.

"It seems your expedition was a success!" a jovial, overweight man, that Lissandro supposed to be Bertrant, exclaimed, coming to them.

"We freed the men, Commander. Elye is dead," Louis answered. "I come back with an old friend and his companion. I considered they could be good recruits."

Bertrant gazed at them. "I don't want to misjudge your perception, Louis,"

Bertrant said, doubtful, "but you are conscious that one of them is a woman, a real woman?"

"I'm not blind," Louis sighed. "She is, above all, a warrior. She killed Elye." Louis held Bertrant's look.

"Your rules…" Bertrant insisted.

"Do you really think someone could confound this woman with a prostitute?"

Lissandro looked at Kilda. The adjective ferocious suited her better than sexy or lascivious, if these terms could ever be applied to her.

"Well, we only have one decisive battle to fight. It's not as if we were preparing ourselves to pass winter. But she stays in her tent."

"She will. I insisted on that. Thank you, Commander," Louis said.

"Lady Hewald!" Pembroke stood by the headquarters' entrance. He looked aghast.

Lissandro saw Bertrant's puzzled face and the appealing look Louis gave Kilda.

"Lord Pembroke," she answered with an ice-cold voice.

There was a moment of silence where no one dared to react. Pembroke drew nearer. "I know you have reasons to hate me, my lady," the lord said, "and I have no excuses. If I am responsible for your presence today, and your present state, I will do all that is in my power to help you." The count bowed and looked down. Lissandro judged the man sincere.

"I want to fight, and I want justice," Kilda said.

"Then, we welcome you in the Rebellion," Pembroke said.

They dismounted. Soldiers took their horses to the corral.

"Any news from the east?" Louis inquired eagerly.

"Nothing," Bertrant answered with a troubled face. "We must wait." The commander turned to him. "What is your name, young man?"

"My name is Lissandro, Commander. I am an archer from the Windy Isles. I can tend to the security of Lady Hewald if you wish, my lord," he proposed.

"Do it," Bertrant approved. "You will have a tent next to hers."

They heard shouts come from the east side of the camp. Soldiers ran towards them. "My lords! Commander!" The men looked troubled.

"What is it?" Louis asked sharply with apprehension.

"Refugees coming from Earthfell. The city has been burned!"

52

The man had looked sincere. Yet, she still hated him. However, her friends could suffer from her actions. Kilda decided not to take her revenge, after all. Pembroke may die during the war anyway.

As she had to stay in her tent, she had used her time cleaning her armour and weapons. Lissandro had visited her a few times to see if she needed anything. He had brought her food and found her new linen. They were men's clothing, but they were still in a better state than her tattered clothes.

The whole day had passed, and she was getting bored. She thought that maybe she could venture to the infirmary. She could always pretend a headache or a sickness of some sort. Kilda put her armour on and plastered her short hair to look even more masculine. Hopefully, the scar on her cheek would repel the men. She went out.

The evening air was fresh and moist. The first stars shimmered in the sky. Between the braziers, the soldiers strolled back to their tents, casting long shadows on the white fabric. Kilda walked by the tents, unnoticed. The atmosphere was jovial. There were no drunkards or fights as she would have expected. Confusing her for one of their own, some men hailed her for a drink. She gestured a refusal.

The infirmary was generously lit. Most of the refugees of Earthfell occupied the beds. There were people of all ages. They had probably thought that the Rebellion would protect them from the dragon. Obviously, they could not stay in the camp and would be sent to Millhaven on the morrow, unless some men decided to join their ranks. Kilda walked between the beds, looking at the sobbing faces and burned limbs. She remembered the villagers in their cages. So many innocents. What would happen with these? While she was lost in her thoughts, someone handed her a bowl of water and a rag.

"You there. Make yourself useful," a man in a brown cloak told her.

Kilda looked around, holding the bowl in her hands. "I'm no nurse," she replied, but the man was gone. She looked at the wounded on the beds and spotted a man who looked to be a soldier. At least, he had parts of an armour on. He was different from the other villagers. Kilda walked towards him. The man was unconscious. His blond hair was plastered with sweat to his forehead. He must have been badly injured as he had a long scar on his face. It made her own scar look like a scratch. She dipped the rag in the water and wiped his forehead. He was warm. There was something pleasant in his features on the unharmed side of his face. She moistened his throat and neck. As she moved closer to him, the blanket slipped. Kilda noticed with sorrow that the man was missing an arm. The wound had been cauterized with fire, probably with a blade. Some salve had been applied to heal the skin. She put the bowl away and decided to remove the man's last pieces of armour. It must be unbearable for him to have that weight on his body. As she unlaced the pauldrons, the man opened his eyes.

"Don't move," she said with her kindest voice.

"Am I dead?" the man whispered.

"No, you're not. This is the Rebellion's camp infirmary," she answered.

The man tried to chuckle but coughed. "Tell Louis that Josselin succeeded," he muttered.

"Are you Josselin?" Kilda asked.

The man did not answer, but he raised a frail hand to her cheek, grazing her scar with his fingers. While she removed the rest of his armour, the man fell unconscious again. She decided to carry his message to Louis.

Kilda left the infirmary and headed to Louis's tent. The man was busy reading papers at his table. He noticed her presence at the entrance.

"What are you doing here? I said you should stay in your tent," Louis exclaimed, upset.

"I know. I'm sorry, but there is a man in the infirmary who has a message for you. His name is Josselin."

Louis got up and hurried out of the tent. The man was shorter than her but strode fast. Kilda trotted behind him to the infirmary. He entered the pavilion and stopped.

"Which bed?" Louis asked.

Kilda pointed at Josselin. They reached the man.

"How long has he been unconscious?" Louis stood by the side of Josselin's bed, his arms crossed over his chest.

"I don't know. I removed his plate, and he fell asleep. I came to fetch you right after. He only told me that he succeeded," Kilda said. She sat on the side of the bed, holding Josselin's wrist to check his pulse. "It doesn't seem that he has more injuries besides his missing arm. He has not been burned."

"Do you think you could find someone who could tell us what happened to him?" Louis asked her. His tone had softened.

"Of course."

"Summon Brother Benedict if you see him," Louis added. "He is a monk with a tonsure," he said as she hesitated.

It was easy to find the monk. The man brought broth to a wounded woman.

"Brother, excuse me. Louis calls for you." She pointed towards Josselin's bed.

The man opened his eyes wide. "A female soldier. That is interesting. Welcome to our ranks, my lady." He minced away towards Louis.

Now, she had to find a villager who knew about Josselin. She went to the refugees who stood between the beds.

"Excuse me, does any of you know the man over there?" They looked at her with incomprehension. She could see she was bothering them. "The soldier with an arm missing, do you know him?" She turned towards a woman who had burns on her shoulders and neck. "Do you know the blond man over there?"

"I know him," a soft voice said behind her. "I saw what happened." A young woman sat on a bed near an older man. The girl's hair was a mess and she had black rings under her eyes. She was in shock but unburned.

"Could you come with me?" Kilda asked. The girl nodded. Kilda brought her to Louis. As the women approached, the monk left the bedside.

"What did the monk say?" Kilda asked.

"He said that Josselin's wound is healing and that he could live, should his temperature fall," Louis said. "Did you find a witness?"

"I have. Can you tell us what happened?" she asked the young woman.

"The knight faced the dragon," the girl told them. "The city burned, and everyone fled. I was leaving the keep when I saw him. He stood in the yard, facing the beast.

He attacked the dragon with his sword, but at some point, he just ran towards it. The beast took him into the air and ate his arm. When we saw the knight fall into the stream, a few of us hurried towards him. The men burned his arm, and we carried him with us." She paused. "The dragon burned our city to the ground." The girl looked at the ground as if contemplating the remnants of her world.

"You will head to Millhaven tomorrow," Louis said to the girl, "and when the war is over, you will return to Earthfell to rebuild your city. Nothing stays burnt forever. Rain will come, and life will grow back."

The girl looked at him as if pondering his words.

"Was he on a mission for the Rebellion?" Kilda asked.

"Yes. It's a miracle that he even survived," Louis answered. He bent over the man. "We know you succeeded, Josselin. You fought bravely. Songs will be sung about you," he whispered. "Kilda? Do you think you can check on him from time to time? I would not like him to be left alone here."

"Of course. I will do it with pleasure," she answered. The man had faced a dragon in a single combat in the name of the Rebellion. No one with such courage should be left to suffer alone.

She stayed by the side of the bed throughout the night. She drowsed a few times. As dawn came, she rose. The monk attended to a man next to her. "I will rest a bit. I will come back later during the day," she said.

Kilda walked to Louis's tent first. She wanted to reassure him of Josselin's condition. The flaps were closed. She cleared her throat. "Louis, may I enter?"

"Yes, of course," Louis answered from the inside of the tent.

Kilda came in. Louis sat at the table, already working on the morning reports. "It's sunny outside. Should I open the flaps?"

"No, please. This tent is a mess. I don't want the men to see it."

Kilda looked around, searching for the mess. The bed was undone, and some bowls were probably in the wrong place. She gazed at Louis. "You look tired," she said.

"I could not sleep." He rose and buckled his belt and sword. "How is Josselin?"

"He sleeps soundly." There were noises coming from outside. Kilda guessed that the soldiers moved towards their daily occupations. "He woke up a few times, but he is still too weak to speak. I will watch over him until he understands where he is."

Behind her, someone pushed one flap of the tent. Kilda stepped to the side, hoping to be unnoticed. According to the orders, she should have been in her own tent.

"Don't come in," Louis said, fixing his dagger. "If it's for a report…"

"Should I stay outside?" a soft, silvery voice answered.

Kilda turned around.

The man standing at the entrance, at least by the shape of his arms and chest Kilda guessed it was a man, was stunning. As Louis had struck her with his cold beauty, this man had something entrancing, and judging by his hair, exotic. In an instant, the two men rushed forward and enfolded in a passionate embrace. Their mouths smiled and played with each other.

Taken aback, Kilda was at first shocked, then she was moved by their sincere affection. When he noticed her, the mallow man interrupted their long kiss.

"Don't worry," Louis told him. "It's Kilda. She is a friend of…" Louis beamed as if he remembered something.

"Of?" the man inquired.

"So! Is it here you ran without saying hello?" Lissandro appeared in the entrance.

"Lilo!" the man screamed with joy and jumped into Lissandro's arms. "I'm so glad to see you!"

"Me too," Lissandro coughed. "Selen, you are squeezing me. Armour."

"I'm sorry. Lilo, when did you come back?" Selen inquired.

"I found him in the prison. It was quite unexpected," Louis said.

"Now, you won't get rid of me," Lissandro joked. "And I have so much to tell you."

"I know, but Selen has to report to Bertrant at once," Louis said. He turned to her. "Kilda, about, um… "

Kilda looked at the three joyful men with a broad smile on her face. "Yes, I know. I will take it to my grave," she laughed. She, who had been so scared at first to wear her husband's armour, and who still felt uneasy walking through a military camp, wondered how much effort and sacrifice it must have taken such men to win their place. A heavy weight was relieved from her soul. For the first time in a long time, she felt good. She went out and headed to her tent lighthearted.

53

Louis and Selen entered the pavilion. Bertrant still couldn't believe that he would never see Faremanne again. The captain had fought at his side for a long time and had been like a friend to him. Louis had avenged his death, but it would not bring the man back. Many men died during war, but usually, it was on the battlefield or in the infirmary after the battle. Faremanne had died under the blow of a coward and a traitor, when he deserved a more honorable death. At least, they had cremated the captain's body with all the honors and in the presence of all the soldiers left at camp.

"I see you both look happy. I suppose the mission was a success," Bertrant said.

"We defeated the orcs and killed their general, Commander. There are no survivors," Selen said with joy and a hint of pride.

"And the dam?" Pembroke asked.

"Intact, Commander."

"Good. This means that we can cross the Lowlands. Louis, I'd like to hear your report on our current situation," Bertrant said.

Louis bent over the map and pointed at their position. "We are here to the north of the Lowlands. The mountains close the Crysas Peninsula like a bottleneck. Once we reach the Falst River, we will probably be within sight of Nysa Serin. We can count that Agroln will throw all his forces against us and unleash the dragon. I have sent scouts to the north. No army is closing in on us from that direction. Nothing should come from the east and west either. We will have a frontal assault."

"How do you suggest we organize our troops?" Bertrant asked.

"Spies mentioned orcs. This means they won't have a cavalry. Yet, they may get reinforcement from the city. They will probably wait in the plain here where the ground is to their advantage," Louis continued, moving the wooden pieces on the map. "Most of our forces are mounted. I suggest three blocks of cavalry here and there on the sides, and here in the back a line of archers who will join the footmen once the melee starts. The footmen can form a block between these marks. I want every single man on the battlefield."

"This sounds good," Pembroke said, "but where will we stand?"

"I don't understand your question," Louis answered.

"I think what Lord Pembroke asks you is where he should position himself," Bertrant clarified the count's thought, knowing already what Louis's answer would be.

The answer fell like a razor blade. "There," Louis said sharply, pinning a flag on the front line.

Bertrant looked at the count. The man was ill at ease. Bertrant thought he could give him a little push. "Whatever the result, it will be our last battle. I intend to get the best view of it, and what better place than the front?"

"Yes, of course," Pembroke mumbled.

Louis stared at the count with a condescending look. Bertrant cleared his throat. His captain turned to him. "And what of the dragon?" Bertrant asked.

"Josselin confirmed that the beast swallowed the artifact. We can only pray it works," Louis answered.

"And where will you and your friend stand during the battle?" Bertrant knew that there would be a thorn here.

"I suggest Selen rides in the middle of the front line. As for myself, I intend to be here," Louis replied, pointing at the front.

Bertrant looked at him with hopelessness. "Louis…"

"Or you may want to stand there," Louis mumbled.

"Well, then it's settled. We will march at dawn. Have the men rested and ready. And it includes you as well." Bertrant told his captains. They took their leave.

"I guess tomorrow is our last day," Pembroke said.

"Probably. Will you keep your word and stand until the end?"

"I will." The look in Pembroke's eyes was resolute.

Bertrant left the tent and sauntered around the camp. He looked at the men he had shared his life with over the last four years. They saluted him and hailed him cheerfully.

"Shall we slice some orcs tomorrow?" Bertrant exclaimed.

"Yes, Commander!" the men cried out.

"Good! Then I hope to meet you after the battle so you can tell me all about it."

"We will, Commander." They raised their mugs towards him and laughed.

Bertrant did not discern fear in them. This would come tomorrow when the enemy would be in sight. Now, the men longed for action. Louis had filled their hearts with pretty thoughts of honour and victory. Bertrant had added an extra ration of beer to it. Just in case.

He passed in front of the infirmary and met Kilda.

"My lady. I hope your stay among us has been without incident," Bertrant inquired.

"Your men have been very polite, my lord. I look forward to fighting with them tomorrow."

"Will you be on the battlefield too?" Bertrant asked, still unsure if it was a good idea.

"I will ride with the cavalry in the front row. That was where my husband fought."

"Lord Hewald," Bertrant said. "He was a good, honorable man. He fought bravely. I was there when he fell. You honour him, my lady. I do not wish you for you to meet the same fate." He remembered Lady Hewald when she was still wearing dresses, strolling at the side of her husband. He had not even recognized her in her husband's armour. The woman had been through so much. He admired her courage.

"I thank you, my lord, for giving me this opportunity to fight in the Rebellion."

"And I thank you, my lady, to have given me the chance to correct my foolish decision to deny you this right the first time."

Kilda smiled and went on her way.

Bertrant remembered the words he had had with Louis. They all wanted to win this war. And who were they? Exhausted soldiers, young boys, wench-looking men, cowards, a revengeful woman, rascals, and an ex-drunk commander. All misfits. No noble court would have lowered its gaze on them. Yet, tomorrow they would write history; they would fight the last battle. "Four years and here we are," he whispered. He was proud to have escaped his own demons, to be himself again. Still, most of all, he was proud of the Rebellion.

Bertrant headed back to the headquarters. He had to talk to Pembroke. He had changed his mind.

54

Lissandro, Selen, and Louis had gathered in Louis's tent. Louis had closed the flaps and hoped that no one would interrupt their discussion. Selen sat on the trunk near the bed. He had exchanged his armour for his plain, green tunic. Louis was on his chair, one elbow on the table. He looked at Lissandro, who sat on his bed, ready to tell his story. His friend was impatient, and his mouth twitched in nervous smiles. Louis wondered if Lissandro was waiting for his permission to speak. This was ridiculous. He was his friend, not a footman.

"So, Lilo, what have you learned that is so important?" Louis asked with curiosity, breaking the awkward silence.

"First, I need to know if you both have recovered your memory as well. What I am going to say may be a bit…perturbing," Lissandro said. Louis and Selen nodded. "When I was in the Ebony Forest, I met an enchanting creature, a dryad. She revealed to me the truth about us."

"Are we dead?" Selen asked.

"No. But we died," Lissandro replied. "Let me explain. Agroln used blood magic to take over the throne. To be invincible on the battlefield, the wizard needed an army and a dragon. Therefore, he opened portals to hell, which created an imbalance with heaven. We are souls that heaven sent back into this world to fight the darkness."

"Is this why we woke up naked in the middle of the wilderness? We materialized from a portal?" Selen asked, confused.

"I think so, yes," Lissandro said. "Yet, I still don't get why it took four years for us to start dreaming."

Louis chuckled. "Let me guess. It is because we did what was natural for us. Hide from the world in a place where we felt secure. Maybe heaven grew desperate of our inaction and decided to kick our lazy asses by showing us the way."

"It is one thing to show us the way, but are we supposed to fight darkness with our bare hands?" Selen asked.

"I did not get magical tips. I suppose we are good at fighting, but I know many who would be better than me. Maybe it's something we have in us, or maybe they needed three fools to do the task," Lissandro said.

"And if we kill the dragon?" Louis asked. "What will happen to us?"

"Even if we kill the dragon and Agroln, we will have to live here until we die. There is no turning back," Lissandro said. "We have to take it as a second chance."

"It is fine with me. I don't think I have a world to go back to anyway," Selen said.

"The dryad also said something quite interesting," Lissandro carried on, staring at them with curiosity. "She said that we are from the same world but not from the same period. For example, I am an American from the twenty-first century."

"You are from the future?" Louis inquired, taken aback.

"Twenty-first what?" Selen asked, puzzled.

"Oh! This sounds interesting," Lissandro said. He turned to Selen. "Don't say anything. Let me guess. Hmm, you can't be from the Middle Age… Year of our Lord Jesus Christ?"

"Of who?" Selen asked, lost.

"I knew it," Lissandro said, all excited. "You're pale as a Swede, but considering your knowledge, you must come from the south. They had contacts with the north anyway… Roman Empire? No, something more exotic and yet European… Greece! You're from Athens. You're an Achaean," Lissandro exclaimed.

Selen laughed out loud. "Those rustic goat-shaggers! We kicked that scum back into the sea."

Louis felt offended to have his references insulted and gazed at Selen with an angry look. "They may have been your rivals, but you should not use such words against a brilliant civilization." Selen gaped at him, speechless. Louis turned to Lissandro. "Besides, that's stupid. It has no importance who we were before. You said it was a new start." He had just gone over his past, he didn't need Lissandro to twist the knife in the wound.

"But I'm curious," Lissandro said. "This is a unique occasion. We could learn from each other's periods."

"I can hardly believe we can learn something from the future," Louis objected sardonically. "I don't want to hear you praise the worth of abject physiocracy."

Lissandro looked at him now. His friend's eyes narrowed. "You are definitely special and not that easy to situate. You are at least from the Enlightenment, maybe later... Well, you're obviously a frog."

"At least, I am not the result of a rascal and a prostitute," Louis snapped back.

"My mother redeemed herself," Lissandro grunted.

"I'm sorry," Louis said, confused, "I did not mean it literally."

"Just tell me when you're from then," Lissandro insisted.

"I can't. I was…" Famous? Lissandro would probably not know him. Yet, there was still a risk, and Louis did not want Selen to know too much about who he had been, definitely not his name.

"You were? You mean you were *someone*?" Lissandro sat on the edge of the bed and hung on Louis's lips for an answer.

Louis sighed. "All right, but keep it to yourself." He walked to Lissandro and whispered his full name in his ear. Selen stared at them puzzled but did not ask.

"That crazy, bloodthirsty bastard!" Lissandro exclaimed.

"What?" Louis said, offended. "Oh, yes, scapegoating." They did drown his name in a lake of blood. "Nice you know about me, though," he said, half smiling.

"You're kidding! I was in your city during the insurrection, some forty years after your death. I was searching for my next butler. I liked them with some style. The man I found told me a lot about you and your…" Lissandro had a quick glance at Selen, "…friend. Not in your favour. He complained you got his family arrested, that he lost a brother and some nephews, something like that. Yet, it awoke my curiosity, and I read a little." Lissandro stared at him with amazement. "I can't believe it… You look even better in reality."

Louis did not know which details were the most confusing, the insurrection or that his friend had a serious problem with his longevity. He decided he only wanted to know more about the latter. "You said twenty-first century. It would make you around two hundred…"

"I had an exceptionally long life," Lissandro answered. "But I can explain it another time." Lissandro looked at Selen and at him again. "Now, I get it." Lissandro grinned with a provocative glance. "I'm not the only one to get lucky."

Don't even dare mention it, Louis thought. "I suggest we plan tomorrow's battle," Louis said and frowned at Lissandro. He did not want to hear more about their past or Lissandro's opinion on them.

"I can stand on the front line as you proposed," Selen said.

"Should I stand with the archers?" Lissandro asked.

"I had thought you could ride in the left front line with Kilda. I want men I can trust behind my back. We will charge directly towards the dragon as soon as it appears," Louis said.

"Oh, so you want to launch a suicide mission?" Lissandro chuckled. "Well, at least we will die like heroes. Even if the artifact works, it's still a dragon."

"This is why I want to take care of the beast myself. I can't ask that from you. However, I would like you to cover my back," Louis said.

"No, Louis. This is madness," Selen objected.

"You *are* crazy," Lissandro said with disapproval. "Besides, the commander will never agree that we launch a separate attack."

"This is why I need to get the command of the army before tomorrow," Louis insisted.

"To take over the command from two Lord Commanders. How do you plan to manage that? With a lap dance?" Lissandro sneered. "This is mutiny, and it's not you."

His friend was getting on his nerves. How could he even consider that he wanted mutiny? "I mean to talk to the lords. Do you have a better idea, perhaps?" he snarled. Louis knew there was but little hope he could manage to convince the two men, and he trusted none of the commanders to win the battle. If they showed hesitation as he feared, all would be lost.

"Please, stop. Both of you," Selen said with a tired voice. "We can't plan an attack on the dragon. We have no idea where it will appear and how. Louis, he is right. You have to stay at your post. You are second-in-command after Bertrant. The men need your leadership, at least until the melee starts. But you can count on us, whatever happens."

"I know," he said, looking at Selen as if holding on to a buoy. He needed to think about all of this alone. It had been too many emotions lately. "I have to make a last check of the camp. We will see each other tomorrow on the battlefield."

Lissandro rose and came towards him. "Whatever happens tomorrow, it will be an honour to fight at your side." He grabbed Louis's hand tightly.

Louis pulled Lissandro to him and hugged him. "We will fight like brothers, my friend."

"Lead us to victory. I know you can. You've done it once before," Lissandro whispered, holding him.

Selen smiled at him. "Can I have some words with you, Lilo?" Selen asked.

Lissandro let go of Louis and turned to Selen. "Of course," he grinned.

They went out of the tent and parted ways.

Louis walked through the camp, encouraging the men and controlling their materiel. The blades were sharp and the plates glittered. Bertrant had distributed an extra ration of beer, but Louis did not mind. Greasy sausages grilled over braziers, spitting their juices into the fire and spicing the air with the scents of garlic. Louis wondered where the men had found such meat. Yet, as he may have to eat some, he preferred not to know.

"Would you drink with us, Captain?" a man from a group under a tent hailed him.

"I think I can take the time," Louis replied and took the mug the soldier handed him. He walked forward and joined the group. Looking at their seasoned faces, he refused to think of how many would fall during the battle. The men were cheerful and boasted of their success at the dam. A bearded, chubby soldier in a leather armour told the events to a captivated audience.

"We smashed the orcs and pushed them down towards the third line. I stumbled on one of these filthy creatures. We struggled hard, but I ripped one of his tusks with my bare hand and shoved it in his eye." The man accompanied his description with explicit gestures. The soldiers laughed. "I got up, and I was hurrying down the hill with Peter when we saw the purple mongoose—"

Louis choked on his beer.

"Oh, I'm sorry, Captain. I mean Captain Selen rushed towards that giant orc general! A walking horror. The captain must have balls of steel. The beast was over eight feet tall, with green arms like trunks, and carried an axe large as my chest! But the captain was swift as always. At one point, we thought the orc had him, yet we saw black blood spurt everywhere, and the monster fell down the dam. That was a fight."

The soldiers around sighed with awe. Louis regretted he had not seen it himself. He would have to ask his friend for the details.

"Can you tell us about Mighthorn, Captain? How was it?" a young boy in a grey brigandine asked him.

Louis was not sure he could make such a vivid description of their story. He glanced around and spotted a man who had been with him that day. He pointed at the soldier. "You can ask him. He was there with us. He will tell you all the details."

The soldiers rushed to the man. Louis could hardly believe how much the soldiers had improved in such a few weeks. He was proud of them. He did believe that they could win tomorrow. If the lords did not fail them. He put the empty mug on a table and left the tent.

He encountered Folc near a brazier. The boy was dressed in his armour.

"Will you fight well tomorrow, Folc?" he asked.

"For sure. I asked Bertrant if I could ride on the front line. I want to honour my family name."

Louis smiled. The boy was incredibly brave. He was worried to know that Folc would be right behind him at such a dangerous place, but he could not deny him that. "Show Pembroke how a real man can fight." He hugged the boy. "And don't get killed."

"I won't. I know you two need me to watch your backs." The boy smirked.

Louis laughed. He waved at the boy and returned to his tent.

When Louis opened the flaps, Selen was waiting for him inside. He smiled. "I knew I would see you a last time."

"I have something for you." Selen came forward. He unfolded a piece of cloth. At the sight of the object, Louis was not sure he understood and did not know what to say. "It's an earring," Selen said, blushing. "You have a hole in your earlobe ... I had it made with scraps of my armour." The ring shone white with tints of gold.

"That is really sweet." Louis took the earring and looked at it. He felt deeply touched by his friend's gesture. "I'm sorry. I have nothing ..."

"You know I only need a smile," Selen said with infinite kindness.

Blood rushed to his heart. Louis cupped Selen's face in his hands and kissed him. With his burning lips, he opened Selen's mouth and plunged his tongue deep as if to suck the life out of his body. Surprised, Selen struggled before his hands tightened on Louis's shoulders, and he tugged Louis against him.

"If it wasn't for the thirty thousand men outside..." Louis whispered. His blood burned with lust.

"I know," Selen whispered, kissing him back and tugging on his lips. "I crave it too." Selen's hands ran over his body.

Louis grabbed his friend's hands before their need became irreversible. "We can't," he forced himself to say. Louis did not release his grip. He needed the touch. They breathed deeply and calmed down, their foreheads touching.

"Do you think we can survive the battle?" Selen asked softly, anxious.

Louis stared at him. "We have fought so hard for this sacred aim. I know our war is right, and I believe in us, in our men. We will win tomorrow, and we will see a new world rise. A better world. Just don't lose your smile."

"I will watch your back, and we will live together in this new world," Selen said, moving backwards to leave. "I love you."

Louis kept holding his hand. "Please, my love, survive tomorrow."

"I am your harsh, trained, fearless warrior. I can't lose," Selen teased him.

Louis smiled, biting his lip. *Damn you, Lissandro*, he thought. He let go of his friend's hand. Selen left.

Louis moved to the table and checked the maps again. At the same time, he fixed the hoop earring in his earlobe.

"You don't need such an accessory for the mission we are going to give you," Bertrant said reproachfully while entering the tent. Pembroke followed him. Louis gazed at the lords with surprise.

"We have had a change of mind," the lords told him.

55

Louis stood in front of him. His look was tense as if under great concentration. His full lips were slightly opened, twitching in silence. A lock of hair caressed his cheek. He pushed it back with a toss of the head, revealing a faint sparkle from his left ear. His friend stood alone on his white horse, isolated from the rest of them. The line of riders stretched long on both sides. It curved slightly on the extremities like a crescent. Bertrant was in front of the left wing, Pembroke in front of the right one. Louis stood in the middle.

At the last moment, the lords had made him Commander of the Rebellion. As he had eagerly wished, his friend would lead the assault. Selen approved the lords' decision. Just like them, he considered that Louis deserved this. He had brought them here; he would lead them to victory.

Selen's heart raced. He closed his eyes and took deep, long breaths. He felt the throbbing of his horse under him and the slight jolt when it moved its front legs to stomp the ground. The mounts were growing impatient. In the deafening silence, he heard some whinnying in the distance. His horse blew air from its nostrils. Selen sensed the rigidity of the leather between his fingers as the animal tugged on the reins. He patted its neck. Selen took another breath. It smelled iron. He could taste it on his tongue. There was something else, a more acrid odor. The men were sweating. He too was sweating already. It was summer, and the sun was high in the sky. Selen opened his eyes and lifted his head. The sky was blue as the sea. He spotted a line of white birds in the east. His gaze followed them. As he turned his head, the wind blew right in his face. His green eyes narrowed. His long hair swirled high. Selen wondered for an instant if he should have braided it for once. He lowered his head. Further down the row, standing beside Folc and Kilda, Lissandro looked discreetly at him. His friend nodded and smiled. Selen turned his head forward again. He unsheathed his sword and held it in his left hand. With the other hand, he picked up the spear attached to the saddle.

Selen did not feel fright. He was not afraid of the pain. He felt sorrow. He thought of his journey, of the shack he had left. He wondered if it still stood in one piece. All the lambs should be born by now. He had been so ignorant. Now, he felt as if he had seen too much, too much misery and death. Or not enough, not enough life and love. He yearned for more. He wanted to live. A tear ran down his cheek. He saw Louis's head tilt. He forced a smile. Behind his friend, Selen saw movement on the horizon to the south. The enemy was approaching.

The black battalions of orcs drew nearer. They had no cavalry, but they were numerous and threatening nevertheless. Even at such a distance, Selen saw that they were manifold. Some crawled and limped, while others, without being as impressive as Kraalh had been, towered several feet over other orcs with their tall frames. Their red standards floated like rags in the wind. Though of dark metal, their plates glittered in the sun, as well as the blades of their axes and swords. The orcs halted. He heard distant shouts.

Selen saw Louis bite his lips and take a deep breath. "You can do it," Selen whispered, "you can." Louis raised his head. His sapphire eyes burned with flames of ice. Louis twitched his legs. His horse piaffed and danced on its spot. Louis's hair floated around his shoulders, whirling with each move of his mount. Selen had never seen him so sublime. Louis raised his sword in the air. As his horse cantered down the line, he shouted loud with an orotund voice that took Selen aback.

"Soldiers of the Rebellion! Warriors of Trevalden! Shall we bend and creep forever?"

"No!" the soldiers yelled in unison.

"Shall we let them rape our land and behead our children?"

"No!" the men roared louder.

"Have we fallen so low to give up our country to rascals and imbeciles without even a fight? We have no home left. We have lost so much. But have we also lost our dignity?"

"Never!" the clamour thundered.

"There is no king but a tyrant! And we are the people. We create our own future! We are the Rebellion! We are soldiers of light! Burn our hearts, burn it out! This is the last battle! The glory will be yours only! Bathe in their blood! Send this shit back to hell! Are you heroes or are you cowards? Take up the spear of your fallen brother! Avenge the dead! For a new dawn!"

Louis was exalted. His horse progressed up and down the line, and turned the sand into clouds of dust. The soldiers roared like a growing thunder. They shook their spears and banged their swords against their shields. Selen raised his sword and shouted with them. Louis's horse reached the middle of the line again. He jerked it around, the long white tail flowing in the air.

"No prisoners! No surrender! No retreat! For the people of Trevalden!"

Louis's horse reared and plunged forward. Selen spurred his mount at a hard gallop. The whole line followed its commander. The orcs ran towards them from the other side. The creatures halted and formed a wall. Selen heard the whizzing of arrows passing over their heads. Orcs fell. On the sides, the lords led their riders in a curve, aiming at the enemy's flanks. His mount's breathing was harsh and husky. The pounding of the several thousand hooves on the ground was deafening. Metal chinked, men shouted, and horses whinnied. Selen was panting. His heart palpitated. He focused on the kill. There could be no place for fear. The orcs shot their first range of arrows. As they drew nearer, their horses increased their pace.

Only a few yards left. The riders lowered their lances, as did the orcs. Selen raised his spear high and aimed for the orc in front of Louis. The stick pierced through the orc's chest. The creature fell, creating an aperture. Selen spun his mount behind his friend's mount. Louis's horse rammed into the mass of orcs. Some were trampled under the hooves. Others had their bodies smashed into pulp against the metallic peytral. Louis lowered his sword, mowing down the creatures. Black slime squirted out of severed necks and splashed on Selen's face. His whetted sword hewed all that stood in the way. Selen pressed his heels against his horse's flanks to hold the distance with his companion. Their cavalry spread like bloody streaks into the orcs' battalions. The mounts could not be stopped. They crushed and slew the foes. Concentrating on his moves, Selen lost all notion of space. He had no idea where the rest of their battalion was or if soldiers followed. He fought for survival.

A dark shape covered the sun for an instant. Selen looked up. "The dragon!" he shouted. The beast let out a tremendous roar. Louis raised his head and pulled brusquely on the reins at the last second to avoid the giant orc in front of him. Cut in his run, Louis's horse sidestepped, stumbled, and crashed on its side, throwing man and beast to the ground. Selen jumped from his mount onto the orc. His sword cleft the beast's throat. He rushed to Louis, who disentangled himself from the reins and rose laboriously. Placing himself between his friend and the sea of foes, Selen sliced through the first orcs approaching.

"Where is it?" Louis yelled.

In the distance, the dragon plunged into the melee, attacking indistinctly all that his jaws could reach. Yet, there was no fire.

"He can't spit flames!" Selen shouted. With the flat of his sword, he blocked a blow coming from the right, rotated the blade, and chopped off a hand.

"We need to reach it!"

Selen glanced around. The dragon was far, and mayhem lay between. Selen saw the banner of Bertrant in the east, circled by the foe and with few men around him. The Rebellion had progressed so erratically through the enemy lines that it was widely scattered. Wounded horses and men thrown off the saddles, screamed of pain. Yet, the orcs drew back.

"No. It must come to us!" Selen shouted, dodging a blow. He ran his sword through a chest. The dragon took to the air again. "Call the men to reform the ranks!"

"No one can hear me from here!" Louis shouted. His friend pulled his sword out of a skull. "Let alone see me!"

Selen looked around and glimpsed a prominence that was not covered with orcs. "Up there!" More orcs came towards them. They placed themselves back to back and progressed slowly towards the hill, chopping and cutting the enemies with powerful counterstrikes. United as one, they fought with ardour. Swords clashed. Maimed orcs fell. Cold and sticky blood squirted onto their faces. The orcs were legion, but Selen and Louis were skilled. Finally, they reached the middle of the hill.

"I will call the men!" Louis shouted, searching for the nearest group of soldiers.

They heard a strident shriek. The dragon was flying towards them, its giant, golden wings flapping slowly. Its devilish, vermilion eyes looked right at them. The jaws opened, revealing rows of soiled fangs. It came down on them. "It can't spit fire," Selen muttered, terrified.

"No, but it can bite!" Louis shouted, pushing him to the ground.

He heard the sharp teeth snap. The long, amber body passed over them. The dragon landed on the top of the hill. It turned around. Its razor-sharp claws crumbled the stone under them. The beast stretched its long, muscular neck in the air and uttered a cavernous rattle.

"I must face it, Selen," Louis said, resolute.

"No! It's suicide. Please," Selen implored. He held to him and looked at his love with appealing eyes.

Louis grabbed Selen's neck. "I am the only one who can kill it. It is our fate. We live—or we die," Louis said with fatality in his voice. "I love you. Goodbye." Louis escaped his grip and ran up the hill.

The pain in Selen's chest went out in a mad scream. Selen turned to face the orcs again. The filthy creatures climbed the slope. "We live or die," he whispered. "Go face the dragon. I will be the shield to your back." Selen stretched his arms, sword in hand, like a wall against the sea. He took a last breath. "To the end." He extended his sword forward. The first wave was on him.

He slashed, sliced, and hacked with frenzy. His hair swirled around him, following every move. For each fallen enemy, gushes of blood ran down the hill. Bodies piled up at his feet. He kicked them down. At least, these improvised logs slowed down the progression of their followers. Selen's legs were sore, and he could not feel his arms anymore. Still, he held. With each sensation of despair rose a spark of anger. He would not give up. His rage against the orcs was nothing compared to his rage to live. What kept him alive was not the cause, but to know he fought for the one he loved.

The flow of enemies became scarcer. The orcs had favored the melee. He gazed downhill, searching for his next opponent, when pain rose from his right leg. Selen lowered his gaze. A black arrow was stuck in his outer thigh. Though he tried to stay up, his exhausted legs gave in under him. He fell on his back on the green grass. This time, no anger blocked his sorrow. His strength left him. He turned his face slowly towards the top of the hill. A curl of hair slid down his cheek. Louis was still alive. Yet, the dragon was unharmed and had the advantage. Selen thought he saw a faint white light come from where his friend stood, but blades of grass stood in the way. Tears pearled in the corner of his eyes. Selen felt a presence towering over him. He turned his head slightly. A muddy sabaton compressed his chest. A stout orc stood over him, holding a serrated blade. Selen's hand searched for his sword on the grass in vain. With his last strength, he tried to move and grabbed the creature's ankle. The foot pinned him harder to the ground. *I'm sorry*, Selen thought. The orc grinned and raised its blade.

A sword ran through the orc's flank. Another blow fell on the creature, and a fountain of blood spurted where the head had been.

"Get up!" Lissandro shouted, shoving the heavy body of the creature out of the way.

"I can't, it hurts," Selen answered, rising laboriously on his elbows. Lissandro slapped him hard in the face.

"It's only an arrow on the wrong side of the leg!" Lissandro twirled the shaft of the arrow. Selen shrieked. His fingers dug into the ground. "And it's loose!" His friend unsheathed his dagger and pushed it into the wound to remove the head of the arrow. Selen howled with agonizing pain. Blood jetted as Lissandro pulled the whole arrow out of the open flesh. "See? Now, get up!" he shouted, dragging Selen up by the arm.

Holding on his friend's shoulder, Selen turned towards the top of the hill.

"The beast is going to eat him," Lissandro whispered in horror.

"No." Selen felt his wrath come back. "Give me a spear."

56

Louis was scared, but he would not show it. He walked towards the dragon, sword in hand, forcing himself to ignore Selen's heartbreaking scream. The dragon had been his call from the start. It had haunted him, provoked him. This fight was more than saving the land. The beast turned its ruby eyes towards him and frowned. It crawled and flapped its vast bat-wings with slow movements. A low hum came from its throat. Like a predator, it waited, gazing at its prey. Louis stopped and stared at it with repulsion.

"Do you believe you can kill me?" he heard a low, guttural voice say in defiance. The dragon had not moved its jaws, but Louis had no doubt on the origin of the voice.

"I will kill you and put an end to all this," Louis said.

"You think so?" The dragon's tail snapped into the air and spun towards him. Louis threw himself flat on the ground. The tail passed only a few inches above him. Though supple, he knew he was not as trained and nimble as Selen. He would have to engage and stay near. As he rose, the dragon stretched its head to grab him. Louis sidestepped and moved under the neck. He delivered a blow to the throat, but the blade bounced on the scales. Astounded, he stepped back and hit a paw. Raising his head, he realized that the beast's front paws were twice his height.

"You are no match for me. You never have been," the voice said with scorn. "I can see in the innermost of your soul, crystal clear."

"I am deaf to your provocations. God brought me here to defeat you," Louis answered, challenging the dragon.

"Do you hear yourself?" the beast chuckled. "Pretentious fool! I rule the Earth. I am invincible."

Anger grew inside Louis. He aimed for the paw again, but the blade did not even leave a scratch. The dragon walked around him, encircling him.

"See? You can't pierce my skin. You are powerless. Your words and your sword are useless." The voice ringing in his head laughed.

Louis tried to pierce the dragon's flesh. Despite the strength of each blow, the point of his sword would not break the skin.

"This world will be consumed to ashes. This country will drown in its own blood as yours did. And why should you care? Look at these men, pitiful cowards wallowing in depravity. Imbeciles and rascals. Those were your words, right?"

"You're twisting the truth," Louis muttered, confused.

"Am I? Look at them, for once! Look how they really are! They let you down once. Would you fight for them again? You despise them more than I do. I actually like them. I encourage their vices. And these are deeply rooted in their souls," the voice whispered. "And by the way, they dislike you. You are not one of them, and you will never be. Your name will forever be soiled with blood. The only thing they will remember about you is the insufferable conceit of a pretty face."

"Liar!" Louis hit the scales once more in infuriation. The dragon's words had upset his heart. Something within him was amiss. He could not have lived in vain. "You are nothing more than lies and delusion! There is always hope for justice and virtue. Innocence will prevail!" he shouted, but his voice was weak.

"Is it doubt I hear? You can't escape your own nature. The fairy tales in your head you force yourself to believe in will be submerged. Your will will be crushed, and you will learn how to serve me. Remember the faces of your enemies."

As the dragon uttered these words, Louis's mind blurred, and he saw them, the hundreds of hatchlings, but their faces were human again. Some stood out. Traitors' faces. He saw one that should not have been there. Rising proud like the Hydra's head, it smiled at him with a rictus. Louis clenched his sword and twisted his features with ire. *It can't be. I killed you.*

"Yes. Unleash your hate once more. Because it is all you are. God is dead, and heaven rejected you. You should have accepted your place in hell," the cavernous voice carried on. The dragon kept on crawling around. "This is where you belong."

Louis raged. *No, I don't*, he thought. He rushed to the other side of the beast and ran up the bent rear paw. He turned around and jumped on the left wing, sword forward. The blade passed through the membrane. As he fell, he ripped it like a piece of cloth. The dragon's tail hit him hard and projected him to the ground. Blood ran down Louis's face. He tried to rise but lost balance. As he bent to pick up his sword, drops of blood fell from his head onto the blade. The stained spots briefly shone like crystal. The dragon reached him with his paw and blocked him down between two claws.

"You are a failure, for both sides," it drawled, "and I will feed on your flesh."

Its muzzle drew closer. Louis could feel the hot breath on his face. He wiped his forehead with the palm of his hand and applied it on the scales of one of the dragon's fingers. In a second, the beast drew its paw back as if it burned. Louis crawled back and took up his sword. He removed his gauntlet. "We live or die."

The dragon realized what Louis was doing. It was preparing itself to jump when a spear hit it in its eye. The dragon roared and looked for the foe. Louis cut through the flesh of his arm with his sword, bathing the blade in his blood. Before the dragon turned its head towards him again, he ran and climbed on one of the bent front paws. Louis's sword pierced the skin at the top of the neck and buried itself deep. Louis held to the hilt and let himself fall. The blade severed the throat from top to bottom. Buckets of blood showered him. The voice in his head turned into an agonizing shrill. The dragon collapsed in a heap of limbs and wings, dead, its neck half sliced. Louis raised his sword and chopped the other half in frantic slashes. He moved towards the head.

"I am not a failure!" he shouted to the blank eye before running his sword through it.

"Louis!"

He turned around. Selen hurried towards him, limping on his right leg. Blood ran down his thigh. Lissandro followed close on his heels.

"Selen!" He hugged his friend as tightly as his strength allowed it.

"Never dare to say goodbye again," Selen whispered with anger as he clenched him. "Now, show them."

Louis climbed on top of the dragon's head and raised his sword high. A loud clamour rose from downhill. He gazed at his soldiers hailing him from the battlefield and smiled.

"Victory is ours!" he shouted. The Rebellion had won the battle. Louis had learned that dragons could be defeated. "There will be a new dawn," he whispered.

While he got down the beast's head, his vision blurred. Louis saw his friends run towards him before he collapsed against the massive jaws and lost consciousness.

Louis woke up in bed. He had been washed, and a bandage covered his left arm.

"How do you feel?" Selen asked him, anxious. His friend came to him, still limping, and sat on the side of the bed. His sweet eyes were swollen.

"I think I'm fine. Why do you look so sad?" Louis inquired.

"Come." Selen helped him get up. The infirmary was crowded. The beds were filled with wounded men, and male nurses hurried through the rows. The whimpers and screams were incessant. Holding each other, they walked laboriously to another aisle of the pavilion. Soldiers standing up crowded around a bed. Among the group stood his friends Lissandro and Folc. Louis felt deeply relieved to see that they were alive. When the group saw him, the soldiers stepped back and made a way to the bed. Louis's face fell.

Bertrant lay on bloodstained sheets. His eyes were half open. His armour had not even been removed. Louis understood at once. Sadness swept over him.

"He has lost a lot of blood," Pembroke said.

Louis sat next to the commander. When he saw him, Bertrant chuckled. Trickles of blood ran down his chin. Bertrant grabbed Louis's wounded arm.

"A scratch," the commander muttered with provocation.

Even on the brink of death, the man kept his biting. Louis admired him. He half smiled and grasped the commander's wrist. He felt a tear roll down his cheek.

"You fought bravely," Bertrant muttered. "You may be a bloody pain in the ass, but you are a true leader."

"It was an honour to fight by your side in the Rebellion, my lord," Louis said. "The bards will sing your name for many years to come."

"The army is yours now," Bertrant sighed. "Win this war for me."

With a heavy heart, Louis watched his commander fade away. He did not hold back his tears. Around him spread a grieving silence. The battle had been long. Louis hoped that, from the stars, Bertrant would see the light they would spread over Trevalden. Agroln's darkness was soon over.

57

The crows circled in the blue sky. Some were already perched on skulls, pecking at the eyes. Segar watched the last wounded being carried away to the infirmary. He cleared his throat and spat. His boots were clogged in the mud soaked with blood. Dead horses, mutilated corpses, and severed limbs lay scattered in heaps. Judging by the faint moans here and there, not everyone was dead, but they would be soon enough. The battlefield smelled of iron and shit. In a few hours, it would stink even more. By night, the place would be infested by scavengers. He walked to the dragon's carcass. Disturbed by his tramp, fat, blue flies flew in swarms.

The beheaded carcass still stood on the hill. The head had been taken to the camp. The body had been left to rot. Segar would not let it happen. This was probably the only dragon Trevalden had ever seen. Everything to its piss was valuable. Only with the scales and bones, Segar planned to become one of the richest men of Nysa Serin. His men would be there in a moment. He had come alone first to admire the beast himself. Such a beautiful creature butchered by that mongrel. And the man was still alive. Every survivor of the melee had seen him parade on the head of the dragon. The last thing the brat needed was a boost to his ego. All that because of Bertrant. At least, the commander drowned in his blood by now. Segar hoped the man would die. It would be one ally less for the two pretty captains.

Segar looked at the dragon and calculated its weight. He would never manage to get all of it. Besides, the flesh was already corrupted. Maggots would crawl all over it in a few days. He noticed something sparkling in the bloody mess. He took out his dagger and scraped the tissues. There was an object stuck in the gizzard. Probably something the beast had eaten. It was carved in silver and looked like folded wings. The object was certainly of some value. Segar regretted that the flask in the middle was chipped. When he put a finger on it, the glass splintered. The watery liquid inside the flask spread on his hand and disappeared, as if absorbed into the skin.

"What kind of shit is that?" he said, dropping the object. He looked at his hand and saw nothing. It did not hurt either. He picked up the metallic object again and tucked it into his pocket. On the slope, his men approached.

"Cut as much as you can of that thing," Segar ordered them. "Use crates from the supply train. Soon, no one will use them anymore."

They would probably enter the city tomorrow. He would have to find a way to smuggle the crates inside the city gates, unless he made the boxes look like leftovers of the supply train. The stench had become unbearable. Segar trotted back to the camp.

"The commander is dead," Jamys told him when Segar entered his tent.

"Good. One less," Segar replied. As a pathetic drunk, Bertrant had been harmless. Since he had been under the influence of the pretty bastard, he had only been a nuisance. His reputation and prestige would have opened many doors in the city for the captains. Now, unless Pembroke backed them, they would lose the support of the nobles.

"They will burn the body in the evening. Will you assist?" Jamys asked.

"I will. It would be suspicious otherwise," Segar answered.

"Who commands the army now?"

"That, we will see tonight if it's Pembroke or the whoreson." That last possibility was still highly probable considering how the soldiers had cheered him today. Should the man win the war, Segar would have to disappear in the shadows of the capital. All would depend on the turn of tomorrow's events. He had definitely planned to have a hand in the black market, a trade highly facilitated by his access to the army's supplies. The slave trade would probably come to an end, but he would find other sources of revenue. Yet, he would not forget to take his revenge. Segar would not have minded to extend it to the whole gang. The scarred wench and the dashing archer were probably of the same sort. Still, he wanted to act discreetly, and his hate was centered on the arrogant fool. Now that Segar thought about it, he even had nothing to complain about when it came to the purple slut. The man used to shut his mouth and stay out of the way. But to strike one meant to hit the other. Besides, Segar wondered how pleasurable it would be to torture the slut in front of the flaunting bastard.

The torches burned brightly in the dim glow of the evening sky. Above them, the first stars glittered. The twilight air was cool, and a light breeze blew. Every man who had survived the battle and could stand on his feet had gathered on the plain outside the camp. Segar had rarely seen such a dismal and solemn party. Wood had been gathered in a large heap. On top of it lay Bertrant's corpse. The commander had been dressed with care in crimson robes, and his sword had been placed in his grip, in the style of the recumbent statues of the kings. Behind the pyre, Pembroke and the two captains stood side by side, all dressed in their armours. If the men had been wounded during the battle, their appearance did not give a hint of it.

To Segar's great annoyance, the whoreson stepped forward, a torch in his hand. Walking slowly in front of the men, he chose four soldiers. Each received a torch and placed himself at a corner of the pyre.

"Here lies Lord Bertrant Heymon, hero and commander of the Rebellion. May his soul rest among the stars," Pembroke said.

The captains and the four men lowered their torches and set the wood ablaze. The whoreson stood grave, his hands behind his back. Much to Segar's surprise, the man sang. His clear voice was sad and, Segar had to admit it, beautiful.

"Lo, the eagle's funeral pyre,
Proud father of the Rebellion,
Glorious heart bursting into fire,
Though wounded by hostile iron,
With a devotion we admire,
Bertrant upheld, with the honour,
The valour,
The ardour,
Of warriors.
Our brave, alas, when he expired,
Still shouted to his companions:
We're marching on!"
"You gave your life the sword shining,
Women such a hero will weep,

The hills and fields no more strolling,
Rest, brother, in eternal sleep,
To your wife, now returning,
In revenge we take up the spears,
Grey as tears,
Darkness leers,
Show no fear.
A new dawn comes at day's ending,
Gather once more, fierce battalions:
We're marching on!"

In a roar, the soldiers repeated the last verse over and over again, clapping their breastplates to the rhythm of the song. The captains raised their fists in the air, imitated by the whole army. The flames grew high on the pyre. The heat spread over the plain. The golden light reflected on the men's armours and staunch faces. Segar gazed at the whoreson's haughty look and knew that from now on until tomorrow, it would be *Commander*.

58

The army marched on Nysa Serin. They had lost many men during the battle, but what was left of the Rebellion was still impressive. Besides, as the enemy's forces had been crushed, a fierce resistance would be highly improbable. Lissandro rode at the front, behind Pembroke, Louis, and Selen. Louis had replaced Bertrant as commander of the Rebellion. His friend had given Bertrant a beautiful ceremony. Lissandro had still goose bumps when he thought about it.

Lissandro looked forward to arriving in the city. Louis had insisted that they drag the dragon's head with them, as a clear message of their strength and intentions. As it was obviously too large to be put on a spike, they had fixed the head on a chariot behind the first lines. The stench coming from it was obnoxious and the swarm of flies, unbearable. Louis had said that, once they reached the city, the head would be boiled and its bones bleached before being mounted as a trophy. Until then, it had to look as frightening as possible. Lissandro could confirm that this part was a success beyond all expectations. Fortunately, the journey would not be long.

Nysa Serin appeared in front of them. The size of the capital could not be compared to the cities of his world, but Lissandro thought that Rome must have appeared as sublime to the victorious legions returning home as Nysa Serin was to him now. The city was built on the flank of the mountains in the west. Its imposing outer wall was made of ochre stone and contrasted with the whiteness of the last levels of the rich houses on the inner side. Here and there rose the red tile roofs of some imposing buildings. Among them dominated a large dome circled with narrow towers. It gave the impression to be the main temple of the capital. In the west, uphill, stood the king's palace. It was wider than high, with three massive, angled towers and what looked like an immense great hall. A path rising from the city wound its way up the slope. The palace could be reached only from the southeast. The north and east sides were cut into a cliff. It did not have an outside wall. Such an eyrie did not need one.

Lissandro turned his gaze on the heavy gatehouse. It was at least a three stories construction and was riddled with arrow loops. The oaken doors, reinforced with metal and stamps, were still closed. As they drew closer, one of the doors opened, and a man came riding towards them. He was richly dressed and too plump to ride such a nervous horse. He bounced on his saddle like jelly. There was something grotesque about this vision. He halted a few yards from the front row. Louis rose his right hand. The army stopped.

"My name is Lord Honfroi Tollbridge. I come to you in the name of the inhabitants of Nysa Serin," the man said, panting. "I would like to have a word with you, Commander."

"Speak," Louis said as straightforward as usual.

"Humph." The man who had addressed himself to Pembroke was obviously disconcerted. "As we have understood, you came here to free us from Agroln's grip and his creatures. We would gladly open the doors of the city to your army. However, we would like to be assured that no harm will be done to the population."

"It is not in our intention," Louis confirmed. "Is there any resistance left in the city? Orcs?"

"There are no more orcs in the city, my lord. None came back from the battlefield."

"And where is Agroln?" Louis inquired.

"He is still in his palace, my lord. At least, that is what we think. We have not seen him for a long time, but the coming and going of his minions confirms his presence," the man answered.

"We will follow you to the city and control the palace ourselves," Louis said.

The fat lord turned his horse back towards the capital. The army followed him on his heels. Lissandro though that, should the invitation be a trap, the lord would never escape them alive. He gazed at the gatehouse's turrets and saw neither archers nor the reflection of a weapon. They passed under the gate. He looked at the sharp teeth of the portcullis above his head. For a short instant, his heart stopped.

When his horse stepped on the cobbles of the inner yard, the splendor of the city took him aback. The white houses were high, most with wattle and daub walls, but a few were made entirely of stone. The small windows were glazed in green and orange glass. Shops displayed baskets of goods and colorful fronts. It smelled of pepper, oranges, and cinnamon. Some roofs had been converted into terraces with gardens. Grapevine and ivy grew around the balustrades. Some front walls were decorated with paintings representing scenes of life or animals. Lissandro guessed that they must be in a rich shopping part of the city. The main street was large and clean, but the alleys on the side were narrow, dark, and a watery liquid flowed in the gutters. There were squares decorated with fountains encrusted with mosaics, statues of lascivious women or heroes, and closed wells under the shade of green trees. However, besides the birds and some cats, the city was empty of life, as if the whole population had abandoned their activities in a panic. Lissandro guessed that no one would dare to go out of his house as long as their intentions had not been made clear. Still, he had no doubt that behind every shutter, eyes spied on them. They arrived on a square situated at the bottom of the cliff. The way to the palace stretched at their left, upwards in hairpin bends. When the first battalions of the army halted, the rest of the men still filled the streets that his group had crossed.

"Not everyone needs to climb up there," Louis said. "I suggest we only take a battalion with us. The rest of the men will watch over the city and look out for enemies until we return."

It took some time for the thousands of men to climb the hill. The path was steep, forcing the horses to walk slowly. On their left, cold water from the mountain cascaded in a whirlpool between rocky spurs. Lissandro felt unsecured. This bottleneck would have been the perfect place to trap them. Yet, nothing happened. They reached the gatehouse leading to the esplanade outside the palace. A barbican stood at the front, defending the entrance. A few yards behind, a broad stone bridge stretched from the main building on the left to a large tower on the other side of the path. The portcullis was raised. No guard was to be seen. They passed under the gate. From the courtyard, the view of the city and the Lowlands was breathtaking. Lissandro saw the eastern mountains on the horizon and the Eryas Lowlands where they had fought the day before.

Lissandro swiveled and gazed at the palace. At the right of the long wall, stood a wide staircase leading to massive wooden doors set with flower-carved metal plates. With its pinnacle turrets, the building looked like a church, but considering it couldn't be a cathedral, Lissandro supposed it was the great hall. There were no traces of soldiers or people anywhere. The place was utterly silent. Louis, Selen,

Pembroke, and Lissandro dismounted and approached the steps.

"Behind the doors is the great hall. It has a narthex," Pembroke said. "I don't like this silence."

They pushed open one of the heavy doors slowly. Louis, who stood first in the line, stopped in his move.

"Pembroke, wait for us outside, if you please," Louis said. "It is best you stay with the men on the esplanade. We will call for you if we need reinforcement."

"Yes, Commander." Pembroke stepped back and returned to the esplanade.

"What is wrong?" Selen muttered once the lord was gone.

"Look," Louis said, opening the door wider. As light entered the narthex, Lissandro understood. The walls were not brown but red. The tiled floor was also stained as if wiped with a bloody cloth. Candles flickered on a stone table. They stepped inside the narthex.

"Close the door," Lissandro said to Selen. "The men don't need to see this."

"I don't like it," Selen whispered. "It's too quiet."

"It's not the silence that perturbs me most," Louis said. "It's this sweet, foul smell."

Selen went to open the next door.

"No!" Louis exclaimed. "Don't. There is something carved here." He took one of the candles and raised it up to the wall between the two interior doors. An inscription had been cut with a blade. "I can't read it," Louis said.

"I can," Selen said. Their friend stood silent for a while. Lissandro saw beads of sweat on his forehead. Selen was scared. "It's Sumerian."

"Can you read Sumerian?" Louis asked, surprised.

"It is a widespread literary language, in my world at least," Selen answered. His voice was dead. He was still focused on what stood on the wall.

"No," Lissandro whispered. It was more than that. "It's the language of the great ancients. The language of the rituals." He could not read it, but he had seen it in old books when he had studied the arcanum of his lineage.

"What stands on the wall, Selen?" Louis asked, anxious.

"Abandon all hope you who enter here, for my body is a thin rope between two realms."

"In any case, don't open that door," Lissandro muttered, insisting on each word. Louis had dreamed of the dragon, but what Lissandro had dreamed of was beyond words.

"But we must. This is exactly why *we* have been sent here," Selen insisted, fighting back his fright.

"We should listen to Lissandro," Louis said, stepping back.

"No! We have to end this war." Selen grasped the handle and opened the door.

They stepped into the hall. Though he never had seen it with his own eyes, Lissandro recognized it at once. He had read the descriptions of such constructions in old ceremonial books. His mentor Alexei had told him about it, creations born in the depths of darkness, old as humanity itself. Yet, it was not a legend, the fruit of a sick mind. It was there in front of him. In all its infernal splendor.

The walls had the appearance of flesh, in various shades of red. Stuck in heaps of bones, ceremonial candles reflected their swaying lights and gave life to infernal shadows. Stalagmites rose from the ground to the invisible ceiling, dark as the night. Some half-formed supports had been carved into stoups of blood. Vitrified bodies poked out of what had been columns once. The corpses had been flayed and were twisted in agonizing poses. Their empty eye sockets gazed at them in reproach, as if the three men were guilty of their damnation.

"Are they...?" Louis muttered.

"The gifts from Elye," Lissandro answered. "His experiments."

They progressed through the hall. The ground was moist and soft. The smell was sweet, like rotten fruits. But the flesh was not corrupted. It was made to be preserved for eternity. Above Lissandro's head, membranes floated as veils. *The standards of hell*, Lissandro thought. On the dais stood a throne of bones and spikes, and someone, or something, sat on it.

The human creature dressed in golden robes rose. His yellowish limbs were elongated, unnatural. His face was more than emaciated, bones had grown out of his skin and pointed out like spikes, as if the result of a malformation or a terrible sickness. Scales covered one of his eyes. The other looked dead. He twitched his long clawlike nails, inviting them to approach. Lissandro and his friends did not move.

"Are you Agroln?" Louis inquired with a faint, taut voice.

The creature had a circlet on his head, but his body was too deformed to be the one of a king.

"Agroln," the creature answered slowly. "Agroln...has touched knowledge beyond his control. I carve his throat with the sound of my voice. I shape his face in my image. Sometimes screams from his wretched, drowned soul pierce to the surface, before sinking again into the depths. A slave condemned to rot away in darkness." As the thing spoke, the smell spread stronger like a perfumed poison. Lissandro almost gagged.

"Whoever you are, the war is over," Louis said with an unyielding self-control, though his face had turned grey, and his throat looked on the verge of retching. Lissandro speculated that, even facing Satan himself, Louis would break before he gave in. Lissandro put a hand on Louis's shoulder.

"Don't talk to him," he whispered. "It's not a human anymore."

"The war," the creature muttered in a guttural, hypnotizing tone. "The war is everywhere. It resounds in these walls. Can't you hear the screams of the blades? Look at those faces. Unrested souls, offerings to the Devourer. Death and war are carved unlaced in the hearts of men. There is no escape. The serpent devours the rich as well as the poor before resting under the cypress, near the poisonous waters of the stream of sorrow. I do not need to subdue the earth to the yoke of slavery. It is already in chains. I have won the war."

Lissandro saw the panic on Selen's face. Selen unsheathed his sword and dashed towards the creature.

"No!" Lissandro shouted, but it was too late.

The long fingers cast a wave of energy towards his friend. Selen rose into the air and shrilled harrowing screams. His body trembled, as if taken over by an epileptic seizure. His head tilted backwards and his eyes rolled upwards. His howling froze Lissandro's blood in his veins. Only infernal creatures could display such psychic powers.

"Nothing that pure can raise a hand to me. I feast on such essence," the creature hissed with a savoring grin.

Lissandro saw the hand twist to increase the torture, but Louis was already on the creature, ready to strike. The creature let go of Selen and swiveled towards Louis. With the twitch of a finger, he flung the sword away. Louis had no time to notice before one bony hand closed its grip on his throat and raised him high.

"What an interesting soul," the creature hissed in Louis's face. "A much better vessel than Agroln."

The nails cut the flesh on his friend's throat. Blood pearled. A drop dripped along one nail slowly down to the finger. At the sight of the scarlet liquid, the creature curled up its wrinkled lips. And there, Lissandro saw. He knew what he was facing. He smiled.

Under the iron grip, Louis panicked. He struggled and scratched the elongated arm. Lissandro saw the terror in Louis's eyes. He knew that the grip was not the only reason; there was more than the eye could see. The creature tortured Louis's mind, feeding on his thoughts and fears. His extended, reptilian tongue licked the beads of blood in delectation.

"Let him go," Lissandro ordered.

"Your turn will come," the creature told him without turning his head. Drool slid on his chops.

"Are you deaf?" Lissandro insisted. "I told you to let him go, putrid pile of feces."

The thing turned his head in irritation. His face was as nasty as the one of a lizard. "If you insist," he hissed.

The hand let Louis fall to the ground. A white, scrawny arm stretched towards Lissandro. He thought of his nightmares. He deeply hoped he was right. In the corner of his eye, he saw Selen awaken. The creature's arm cast a wave of energy. Lissandro felt nothing and moved forward. He sensed the teeth grow in his mouth. He rubbed his tongue against them, relishing the feeling. The creature cast another wave, in vain.

"It's impossible!" the creature snarled.

"It's not," Lissandro replied, showing his two long, sharp canines. "I am of your blood."

"If you are my kind then you can't kill me. You are young. I am stronger!" the creature exclaimed in rage.

"I *was* your kind," Lissandro pointed out. "I have reached salvation. My soul has been washed of our ancestors sins. I am a child reborn." Now, he could see the terror in the creature's eyes.

"No! You can't be! Not in this world!"

"But I am not from this world." Lissandro grinned. *Selen, Louis, now!* Lissandro shouted in his mind. His friends grabbed the creature by the arms and held him as hard as they could. Lissandro rushed forward and bit deep into the flesh. He severed the throat like a wolf on its prey, ripping it apart with his hands. Black pus squirted from the torn flesh and the splintered bone excrescences. Lissandro spat. He knew he could not swallow a gulp of this blood. It was poison for any man and probably worse in his case.

The body of Agroln fell on the floor, the head attached by pale ropes of tendon from the spine. The flesh structure around them went ablaze. It disappeared into nothingness, leaving only heaps of mutilated bodies and bones behind.

"It is going back to hell," Louis said, his voice hoarse. He crept and leaned against the throne. Slowly, Louis turned to him. "I will try to remember never to make you angry," he chuckled. "Are you even human?"

"In this world, I am human, but it was not always the case. I could do this because the creature's presence compelled me to. I have no power anymore."

"Good. We don't need to stick you with a stake," Louis teased him. "Selen, are you all right?"

"I am," Selen answered. Lissandro saw Selen creep towards Agroln. His friend unclasped the circlet from the dead king's forehead and came back to them. "Put it on," Selen said to Louis.

"What? No! There is no way *I* am going to be king," Louis protested.

"You are the best fitted to it. You are a natural leader. You are honest," Selen insisted.

"It is against all my beliefs," Louis objected. "Lilo, tell him."

Lissandro knew what giving absolute powers to Louis meant. At the same time, he understood Selen's motivations. "Selen is right," he finally said, knowing he would regret it one day. "Take it as a second chance to make things right."

"But it belongs to the people," Louis insisted, looking at him in dismay. "You know that."

"What I know is that if you don't take that crown, unscrupulous men will fight for it, and it will be mayhem again," Selen said. "Is that what you want?"

"No. But, the institutions …" Louis said.

And now it started. "This is the Middle Age! If you want things to change, you do it yourself," Lissandro said. "Well, with us by your side." He would insist on that, should he delay his journey a few months.

"Think if Segar Mills takes the crown," Selen said.

It took two seconds. "Give me that thing," Louis said.

Selen fastened the silver circlet on Louis's brow. With this simple gesture, Selen had crowned his king and had sealed their fate.

They rose and were heading for the door when Pembroke entered the hall. At the sight of the corpses, he stepped back and put his hand to his mouth as if to retch. "What on earth!" He turned to them. "We started to worry. Have you killed Agroln?" The lord stopped, looking at Louis, aghast. For a moment, no one dared to move. "If it is so," Pembroke said, "we will do it by the rules." He moved towards Louis and picked the circlet from his forehead. "Follow me."

The four men went out of the great hall. Outside, the soldiers were waiting anxiously for the outcome of the events. When they appeared, the men expressed their relief and contentment.

"Agroln is dead!" Pembroke shouted to the crowd.

A clamour of triumph rose in the air. The men embraced and congratulated each other. The long years of war were finally over.

"And we have a new king!" Pembroke carried on. The men fell silent and listened with attention. Pembroke fixed the circlet on Louis's forehead. "Pray they approve," Lissandro heard the lord whisper to his friend.

The soldiers did approve and acclaimed their commander with glad shouts and exalted roars. Ignoring his new status, Louis walked through the crowd to congratulate the men for their victory.

"Are you sure you both know what you're doing?" Pembroke muttered to Selen and Lissandro.

"He will need help," Lissandro said. "Will you help him?"

"As much as I can," the lord answered.

"Why did you vouchsafe for him in the first place?" Lissandro inquired.

"I have seen what the man has done with the army. I'm curious to see what he will do with this city," Pembroke grinned.

Lissandro would never have guessed that the lord was such a gambler.

59

An hour after the death of Agroln, the captains and lieutenants were gathered on the esplanade in front of the palace.

"I know that many of you and our soldiers long to return home to Embermire or Millhaven," Louis said, "but before you all get your leave, we need to be ensured that no threat hangs over the capital. At the same time, we will need a force to assure the security of the population. I give you the task to recruit a city watch, as well as guards for the palace, among our bravest men. I will choose the royal guard myself. Have the infirmary installed in one of the cathedral outbuildings. One more thing, have a group of men pick up the bodies in the great hall. I want the place cleaned. Take your leave." While the men dismissed, he turned to Pembroke. "Find the list of the stocks, spare rations for four days, and have the rest distributed in the slums." He hoped there would be something left to give to the ones in need. The night before, he had denied Segar access to the supply train and had ordered that the man be arrested. Yet, Segar and his accomplice Jamys could not be found. "How long before we can gather a high council?" Louis asked Pembroke.

"Now that Agroln is dead, I guess it will only be a matter of hours before the city notables swarm around you. Yet, you can't gather a high council as long as you are not officially king."

"Well, let's have the coronation ceremony tomorrow then," Louis replied.

"Are you serious?" Pembroke looked at him, astounded. "It takes days to organize…"

"And it takes even longer to reorganize a country. The people wait for help. Tomorrow will be fine. Besides, I want to be crowned before I dismiss the army."

"You could keep the army mobilized until you consolidate your power," Pembroke suggested.

"And be a military tyrant as Agroln had been? No," Louis felt already like a usurper, but he would not say it in front of Pembroke. "The people will accept me or they won't. I won't hold the men longer than a few days. The war is over. Everyone needs to return home. Pembroke, you know the city and its people. It should not be too complicated for you to contact the right persons."

"I will make the arrangements. In the meanwhile, I suggest you explore the palace. It is your new home, after all," Pembroke said.

Louis gazed at the palace. *Your new home.* The words sounded weird in his ears. He joined his friends.

The castle was bigger than what it looked like from the outside. The prison tower was situated at the outermost corner, north of the stables and the inner courtyard. At the south corner of the yard stood a large tower with the library, the chapel, and the undercroft. A long gallery connected the tower to the great hall and to the long south aisle with the guests' apartments, the kitchen, and the pantries. In the west of the gallery, stairs led to an inner garden. Over the roof in the west, there was a beautiful view of the mountains overhanging the palace. A peristyle of red tile circled the yard. The mullions of the first floor's windows were chiseled, while the walls of the ground floor had only one door each and no windows except towards the gallery.

"I suppose the royal apartments are in that aisle," Lissandro said looking at the luxurious, oaken, golden door on his left.

"Not a single window. With two guards in front of it, it will look like a cell," Selen complained.

They entered the solar. There were mullioned windows, stained glass in light green and all opening to the south. The walls were painted in ochre, and heavy tapestries covered the windows' sides. The desk, the guéridons, and the cabinets were made of varnished chestnut. There were fauteuils and a love seat of crimson velvet and green satin. From the fireplace to the south wall, red carpets embroidered in gold treads littered the floor. They matched the long curtains circling the high, comfy, canopy bed. Golden and crimson patchwork covered the comforter. Here and there lay blue porcelain vases with dried flowers and silver, ornate candelabra.

Louis regretted the vases were the only blue things in the room.

"This is a nice cell," Lissandro said with amazement.

"It's so beautiful," Selen sighed.

"It looks like Versailles," Louis said. "At least, the idea I have of it."

"The door here leads to another bedroom, but I see no bed," Selen said, puzzled. He had opened the door to the right of the bed.

Louis came closer. "It's a boudoir. It's not made for sleep. It's a kind of meeting room where you can…play."

"And I've found the toilets," Lissandro said from the other side. "I mean, the garderobe."

It was the first one they found. "Thank God," Louis said. "For a moment, I thought the court released itself behind the curtains."

"Yuck! That's disgusting," Selen said.

"I agree, but so were palaces at my time, as I had heard." Louis gazed at the bedroom again. He felt already uncomfortable to be in there, as if he were betraying himself. "I should not live here."

"You will get used to it sooner than you think. I, on the other hand, will forever miss running water. I would exchange any solar against a shower and a toilet with real paper," Lissandro said with melancholy. "And toothpaste. A kingdom for a menthol toothpaste."

"Before you finish your list of your bathroom accommodations, maybe we could discuss the organization of the following events?" Louis suggested, slightly irritated by his friend's superficiality.

"Well, it's simple. You become king and you can do pretty much whatever you want," Lissandro responded while testing an armchair. "Besides, this is a kind of medieval society. It should be quite loose with the etiquette."

"I was not thinking about me. I was thinking about you two," Louis said. He had a pretty clear idea of what he wanted. "You are no nobles, you have no power and no money. At least Selen is a knight." He paused and sat behind the desk. "I can't give you important charges in the government. It would sound as if I favored my friends. Therefore, I thought I could make you my counselors. We won't share the crown, but you will stand at my side."

"This could work, indeed," Lissandro said, "but we will need some responsibilities." Lissandro was silent for a while, thinking. "I managed a company in my world. I could take care of the library and the crows. Archivist is a respectable task, not much coveted, and suits well with counselling."

"What kind of company?" Selen asked.

"Fish sticks."

"Good you want to take that charge," Louis said. "I will need a lot of documents. You can start your functions by finding me the codex with all the laws in application. I need it as soon as possible. Try to search for it today if you are not too exhausted. All my decisions must be in total respect of the laws."

"Prepare yourself to be deceived, then." Lissandro chuckled. "Ever heard of primae noctis?"

"Oh, please. It's a legend," Louis responded. "No one can come with such ideas."

"Yes. Men like Elye do," Lissandro said. "What I mean is that you may have to adapt the laws."

"Louis," Selen called him, sounding desperate. "I'm not sure I can do anything. I have never been more than a guard, and all my previous knowledge is useless here."

"You are not useless. You have been in a royal guard. You must know a lot about court organization," Louis said. He thought of what his friend could do and how he could adapt it to the court. The answer appeared at once, obvious. "You are a physician. You will be the court's official physician. You can use the garden outside, and I will install Brother Benedict in the palace. He will help you." Louis saw Selen's eyes gleam at the news.

"Will we have our own apartments in the south aisle with the guests and nobles?" Lissandro inquired.

"I have a better idea," Louis said. "If all castles are organized the same way, the royal apartments should have many rooms, boudoirs, and such. I just need one room."

"You mean you want us three to live in the king's apartments? Won't it look strange?" Lissandro asked.

"There is a whole aisle, two floors, and it's better three than two," Louis said.

"That's true. Yet, we have to remember that this is a palace. There are servants, maids, and guards roaming around all the time, and probably several dozen of nobles," Lissandro said.

"Do you mean that my life will be a permanent display?" Louis asked, frightened. He had heard of how the monarchs liked to make a show of themselves. Some kings wanted to be observed in the most awkward and intimate moments.

"No, not at all," Lissandro said, reassuring. "I mean that if you want privacy, the doors must imperatively be locked, or you put guards in front. Besides, people will make your bed, wash your clothes…you know," he added, looking at Selen.

"Can we refuse?" Selen asked.

"No. Lords are served. You can do all you want: gamble your whole fortune, plot against your peers, shag maids in a corner, but not your laundry," Lissandro said to Selen.

"I have to go now," Louis said. "I want to talk to Pembroke about tomorrow. Maybe I will meet some flies on the way."

"Flies?" Selen asked.

"Solicitors," Louis said. "Find yourself some rooms and make yourself comfortable." He went out and headed to the great hall.

The bodies had been removed, and groups of men cleaned the whole place. At this pace, it should be done before tomorrow. He met Pembroke on the esplanade. The lord came back from the city accompanied by Honfroi Tollbridge and a slender man Louis had not seen before. Judging by his elegant, crimson robes, the man could be a merchant or a noble.

"Are the preparations going well, my lords?" Louis asked, staring at the stranger.

"We came here to talk to you about it," Honfroi said. The man had avoided referring to him with titles. Louis did not know which of both titles the man had not dared to use. "But first, let me introduce Evrardin Delnay of the most glorious noble family of Nysa Serin."

"My lord." Louis disliked him at once but saluted him with what he hoped to be a convincing smile.

"My lord," Evrardin answered with a honeyed voice. It was the wrong title, but at least it was something.

"So?" Louis grew impatient.

"It is about the preparations. We think that a coronation tomorrow may be a little...hasty," Honfroi said.

"I don't think so," Louis objected. "The people will gather on the streets as usual. I will ride to the temple, and I will be crowned. As simple as that."

"But it is the tradition to organize festivities during the whole day," Honfroi puffed with stupefaction.

"Oh, I see." Louis did see indeed. The men would have him put the Crown in debt from the start for festivities *they* would enjoy. "Well, I was thinking that the glorious families and richest notables of Nysa Serin could reward their brave liberators by taking the charge of these festivities. I am sure that the men of the Rebellion would be grateful for this honorable gesture." Louis paused to enjoy the sour look on their faces. "We crossed the city a few hours ago, and I remember smelling the most delicious perfumes of spices and fruits. Surely, it would not be too difficult to satisfy our guests with one single dinner, and the soldiers would be pleased with some salted pork and beer." Louis held Honfroi's look, making it clear to them that this would be the way things would be done and no other.

"This is a brilliant idea! Don't you think, my lords?" Pembroke exclaimed. "There is no better way to carve your names in the Rebellion's glorious story. The Nobles who rewarded the heroes. Bards will sing of you."

"Indeed, indeed," Honfroi stammered. "Everything will be ready by tomorrow." The two rich men took their leave.

"This was a good start," Pembroke chuckled once they were gone. "Good you will be crowned tomorrow. At least, it was entertaining."

Louis thought he would have to give the nobles something in return to occupy them. An honorific function or titles. Some people craved that kind of things. He had not liked the look in Evrardin's eyes. "Can you tell me about the ceremony?" Louis asked Pembroke.

"You will ride to the temple. Your friends and the captains of the Rebellion, me included, can ride behind you to give a mass effect. You will enter the temple. Then, it's the usual religious ceremony. The priest crowns you. You leave the temple and ride back to the palace where the celebrations begin."

"No," Louis said.

"What do you mean, no?" Pembroke asked, taken aback.

"I will ride to the temple with my captains and the Rebellion army behind us. It is the soldiers' day as well as mine. We will have the coronation outside the temple, for the whole population to see. Then, they can have a ceremony inside the temple if they wish. Oh, and I want a child of the slums to crown me, not the priest. It will be done in the sight of our Lord, but I am, above all the people's king," Louis told Pembroke, looking directly at him.

"They will hate it, especially the high priest," Pembroke uttered in disbelief.

"And you? Will you hate it?" Louis asked. He tried not to say it in a challenging tone. He had no grudge against Pembroke.

The features of the lord changed. "I think it will be…entertaining." Pembroke half smiled.

Louis smiled. He liked the man after all. "When I will be king, I would like you to be my treasurer." Louis considered it the most crucial function. Therefore, he needed someone he could trust.

"You honour me with your trust," Pembroke said. "Now, if I may, I suggest you take some rest before tomorrow, and this includes removing your armour."

Louis realized that he had not even changed since the morning. He squirmed. "I will."

"The palace stands on hot springs. The king's apartments are famous for their bathroom. You probably missed it during your first visit," Pembroke said. "I will go back to the city and fix the preparations. We will meet tomorrow for the last details." The lord took his leave.

Louis strode back to the palace, through the great hall, and up the steps to the inner garden. The baths were situated on the flank of the mountain, in the aisle adjacent to his apartments. Louis understood why the bathroom was famous. There were pools of different sizes carved in the stone, and water poured out of granite figures onto the floor. There were racks for armours, tables with towels, rudimentary mirrors, and what he supposed to be a medieval version of hygienic utensils. The place was hot and slightly misty. Louis removed his armour. The damp air made his linen stuck on his body. He undressed and put a hand on the side of his throat where he had bled. The blood had clotted. He scratched the crust. He walked under one of the waterfalls. The feeling of the hot water pouring on his head was a bliss. Louis washed the disgusting marks the creature had left on his neck. He disliked he could not as easily wash away the feeling the rich men had created by their presence. He feared he would have to keep the men close to have an eye on them. If they had been the first to cross his way, it meant they were the most powerful in the capital, or worked for the most powerful. He would have to instruct his friends about all this.

Louis walked back to the table, dried himself, and looked at his linen with disgust. Plain robes lay folded on a shelf. He put some on and went to his apartments. As he opened the door, his heart rejoiced. "I knew you would be there."

"I am reading about the history of the capital. It's fascinating," Selen said with a smile.

He sat on the windowsill, a book in his hand. He had bathed and changed clothes. The tips of his hair were still wet, dropping silently against the stone wall in dark streaks. Louis stared at him. If he had not known him intimately, this choice of outfit would have been confusing. Selen noticed his expression.

"Yes, I know. It seems they like robes here. It would not be my first choice either," Selen said, embarrassed.

Louis walked towards his friend and hugged him. "It doesn't matter. We can adapt as long as we don't have to wear our armours again." He sighed, his chin on Selen's shoulder. He could smell the honeysuckle perfume of his hair again. He had missed his love so much. "Can I have the book once you're done with it?"

"Of course." Selen put the book on the side.

Louis looked outside. The view of the south plains was breathtaking. The sun was setting in the west and bathed the fields in a pink, orange light. Louis noticed a persistent noise. The cascade flowed right under the window in a loud rumbling. "At least, no one can enter through the window," he whispered.

"This room is a golden cage," Selen sighed. His friend turned his face to him, his green, doe eyes staring at him. Louis felt like gazing at the sea from a cliff. It felt like ages since the last time Selen was this close to him. He still found it hard to believe that they would see each other every day from now on—and not only see. He had not forgotten to lock the door.

"Do you think it's all over?" Selen asked.

"No," Louis whispered. "It has just begun."

He took Selen's lips between his and grazed his tongue on the edge of Selen's teeth. Selen welcomed the kiss. His mouth opened to meet him. Louis was surprised to taste almond and peach. Selen's long fingers ran through his brown locks, tugging at his earring. Louis had noticed Selen's fascination with his hair. The way his friend looked at him in public made him sometimes feel ill-at-ease to the point that he had to repress blushing. He would have to talk to Selen about it again. No one could know. One of his hands slipped under Selen's robes, along his firm ankle and bare leg.

"I don't think robes should be worn with nothing under," he said, teasing, his hand slowly moving upwards.

"I can't tell you how many times I wanted your firm hands under my clothes," Selen whispered between two kisses. His words sent hot sparks through Louis's body.

Before Louis's hand reached his thigh, Selen climbed down from the windowsill. Louis pressed against him, blocking Selen's bottom against the wall's edge. He nibbled at Selen's earlobe and ran his tongue down his throat to his collarbone. Selen breathed faint moans. They were nearly squeaks. Selen's hips wriggled against his. Louis stepped back and removed his clothes. Biting his lip, Selen stared at his naked body.

Louis looked at his friend. "You really should not have put the robe on," he said, smiling.

Selen understood and blushed with embarrassment. He went to remove his clothes, but Louis stopped him. "No. Come." Taking Selen's hands in his, he led him to the bed and made him sit on the edge. Louis knelt between the open legs of his friend and kissed him tenderly. With a sigh, Selen lay down on his back.

His hands grazing up Selen's graceful, spread legs, Louis raised the cloth to the waist. Selen's shivering body waited as a chalice, and Louis couldn't wait to soothe his thirst. Louis covered both inner thighs with delicate kisses, up to the crotch. When he opened his mouth on Selen's tender perineum, his friend uttered a deep sigh, and his body tensed. At this delicate sound, the urge in Louis's crotch intensified, but he would not touch himself. Keeping his full lips moist, he brushed them on Selen's most sensitive parts. He knew Selen's hand would soon be on his head. Louis welcomed his grip. It meant Selen enjoyed the tease, and Louis could spend hours between his legs.

"Lower," Selen mewed between two gasps.

Louis complied. The tip of Selen's fingers ran through his hair. Louis put two of his fingers in his mouth and used them to fondle his friend, pushing them inside the tight entrance one knuckle after the other. While his fingers slid in, his lips ran up through Selen's fair curls, and onto Selen's shaft. His tongue trailed on it, licked the beads on the slit before he swallowed Selen deep. He was pleased to find the familiar taste of honey blend with salt again. His attentions were rewarded with intense purrs. Louis forced himself to stop and rose.

While Selen took his robes over his head, Louis climbed on the bed and knelt between his friend's long legs. Selen's lilac hair fell wildly over the side of his body. Though not larger than his, Selen's chest was fit, the mark of long, intensive years of training. Biting on his lip, Louis savored the sight. He lowered his head. With his hungry mouth, he sucked at Selen's nipples, pulling until the tips hardened. Selen moaned. His friend grabbed his neck to kiss him. Louis embraced him.

"I love you," Louis whispered, desperate with love and burning with desire.

"Me too," Selen cooed. "Take me," he whispered, folding his soft fingers around Louis's erection.

Selen gave a light pull that made Louis gasp. Louis looked down. Selen's forehead, still resting against his, followed his move. He removed Selen's hand from his aching member and entered his friend slowly, relishing the tight and warm feeling. Selen arched back with a scream of pleasure. Louis grabbed his friend's legs and raised them onto his shoulders, holding the muscular thighs firmly in his hands. He knew he would not last. It had been too long since Millhaven. His heart was already pulsing fast, and he was horny. He looked down and observed how his length disappeared in long strokes into Selen up to his hair. Raising his gaze, he stared at Selen's stretched, swollen member, so inviting. His body craved it more than ever. Louis realized he should not have thought that. He closed his eyes shut. His climax overwhelmed him, unexpected and intense. Louis released himself inside Selen with a scream.

"Please, touch me," Selen begged him.

Panting, Louis lay down on top of his friend and kissed him lovingly. "I want to be one with you," he whispered. "I want us to be as equals. I need you." He had dared to say the words and hoped Selen would agree.

It took time for Selen to understand. His eyes grew wider. "No. I can't do that," Selen whispered, confused. "You are… I can't top. I don't want to."

Louis refused to force his love. He regretted his words, and his frustration was tainted with the shame to have revealed such an intimate urge. He saw Selen smile.

"Wait," Selen said, placing his hands on Louis's waist. His friend swiveled him until Louis lay with his back on Selen.

For what seemed an eternity, Selen caressed his chest and prepared Louis's willing body with his delicate fingers. It was not the first time Selen had fondled him deeply but never with such dexterity. It sent shivers down his spine. Louis heard Selen inhale the scent of his hair.

"I have never…" his friend breathed with his fetching candor.

"Yes, I know," Louis whispered, "but I have." Only it was in his previous life, so ages ago. Yet, he would give a hint of his stress. His mind wanted it, and so did his flesh. He wanted to be held, to be taken, to feel he was loved. As Selen positioned his member, Louis gasped with expectation. His breathing was short, and his heart hastened.

"You need to relax," Selen whispered.

Selen grabbed Louis's neck with his mouth and sucked it while gradually lifting his hips. The sudden heat on Louis's neck loosened the tension in his lower parts. Still, it was painful. Louis's fists twisted the sheets. He bit his lip. *I'm his first time.*

Once entirely inside, Selen held him fast, breathing hard. Louis understood and lay still until his friend had calmed down. His own body relaxed as well, and pain disappeared. He stretched his arms behind his head to reach Selen's neck and hair. He felt Selen's mouth grab his fingers and suck at them, swirling his tongue on the sensitive skin. Louis gasped. His friend was naturally skilled. Gently, Louis rocked his hips. It felt incredibly good, filling him and tearing him apart in pleasure. He noticed he was getting hard again. Selen's fingers pinched at one of his nipples, while the other hand clenched the inside of his thigh, holding him as Selen buried himself inside with long, slow moves. Louis did not hold back his moans. The voluptuous delight on each part of his body awoke all his senses. "I'm yours," he breathed. "As I made you mine."

The embrace around him tightened. The worship they felt for each other reached its peak in a complete abandon of their bodies. They merged like one mind, one flesh. And Selen was his perfect warrior. When Louis remembered what he had heard about Selen's battle by the dam, he grasped Selen's hand and carried it from his chest to his mouth to suck avidly at Selen's fingers. In response, Selen's hips increased their pace upwards. Louis could barely feel his mind. Greedy, he thrust his bottom down. Selen's teeth bit on his fingers as Selen came, long and deep. Once Selen's body stopped shaking, Louis moved to the side to stare at his friend. Selen's eyes sparkled with amazement.

"Wow, that was..." Selen whispered, panting, "...great."

"And it was only the first time of many. Turn around," Louis whispered in his friend's ear. Selen's big, emerald eyes looked over at him. Selen grinned.

"Did I cause that?" Selen teased, gazing at his loins. "It shouldn't be wasted." Selen was exhausted but still eager. After weeks of repressed desire and intense emotions, his friend was crawling the walls.

Selen kissed him and placed himself on hands and knees, his hips up. He turned his head to look at him. Selen's smiling mouth was slightly open, and locks of hair stuck on the side of his face. He could not be more inviting. Louis placed himself behind Selen and cupped one firm cheek with his hand. His friend's thighs were sticky. As it was the second time, Louis knew he would not hurt his love. Considering the sudden rapture on Selen's features when he plunged his hips forward, he did not. His hands stretched on Selen's back and took hold of his arms. Selen pushed his hips backwards. Louis wanted more than to satisfy him, he wanted to blow out the last sparkles of his friend's mind. He rode Selen long and ardently, his hips high to press on the sensitive spot. Louis pulled on Selen's arms to reach Selen's mouth with his, partially covering their frantic moans.

"Come, my love," he breathed.

Selen's screams of ecstasy, tinging like fragile crystal drops, were music to his ears. Selen's body contracted, closing around Louis like an iron grip. Louis threw his head backwards and cried out. His mind exploded as he climaxed again.

They collapsed on the bed, panting, their warm skin covered with small beads of sweat. Louis held his love tight against him. Their arms entwined. The urge was gone, only their unbridled affection lingered. Their faces rubbed against each other. They smiled and chuckled.

"Until we die?" Selen whispered.

"Until we die," Louis breathed. His heart burned. *And I swear to make you smile,* he thought.

Listening to his friend's breathing, Louis rested until Selen fell asleep in his arms. Bathed in the moonlight, Selen looked even more innocent and pristine. Never had Louis wanted to be king, but now that he had accepted, he would do all in his power to build a world where the guiltless like his love would be happy and protected.

Silently, he got up and walked to the desk. Inside, he found some paper, ink, and a quill. Louis went back to the bed. He searched for a dry spot to sit on but gave up. They would probably need to burn the sheet anyway. He lit a candle. His left hand coiled in a lock of Selen's long hair as he wrote.

60

The first time they had crossed the capital, it had been empty and silent, like a ghost city. Today, Lissandro had the impression that all the people of Nysa Serin and around had gathered on the streets. Everyone wanted to see their liberators, and above all, their new king. Flags and banners of different colors, representing Trevalden, the city, or its areas, hung from the terraces and windows. Roses and daisies had been twined with ribbons on poles and columns. Men in working aprons saluted them. Lissandro saw butchers, tanners, clog-makers, smiths; all had left their activities to see them. Women carrying their children high in their arms wore crowns of flowers. From balconies, maidens tossed petals as their horses walked up the street. The jubilation of the commoners warmed his heart. Lissandro wondered how it must feel for Louis to see all these joyful, gleaming faces cheer him. His friend had insisted that it was the Rebellion's victory day, but as it was also his coronation, he had been forced to ride at the front.

Louis wore long, royal blue robes with large, silver arabesques around the collar and shoulders. The sleeves were split open on the ample white shirt underneath. He had dark blue pants and his usual riding boots. His outfit was elegant but as sober as it could be. Lissandro rode behind him, in parallel with Selen. His friend was radiant. *Not too hard to figure out why*, Lissandro thought, amused. He had to admit that Selen was a man one would love to cherish, and Louis never did things halfway. Selen was dressed in light beige robes and pants of the same color. He had braided a silver chain around the length of his long, lilac hair. It was held on the side of his head by small pearls that glittered in the light. Selen looked like an elf who had escaped from his magical land. As for himself, Lissandro had opted for embroidered, pale green robes, which did not make him look less from an enchanting place. Like Louis's, his hair floated in light brown curls around his shoulders, but in a slightly fairer tone. Their horses had been combed and braided. Judging by the three riders at the front, Lissandro considered it was more an elven king invading Nysa Serin than Caesar returning from the Gauls. This blatant lack of virility was barely rectified right behind them by Pembroke and Folc, restricted in their colorful, puffing doublets and exuberant burgundy hoses of the latest fashion. The two men wore golden necklaces and large hats with feathers. The whole army of the Rebellion followed them in a bright line of polished plates and greased leather.

The street opened wide. In front of them, the square leading to the temple was littered with thousands of people. It had a sloping pavement in red bricks and ended in a long flight of stairs. A prestigious assembly composed of the nobles, the high priest, and his deacons waited for them in front of the gilt-bronze doors of the majestic, white building. The temple was as large as the cathedrals Lissandro had seen in his world and was surrounded by four spire towers. Column statues of white marble representing the twelve gods adorned the façade. It was also embellished with a colorful mosaic on the tympanum. Lissandro regretted that he would not see the inside of the temple, not today at least.

The cortege halted. Louis dismounted and climbed the stairs. Lissandro, Selen, and the captains followed him and placed themselves on the side with the nobles. The high priest was a chubby, short man with a thick, white beard dressed in an embroidered golden chasuble. Lissandro could tell by his surly look that Louis's decision had deeply offended him. The nobles did not look more joyful. Still, they were curious and observed their future king with inquisitive eyes half hidden under hats with large rims and pastel organza.

The high priest opened the ceremony with a pompous speech about the ancient lineages, the calamities of war and the gods above. His interventions were broken by hymns sung by a choir of young boys. Lissandro listened with only half an ear. He stared at the crowd. While some people bore on their faces the scars of the pangs of war, others displayed shameless wellness. The four years of Agroln's tyranny had not affected everyone the same way.

The crowd cheered. Louis stepped forward and addressed the people, glorifying the bravery of the soldiers of the Rebellion and the peace to come. Lissandro had beseeched him to keep it as simple and short as possible. The crowd wanted a show, not a monologue on the constitution.

The high priest recited a prayer and walked towards Louis. "In front of the gods, in heaven and earth, the king will now swear the oath concerning his people and the Church," the old man said towards the crowd.

Louis stepped to the edge of the stairs and knelt, his arms open as if to embrace the multitude. "I, Louis, King of Trevalden, swear to guarantee the security and the peace of my people, to administer justice, and to protect the faith." Lissandro noticed how his friend twisted the last word. While incense dangled around them, the high priest said the prayer of the consecration.

There was a religious silence as a little girl in a plain white dress climbed the stairs. Under her crown of flowers, her auburn hair flew around her face. Her broad, innocent smile revealed her white teeth and the gaps where the milk ones were missing. With her small hands, she fixed the circlet on Louis's forehead and, in a childish reflex, brushed his hair back. Louis raised his head and looked at her with the kindest gaze. He took her hand in his and rose, smiling at the crowd. His people broke into loud demonstrations of joy and enthusiastic hails.

Congratulations, you have crowned a regicide, Lissandro thought. *May the king live forever, amen.* He turned around. The reaction from the esplanade was ice-cold. Lissandro had no illusion about how things would turn out in the future.

The festivities were held in the great hall. The place had been scrubbed clean, and the floor was now covered with long benches and tables decorated with wreaths and bunches of flowers. On the dais, a group of musicians played charming songs. There were three tables, one for the king and the most eminent men of the city, and two long ones, perpendicular to the table of honour. The guests entered the hall. Pembroke sat down at Louis's right side. To honour him for his deeds, Louis had proposed the seat on his left to Josselin. Lissandro noticed Kilda's absence. He guessed that the change would have been too hard on her. Lissandro chose a seat at the long table on the right.

"May I sit next to you?" Selen asked. His friend wore long watery green robes with gold threads that suited his hair color perfectly. His appearance was the evocation of spring reflected on water.

"Of course," he answered. "Are you afraid to mix with the crowd?" Lissandro grinned.

"Yes," Selen answered feebly, candid as usual. His voice was barely audible under the notes of the hurdy-gurdy. "I should not be here."

"Louis has dedicated this day to the Rebellion. You have every right in the world to be here," Lissandro said, carving his bottom in the cushions on the bench. "Besides, I do enjoy your company."

When everyone had taken a seat, the servants came with the wine in golden carafes. Once served, Lissandro put the filled chalice to his lips. The claret had the color of cherry and was fruity with notes of raspberries. At his side, Selen took a large sip of his cup. Lissandro wondered how many cups his friend would need to survive his environment.

There was no boundary in the luxury of the table settings. The plates were of punched tin and the silver cutlery was gold rimmed. Lissandro took his knife in his hand and admired the sparkle on the pointy end. Dishes were served. A whole wild boar stuffed with cherries was placed in front of them. Lissandro sliced an ear and gnawed at it.

"I always thought it was only a dog snack until I tasted one," he said, chewing. Selen struggled to move a pheasant leg onto his plate with his dagger. "You can use your fingers," Lissandro suggested. Irritated, his friend stabbed a pink apple instead.

"I don't really wish to give the same sight as what I see around me," Selen replied. He put the fruit to his full lips. Lissandro watched him take a bite. The apple crackled under his white teeth. Droplets of juice dribbled from the peel onto his skin. Lissandro broke his stare and looked around.

The guests helped themselves to civets of hare, salted stags, or swans stuffed with mushrooms. The nobles sucked on their greasy fingers and tore the roasted flesh with gluttony. One man swallowed oysters. The salty water ran copiously on his chin. Another lord in front of Lissandro took a whole mutton leg from a platter and gnawed at it. There was no end to the cortege of plates. The guests were offered capons flavored with cloves, sturgeons in ginger, plums stewed in brandy, sweet tarts, candied fruits and many more expensive dishes Lissandro could not see.

"I do hope Louis did not pay for this," Lissandro whispered. The capon wing in his hand tasted like paradise. He relished every bite as if it were his last supper.

"He didn't," Selen said, picking at the mulberries on his plate. "They paid."

"Oh? We will count this as his first miracle," Lissandro picked a hare leg and put it on Selen's plate.

The nobles fluttered about in their glimmering clothes, sharing amiabilities and compliments on the ceremony and on their overdone outfits. It was a ball of mannerism and syrupy smiles.

Lissandro's neighbor leaned towards him. The man was young with an amber complexion. He had dark eyes, and Lissandro would swear that his eyebrows were enhanced with kohl.

"And you, what is your task in the government?" the man asked, all toady.

"I am responsible for the archives and the library," Lissandro answered.

"Oh," the man raised an eyebrow with indifference. "Did they have well-read people in the Rebellion beside Pembroke?" Lissandro just learned where an archivist could situate himself on the social echelon.

"Do you suggest that the king is uneducated?" Lissandro inquired.

"Well, you have lived in the mud for four years, as I have heard. Quite a rustic way of life for civilized people," the man said, biting at a plum.

For his own safety, this man should never pass less than a hundred yards from Louis. Expatriation would even be recommended. Lissandro decided not to share the precious counsel. "If I may suggest his lordship to step back. You may fall down looking at me from such a height," Lissandro sneered. The man pivoted contemptuously to his other side. "So much for making new friends," Lissandro muttered to himself and turned to Selen again. His friend had finally decided to eat something consistent and chewed on a quail's bone.

"So, how is the life in your apartments?" Lissandro asked. Considering that Lissandro had kindly agreed to sleep simultaneously in two bedrooms, he guessed that Selen understood his insinuation. "Still feeling in a cage?"

"I still do," Selen replied, "but I have to admit that you were right. One gets easily used to comfort. I could spend half my day in the bathroom and the other half in the garden. Yet, I still can't wash away the filth of these last months."

"I can assure you that you are beyond clean, especially if we take the present assembly as a point of reference. Rub harder with your soap, and you will polish your bones." Lissandro decided to taste the sturgeon. The fresh ginger burned in his mouth.

"I have found interesting books in one of the solar's cabinets. Are there some in your apartments too?" With his greasy fingers in the air, Selen searched for a napkin. "Have you seen bread?"

"Don't search in vain. It's the bowl of water in front of you, or the tablecloth," Lissandro whispered. "Yes, I have some books as well. I found one about ornithology. Are you interested in something in particular?"

Selen had opted for the tablecloth and cleaned the tips of his fingers with an expression of slight disgust and shame. "Actually, I would be interested in learning more about the history of the land and politics." Selen leaned towards him. "Sometimes, I don't understand what Louis wants to say, and I don't like to feel stupid."

"Don't worry about that. It's not you. All the books in the world won't help," Lissandro said but realized it might have hurt his friend's feelings. "Still, I will give you all I can find about politics and history." He smiled.

As the wine and hippocras flowed, the manners loosened. Men shouted lewd jokes and women chirped. The man in front of him was fed fried duck hearts by a giggling young woman sitting on his lap. In her corsage, she put a morsel that the man tried to fetch with his mouth. The guests around them laughed coarsely. One mimicked the sound of a pig and got applause for his interpretation. Even women displayed tasteless behavior. A red-haired woman got a golden coin to have her breasts kissed.

"Wealthy and greedy for more," Lissandro sighed.

Some guests rose to dance in the space between the tables. The colorful satin, the rich brocades, and the organza veils twirled around the emerald lace in the rhythm of voltes. Men in silk and carved leather raised hats decorated with beads and feathers.

"May I have this dance?" he whispered to Selen, teasing.

"Don't make me say yes," Selen grumbled. Lissandro was surprised to notice disgust in Selen's eyes. His friend who had been radiant during the ceremony this morning, gazing at Louis like Hephaestion at his Alexander, had now turned morose.

"You're right. It may not please the king," Lissandro said, turning his eyes on Louis. The look on Louis's face was even worse than Selen's. Lissandro wondered if they had crowned a raptor. His smiles were hints of bites, and all in his features displayed a blatant condescendence. The articulations of his fingers looked sore as he twisted them together in anger. Fortunately, this rude sight was compensated by Louis's cold appeal.

"My dear," Lissandro heard Honfroi address the giggly company sitting around him. "How dreadful the preparations of this day have been. The servants were so terrible at their tasks. It was a miracle that I could find enough brandy in that damn city. And you should have seen my terror when I learned that the shops were out of figs."

"What do you know of terror?" Louis snapped. "Has your neck been near a blade once except to shave your chins?"

The fat man fell silent. He probably had sensed the wind of the blade.

Pembroke rose and left his seat to dance. Lissandro took advantage of the situation to slip away from his place and sit next to Louis.

"Work on your smile. It's turning into a rictus, and it's scaring me," Lissandro whispered to his friend.

"Look at those indecent imbeciles," Louis whispered, raging. "Talking only about debauchery, mode, lifestyle, and horses. We should be celebrating the Rebellion, the soldiers. These men take the laurels for deeds they could not achieve. Such decadence. Look at this scene. It's only missing the buffooneries of fools and the fondling of courtesans, and only because I can't see behind the curtains. Their words are poison in wicked mouths. And to display such prodigality right after a long war, when our people starve. Their despicable baseness is barely conceivable."

Louis's anger was so sincere and passionate. Lissandro had to admit that there was something enticing to it. No wonder Louis had led the Rebellion with style. Lissandro would have picked up any sword, should Louis had said the right words. "It's called a court, and you know that," Lissandro said. They watched Selen rise from his place and leave the hall with dignity. Their friend could not endure it anymore.

"I know," Louis sighed, "and I'm the king of that flock. Wait until tomorrow. They will have to justify all that."

"Careful, Louis. I know what you want, but they are powerful. Move cleverly." As Lissandro spoke, a drunken young lord from the table on the left had opened a serving maid's corsage and poured wine on her tits. He dragged her onto his lap and raised her skirts. The giggling girl sat astride the lord and wiggled while the man licked the wine. There could be no misinterpretation of their actions. The men sitting on the side encouraged their friend.

"That's enough," Louis snarled, infuriated. As he rose, all the faces swiveled towards him. Lissandro looked at Louis with appealing eyes and moved his lips in a clear no. The veins on Louis's throat bulged. "In the name of the Rebellion and the Crown, I wish to thank all the noble families for their generosity and wonderful festivities. I will now retire myself and hope you will enjoy the rest of the evening." The lords rose and hailed him, raising their goblets. Louis bowed his head in a short salute and left the hall with the dignity and coldness of death.

"Back in the saddle," Lissandro whispered. He took a last sip of his wine and gazed at the crowd. His friend had seen pigs, and he would make them squeal.

61

"Strength is neither justice nor law. But it's impossible not to use it to enforce law and justice. The government, and here I mean the institutions, must be strong to be just. It is neither oppressive nor harsh, as only evil will suffer. The citizen is accountable to his conscience and the ethics; should he forget it, he is still accountable to the law; should he despise the law, he is no more a citizen," Selen whispered, reading the papers. Such hard words and yet so true. There were more pages to read, all covered with reflections and thoughts. Some were crossed out and some had been hastily written in a corner.

Selen caressed his love's soft curls. Louis slept, his head resting on Selen's bare abdomen. He looked so peaceful and fair despite the shadow of a morning beard. Selen wondered which pages had been written last night. The festivities had awoken dark memories in Selen's mind, but it had infuriated Louis. His friend had not shouted. He had thrown one of the porcelain decorations on the floor and had sat on the bed in silence, his ice cold gaze lost in thoughts. Selen had crept behind him and had held him. Though he had wanted to assure Louis of his support, he had not forced him to confide in him. Once his temper had cooled down, Louis had taken the quill and had written pages throughout the night. Selen was curious to know what kind of reflections had followed from it.

"What are you reading?" Louis asked. He had woken up and his half-opened, blue eyes looked up at Selen.

"Your notes," Selen answered. "They were scattered on the bed, so I guessed I could. It's very interesting."

"Do you think so? I mean, do you agree?" Louis inquired, surprised.

"I don't understand some concepts, but I agree."

"So you will probably agree with my intervention at the high council today. I wonder who will sit there. Pembroke said we will be eight." Louis grazed a finger around Selen's navel.

"Probably Honfroi Tollbridge and the other, that weasel…" Selen's eyes narrowed. "Evrardin," he said with disgust. He had met the man the day before and had noticed something vicious in his smile. "I am more worried for this afternoon." They would face the whole court in the great hall. Everyone would look at him at one point.

"Me too, but you don't have to say anything. Maybe they will be too drunk and sick to show up." Louis pushed back his hair. The earring felt cold on Selen's abdomen.

"You would hate that," Selen said, "or maybe it would be a way to sort out the ones to trash."

"Nice you got it." Louis smiled.

"About the royal guard. I made the list you wanted. Here is my proposal." Selen handed him one of the papers. Louis read through the names. Selen had chosen among the most faithful and honest soldiers of the Rebellion that he had judged apt to the task.

"Folc?"

"I know he will stick out by his youth, but he will never betray you." It was also a way to give the boy a roof over his head and to keep him close.

"I was not objecting. We will acknowledge them this afternoon." Louis crept up and kissed him, an arm around his waist. Selen gave back the kiss and the cuddle. "Shall we prepare ourselves and see who those three mysterious counselors are?" Louis said.

As foreseen, Honfroi Tollbridge and Evrardin Delnay were present. Another counselor was Hernays Dunstan. Selen had seen the man dance during the festivities. A jovial, handsome, blond man who apparently had abused the wine. Hernays's eyes were hollow, and by his features, Selen presumed the man still drowned in his hangover. The fourth man was sober and aware. His name was Mauger Hayward. The strong, bearded man with brown skin looked stern and ready to begin the discussions. Selen had never seen him before. All were nobles. It seemed it was the main condition to be in the high council. Louis stared at the last man.

"What on earth are you doing here?" Louis inquired.

"I assist at the council, Your Majesty. As all my predecessors have done before," the high priest answered.

"I ask you to leave this table. I would like to begin the discussions," Louis said. All the counselors, Pembroke included, looked surprised.

"Your Majesty, the high priest—" Pembroke said.

"Has understood my command," Louis insisted.

"But I am one of the most important men of this city. My word weights," The high priest objected with indignation.

"It would be if you led people to a social harmony and an inner communion with our Lord," Louis said. "But you use your function to maintain the people in ignorance in the fear of the powerful. You are a rampart for tyranny. Anyway, I don't want a religious man at my table."

"I have to give shelter to your men in my outbuildings," the high priest snarled. The clumsy threat was badly received by everyone.

"Would you dare refuse assistance and compassion to men in need?" Louis retorted, looking at the priest with daggers in his eyes. "And it's *Your Majesty*. This is your last warning."

The man looked around him for support, but no one spoke. "Your Majesty, I am the high priest, I represent the gods on earth."

"I don't mistake the censer for the God," Louis replied crisply.

Infuriated, the high priest rose and left the room.

Louis turned to Pembroke. "How much does the Crown give to the Church through donations and granted taxes on the population?"

Though Selen had only simple notions of economy, Pembroke's answer sounded excessive if Selen compared the sum to the cost of yesterday's festivities.

"Cut all. Let him live on roots. It will teach him the meaning of charity," Louis said. "And as we talk about religion, I forbid public manifestations of faith that are not related to a traditional celebration day. I want the doors of every temple open as a shelter for the poor and to remind these priests that they are a part of this city. Temples are not private property. At the same time, besides their holy occupations, every priest must exercise a profession useful for the population. Finally, the new laws will be proclaimed in the temples, but I don't want any mention of God in the documents. Regardless of God's infinite grandeur and the merit of his Church, the earth belongs to men's hands, and priests belong to the laws of this world in the spirit of truth, and truth itself comes from God."

Pembroke took notes. Selen thought that if Louis's words were put into action, the blow would shake one of the pillars of the framework which hemmed in this society. Selen still had difficulties in understanding this concept of religion and the ridiculous importance these people put in the men guarding the temples. The gods were everywhere, not locked in temples, and anyone could talk to them. He covered his smile with a hand and looked at the gaping counselors.

"So, my lords, shall we begin?" Louis asked.

"Well, Your Majesty, there are the functions of your ministers, the Crown's finances, and your name," Pembroke listed.

"What about my name?" Louis asked astounded.

"Yes, Your Majesty. We will have to fix the heraldry and the protocol," Pembroke explained. "But we can talk about it later," he added, noticing that the subject embarrassed Louis. "So, the functions of your ministers."

"As you probably know already, Selen will bring his voice to this council as a physician of the court. As for the ministries, I have decided that you, Pembroke, will be treasurer. Honfroi, you will be chamberlain."

"It will be an honour, Your Majesty," the round man said. Selen did not see where the honour was in being in charge of the palace. Still, the title sounded important.

"Mauger. You will be keeper of the seals," Louis carried on.

This was an important function, and by the disappointed look on Evrardin's face, much coveted.

"Hernays, you will be in charge of the city watch," Louis said.

Selen stared at the man. Hernays was probably a few years younger than him. He must come from an important family to receive such a post, usually entrusted to seasoned knights. Hernays winked at him with a lewd smile. Selen looked away in confusion. A very important family.

"And Evrardin, you will be responsible for the city's planning and architecture," Louis said.

Evrardin looked at Louis aghast and puffed up like a frog. "Your Majesty…"

"It is an important post. I intend to make changes in the capital. I need someone who knows the place and its people," Louis said.

And with Pembroke holding the purse strings, the man had his hands tied. He would be important but powerless.

"But, Your Majesty, you have not named a high constable," Evrardin said.

"Because I don't need one. I am the king and commander of the army in case of war, and there won't be any more war," Louis responded. "What of the state finances?" his friend asked to change the subject and close the discussion.

"Well, Your Majesty is not broke…but the treasury has seen better days," Pembroke said, embarrassed.

"If I may suggest something, Your Majesty," Honfroi said, "we could trade more goods with the Iron Marches."

"The answer is in the quantity, Your Majesty. We need to create more money to invest in long-term projects," Evrardin proposed. "I could come up with a few ideas for buildings."

"Ah, Your Majesty. Taxes. There is nothing that works better than new taxes," Hernays exclaimed.

"Indeed, indeed. Any more useful suggestions?" Louis asked. Selen heard the sarcasm behind the amiable tone. Mauger stayed silent. "Then, I thank you for your counsels, my lords. You can take your leave. Pembroke, I will have a word with you." He made a sign to Selen to stay as well. The ministers rose and left the room.

"You have not told me your decision about the taxes, Your Majesty," Pembroke said.

"Apply a tax on the foreign trade. The bread is needed here. All transactions of lands done by the Crown under Agroln's reign are considered invalid. Take back all the lands and divide them into useful parcels you will share equally between the poor to eradicate mendicity. At the same time, all the nobles who have not shown active support to the Rebellion during the war will have a part of their lands confiscated," Louis turned to Pembroke. "Yes, impose a tribute, not taxes, we make it simple, but proportionated to the incomes. I mean, increasing. And everyone has to pay. Remember that a man doesn't need more money than he needs to take care of his family and live decently on his own parcel of land. Do not create a single coin. What we need to eradicate is speculation. Maybe these measures will unblock money and give work to the people."

Pembroke looked at Selen, who nodded. "They won't tolerate…" Pembroke said.

"I know, it will be hard," Louis interrupted him. "You don't need to do everything in one day. Yet, we have to be firm, and make it public to have the support of the population." Louis rose. "They showed us yesterday how filthy rich they were. I will show them that opulence is infamy." Louis and Selen headed for the door. Louis turned back. "What of my name?"

The big books were spread open on the desk. Selen tried to understand something in the long, obscure lists of sums and accounts of the treasury while Louis had buried himself in the laws register.

"It is a nightmare," Louis sighed. "These laws are abstruse, outdated, and unjust. I would not follow them myself, let alone force them on the people."

"Can't we brush out the oldest ones and insist on the most important?" Selen suggested.

"This is what we will have to do until we have new laws. God knows what they apply in justice courts right now," Louis exclaimed.

"It is a lot of work, but you could administer justice yourself until you have written new laws," Selen said.

Louis raised his head and stared at him. "No, my love. You don't understand. If I administer justice without following the law, it will only be my own subjective opinion. Everything has to be done according to the laws, and I can't write them myself. They must represent the people's will. If the people are consulted individually in the creation of the laws, everyone will come with what is best for his own interest, and the sum of all those interests will be the best for everyone. With wise and inflexible laws, the whole system will work in a harmonious, natural way, without weakness or constraint."

Selen gaped at Louis. He progressively understood the level of social justice his friend wanted to reach. It nearly made his head swim.

The door of the solar slammed open and closed briskly. "Jesus Christ, Louis! What on earth have you done up there?" Lissandro shouted.

"I know you are my friend, but it happens I am the king. Don't make a scandal," Louis threatened him.

"The high priest *and* the nobles at the same time, on the first day. Are you out of your mind?" Lissandro hissed.

"I did what had to be done," Louis snarled, getting up.

"According to your handbook or to the situation? Louis, you could kill all the nobles of the city, maybe it would still be *what had to be done*. It doesn't mean you have to do it," Lissandro said. "Do you have any idea of the ascendancy a priest has on his community? And it's still nothing compared to the nobles' power of destruction."

How can you preach inaction? Selen thought. "These nobles deserve to pay," Selen exclaimed.

"Don't tell me you encourage him in his madness!" Lissandro shouted, pointing at Louis. "You don't know him." This remark hit Selen in the heart.

"My madness?" Louis shouted, striding towards Lissandro.

Selen saw what was going to happen. "Enough!" he yelled, rising from his seat. His friends stopped dead. "You have no idea how much horror and debauchery I saw when I was a royal guard," Selen raged. "I know what we are facing. Pigs, perverts, rapists, traitors, and plotters… They think they are superior, but I heard the screams of their victims. I saw them shag in front of my eyes, as if I was nothing more than another vase in the room. They have no decency, no honour. They don't give a shit about the people! But Louis does. And we are going to help him."

Lissandro gaped, aghast. Louis was enthralled and looked as if he was going to kiss him.

"Of course, I will help him," Lissandro said. He turned to Louis. "We have to act wisely. We will give the people justice, Louis. But this is not your world. And you know how it failed the first time. This world is even worse. I suggest we start with comforting your positions on the high priest, and we can make invalid the lands acquisitions under Agroln's reign. The rest will come progressively," Lissandro said. Louis gazed at him, suspicious. "In a few days or weeks."

"All right, I will slow down, but I won't wait," Louis said. "The people expect changes."

"If we take our time to plan and organize better, we can create the society we want," Selen said, trying to sound positive.

"And then, there is your name. You can't be just Louis. You need a family name," Lissandro insisted.

"Doesn't he have one?" Selen inquired.

"Of course he has one. S…"

Louis picked an object on the desk and threw it at Lissandro. "Don't you dare say it out loud!"

"Ouch!" Lissandro cried out as the object hit his shoulder. "Why? It suits you perfectly."

"I want a new life and a new start," Louis hissed.

"With the same projects? You are a living paradox in words *and* actions," Lissandro snarled. "Well then, use a number or a nickname…before they find you one."

"Considering your opinion about me, I suppose I can choose between the Bloody or the Mad."

"Oh, stop this pettiness. I have a high opinion of you. Can't you understand that

I do it for your own good?"

"I don't even know why I'm having this conversation," Louis said, grabbing his head.

"You need a name. You are the king, for God's sake," Lissandro insisted.

"Please stop," Selen squeaked, on the verge of crying. He hated to see his friends argue. They needed unity to face the court. He remembered he had not eaten for the day and felt nauseous. He grabbed the desk.

"I'm sorry," Louis said. Seeing him faint, his love came to him and hugged him. His shoulders were warm. Selen held to him, burying his face against Louis's neck. "Find me something, Lilo. But not *that* name."

"I've found you a name," Lissandro said kindly. "Domgeornan."

"I like it. It fits this world. What does it mean?" Louis asked.

"It means virtuous." Lissandro went for the door. "We will see each other this afternoon." Selen heard the door close.

"Are you all right?" Louis asked, cupping Selen's face.

"Yes." Selen sat down on one of the armchairs, still feeling dizzy. "If we want to create something of our situation, we need unity."

"I know. I don't understand why he nags me all the time," Louis said. He sat in the chair behind his desk, a hand against his head.

"He is trying to help you. He is also your counselor. You must take into consideration that Lissandro has seen more of life than we have."

"Then he should know I am right and back me up instead."

Selen searched for the most diplomatic words to make Louis understand. "Maybe he is right as well. Lissandro may have another interpretation of the same opinion. This is why you should collaborate. I have no experience myself, but I have heard such royal debates many times. Patience is a precious ally." Louis frowned. "I said patience, not ruse," Selen insisted.

Someone knocked on the door. Selen rose and opened it.

The servant behind the door stepped back with surprise. The maid dressed in a brown gown and apron carried a covered tray. Selen realized that she waited to step in and moved aside. The maid walked to the middle of the solar and stopped in front of the desk.

"What is it?" Louis asked.

"I…I bring you your meal, Your Majesty," the maid answered.

"Is this how it works?" Louis asked. "I mean, does someone bring me food here every day?"

The maid was as confused as they were and stood still with the tray riveted in her hands. "Yes, Your Majesty. We bring food from the kitchen to the solar two times a day, Your Majesty. More if you wish so."

At the mention of food, Selen's stomach rumbled. He picked the tray from her hands and placed it on the desk. He uncovered it and winced. Roasted meat chops swam in a brown, thick sauce. On platters stood blue cheese, white bread, and what looked like hare crusted pâté. Selen shared a look with Louis.

"Do you have fruits and biscuits in the kitchen?" Louis asked.

"We have everything, Your Majesty," the maid answered.

"Could you please take back the tray and bring me something more…fresh?" Louis said.

The maid stared at Louis, gaping with incomprehension. Not even a muffled sound came out of her mouth.

"A soup? Fish? Cherries?" Louis insisted, waiting for a reaction on the maid's face. She closed her mouth. Her eyes brightened. "The bread is fine," Louis added.

The maid picked up the tray. "Yes, Your Majesty." She curtsied and left the room.

"I always wondered about the transformation of the sovereigns on the royal portraits. Now, I know," Louis said.

"It could be seen as a passive regicide." Selen smiled.

Louis chuckled. "Henry the VIII, one of the ancient kings in our world, was so fat when he died that his servants had to wash him lying down. His body was covered with boils," Louis said. Selen made a face. "And he had six wives."

"Rich food, casks of wine, horny wenches in their bed, and hunting parties. That is what kings need," Selen exclaimed, raising his fist. They laughed.

"I am sure it is what they expect of me," Louis sighed. "A royal pig in silk."

It made Selen chuckle. "You would become one of their peers. But don't feel down, I would kill you before it happened."

Louis's face brightened. "Please do, and I promise I will do the same for you. Still, I can tell you that I won't give them this pleasure." His hand played nonchalantly with the lock of a box on the desk. Selen sighed and gazed through the window. His belly ached. "I will miss eating with the soldiers," Louis said, sounding melancholic. Selen looked at him inquiringly. "Not that I miss the bawdy jokes, but a leader must know his men. How can the people like me if they don't know me? How can I know about them and their needs if I live in a golden cage?"

"Should we go down in the city and visit a tavern?" Selen asked. The idea of sitting in such a place with people staring at him with contempt did not cheer him up. Besides, the king would not leave the palace without the king's guards. It was the rule. "Yet, I'm not sure the court will see well that you mingle with the population. Maybe later."

The maid was back by the door. Selen picked up the tray, thanked her, and closed the door.

"Hungry for salted pork in jelly or quails in wine?" Selen said. He laid the tray on the desk.

Louis raised the metal dome, uncovering a pumpkin soup, cold salmon pie, fish eggs in gravy, bread and strawberries. Selen's mouth watered. He cut himself a part of the pie and wolfed it down until the pain in his empty stomach disappeared.

"Did you often go to taverns?" Selen asked, still chewing.

Louis had ripped off a chunk of bread and dipped it in the bowl of soup. "I did go to taverns when I was young, in my previous life, of course, but I got pretty bored of it. Unless you go there with a friend, it is not a place where you can share interesting conversations. Even then, it is a noisy place of idleness where half-drunk men display the worst of themselves. When it's not a place of debauchery crowded with harlots."

"I see you like to mingle with the crowd, indeed," Selen said sardonically. He did not enjoy taverns either, but he had always considered that the problem came from his own reserved attitude, not the opposite. He poured soup into a bowl and sipped the tepid liquid. "What do you expect to talk about with a half-drunk commoner? Philosophy? Music?"

"Aren't those interesting subjects? I want to know more of the commoner's way of life. I could learn from their works. Masons, smiths, tanners must have so much to talk about. I could also learn of their problems."

"I can count on one hand the number of times I was in a tavern, but I am pretty sure that if the people go there, it's to forget about their problems. For such talks, you should walk the streets and visit shops. You don't need to constrain yourself to socializing at a playing table."

Louis's eyes shone. "That sounds like a better plan, indeed," Louis said with a hint of relief. He picked a handful of strawberries from the plate.

Selen wondered what he would do of his time in the meanwhile.

This was the first court session of Louis's reign and a major event after yesterday's coronation. At the call of his name and titles, Louis, followed by Selen and Lissandro, entered the great hall by the door behind the dais. Louis was clad in a long, blue brocade tunic with a sleeveless cloak of the same fabric. The royal circlet encircled his brow. He sat on the massive carved throne, proud and solemn as usual. As he crossed his long legs, his waxed, black boots shimmered. Selen and Lissandro stood up on each side of the throne at a respectable distance. The ministers stood a bit further away. Except for his long, ivory robes, it was not such a big change from Selen's previous functions, and he considered he could manage it easily.

The air in the hall was hot. It was summer and the days were warm in the south. The nobles packed themselves on rows of benches. They looked surprisingly fresh and bright-eyed. Some wrinkled their noses. Louis had wanted the gates open to commoners who gathered under the galleries. Selen spotted Kilda in the front row. She hid herself under a cloak, likely ill-at-ease to be there. At her side stood a one-armed, blond man with a crimson doublet and a black cape. Selen had no difficulties recognizing the hero of Earthfell. He was happy for his friends and hoped he would share words with them later. The herald's clear voice rang out again, opening the session with the presentation of the new ministers. Everyone rose.

Louis stood up and spoke. "Our country fell and bled under the tyranny of the forces of darkness, but we prevailed. Now, united in peace, we rise from the ruins, and, confident in our strength, we rebuild. A new dawn means a social reorganization. Much will have to be reformed. The people of Trevalden need to work, to eat, to live. The time of enslavement and idleness is over. To succeed in this good, patriotic task, essential measures have been already created. Minister Pembroke, would you please read the decrees."

Pembroke declaimed a polished version of their morning discussion. Louis's decisions on the noble's properties had been eluded, for the time being, but the tribute and the point on Agroln's transactions still stood. The lecture of the decrees launched vivid discussions among the crowd. The decisions were so sudden and unusual that most didn't seem to realize their scope.

Louis was back on his throne and sat imperturbable, gazing at his subjects, ready to mow down any outward objection. Others would have had the controversial decrees proclaimed directly in the streets, but his friend always assumed his decisions. *I admire my king*, Selen thought, relishing on the *my*. He brushed the torrid fantasies off his mind; eyes were on him.

A man clad in brocade silk stepped forward. He stopped in front of the steps, pulling nervously at his pointy beard.

"Your Majesty, my name is Hallecos. I have investments in the spice trade and other exotic products. I fear that the decree concerning the taxes on the foreign trades will create difficulties in my transactions, and probably in the ones of my fellow merchants. It may jeopardize our activities, create inflation," the man wailed.

"I would be sorry if you should lose your activities. Maybe I can ask Minister Pembroke to go through your accounts to verify your profits and loss in details? He will certainly find a solution to your problems," Louis proposed to the man.

"Your Majesty is kind. Yet, I think I can find a solution. If I change some investments." The man lost himself in words and stepped back into the crowd promptly.

As no more objections rose, Louis made a sign to move on to the next subject. Selen sighed and stretched one ankle. These ceremonies were always too long.

The herald called the names Selen had chosen for the king's guard. The ten men came forward. Folc stepped out of the crowd and looked at him. Selen smiled. The boy was proud in his shiny, white armour. The soldiers aligned in front of the king. They received a cloak of heavy, white wool with a blue hem. A silver brooch representing a unicorn clutched the woolen folds. Louis had chosen the mythical animal as his heraldry. The king's guards knelt down and were asked to swear their vows to Louis. As they pronounced their oath, Selen detected a furtive motion out of the corner of his eye.

Someone hid behind the pillar in the front row. Selen could not move from his place. He tilted his head to see. Cloth slithered from behind the stone. Should he glimpse a weapon, he would throw himself into the crowd. Even unarmed, Selen was ready to act to protect the king. A hooded man pushed his way through the crowd towards the back. His face swiveled a fraction of a second. Selen's eyes opened wide. Segar Mills. Their gazes met. The man disappeared.

The session had been long and tiresome. Selen rested on the fresh grass in the inner garden. The sun shone bright and the temperatures rose with each day. He was glad to sit for a while. During the ceremony, he had felt a throbbing pain in his arms and chest. He wondered if it was due to the lack of air, or to the fact that he had been upset to see Segar. Selen winced. The pain was coming back. He pulled on his sleeves and looked at his arms. The skin was paler than usual. He put a hand on his brow. Nothing indicated that he was sick. He rose and headed for the bathroom. Once inside, he removed his robes. He could feel the pain like a cramp stretching from his wrists to clamp at his heart. Yet, he saw no marks. He finished undressing and stepped into the pool of warm water. In contact with the heat, the feeling disappeared, and his skin took on a light shade of pink. His arms looked normal again. Selen plunged his head into the water and swam.

The face of Segar came back to his mind again. What did the man want? Was he after them? Louis had declared him a fugitive. Should he be arrested, he would be executed. Why would Segar stay in the city and thus risk his life? Something was up, but he didn't know if he should alarm his friend. It would probably be better to wait and see.

He swam to the edge of the pool and pushed himself out of the water. Droplets ran down his body as he walked towards the towels. He dried himself and put new robes on. Selen walked back to the garden. The place was empty, and no guard was stationed in front of the stairs in the gallery. It meant that the king was absent from his apartments.

Selen entered the solar. Flowers lay on the desk. A note had been scratched on one of the papers under it. *Dinner with Pembroke*. Selen picked up the flowers and walked to one of the windows. His book still lay on the windowsill. He opened it at the right page while breathing the perfume of the bouquet in his hand.

"I could do a painting of you. I would title it *The Lady-in-Waiting*."

Selen raised his head but already knew who had entered the solar. "Do me a favour, Lilo, and remove all the robes from this aisle."

"One must learn to live with his time. I thought the robes were fashion during your period. Didn't you guys used to walk around with yards of sheets wrapped around yourselves?" Lissandro said.

"Toga are not robes. There were robes indeed, but I was a soldier. Soldiers have their armour on or leather outfits."

"Leather outfits…" Lissandro gazed at him with narrowed eyes. His friend shook his head. "I see you are alone. Would you mind to join me in my, or should I say your, apartments? I am pretty sure no one is allowed to stay in the king's solar in his absence, and we haven't talked for a long time."

Selen closed his book and put the flowers in the water jar. He made a few steps towards the center of the room and stopped.

"The door at the right of the bed. Your room is two rooms further," Lissandro coughed.

They left the room. Lissandro's apartments were of the same size as the king's solar, but the decoration was in shades of light blue. *I must bring Louis here*, Selen thought. The profusion of porcelain and lace gave a somewhat feminine touch about it. Selen guessed that it must have been the queen's chambers once. Near the window, a guéridon had been dressed. There were fried chicken legs in a bowl, grapes, and oranges. Two goblets stood by a wine carafe.

"Were you waiting for someone?" Selen asked.

"I thought we should have a discussion without our tempestuous friend. Please, make yourself comfortable," Lissandro said with a short gesture towards the chairs. Selen sat down on the love seat while Lissandro filled the goblets with wine. "Tell me, why did you crown him? You did not actually believe it would improve your lives, did you?"

"I meant what I said when I handed him the crown. He is the best suited to be king. If someone can rebuild this kingdom, it is Louis," Selen answered. Lissandro handed him one of the goblets.

"Pembroke could have done it. He has the experience, the intelligence, and he is from this world. Now, the truth, Selen," Lissandro insisted.

Selen folded his legs under him, pushing himself deep into the cushions of the seat. He took a sip of his wine. "Louis lives through his dreams. He doesn't want the power—he wants to feel alive. Without the war, there is no army, thus forcing him to face the real world. Louis sees flaws and corruption everywhere. He has ideals. He will impose his views, whatever the cost. Put the crown on someone else, and he will fight to depose the man. Louis's golden cage is a life in the archives of Neolerim. I did not want to see him unhappy."

Lissandro stared at him. "You took the cage so that he could live his dreams."

"What is a cage if you can spend your life at the side of the person you love?"

Lissandro sat in the armchair on the other side of the table. "I am impressed by the insight you have of him. Would you care to know more about his previous life?"

"I only want to know what he is ready to share with me." Selen still felt an ache in his heart to know that Louis had loved another man in his previous life, and by what he had understood, it had been as deep as what they had now. Sometimes, Selen wondered if it was the reason his friend would not tell him his full name. Selen knew it was foolish and selfish, but he could not help himself.

"You know he doesn't use gloves to apply his ideas. How can someone as kind as you cope with it?" Lissandro asked.

"I agree with his views if it is what you are curious about. I know the process can be ... messy, but as I said, he is not facing innocents. These people..." Selen shook his head. For six years, he had been a royal guard. What he had witnessed had marked him for life. So much violence, debauchery, and treachery. It was a miracle he had come out of it untainted. This palace could not be different.

"You are probably right. I have never been in a royal court, but in my world of darkness, as I would call it, there are princes. I have faced monsters beyond imagination. Yet, I have to tell you, Louis's ideas have flaws, and he doesn't learn."

"Your warnings sound as if Louis tries to reproduce his tragic fate once again. I do not have your knowledge, I am but a simple soldier, but I think we all deserve a second chance."

"I can see it pains you to talk about it, so I won't insist. I will only give you one last counsel. Temper him, calm him down, do all you can so that he acts wisely. Louis is a wild horse. He needs a firm, but calm and patient grip."

Selen would remember Lissandro's words, but he would judge by himself what his love needed best. "You are one wild horse yourself," Selen replied.

"I know. I speak from experience. Like Louis, I too grew up without a father. Except that mine did not die but turned against me for what I am. What we have, what we are, men like Louis and I built it with our will. I was stubborn and lost, but I found my master." Selen noticed that his friend's eyes twitched. "I look young because this is how I was when I died. My first death. Yet, I lived two hundred years. I know about solitude. At some point, you give up having friends. No one can bear to have the ones he loves die one after the other. You two are my first mortal friends. And damn, you are like water and fire." He chuckled.

They both laughed. Lissandro poured himself more wine. He picked up a chicken leg and proposed one to Selen, who took it.

"Did you never get bored to live that long?" Selen asked, chewing the meat off the bone. The golden, crispy skin crunched under his teeth.

"There are good sides. You have powers, you are young, you can see the world, and read all that exists. Then, there are the bad sides. You have to work for eternity, you can't eat, and you get bored to death. Moreover, a lot of people you sometimes have never met want to see you dead for different reasons."

"According to them, you were twice a monster." He picked up a new chicken leg from the bowl. "What do you miss the most from your world?" Selen inquired.

"Beside the toilets and my bathroom accommodations, as Louis would say, maybe underwear, and, oh, the technologies. A good movie for example." Lissandro probably noticed Selen's puzzled look as he explained his thoughts. "A movie is a story, like in a book, but instead of text, there are moving pictures. See. Imagine this is a rabbit." Lissandro made a shape with his hand, raising two fingers which looked like ears. "If I move my hand in front of grass, I can pretend the rabbit is moving in a field, eating…grapes." Lissandro put grapes in front of his hand. "This would be like theater. Except that in a movie, there is no real rabbit because it would be an image. A lot of images moving. Yet, you believe in it. It is the story of the rabbit. Like if you read a book but all that happens in your head, happens on a flat surface." Selen nodded. It sounded fascinating. "Well, that is a movie. It is like a book but with moving pictures."

"And what kind of stories did you like?" Selen asked curiously. He put down the bone on the plate and sucked his greasy fingers.

"Especially stories about knights, swords, and magic kingdoms." Lissandro laughed. His friend stared at him. "I am curious. How does a man like you end up being a soldier? You must be the sweetest person I have ever met…after my rabbit," he added, raising his hand with the two fingers. Selen chuckled.

"I had no choice. I was forced to train when I was a child. Many died. I wanted to live. I had no family nor friends, but I was allowed to have pets. It may sound stupid, but they gave me the will to keep on fighting. Now that I have friends and a soul mate, I am probably a better fighter than I have ever been." Selen flushed. He knew he didn't look fierce curled up in his white robe with his long, lilac hair falling around him and over his brow.

Lissandro looked at him, serious again. "I saw you on that hill on the battlefield. What you did that day, not even a seasoned warrior would have accomplished. Never underestimate yourself. I won't."

"I saw Segar today, at the session." Selen did not know why he had said it, but he felt better to have shared his worry with his friend. "The man loathes Louis."

"A court is a dangerous place, and more enemies roam in the shadows. In his previous life, Louis could count his friends on one hand. Don't worry, he has dealt with many Segar Mills already. Just be on your guard. I will keep my eyes open." Lissandro cupped his goblet, thoughtful. "You know what I miss? Music."

"But there is music in this world as well," Selen answered. Though he never had the occasion to hear music, he liked the new sounds he had heard during the festivities.

"No. I don't mean classical or whatever kind of folk music they play here. I mean modern music, songs. Good hard rock, even metal," Lissandro's eyes sparkled.

"I fear you have lost me again," Selen said.

Lissandro stood silent, concentrating. Selen saw that his friend had an idea. Lissandro stood up and sang. Selen had never heard something similar. He wondered what kind of instrument could accompany such a song. The story was about a place that had all he wanted and getting on the knees. Though Selen did not understand the meaning of every word, it was entertaining. He would have clapped his hands if he had not feared to cover Lissandro's voice. Lissandro jumped and danced as in a trance, shaking his head. Selen stared at him, fascinated.

When he was done, Lissandro looked exhausted. He took a sip of his wine and sat down.

"Is this what they call music in your world?" Selen asked.

"That is good music." Lissandro grinned.

"Will you sing more for me?" Selen looked at his friend with his best appealing eyes.

"My dear, sweet puppy, I am not a jukebox. Yet, I know a few songs I could share with you. Would you like to learn one?"

Selen nodded with enthusiasm. Lissandro got up and sat on the love seat next to him. The song he sang was beautiful and the text was filled with passionate love with a touch of sadness. Selen asked Lissandro to repeat the text until he learned the lyrics. Lissandro made him sing the song a few times.

"You have a beautiful voice once you pass over the level of the whisper. Not many men can reach such high notes," Lissandro said.

"Thank you," Selen said with a blush. "I think I will go back to the solar. It was a very pleasant evening." He got up and pushed his hair behind his back.

"I am just two rooms away if you need company," Lissandro said.

Selen smiled. "Good night."

He left the room and headed to the solar. When he opened the door, Louis was already in bed, writing. His friend leaned against the wooden headboard.

"I thought you had decided to sleep in your apartments," Louis said. He looked weary but glad.

"This bed is too big for you to warm it alone," Selen said. He removed his robe, climbed onto the covers, and sat astride his love. "I had dinner with Lissandro. Thank you for the note."

Louis put away the papers. His hands closed around Selen's waist. Selen slipped under the bedsheets and pulled them around his hips to keep the warmth of their bodies, creeping closer into Louis's embrace.

"You look like someone who has learned something new. What did Lissandro talk about?" Louis asked suspiciously with a twisted smile while his hands skimmed Selen's back.

"I have learned about his world. I have learned about music." Selen still felt dreamy from the songs. He ran his fingers through Louis's hair and sang.

62

He could swear the wench had recognized him. He had seen it in his wide, green eyes. Segar wanted to assist with the court sessions. He needed to know what they planned, and how the whoreson's decrees would be welcomed by the crowd. It burned his eyes to see him sit there in self-satisfaction with the crown riveted on his brow. After his over-the-top performance at his coronation the day before, the new king had decided to keep on poking the anthill. Segar did not care if the insufferable fool was a basket case; he had understood by the cheers of the commoners that the man would not be so easy to overthrow. Yet, Segar would be the sand in the gears. He did not care about the nobles, but they were good customers of the black market. If they lost their fortune, he would too. However, it would not be long before they despised their new king.

Segar strode through the city. He entered a private house with closed shutters. His headquarters were sober on the outside but richly furnished on the inside. Discretion was crucial. The room was comfy with seats, cushions, and carpets. Small cherry tables decorated with fruit baskets filled with pomegranates and grapes stood under the windowsills. The windows opened to an inner yard. Birdsongs and the chanting noise of the fountain's flowing rose from the garden. Segar was sweating. The air was warm, but not as suffocating as in the great hall. Jamys sat on a couch near the window, fanning himself. His blond chest hair stuck out of his open shirt.

"How did it go?" Jamys grunted.

"As expected. I had to endure a speech on peace on earth that sounded like a war declaration. Is everything ready for our visitor?"

"The wine is on the table and the package is in the next room," Jamys responded. "Should I move out?"

"I think it's best. The man did ask for discretion."

Jamys left the room. Segar walked around to check that everything was ready. He pulled the shutters, but let the windows open. Someone opened the door downstairs.

"I am pleased to see that you accepted my invitation," Segar said with a honeyed voice.

"Is the place safe?" the high priest asked.

"As safe as it can be. No one will find you here." And Segar would hold to these words, should the man refuse his proposal.

"Good," the old man grumbled and sat on an armchair.

Segar poured the high priest a cup of wine and sat in front of him. "I have heard that you had some words with our new king this morning?"

"The news spread fast."

"I don't miss a thing in Nysa Serin," Segar said with a mocking smile. He grabbed a grape. "So tell me, what do you think of our new king?"

"It's a scandal! A humiliation," the high priest snarled, wiggling in his seat. "Who does he think he is?"

"The king, my dear. A king who thinks he is better than you, better than the nobles, and better than everyone." Segar took a sip of his wine. The high priest gazed at him with interest. "Maybe the king could learn some humility," Segar suggested.

The high priest looked wary. "He is, above all, the king," he mumbled.

"He is," Segar said. "How did you cope with Agroln?" The dead king had been a damn hellish creature. Yet, the high priest did not seem relieved by his death.

"He pretty much left us alone. Always locked up in the palace. Of course, some commoners disappeared, people wailed, and the prices were high. Yet, nothing alarming. Still, I am glad to be rid of these stinking, greenish creatures."

"And I assume you still got donations from the palace until now? Agroln must have been quite generous." Segar squeezed a grape between his teeth.

The high priest was uneasy. Sweat pearled on his forehead. He grunted, scratching his beard. "We could not complain."

Don't say you got rinsed, Segar thought. "It may turn a bit rough now, with our new king?"

The high priest flushed red. "How dare he?" he grunted. "How will I live?"

On your fat, was the first answer to pop into Segar's mind. "What if I told you that you could have everything back?" Segar smirked.

"How?" the high priest inquired. His sunken eyes narrowed.

"Like this," Segar said, snapping his fingers. Two buxom wenches dressed in veils appeared at the door. They stepped forward, dancing lewdly. One came to Segar and sat astride him, while the other one rubbed herself on the lap of the high priest, pushing her round breasts to his face.

"I don't understand," the man stuttered. Yet, as the girl slipped a hand on his crotch, he did not move.

"It is quite easy." Segar pulled off the veils of the wench on top of him. He moved his face and pulled at a thick nipple with his teeth. "I could never offer such a gift to our king. Though I tried."

The high priest stayed silent. Segar wondered if the man had not understood, or if he was too busy fondling the inner thighs of the wench. Though he had judged the priest's weakness well, this lack of attention irritated Segar. Finally, the man showed interest to his words.

"Why?"

"What does our good king look like?" Segar asked, opening his pants. The girl bent down, took out his cock, and sucked it deep with enthusiastic moves. It grew hard in the whore's throat.

Busy fondling the girl's tits, the high priest took some time to think. "Long hair, a slut's thick lips, piercing blue eyes…and this earring. He looks like a wench." The high priest gaped at Segar. "Is he a wench?"

"No! Of course, not," Segar said. He grabbed the girl by the hair and moved her up. "Bend over," he snapped. He knelt behind the whore, took his cock in his hand, and pressed it between her cheeks. Segar turned to the high priest. "And have you seen the purple thing?"

"The horror. I thought it was a painted woman until I saw his arms," the high priest panted as the girl rode on top of him, moaning loud. He grasped a loose breast with one hand. "Perversion. Immoral aberration. It should be burned at the stake."

"You can't. Our king shags him…or is shagged. It doesn't matter," Segar said as he rammed into the screaming wench. The girl was horny, but it was not as savoring as the wince of disgust on the high priest's face.

"This is repulsive! Is it true at least?" The man let out a grunt when the girl moved faster. Segar could barely hear him over the girl's overdone, fake moans.

"As true as it can be," Segar insisted. The fury in the whoreson's eyes in Millhaven had been worth a thousand words. Lost in his frenzy, he had not even tried to deny the blatant truth. The cut of his dagger had left a scar on Segar's arm. Yet, it was nothing compared to what Segar would leave on his body once the insolent brat was in his grasp. "If I remember well, the words of the gods are clear in the Holy Book on buggery and effeminates."

"Crystal clear," the high priest gasped. "It is one of the worst sins. This filth will burn in hell for that."

"I'm not preoccupied about their souls," Segar gasped, releasing himself onto the wench's bottom, "but about the views of the population on the matter."

The high priest swore and jerked. He slapped the wench away. "Give me solid proof or a witness, and I will have my flock build a pyre for these repulsive perverts." The high priest grinned nastily. The man rectified his clothes, rose, and left the room.

Segar lost himself in his thoughts. Now that he had the high priest, he needed to convince the rich families. It would be more complicated to reach them. They were sly and greedy. He would not corrupt them with cunts or gold. They drowned in it. He had noticed a few potential allies among the new ministers, and some nobles had protested against the new decrees. It would probably take some weeks, but the whoreson was digging his own grave. It was just a matter of time until the nobles became desperate. Once their gold was at risk, they would listen, and together, they would strike. "Oh yes, whoreson, united we build." Segar smirked. He rose and decided to tidy up.

As he picked up the used goblets, he felt a pain in his right arm. It radiated to his chest. It was not the first time he had felt that throbbing ache. He wondered if he had caught a disease during that stupid war or maybe it was the stress. All this plotting and trade building was a lot of work.

Segar heard screams come from the street. He watched through the shutters. The noises came from the large house on the other side. A plump man in ochre, silk clothes argued with the men of the watch. A young woman Segar supposed to be the rich man's wife cried. Segar listened with attention.

"I don't care what your orders are! I bought this house legally two years ago!" the man shouted, infuriated.

"This house previously belonged to the city watch. It was property of the Crown," the guard responded. "Unless you can show me tangible proof that you don't own or can't afford any other residence, you have until tomorrow to leave the place."

Segar smiled. It had already begun.

63

"Monarchy will always be popular, whatever its tendencies to tyranny. And, whatever its love for freedom, the people will always show it…its…" Louis muttered, rolling a plum in his left hand. The quill stayed suspended in the air. Louis sat on the chair by his desk. The board was covered with papers and books. There were also two goblets of wine and a plate of fresh fruits, nuts, and olives. Louis let go of the plum and ran his hand through his hair, sweeping it back. Though he had bathed the day before, it was already sticky with sweat. Even with all the windows opened on the cascade, the solar was ridiculously hot, like any room in the palace.

He turned to Selen, who sat on the floor, the book about the history of Trevalden open in his lap. Selen had only his pants on, and sweat pearled on his chest and neck. His usually neat hair was matted and negligently pushed to the side. "Do you have a synonym for ardour?" Louis asked.

"Zeal? Like your zeal to work by such a beautiful, sunny day?" Selen answered. His friend picked a fresh fig from the plate beside him and tore it apart with his teeth. "We should go out," Selen suggested with a pleading look.

"To be seen eating and reading together?" Louis asked with a smile. Zeal was a good word indeed. He wrote the end of his sentence.

"There is nothing wrong with that," Selen replied, still looking at him.

"You're half naked. Not that I complain." Louis raised the quill again.

"Or at least to the bathroom. We could swim. It's Folc's watch right now."

It was Folc's watch most of the time. As the most trustworthy of the king's guards, the boy spent all of his mornings and evenings guarding the entrance to the garden. "I don't know. I would like to finish writing this speech before this afternoon, but I can't think clearly in this heat," he sighed. Besides, he had no idea of how the delegation would be and who composed it.

"You could drop some clothes. Starting with your shirt." Selen's hand crawled suggestively on Louis's bare ankle.

Louis thought that, as the king, he had to look a minimum presentable should someone show up at the door for an audience. Yet, his shirt was open and stuck on his skin. He needed to bathe again. The ink on the quill dried.

Louis gave up and opted for an improvised speech. He dropped the quill, got up from his chair, and sat down next to his friend, his back against the desk. "What can you tell me about the history of this land?" he asked softly.

"The author talks about populations arriving from the east, but he can't date their arrival," Selen started. "It was a long time ago. The migrants met the Children of the Forest. I suppose it is the folk who lived in the Ebony Forest, the ones Lilo talked about."

Louis brushed away Selen's disheveled hair and grazed his lips on his wet shoulder and neck. "Carry on," he whispered.

"They lived in peace for a while under the reign of the first kings," Selen went on with a tremulous voice. "The migrants plowed the earth, built cities, and populated the land. Forcing the indigenous to live in the most inhospitable parts of the land. One day, a disease spread. It took away many migrants, especially their children. The Children of the Forest were accused. It is said that they used to celebrate dark rituals on magic stones. To prove their innocence, the Children of the Forest sent some of their own children to be raised in the cities. Many died from abuse. A war started. Many people were killed, and the Children of the Forest were exterminated. The survivors lingered in the deepest of the forests, preserving the remains of their civilization."

"That is horrible," Louis muttered.

"The chapter is entitled *The Way to Civilization*," Selen sighed with sadness.

"This is why we should take our references from the past and not look into the future for what they call progress." Louis laid his head on Selen's shoulder and stretched his arms around his moist, warm chest.

"You mean in civilizations like mine?" Selen asked. "If I trust what Lilo said, I am the primitive among us three, and my folk used to burn people. Only interested in riches, they deforested the island. Their stupid wars destroyed our flourishing nature, beautiful animals, and old trees. Not something someone can be proud of."

"The men are not fierce or shy towards each other in nature. They become like that because the tyrants tell them to. It's the tyrants who turn people into savage beasts, who corrupt their souls and call it *natural instinct* to enslave them. If the men had been so fierce and wild in their nature, they would never have built a society in the first place." Louis said.

"You mean that the social order is in nature?" Selen murmured.

"Exactly. Your civilization was already corrupted by the political order. But these Children of the Forest, they were close to nature. They must have had a better society."

"They were small clans living in harmony. They were generous, or maybe just weak. Yet, they sent their children away to the cities. What kind of civilization sacrifices its own children? Send them to the enemy?"

"What do you think they should have done?" Louis asked, holding Selen tighter.

"Teach them to fight. Teach them to die. A population can't keep its freedom without unity and the will to defend it. This is what they taught me when I was young." Louis's heart shivered when he heard his friend's words. Selen turned his face towards Louis's. "Is that what you want to take from the past? To learn how to die?" Selen breathed against his open lips.

"I only want freedom and unity, for everyone," Louis whispered, feeling his heart pound and his loins burn. He closed the distance between their lips. His love's warm mouth tasted of berries. Selen pulled off Louis's shirt and dragged him onto the floor.

Louis, Selen, and Lissandro waited in the gallery, behind the door of the great hall. The court session was about to begin. Louis leaned against the cold, stone wall. They all wore robes of the lightest silk. Yet, it was still too many clothes, especially the pants and the boots on top. Louis and Selen had eventually left the solar for the bathroom for a much-needed shower, and Louis's hair dried in the warm air, leaving cold, wet spots on his shoulders.

"I would love to cut these long heavy robes into a loincloth. I could say it's the orcish mode," Lissandro said. "And when I think I had missed the sun." He too had showered earlier that day, but marks could be seen under his arms. "Is the stench of sweat something you don't even notice or was it less frightful in your times?"

"Live in Paris during summer when it is thirty-five degrees with open sewers, horse dung, excrement, and with people forced to wear three layers of clothes and a cravat. You will see that this stench smells like perfume," Louis answered, smiling.

"I think we would have a pretty similar sight, or smell, of your description if we went down to the city right now," Selen objected kindly.

Those words fell hard on Louis when he realized he had not put a foot in his own city since his coronation a week ago. Soon, he would not be better than the tyrants he despised. His friends must have seen the change on his face as Lissandro tried to cheer him up.

"If you have the nostalgia for your previous home's odors, we can go down for a stroll in the city tomorrow. Preferably for my sinuses, at dawn," Lissandro said.

"That could be a good idea. As we said before, we should learn more about the capital and its people. Besides, they would surely enjoy seeing their king," Selen added, touching his arm gently. Louis smiled.

"So what will we have today? Solicitors? New, unpopular decrees? A judgment?" Lissandro asked with faint, overdone enthusiasm.

"A delegation of princes from the Windy Isles," Louis answered.

Lissandro stopped dead in his twisting dance. "Princes from the Windy Isles? Just that? And you tell us now?"

"There is not much to say about it," Louis replied. "We have to see them first. Pembroke went to meet them on the way to the city this morning. They will stay in apartments in the south aisle for a few days. I assume we will have to meet them a few times to discuss trades and politics."

"I can help," Lissandro said.

"I'm counting on it," Louis replied.

"Maybe we can also organize some entertainment. What do you think of a ball?" Lissandro proposed.

"A ball?" Louis liked the idea of music. "Do you want a ball?"

Lissandro and Selen nodded with enthusiasm.

"I don't want to see the orgiastic scenes of the festivities again," Louis objected. "Moreover, these are the kinds of futile costs I disapprove."

"I was not thinking of a masquerade but something more elegant. You need to propose something to honour the delegation. I could take care of the organization with Pembroke to keep the budget reasonable."

"Do so," Louis said. They heard the herald call for them from the great hall. Louis opened the door.

They walked into the great hall. His friends took their places on the edge of the dais while he sat on the throne. The hall was packed as usual and bright with the shimmering, colorful clothes of the nobles. Sunlight came through the many mullioned windows and the open main doors. Commoners swarmed under the galleries and in the back while some stood outside on the esplanade. Many were curious to see the delegation of princes. It did reek of sweat—not everyone in this world enjoyed a bath—but Louis thought he could endure it a few hours.

The herald stepped forward and cried out the agenda for the day. They would begin with the delegation from the Windy Isles. When the man was done, the crowd split in its middle. Three persons and their followers walked forward to the bottom step of the dais. The two princes carried themselves proudly. One of the young men had short, hazel hair and chiseled features. His body was strong. He wore golden silk, short black boots, and orange satin cloak. As he approached, Louis noticed that he had eyes as black as coal. The other man had smoother features, his frizzy, brown hair tumbling down into his eyes. His slim body was clad in a turquoise brocade tunic, blue pants puffed at the hips, and a shimmering silver cloak streaked with cobalt threads. The first man spoke.

"My name is Philip Howells, of the royal house Howells from the Windy Isles, Your Majesty," the hazel man said with a bow. "And here is my younger brother, Owen."

"I am pleased to meet you, Your Highnesses," Louis said with a bow of the head. He hoped his words were right. He was neither fond nor really aware of the etiquette. "I hope you had a pleasant journey and that you will enjoy your stay in our beautiful city."

"We certainly will, Your Majesty," Philip said. "Our father, King Dywel, sends his salutations and hopes we will have fruitful discussions on both our kingdoms. As you will see, Your Majesty, our father is keen to maintain the peace. He was more than pleased to learn about the death of King Agroln. Our father puts much faith in you. Therefore, he sends us here as well for an important task."

The third person stepped forward. Philip raised the many purple silk veils, revealing a woman of astounding beauty. She had eyes as blue as the sea, red lips, and delicate features. Her long, black hair waved around her shoulders to her thin waist. She wore a maroon gown encrusted with golden pearls.

"Your Majesty, as a sign of his will to unite our kingdoms, our father offers you the hand of the most beautiful jewel of the sea, our sister, the princess Erin."

The crowd sighed with amazement and broke into enthusiastic whispers. Louis was taken aback. Even though he panicked, he had the wits to first look at Lissandro, who nodded and urged him with his eyes to agree to the proposal. Then, he looked towards Selen. He could not see his friend's face, but even from the back, his uneasiness was palpable. Selen's hands trembled, and his fingers twisted nervously. Louis imagined the horror he went through. He rose.

"I am surprised and deeply honored by your father's proposal," he said, trying to compose himself. He stepped forward down the stairs, towards the princes. "Your sister Erin is of great beauty. She would be a wonderful queen and make any king the happiest man in the world." Louis took the princess's hand and kissed it while looking into her eyes. He noticed that she blushed and her hand trembled. She was willing. He gave her a hollow smile to hide his uneasiness. Louis stepped back and looked at the princes.

"Unfortunately, and with my deepest respect, I can't accept your offer." The crowd gasped with shock and muttered its disapproval. He saw Philip's lips twitch and incomprehension on Owen's face. Louis's heart raced. "I have far too much respect for Princess Erin to force her to marry me. I am convinced that arranged unions, as good as they may be for a state, bring only sorrow in the hearts of the newlyweds. I would feel miserable to break such a beautiful heart. I do hope we can still maintain peace between our kingdoms, but I also hope that Princess Erin will marry a man she loves, not a complete stranger. I want only the best for your sister," Louis insisted. Philip's features softened. "To show you my good will and honesty in that matter, I assure you that I won't marry anyone else unless I choose her myself. My queen will be a queen of love," Louis added loud enough.

"These are wise words, Your Majesty," Philip said. The prince still sounded slightly irritated, but Louis sensed that the tempest in his heart was over. "I hope my sister will marry someone she loves."

"And I wish her a long and a happy life," Louis added with a smile. Louis turned to the crowd. "I think we should all ponder on these thoughts. I declare the session over." He stepped towards the princes again. "I trust we can meet later and discuss the future of our kingdoms. I hope you will accept my sincere apologies, but I meant what I said."

"We accept them, Your Majesty," Philip said. "We sensed here no mischief. Yet, we will be sorry not to have you as our brother." The prince half smiled.

"All men of good will are brothers," Louis said.

The princes took their leave. Slowly, Louis went up the dais, smiling and nodding at his ministers. He saw the trouble on their faces. It seemed that no one had understood, let alone approved, his decision. He passed in front of the royal guard.

"Stay here and watch the doors to the gallery." He exited the gallery and closed the door behind him.

His lungs nearly exploded as he took a deep breath. Louis bent over and thought he was going to retch. He cast a hand on the sidewall to hold his balance. He had gone through a lot in his lives, but he had never felt such dread. It had taken him unprepared, and the whole time, he had felt the blade of war and mayhem hanging over his neck. Except it was not only over his head this time but over a whole country. As he calmed down, he thought about his friend. Louis strode to the solar, trying not to run. He opened the door.

Selen stood by an open window, his face livid and his swollen eyes still bathed in tears.

Louis hurried towards him and held him tightly, cupping the back of Selen's head gently. "My love, you don't need to cry."

"You should have agreed," Selen stuttered. "They won't forgive you. The princes may, but not the crowd, not your people, and definitely not the nobles. I could... I could have tried to cope with it," he sobbed. "I should have known it would happen."

"I can't agree to such things. I love you. You are my queen," Louis whispered. To abandon a friend, especially his loved one, was the worst of all crimes in his eyes.

"I am a man," Selen replied angrily, stating the obvious. "And I can't hold you further than that solar," he sobbed. Louis kissed the side of his head.

Lissandro entered the room. "I will try not to shout..." his friend said, attempting to keep his temper. "But why?" he cried out. "How can a man like you, who knows so much about history, ignore that all the kings, whatever their inclinations, have always wed a woman. You must have a queen. There is no other option."

"I know," Louis hissed. He had tried once in his previous life, but engagement loathed him and he had abandoned the idea. It was beyond him. He could not lie, cheat against himself, or betray his real love, not even mentioning the lack of attraction. "I won't break his heart and the heart of an innocent woman for political reasons," Louis answered. "I may get married, some day...in a distant future."

"With him? Because to me, it sounded like you just said, *I will never marry. Don't bother presenting me a queen*?"

"I know how it is. Every noble of the country will step forward with a sister, a cousin, a niece, desperate to match me with a potential bride, and I will be stuck again in the burning of letters and the hundreds of words of excuses to avoid the bride and the offended parent. I already give the people my life, can't I have my heart and my body for myself?"

"No, you can't. You're the king. You are the only man in the whole kingdom who can't be free. If you want to live happily, take Selen and run far away from here," Lissandro said.

"And how far will we need to hide? In the middle of the forest? At sea? We have no future! Two men living together. No society will ever tolerate that. Do you think I enjoyed climbing outside staircases and creeping through windows? That I like to hide under the mask of a coldhearted man to maintain the last shreds of my privacy? All those nonsenses, all those lies about me, because I can't say the truth." Memories came back to his mind as the words burst out of him. Louis felt the tears well up and repressed them with his last strength. "And what of my convictions? I want to change this society. I have the power to do it. I want to prove it can work. I won't run away. I am no coward!" Louis exclaimed. Selen twitched in his arms.

"So follow the rules and get a queen. Even Alexander the Great did. You will need to marry at some point. You will need an heir," Lissandro said.

"An heir?" Louis asked, astounded. "I don't want an heir. For God's sake, Lilo… it's me. I don't want to start a dynasty. Haven't you listened to my words? I want a constitution. I want to install a republic."

Lissandro looked at him, aghast. Selen turned his head, gaping.

"You want what?" Lissandro exclaimed. "Oh my God, you want to start a revolution against yourself. You are mad."

"When all will be ready, I will abdicate. I want the people to be happy. Men are born for peace and truth. If you give them laws according to their nature and heart, they will cease to be unhappy and corrupted. A free society aims at virtue and does not need to be subjugated. We can create that society together. Where there will be no rich, nor poor. Where everyone can live off his land in harmony. Where people will be free to marry who they want and get an education." Louis looked at his gaping friends. "Why do you look at me like that?"

"When was the last time you left your inner world to have a real contact with a human being? They beat me to blood many times just for what I am. Even the kindest ones saw me as a freak. Why do you think I lived on a boat? I've been scared to die every day of my life. I come from the future, and I have never heard of harmony, let alone equality. The world is mean. You fight or you die. Yet, in a thousand years, in some places of our world, there may be hope for you two," Lissandro said. He sighed. "What I'm trying to say is that I fear your subjects may not understand the subtleties of your concepts."

"I know. I will teach them that Machiavellianism is not a tolerable way of life. I have plans for a new educational system," Louis responded. "But we have to bring the nobles to heel." He wanted his friend by his side. "Those are my beliefs, Lilo. Will you stand by me?"

"I would like so much to start my journey," Lissandro looked at him. "Are you sure you don't want to try just to be a good king? No. All right then," he sighed. "A well-known future rolls towards us and I face it with dread."

Lissandro woke up. From his bed, he saw the pink sky turn blue. The temperature would soon rise. He had to hurry. He got up, got dressed, and climbed the stairs to the bedroom on the first floor. Like every morning, Lissandro filled the bowl and a cup before throwing the water through the window. Fresh fruits stood on a plate. He picked up a pear and a peach and crawled onto the bed. While eating his breakfast, he read a chapter of the book on ornithology. Today's chapter was on the sparrow and how the animal engaged in dust bathing. Lissandro wondered how his own dust bathing would turn this morning. When he judged that the sheets had been creased enough, he rose and went back to his room. After a short visit to the garderobe, he fastened his sword to his belt and added a dagger for precaution. He threw a beige woolen cape over his shoulders and made for the door.

Lissandro crossed the aisle to the boudoir and stopped in front of the solar's door. For an instant, he prepared himself to knock but had second thoughts. Delicately, he placed his hand on the knob and turned. The door opened. "Busted," he whispered.

He entered the silent solar and tiptoed to the side of the bed. The sight of his gorgeous friends asleep on each other, half covered by the tangled sheets, was so pleasant to his eyes that he regretted what he had to do. However, their love reminded him of his own loneliness, and the twinge of jealousy in his heart brought him back to reality. Silently, he drew his sword out of his scabbard and held it a few inches above Louis's shoulder. With the cold flat of the blade, he tapped the pale skin.

Louis raised his eyelids a little. At the sight of the sword, he straightened on the bed. It woke Selen up, but his friend noticed him first and showed no sign of panic. Selen's smile faded when he saw the blade pointing towards him.

"Good morning. You're dead," Lissandro said. "Or you would be if it weren't me standing here right now. You can put your best guard in front of the steps in the gallery, and it won't help if the whole aisle is a palace of draughts." Considering Louis's infuriated eyes, Lissandro judged the lesson learned and put his sword away. "Now, I think someone longed to go down to the city? The nobles won't be up for a while, but your people already stroll the streets. Get dressed. I will wait for you outside." In the leaden silence, Lissandro went to the door leading to the garden. This one was locked. He turned the key, opened the door, and went out.

Lissandro breathed in the fresh morning air. Half of the garden was still in the shade. The dew-covered roses spread their light perfume. He walked towards the bench and sat down. He knew he had gone too far, but his friends were still innocent of the court intrigues, and such places were rife with plots. Louis may expect his new enemies to drag him to a scaffold, but he couldn't be more wrong. What killed kings most was not the axe, but the poison on the lips of a mistress, a dagger in a garderobe or a fall from a window. During the court session, Lissandro had seen the offended faces and the daggers in the eyes. Blows could come from anywhere after that.

Lissandro got up as the solar's door opened. Louis stepped out and walked towards him. His blue silk tunic flapped against his thighs. Louis stopped a few inches from his face, which forced Lissandro to raise his gaze to keep eye contact.

"Do that again, and I don't care if you are my friend. I'll kill you," Louis whispered. Now that things were settled, his friend calmed down and stepped back.

Lissandro spotted Selen behind Louis. He wore a brown tunic, a cloak, and had fastened his sword on his side. Lissandro turned to Louis. "I suggest we leave the palace without an escort if you want to talk freely to the population. I see you put cloaks on, so it is probably your intention."

"It is," Louis said. He went down the steps to the gallery. Lissandro and Selen followed him. As Louis pushed the door leading to the outside yard, Lissandro heard a voice behind them.

"You're not leaving the palace." The three men turned around. "Not without me," Folc said.

"We don't need an escort this time, Folc," Selen said.

"I'm sure you don't want one, but it doesn't matter. It is my function and oath to protect the king. Unless the king opposes it, I will follow him into the city. Your Majesty," Folc said and bowed low.

"Don't bow to me Folc, not in private," Louis said. "You can follow, but be discreet. I don't want to draw attention to me."

The boy nodded, and they all went out and down the hill.

They sauntered through the streets unnoticed. Louis and Selen had their hoods pulled down over their foreheads. Lissandro and Folc, who were not as recognizable, walked bareheaded. Only Louis carried no weapon. Lissandro wondered if his friend genuinely thought that the people would not attack him or if he deliberately took a risk to prove that he didn't fear them.

The streets were populous and they sometimes had to press through the crowd to make their way. The shopping area was a colorful place where the precious silk gowns of the nobles grazed the plain cotehardies of the commoners. Though it was summer, wimples and hats were popular among the commoners. Lissandro smelled fresh baked bread, tanned leather, and flowers sold by peddlers. For a while, he forgot the odor of sweat and of the morning waters in the gutter. Sounds coming from the shops pierced the hubbub of the crowd. Here, he heard the clinking of a light hammer, there, the warm, rasping noise of a saw. Sometimes, it was the rattling of coins falling onto a counter.

"It is a thing to read about city life in books, but it is quite impressive to… Hey!" A hand grabbed his sleeve. Selen dragged him backwards. Only strangers walked behind them. Louis and Folc had not followed.

"Where are they?" Selen asked.

Lissandro stretched on the tip of his feet and spotted the white cloak of Folc hurrying towards a shop. "Over there." Lissandro retraced his steps, treading on a few feet, and reached the shop under the insults of the molested passersby.

The heavy scents in the room went straight to his head. Lissandro knew he had entered the shop of a perfumer. Yet, the objects displayed varied from carved boxes to handkerchiefs. The merchant was occupied with two ladies, presenting them glimmering mousseline stoles. Louis stood near the counter, mesmerized by a pair of cobalt gloves embroidered with silver thread. As his friend reached for the precious handicraft, the merchant, who probably had eyes behind his back, scolded him.

"Don't touch that!"

Louis retreated his hand.

"How dare you talk…" Folc exclaimed, turning towards the perfumer, but Louis stopped the boy with a hand on his shoulder.

"How I dare? In my own shop?" the perfumer replied to Folc with anger. "Young rascal. You will leave this place." The man strode towards Folc, hand up, with the determination to give him a good beating.

Louis interposed and was pushed back against the counter. His hood slipped backwards. At the sight of the glittering circlet, everyone in the shop fell silent. The perfumer went down on his knees.

"Please, Your Majesty, have mercy."

Louis sighed. "I only wanted to see your shop."

So much for discretion, Lissandro thought while Selen pushed the curious out of the entrance. Folc unfolded his cloak, revealing his armour and insignia.

"It is an honour for me to welcome Your Majesty into my house. Let me show you around," the perfumer said with a hundred bows.

Lissandro followed them into the workshop. Six people worked in the room. They all rose, startled.

"Please, carry on what you are doing," Louis said.

The workers sat down, insecure. Two worked on a press and one collected the golden liquid in a bucket to pour it into vats. Near a table covered with alembics and retorts, a young man read out and corrected what sounded like formulae. Lissandro walked around, admiring the colorful liquids and the different flasks labelled with names such as apricot, iris, jonquil, musk, and amber. The heady fragrances in the room gave him a headache. He moved towards Louis and the merchant, who stood by two women embroidering tissues.

"And here is where the perfumed textiles receive their final touch," the perfumer explained with pride.

"Where do you get all the ingredients for the scents?" Louis asked.

"A bit from everywhere, Your Majesty. Mostly from the Crysas Peninsula. The amber comes from the Windy Isles."

"How hard does the guild weight on your shop? Do you have to follow oppressive, strict rules?"

The man looked at Louis with surprise. "It is an honour to be a member of the guild, Your Majesty. There are rules, but my trade is free from competition. My work is praised through the city and, as you can see, I have four apprentices.

Without the guild, we would never have survived the war."

"What do you wish from the new government?" Louis asked.

The man seemed puzzled by the question. "I hope the peace will last, Your Majesty."

"Yes, everyone wants that, but more exactly. What do you expect from your king?"

The man turned pale and gaped. "I…"

No one here will dare to answer such questions, Lissandro thought, which actually was quite funny considering that in his world, people would beg, petition, and scream at the politicians to listen to them. When they for once had a genuinely honest leader who cared about their opinions, their minds were as dull and insipid as blancmange.

"Speak freely," Louis insisted. "I command you." His friend was losing patience.

"A…a good king," the man stuttered. The perfumer looked at Louis and must have seen that the answer wasn't satisfying as he added, "not too many taxes."

Considering what the man had said about his ingredients, Lissandro thought that his faint complaint was aimed at the taxes on foreign trade. Yet, Lissandro would not point it out to Louis.

Louis nodded. "And you?" He turned to the apprentice with the book. "What do you wish of the government?"

The boy was livid and cast an appealing look at his Master. The man nodded. "Peace," the boy whispered.

"But there must be more to it," Louis insisted to the boy. "Don't you feel oppressed by the laws? Don't you wish for a house, an education?"

"But…but, Your Majesty, I have already an education," the boy whispered.

Louis opened his mouth to speak, but Lissandro stopped him. "Your Majesty," he said. Louis looked at him. Lissandro could not voice the words, but Louis understood and turned towards the merchant again.

"We thank you for your time. It was interesting," Louis said.

Lissandro did not know if the merchant felt the yoke of the government's oppression on his neck, but if there was a face symbolizing relief, it was the one he had right now.

"It was all my pleasure, Your Majesty," the merchant said with a bow. He moved towards a small trunk and came back. "Please, let me offer you these gloves. They are of better quality than the ones on the counter. They are one of our masterpieces." The gloves in the man's hands were superb. They were made of the finest leather and embroidered with gold thread. Lissandro gave a slight smile. They were purple. "They are perfumed with orchid."

"Thank you," Louis said as he took the gift. "Is there a way for us to go out unnoticed?"

"Of course. Follow me."

The merchant led them to the rear of the shop to a back door. As they stepped outside, they put their hoods on again. The door closed behind them.

"Should we try a tavern?" Lissandro proposed.

"I think I need a drink," Selen said. Lissandro could not agree more. "And something to eat."

"Don't talk about food," Lissandro said. "The smell in there was unbearable." Yet, miraculously, neither he nor the two pallid men inside had retched.

"I know a place," Folc said. He took the lead, and they moved up the street. "Oh, and if you think it smelled bad in there, never enter a butchery or a tannery."

The tavern was a house built of stone with a wooden balcony on the first floor. Flowerpots decorated the windowsills. Light shone through the small windows with green stained glass. A painted wooden sign representing a dancing toad hung over the threshold. The group stopped in front of the dark red door.

"Whatever happens in there, we keep our hoods on. As long as no one pulls out a knife, I can endure a bit of pushing and scolding," Louis said to Folc. The boy scowled but nodded.

They opened the door and entered. As Lissandro had expected, the place was crowded, hot, and the smell of the stew barely won over the smell from sweaty customers. While Folc ordered drinks and food from the innkeeper, they sat down at a table near a window. To be wrapped in their cloaks and hoods in the middle of summer made them look ridiculous. However, Lissandro knew that in such crowded places, you could kill your neighbor on the bench, and no one would raise an eyebrow if the man's head fell in his soup. Lissandro and his friends could well wear cloaks and gloves without raising a single suspicion. At least, Lissandro did not need to push his hood to the rim of his eyes, unlike his companions. On the other side of the table, Selen's face was barely visible. Louis had offered him the gloves, and Selen was busy trying them on. Lissandro smelled a faint scent of orchid every time his friend moved his hands.

"You look more relaxed than I thought, Selen," Lissandro said.

"Oh, yes," Selen said, startled out of his thoughts. "It helps that I am not alone, and though the smell is horrendous, the customers seem calm."

"I am positively surprised that it's not crawling with harlots. Nice choice, Folc," Louis added.

"I don't know what you all are used to, but this is one of the most popular taverns of the city, and it barely smells," Folc said with surprise.

A plump, smiling woman came with their order and placed the foaming mugs at the end of the table. Selen passed the beer around. Lissandro grabbed his mug and raised it up.

"I propose a toast to our noble king. May we smell the perfume of our fellow countrymen once in a while to remember our modest origins," Lissandro said. "To the king."

"To the king," Selen and Folc repeated, raising their mugs.

In front of him, Louis's fingers drummed on the side of his mug. "Do you know the tale of the lion and the gnat, Lilo?"

"Am I that irritating?" Lissandro asked, half offended, half amused. "I have always thought that your compatriots had a cutting sense of humor."

"See mine as thin as a spider web."

"You see! Cutting," Lissandro chuckled. "I like you too." He smiled. Louis smiled back.

"I hope you are hungry," Folc placed the cooking pot in the center of the table. He tossed Lissandro a trencher and served a full ladle of steaming stew on it.

Lissandro saw cauliflowers, leeks, and parsnips but not the tasty meat bits he had looked forward to. "Vegetables only?" Lissandro exclaimed. "Did you order nuncheons?"

"There should be some morsels of eel somewhere. I thought they would like it," Folc said, pointing at Selen and Louis. "I'm sorry I didn't take your diet into consideration."

"Commoners are too poor to afford meat, but maybe for the sake of your delicate stomach, I should promote the concept of a restaurant?" Louis said. Though half his face was in shadows, Lissandro could see the smirk in his eyes.

"Don't be so mean. Maybe the stew is worth the sweating," Lissandro replied sardonically and attacked his stew with his spoon. "Yet, it's a brilliant idea. You could as well promote the concept of fast food."

"What is fast food?" Louis asked.

"It's the future of restaurants. If I describe it in a few words, minced meat, a sauce, and a few vegetables between two slices of bread, the whole served with fries, or should I say for you, *pommes Pont-Neuf*."

"Really? Do they still eat that shit in your time? Besides, I don't see how street food could replace restaurants. You can't prepare a pot-au-feu on the street."

"To favour boiled meat over a hamburger and its delicious fries, Louis, you have no sense of taste. This could explain why you still eat that cow puke." Lissandro's spoon squelched the tepid, grey mixture. Maybe that was how everything tasted once the salt, the pepper, and the grease were removed. Maybe the first fries had been roughly cut potatoes soaked in fish oil. The poor ate shit. It was a permanent trait throughout history. "Folc, you owe me a meal," Lissandro said, shaking his spoon in the boy's direction. "So, Your Majesty, were you satisfied with your meeting with the commoners?"

"I thought they would be more prompt to complain about their standard of living," Louis answered. "The people are happy with their masters' fortune and moan with glory under the yoke of their cruel ambition," he sighed. "But I won't give up. I know it will take time."

"Yeah, happiness is a new idea in Trevalden. While you force the concept of democracy down their throats, you should know that the second time this concept spread throughout the world, it did not turn out as well as in the society of the primitive sitting next to you. Democracy is a sweet word used as a smoke screen by the oligarchy. Elections are a fool's game, and everyone blame his neighbor for ruining his little, boring paradise. The only thing worse than blatant tyranny is the illusion of freedom."

"We are in a completely different context," Louis said.

"Men are men. They want to eat, sleep, make love, and see their children grow."

"Your vision of mankind is depressing," Louis sighed. "But you are American, you can't understand—"

"That moral duty and knowledge is, in every country, the surest basis of public happiness?"

"Well, yes!" Louis exclaimed, his hands open. "Did you just quote La Boetie?"

"George Washington. Your country does not have the monopoly on human rights." Lissandro winked.

"Lissandro, does my country still exist in your time?" Louis asked.

"Oh yes, but you don't want to know what it looks like. You may recognize a bit of the countryside, but it would break your heart if I described the cities. The men who killed you have ruled the world for two hundred years now. The damage is… consequent," Lissandro saw Louis turn gloomy. "My country does not look better, if you want to know, though it has never been brilliant like yours. I hope you will succeed this time. Don't let these bastards win."

"Unfortunately, one must wait for a disaster big enough for the general opinion to feel the need of salutary measures. The good will always come from a disaster. Started too early, these sanitary measures only seem weird or inappropriate," Louis said. "The good is what we must pursue, whatever the price."

Lissandro thought that Louis's words sometimes were so incisive and steadfast that they could be put in a neat, square box. Too bad that the world was round.

"Talking about concepts that could improve the life of the people," Louis said while carving his trencher with his spoon, "I would like to install running water, but I don't have the slightest idea of how it works."

Lissandro chuckled. "Don't look at me like that. It is a complex system which requires years of study in engineering and—"

"Not at all," Selen interrupted him. "I know how it works. We had running water in the palace. Would you like a primitive to explain to you what a siphon is?"

"And electricity? Do you know how to turn on a light bulb? No. That's what I thought, only good at making pottery," Lissandro replied with a sneer and a wink. Selen did not answer. His face had turned pale. "Selen?" Lissandro called. Selen put a hand on his mouth. His body jerked, and he rushed outside.

Lissandro followed his friend and was the first one out of the tavern. Selen stood in the alley on the side of the building. He still leaned against the wall. Vomit lay splattered between his spread legs. Lissandro's attention was caught by a bright light coming from Selen's hand. His friend hastily put his gloves on.

"Selen, your hand?"

"You have seen nothing," Selen hissed. Behind him, Lissandro heard the footsteps of Louis and Folc. "Nothing," Selen repeated near his face.

Lissandro turned around, aghast, and watched Selen join their friends.

"Selen, are you all right?" Louis asked, worried, a hand on Selen's arm.

"Yes. It must have been the food or the heat. Let's go home."

65

Selen went up the staircase leading to the library. His long robes brushed the steps behind him. He opened the door. The heavy cinnamon smell of old paper engulfed him. Bookshelves were cluttered with codices, dusty books, and loose documents. Volumes stood open on carved wooden lecterns. Considering the dust, it had been a long time since someone had taken care of the place. The shutters were half closed to protect the documents from the light. Selen progressed between the shelves, careful not to stumble on a pile of books.

Lissandro sat on a corner of a table covered with manuscripts and unrolled papers. His eyebrows were frowned and so were his lips. The quill in his hand flitted on the paper with small scratches.

"I should have visited this room before I took the responsibility of this charge," Lissandro grumbled.

Selen considered that drawing up an inventory of the documents in this room would take months if not years, and there were two more floors above them. "I came to give you back your book," he said, laying down a book titled *Anthology, Minstrels' Songs, and Popular Dances* on the table.

"I guess you are ready for tonight," Lissandro grinned. "Not too deceived?"

Selen squirmed. "It's not exactly the kind of dances I was prepared for. It's a lot more…sober."

"You can still perform a Dionysian dance. Yet, I'm not sure it is a demonstration the court is ready to see." Lissandro raised his head and gazed at him with his large, blue eyes. "Unlike me. Can you such dances?" he asked with a high, inappropriate interest.

"It is a way to celebrate the gods. Those dances are only performed during festivals and events. And not alone," Selen answered, "but we certainly use our body a lot more than the people in this book do."

"I should probably read it as well before tonight. I used to dance when I was young, but with the decades, the art lost its prestige. I have not practiced for a long time and I have forgotten the steps."

"Do you want to rehearse with me?" Selen thought he had learned most of the steps, but he was still unsure if he could reproduce them with someone. He would not mind a try before stepping on the floor.

"You should know that, as those dances are performed between two people, they require coordination, and often, complicity." Lissandro rose and stepped towards him. "You will need to touch your partner, hold his hand, his waist, to step into his private space, and anticipate his moves. Dance is a game of seduction, of sensuality—" Lissandro stopped a few inches from him "—of lust." His friend kept his gaze down. Selen felt as if Lissandro was almost on him. He smelled his perfume, felt his warmth. It made him feel uneasy. "This is why I won't dance with you," Lissandro breathed before stepping back. "The good thing is that we will only dance with women, thus leaving us the leisure to concentrate on our steps," Lissandro said. "Still, it can be pleasant. You will see." He smiled.

"Were you careful with the costs?" Selen asked. He was not sure he wanted to think of dancing anymore.

"We did the best we could. I even went to the undercrofts in search of materials we could reuse. You will have a big surprise." He grinned. "You can also tell Louis that the situation in the countryside is improving. People are returning from the Iron Marches and the West. It will take time, but the communities will reform and life will start again."

"Any news from Embermire and Millhaven?" Selen asked.

"I don't know about Embermire, but Millhaven has had hard times with the flow of refugees from Earthfell, and some nobles complain about the new decrees. However, the Countess Khorkina supports Louis's measures. It is a fact that the nobles of Millhaven have been more active in the war than the ones here. They won't pay the same price. Besides, they have their gold mines." Lissandro piled the books, blew the candle in the lantern, and closed the ink flask. He took the book about the dancing and joined him.

Selen walked towards the door, Lissandro following on his heels. "There is something I would like to ask you, Lilo," Selen said. He felt uneasy about it, but he had pondered the question. "I would like to know Louis's name."

"If he hasn't told you, it's because he doesn't want you to know. I'm sorry. I can tell you all I know about Louis, but not that. I can't betray him," Lissandro answered. He locked the door behind them and walked down the steps.

Selen followed him. "But it's ridiculous…"

"Yes, I know." Lissandro stopped and turned to him. "Listen, when I told you last time that you didn't know him, it was not to offend you. You do know him as a person, more than anyone. I know who he was, at least, what he did. Louis is a good man, but he is…he won't stop. Whatever the cost." Lissandro stared at him. "It won't end well, Selen."

Selen half smiled. "I will follow him to the grave."

There was sadness in Lissandro's eyes. He shook his head and kept on walking. At the bottom of the stairs, Selen took his leave.

His friend was not in the solar. Selen opened the painted, carved wardrobe. The nobles would probably come in their best outfits, as would the princes. He had to be at his best not to shame his friends. He put on white pants, a white shirt, and chose a knee-length, crimson brocade houppelande, slit from the waist, with long, opened sleeves trimmed with ermine. The embroidery made the cloth tight to the chest and the waist. Still, he buckled a large, carved leather belt over it. The soft straps flapped against his legs. He completed his outfit with dark leather, high-heeled boots that ended above the knees. On his head, he decided to wear the chain he had worn during the coronation. He found a model whose hairpin was shaped like tree leaves. Once he was dressed, he picked up one of his history books and sat on a fauteuil.

A few minutes later, Louis entered the solar. "Oh Lord…" his friend whispered, staring at him.

Selen squirmed. "Should I change?" Under the persistent gaze of his friend, he felt uncomfortable.

"No! It's just that…you put the level quite high, and as the king, I should give the best impression. Not that I want to, but it's a must in such occasions." Louis headed to the wardrobe.

"I am sure we can find something," Selen said, joining him. Louis had already picked dark blue pants and a white shirt. Selen frowned at him. "Something better."

"Something with heels," Louis mumbled.

Louis picked up a long, royal blue brocade vest with split, dagged sleeves. The collar rose high behind the neck. The front was adorned with a double line of embossed, silver buttons. Louis put the clothes on. The vest fit perfectly on his chest. With the high collar, his hair fell on the front to his collarbones like a lion's mane. Around his waist, he tied a long, light blue silk belt, which fell on the side of his thigh.

"Something like that," Selen sighed with amazement and felt the stirring of a feeling he would keep for later. He handed Louis a pair of short, high-heeled, leather boots.

"Oh, musketeer's boots." Louis put them on. His shoulder reached Selen's again. Louis turned to him and grinned. "I think we are ready."

They left the solar. Lissandro waited for them in the garden.

"Jesus. In two hundred years, I have never seen such an amazing sight," Lissandro chuckled. He wore a green embroidered doublet over grey pants. He had tied two long feathers in his hair, which matched its color of dark honey perfectly.

"You wanted a ball," Louis said. "I hope you will enjoy it because it won't happen again for a long time. I want the Crown to show sobriety in the future."

"I can assure you that we were extremely careful with the expenses," Lissandro insisted. He moved towards Louis. "I know how uncomfortable you feel about it, but try to socialize as best as you can. Balls are no battlefields of opinions. Wits and charming smiles are the rule."

Louis put the tips of his fingers to his throat. "Actually, what makes me uncomfortable right now is to be dressed without a cravat. I feel like I'm rude or naked."

"Oh, I do enjoy seeing your throat," Lissandro whispered. Selen noticed that Lissandro's lips parted as he stared at the pale, throbbing skin.

"Please, close your mouth, Lilo," Louis said. "It's awkward."

"Hmm, I'm sorry," Lissandro said, controlling himself again. "Should we move?"

They headed to the gallery. As they walked down the stairs from the garden, a woman walked from the north side of the gallery.

"Kilda?" Selen said.

In her lady outfits, she was hardly recognizable. She wore a dress of thick, red velvet, with an embroidered, open collar, and thin salmon gloves. Her eyes were red and she looked upset. She stopped when she saw them.

"What is wrong?" Lissandro asked kindly.

"I'm sorry, my lords, Your Majesty, but I can't attend the ball," she sobbed.

"Why?" Selen asked.

"Look at me. My hair is a mess, I have a scar, and I look like a horse. And I can't even close my dress." More tears ran down her cheeks. She squirmed and gestured to hide herself. "I'm sorry."

Selen walked towards her. "Don't say that," he frowned. "Look how lovely you are in your dress." She looked at him as if he was making fun of her. "I mean it," Selen insisted.

Lissandro stood at their side. He took her hand. "Selen is right. All you need is to dry your tears." He smiled. He unfastened the feathers on his hair and tied them to her short, black hair. They cupped the side of her head and suited her perfectly. "You look like a native bride," Lissandro said. "It's a compliment."

Kilda half smiled. "Can you do something with my dress?" Her corset was loose, making her corsage look slovenly.

Selen had no idea how to fix a dress and looked at Lissandro. His friend turned to him. His face showed the same helpless look. Lissandro grabbed the ropes on her back and tried to pull on it.

"It's stuck," he complained.

Louis approached them. "Move away," he said, pushing Lissandro on the side. "If you excuse me." He pulled up Kilda's corsage until it was straight. He turned her around, took hold of the ropes, and put his knee on her bottom. Selen and Lissandro gaped as their friend tugged hard on the ropes, closing the corset in a few seconds.

Louis turned to them and stepped back. "Two sisters." He smiled.

With her dress perfectly closed, Kilda was elegant. Many men would probably find her attractive.

"You are beautiful," Lissandro said.

"Thank you," she chuckled.

"But where is Josselin? Should he not accompany you?" Selen asked.

"He went to Millhaven for a few days, but I thought I could have some distraction," she said.

"And you did well," Lissandro said. "Would you accompany me? I'm sure Josselin won't mind." He offered her his arm. She put her hand on it.

Selen smiled. Lissandro was more than a head shorter than her, but they still looked sweet.

They entered the hall. The decoration was completely different from the one they had had for the coronation's festivities. Selen understood what Lissandro had meant with the surprise. Giant mirrors hung on the walls on each side. They reflected the candles' flames and made the hall look infinite. Between the mirrors and around the top and bottom pillars of the aisles, stood long, brocade curtains in dark shades of burgundy. In the subdued light, their color matched the embroidered carpets unfolded on the floor under the aisles.

"And all that was in the undercrofts?" Selen whispered.

Lissandro looked at him with a hint of pride.

Guests were already scattered in the hall in small groups. They turned towards them as the herald announced the king's arrival.

Louis headed towards the delegation from the Windy Isles. The princes and their sister interrupted their discussion with Honfroi and bowed towards the king. Their silk garments were richly decorated with pearls and laces, and they wore puffed-up pants.

"Your Majesty, let us thank you for this charming evening. This place is incredible. I can hardly believe that it is the same hall as the one where we met," Philip said.

"I am pleased to know it satisfies Your Royal Highnesses," Louis replied. "The Crown will do its best to make your stay enjoyable."

"We have no doubt about that. Nysa Serin is known to be a place of luxury and pleasures," Owen said.

Selen wondered how long they would keep on complimenting each other. Probably until they ran dry of pompous words.

"Nysa Serin has suffered the sorrows of a long war, but the city will soon show its virtues of probity and social development to the world," Louis said with a twitch of the lips.

Selen got the answer to his question. It seemed his friend had not appreciated having his capital compared with a medieval Babylon.

Lissandro stepped forward. "If you'll excuse me, Your Highnesses. I need to have a word with His Majesty."

Selen stepped away and decided to have a look at the place. A servant presented him a tray with goblets of wine. Selen picked one. He had noticed that the drink helped him to inhibit his fears in such situation. Yet, he remembered Bertrant and the orgiastic scenes he had faced in his previous life. This goblet was a treacherous friend. A buffet had been set against the south wall. Surprisingly, there were no venison or pâtés, but toasts and a profusion of fruits. Selen picked a ground cherry and turned around. Musicians had taken their places on the dais. The herald stepped forward and announced the opening of the ball.

A flow of dancers stepped on the floor and moved gracefully with the rhythm of the music. Selen listened to the notes and tried to remember the different dances he had learned. He took a sip of his wine. The pink beverage had the sweet taste of strawberries.

"Your friend made a miracle with the decorations," he heard a voice behind him. Selen turned around and faced Evrardin. "I wonder where in the capital he found so many mirrors."

"Then you should probably ask him," Selen answered and realized he was being rude. "I think they come from the palace furniture."

"I have heard that the king projects to write new laws," Evrardin said, showing the true purpose of his conversation. "Will it be the subject of the next council session?"

Selen knew he was not prepared to hold such discussion. At one point, the man would corner him and squeeze out the answers he needed. Selen decided it was time he stepped on the dance floor. "The king is a busy man. I think he may surprise us all with ambitious projects for Trevalden," Selen responded before walking away.

Selen put his goblet on a table and approached a mature woman in a yellow gown. Veils covered the salt and pepper buns on the sides of her head. He held out his hands towards her as he had seen the other men do. The woman looked at him with incomprehension. It felt slightly awkward.

"Are you sure you want to dance with me, young man?" she asked him.

Selen only smiled back. When she saw that he was serious, she stepped forward and took hold of his hands. Lissandro had been wrong on the sensuality, but it was true that he could easily focus on the steps. Dancing was a lot easier than he had thought.

"You are a wonderful dancer," the woman whispered. "You will make the maidens' heads spin tonight." Selen noticed that her chubby face blushed slightly. He was glad to know that he could give a good impression.

After a few dances, he took his leave and was heading towards the buffet when he noticed Kilda. She sat alone in the aisle, apparently scared that her appearance raised sarcasm. Whatever this assembly may think, Selen saw more beauty in Kilda than in any of the overly made-up women in the hall. He walked towards her. "Would you give me the honour?" he asked, holding out his hand.

"With pleasure," she answered, putting her silk glove on his hand. Her voice was warm and noble.

They walked to the dance floor. Selen put his hand on her waist and noticed that, even with his heels, Kilda was somewhat taller than him.

"I hope you do not mind about the corset," she squirmed.

Selen smiled. "No. Don't worry. Louis is very polite, but he would not even glance at a woman. Yet, you are taller and stronger than him. You may attract his attention."

She laughed. "Do you realize how rude that was?" Selen blushed with shame. "No, please. It made my day. None of you can talk to a lady, but your attempts to be nice are always memorable."

Selen and Kilda swirled on the floor like leaves in the wind. She looked happy, and Selen thought that he enjoyed these type of dances. He would not dance with his love, but Kilda was a wonderful partner. They danced together until Lissandro took back his role at her side.

The dances had warmed Selen up. He decided to leave the hall to take some fresh air and stepped outside into the night. Guests stood on the esplanade, but the gardens along the south aisle looked silent. The rose bushes spread their perfume. The air was chilly and moist with the dew. Faint lights shone from the windows above. From the chambers came muffled voices. Selen stopped when he heard Louis's name. He listened more carefully. The voice had something familiar, as he had heard it before, but he could not remember where.

"Did you make all the preparations for tonight?" the voice inquired.

Selen could not hear the answer. He felt that something was amiss and decided to check for himself. The stake for the rose bushes ended a bit under the windowsill. Selen climbed silently on it, hoping it would hold his weight.

"I still haven't swallowed the humiliation in front of the court. This decree will soon bring ruin to my trade. Of course, I am with you in this," Selen heard another voice say. As he could not climb higher, he counted the windows. It must be the fifth room from the west.

"Then let me describe to you what we expect of you," the familiar voice said.

"You don't need to. I already have taken the initiative. Tonight, the king will drink his last cup of wine," the voice sniggered.

"What have you done, fool? We told you to wait!"

Selen's eyes widened as his blood ran cold. He jumped from the stake and ran to the hall.

The party was in full swing. The dancers filled the floor and groups stood here and there under the aisles. It took time before Selen spotted Louis in a discussion with the princes. His fingers discreetly drumming on the goblet in his hand,

Louis looked clogged in boredom with a forced smile that Selen recognized as consternation. Trying not to run or scream, Selen pushed his way hastily among the guests. When he approached, Prince Owen was entertaining the group with a jovial story.

"…We enter the bedchambers, and the man stands on his knees with the chicken in one hand…"

As Selen grasped Louis's wrist, his friend turned towards him with relief mixed with incomprehension. He looked at Selen's grip, pulling his hand away, then at Selen's expression. When Selen shook his head, Louis's features were struck with terror. The goblet fell onto the floor. Louis turned livid and looked at the crowd with panic. Behind him, Owen fell silent.

"Is something wrong, Your Majesty?" Philip asked.

"Stay calm," Selen whispered to Louis. "I will take care of this with Folc. Don't eat or drink anything."

He let go of his friend and hurried towards Lissandro, who stood near the dais with Kilda. She adjusted the bottom of her dress. Selen tapped Lissandro's shoulder.

"Stay close to Louis for the rest of the evening. Be on your guards," Selen whispered. The look in Lissandro's eyes turned grim.

Folc, who stood near the door, understood before Selen needed to say a word. The king's guard followed him out into the gallery.

"Fifth room from the west!" Selen exclaimed. The two men ran up the staircase and along the aisle. The room's door stood ajar. Selen stretched out an arm to stop Folc from rushing in. He pushed the door carefully.

A man lay in a pool of blood. Selen stepped inside and turned the body onto his back. He recognized the merchant who had opposed the decree during the court session. "Hallecos." Yet, it was not his voice that Selen had heard. It meant that Hallecos was behind the plot, but that the merchant had only been a pawn in a bigger scheme. "Whose room is this?" Selen asked.

"His room," Folc answered.

In the garderobe, a man in velvet clothes sat with his tongue out and his eyes rolled upwards. He had purple marks on his neck, but his throat had been severed deep as a precaution.

"I guess he won't talk much," the boy added.

"Ask the commander of the guard to reinforce the security. I think it was an isolated attempt, but we better be careful. However, we have a foreign delegation down there. We have to keep the appearances. Don't cause a scandal."

The boy left the room. Selen felt terribly guilty not to have warned Louis about Segar. It had not been the captain's voice he had heard, but he had no doubt that the events were connected in some way.

Selen sat on the bed in the solar while Louis paced in front of him. His friend still hadn't calmed down.

"I can't believe they tried to poison me," Louis said.

"I think it was an initiative from Hallecos. The man probably felt secure enough to make such an attempt," Selen said. "The other vipers in the court are more cunning. They have too much to lose with a new anarchy." Selen rose and walked towards Louis. "We know that we displease many with our decrees. These kinds of things may happen. You better forget it and concentrate on your work," Selen said with a smile.

"Our decrees?" Louis said.

Selen blushed. "I'm sorry, I didn't want to take credit…"

"Don't be sorry. I like that you feel concerned about it." Louis grabbed him by the waist and took Selen's hand with his other hand.

Selen chuckled. "There is no music."

"Do we need some?" Louis said, staring into his eyes. Louis's steps were graceful and short. Selen let himself be carried along. The music of the evening still rang in his head. His love leaned towards him. "And keep your boots on tonight," he whispered in his ear.

Selen's cheeks burned. His heart beat faster. The feeling he had spared earlier for this moment came back, stronger. He understood what Lissandro had meant with his description of dance. He leaned towards Louis. "Only if you keep your vest on."

It had only been a month since their arrival, but the atmosphere in the streets of Nysa Serin had changed. It was more popular. The heavy decorated litters Lissandro had seen before were now scarce. The exotic fragrances of mango and cinnamon rising from the food shops had been replaced by the more common perfumes of strawberries and lavender. Lissandro missed the smell of cinnamon buns. The bread was cheaper but reduced to a few sorts and not as tasteful as before. *Louis has made sure that everyone ate, should everyone from the palace to the slums feast on pigeon and cabbage.*

Lissandro rode down a street of the shopping area. In the summer light, the people of the city sauntered around merrily, sitting near the fountains, listening to the minstrels. He did not remember ever hearing so much music in a city before, as if the bards had been pushed out of the taverns to perform on the streets. Many songs were different versions of the ballad of "The Hero of Earthfell." In one song, the man had lost an arm. In another song, he had been eaten alive. The maidens yearned at the description of the blond knight, while children ran, mimicking the attack on the dragon. The street opened on to a square. Lissandro halted. His horse was blocked by a crowd.

"…for opposing the guards during your arrest, for refusing to pay the tribute, and for having concealed goods from the Crown, you, Brecken Whitfield, have been sentenced to death by beheading," the herald cried out.

Lissandro saw the guards drag a quivering man from the line of prisoners. Judging by the rests of his torn silk outfits, he must have been someone important a few days ago. As the guards rudely pushed him to the ground and placed his head on the stump, the man yelped some unintelligible words. The axe fell sharp. The head rolled in spurts of blood down the platform to the feet of the crowd. Lissandro heard cheers and bawdy jokes. Another man was pushed forward. This one was shaggy and wore a leather apron. He was obviously a commoner.

"In the name of King Louis and the people of Trevalden, you have been found guilty of charges. For abusing your authority, for the rapes of maids, and for the detention of false coins, you, Gilbert Tikell, have been sentenced…"

Lissandro did not stay to hear the rest. He pulled the reins left and spurred his horse into the street leading to the north districts. There had been complaints that it was an insult to hang the nobles. So Louis had decided that no one would be hung anymore. Every criminal condemned to death would be beheaded. Louis had added that the commoners could see it as a promotion. As Lissandro had foreseen, the decrees condemning the lack of war effort had been a scandal. Some of those stubborn nobles and merchants who had not been able to show proof of their engagement to the Rebellion had held more to their gold and lands than to their lives. Yet, after a few days of examples of that kind, many had submitted. Today, only the blood of the few recalcitrants left tainting the cobbles.

The gold that had poured into the open trunks of the Crown's treasure had been widely reinvested in the construction of hospitals, schools, and a complex sewer system. Lissandro still remembered the face of Evrardin when the minister had approached Louis with the plans for a Pharaonic coliseum and had been charged to build the sewers instead.

Lissandro had no illusions about how this would end. Though he loved and admired Louis, his friend was a lunatic. Unlike Louis, and therefore, he could not blame him, Lissandro had seen the drift of democracy. Louis's precious people were this crowd massed in front of the scaffold, waiting to be entertained, not men like Selen. Once the show was over, and they were put to work in the name of ideals they could barely grasp, the people would bite the hand that fed them. Louis could understand and control an army because he shared the soldiers' values of honour and courage. To understand a crowd, he would need to share their flaws. Yet, Louis despised what made the essence of the people. Therefore, Lissandro's men-loving, ascetic friend wanted to turn the crowd into an army. Lissandro hoped it would work and that Louis wasn't giving them the power and the training to put him down. At least, working with Louis had felt to Lissandro like kicking his heavy boot in the ass of all the oppressors he had met in his lives, and he had loved that!

However, he felt like he would not delay his journey any longer. He longed to look for his soul mate. His position at court had not been as useful to his search as he had hoped. No one in the city corresponded to the description he had given, and he had not received positive answers from Millhaven and Embermire. Maybe he would need to journey east, or even further. Lissandro's heart was filled with sorrow. He often looked at his friends' love with envy. Selen would die for Louis, but Lissandro did not need nor want to go to these extremities. Though he hated the idea of abandoning his friends, his future was not here.

While he was lost in his thoughts, his mount had reached a large townhouse. The building had been seized by the Crown and would be a school for boys. Lissandro got down from his horse and entered the building. The large entrance hall was under renovations. The walls had been bleached, and every bit of luxury had been removed. Lissandro walked around, peeping inside the rooms. Even decorated with sobriety, the townhouse would be a beautiful learning environment.

The atrium had been designed as a garden with orange trees and rose bushes growing in rings of earth among the stone plates. On the wall in front of him, men perched on a scaffold built a giant mosaic. Moving with agility between the levels of the structure, Selen counseled the men. Though it was totally out of his functions and status, his friend had worked with the builders on the different working sites. He was the only one apt to give counsel on the classical architecture Louis had wanted. Lissandro watched him get down from the scaffold. As he swung on the metal poles, the muscles of his arms and shoulders stretched and danced under his waving, flowing lilac hair. Lissandro could see the top of his hips stick out of his pants at the bottom of his long, bare back. Should there ever be an illustration of the men performing at the first classical Olympiads, it must have been Selen. His friend landed gracefully a few inches from him. His innocent, joyful face gleamed at his sight. Selen was catching his breath, and sweat ran down his throat. Most of the time, his two friends' behavior was a deafening slap at his forced celibacy.

"Lilo! I am pleased to see you here," Selen exclaimed.

"Me too, Selen. Don't you see the contradiction between standing on the dais at the court session and climbing a scaffolding half naked?" Lissandro pointed out kindly.

"I can't climb up there with my robes. Besides, there is no one here to stare at me or judge me, and most of the men work bare-chested. The robes make me look a bit too…mannered," Selen answered. He bent closer to Lissandro. "I think the men here like me. They are nice and ask for my help. I don't want to ruin it by acting snobbish."

Selen's need to feel accepted was touching. Lissandro believed that Selen did not expect to make friends, but that gratification for his actions was important to him.

"Do you want me to show you around?" Selen proposed. "There is still a lot to do, but you can have an idea of how it will look. I have followed Louis's plans to the letter."

"With pleasure," Lissandro answered. He was curious to see what kind of school Louis had in mind. Selen dried himself with a rag and put peach silk robes on.

They walked around the townhouse. Selen showed him what would be the library. Hundreds of books were piled against a wall.

"Louis insisted we have as much literature as this world can provide, in every language. There are treatises on nature, poems, books on history, math, and physics," Selen said.

"No novels? I mean, fictional books?" Lissandro asked.

"Only epic tales," Selen answered.

They left the room and progressed along a gallery.

"And here, next to the conservatory, is the kitchen."

"May I point out that the fireplaces are ridiculously small? You will never roast a beef in there," Lissandro said.

"Oh, but they won't. No meat is allowed," Selen said.

Lissandro gaped. It was the first time he heard of a vegetarian school. It would have been inconceivable in his time yet not in Selen's. "They didn't give you meat in your childhood?"

"In my childhood? You mean, in my life. Soldiers did not feast on meat. You could buy some—of course, if you could afford it—or wait for celebrations and the meat from the rituals, but cheese, fish, vegetables, and cereals were our everyday. These children will be just fine. They will even receive fresh fruits. You don't need meat to be healthy." Selen smiled.

Lissandro sneered. "I suppose that with such a diet, your body suffered from severe lack of proteins, thus leading to hormonal deficiencies." Lissandro regretted his words as they left his mouth.

"This is a wholesome diet, but I don't expect someone who fries his food in oil to have notions in nutrition."

Well-deserved and certainly far too nice, Lissandro thought. "I put my foot in my mouth. I didn't mean—"

"Oh yes, you did. You just never care." Selen kept his voice soft, but his irritation was clear. "You've seen me. Do I look like I have deficiencies?"

"No. On the contrary." He lowered his head with shame and shrank in his bones. On an evolutionary scale, Selen was a butterfly, while he was stuck at the caterpillar stage.

"You don't need to pick on friends for what others did to you," Selen said, gentle again. "Come. There is more to show you." They left the room and progressed through the hall.

"I'm curious. Why did you paint everything white and remove all furniture?" Lissandro asked to change the subject.

"It's for the noise."

Lissandro looked at Selen with an inquiring look. "The noise?"

"Yes. To teach the children to be silent. The sound reverberation is so intense that you are forced to whisper if you don't want your head to explode with pain. We noticed how unbearable it was when we emptied the place."

"But it's children. They need to play," Lissandro objected.

"Of course, this is why we have the garden and this place." They arrived on a second atrium. The floor was covered with sand.

"Is it an impression or is this an arena?" Lissandro asked.

Selen looked at him, surprised. "It's a training yard for gymnastics. An arena? It's forbidden to hurt a child. They will learn to fight, but to abuse a child is punishable by death. To avoid such things, the teachers will be rigorously selected from among the best guild masters of the city."

"This sounds ambitious."

"The Treasure can afford it."

"Do you mean the school is free?" Lissandro asked.

"It won't cost anything for the commoners, but education is obligatory, nobles included. Every child from the age of five must stay at the school. This is why we needed such a big building. There must be room for everyone to sleep. There are more schools like this in the city and we will have schools in the countryside for—"

"…military training?"

"How did you know?" Selen asked.

"A feeling." If the population were educated, trained, and armed, they wouldn't fear the nobles anymore. Besides, they would train together to learn unity. This was clever. But once again, it failed to take into account the flaws of the men. The word *play* had been banned from these walls. "I guess you did not plan to have the same kind of schools for girls," Lissandro said.

"A school for girls?" Selen asked, as if he heard the words for the first time.

Lissandro was not a bit surprised. "Never mind. Should we ride back to the palace?"

"Yes. I wonder how it went today with the princes of the Windy Isles."

Lissandro saw that Selen was worried. They walked back to the entrance and mounted their horses.

Once they arrived in the palace's stables, they dismounted and headed towards the main gallery. Folc strode from the opposite direction. The boy hailed them.

"Are you in a hurry?" Lissandro asked.

"I'm on my way to ask the lads to saddle the horses," Folc said.

"Is the king leaving?" Selen asked.

"I don't know. I just follow the orders. If you search for him, he is in the solar," Folc said. "I can't talk too long as I should be at my post in the gallery. It was just a short errand."

Lissandro and Selen headed to the solar.

"The boy is always around. Was it your idea?" Lissandro asked.

"We need people we can trust around us," Selen answered. "I thought that Folc would be glad to live here, and at the same time, I don't need to worry about something happening to him in the city. We would gladly give him lands, but he needs to reach manhood first."

They entered the solar. Louis stood near the door, dressed in a long, turquoise tunic. He fastened a dagger on his belt and barely glanced at them. He looked annoyed and tired.

"Are you going somewhere?" Selen inquired.

"Like every day for the last two weeks, I have discussed with the princes about probably every subject in this world. And yet, I feel like I have lost my time. Some people can't have a real, interesting conversation," Louis grunted. "I suppose it is my punishment for refusing their sister," he sighed.

"They can't be that boring," Lissandro relativized. "Most people enjoy discussions on food, women, horses, and idle talk."

Louis gave him a look that suggested he was not *most people*. "Anyway, now they want to go hunting," Louis snarled.

"Now? In the middle of the afternoon?" Selen exclaimed.

"It's as long as I could make them wait. There is plenty of food in the kitchens, and I see no interest in this aristocratic sport, but I could hardly say no."

"Are you sure they meant that kind of hunt?" Lissandro teased.

Louis turned to Lissandro with a frightful look. "They mentioned boars." His trembling fingers still fought to tie the ropes of the scabbard. The dagger fell on the floor. "*Bordel de merde!*" Louis yelled.

Lissandro knew when to stop with the teasing, and it was right now. Selen picked up the dagger and attached it to his friend's belt.

"Take the royal guard with you. Boars are dangerous. I would come if I could," Selen whispered.

"I know," Louis sighed. He turned to Lissandro. "Lilo, do you think I could consider opening the high council to commoners? I would like to hear the voice of the street, but I can't go down to the city every day. I would like to start working on the laws."

If Louis asked for his opinion on such things, he must really have had his brain mashed by the princes. "If you want my opinion, I would say no. Don't open the high council. You can't trust half of the men who sit there, and it would weaken your credibility. Organize special sessions with Mauger, your keeper of the seals, and masters of guilds. It should help."

Louis put a hand on Lissandro's shoulder. "Thank you. I will try not to kill something for once." His friend kissed Selen and left the room.

"He is wacked," Lissandro said, feeling sorry for Louis. "This function must be torture for him."

"He doesn't sleep much," Selen sighed, "and he still checks the ministers' reports and the reports on the ministers. The princes return to the Windy Isles tomorrow. I think Louis managed to install diplomatic alliances," Selen said. "Sadly, I have heard that the king of the Frozen Mountains will be here in eight days."

"I suggest we share the work here. Louis needs rest," Lissandro said. He saw the plans for his journey drift away as a nutshell on the ocean.

67

The juice of the pomegranate spilled on the table as Evrardin cleft it in two with his knife. For a second, it reminded him of the sight he had observed in the market square. He had known Brecken Whitfield since they had been young knights, scouring the taverns and whorehouses. His stubborn friend had refused to pay the tribute and had paid the price. He had died for a few trunks of gold and a miserable marble country house on the southern shore. Ridiculous.

Evrardin had had to choose between the axe and the loss of a property of ninety thousand acres south of Millhaven. Like all nobles, he still had had the option to move back on to his lands, but it would have meant the loss of his townhouse in Nysa Serin and the loss of his charge as minister. In other words, the loss of his whole fortune and status. The bone was still stuck in his throat.

Of course, he could not have come forward with any proof of active support to the Rebellion. He was already glad that no one had shown the king the proof of his active support of Agroln. The last king had paid well the special packages he and Elye had wrapped up for him. The Rebellion had grown into a threat, but Evrardin had trusted Elye to scheme a solid backstab on the late Bertrant. Unfortunately, the count had failed, and the Rebellion had won. Evrardin had maneuvered Pembroke to get a seat on the high council. Yet, he was no dupe. Louis's piercing eyes had mistrusted him from the start. And now, the king was making a fool of him with this stupid project of sewers.

"Will you eat that?" his wife asked, approaching the table.

She was a tall, emaciated woman with red, bushy hair and beady eyes. Evrardin could barely endure her presence, but her dowry had brought him five thousand head of cattle and lands in Earthfell. The ashes of the property must be cold by now. At least, that one would not go to the Crown.

"No. You can eat it," he said. "And choke on it," he whispered.

"Will you stay here on your chair until they are done picking your last feathers, or do you intend to do something?" his wife nagged at him, pretending she had not heard his last comment. She picked up the half of the pomegranate and sat on the couch in front of him.

"And what do you want me to do?" he growled. He had no army, and the last force of opposition had been swept from the Eryas Lowlands over a month ago. "We can't leave the city without a royal authorization. We are trapped like mice. I would have more freedom were I born in the slums!"

"We managed pretty well under Agroln. Don't tell me you are scared of this brat."

"He has support from the people." The king's decrees had drastically improved the life of many in the commoners' districts and the slums. Evrardin could still smell the stench of that area on his clothes. He remembered how the king had humiliated him when he had presented his project. The coliseum could have brought him and his friends a large amount of money. He already had the contacts in the construction industry. Instead of that, he had been commanded to dig sewers, and they were probably financed by the incomes the Crown had made on the selling of his ninety thousand acres.

"He would not be the first popular king to have an accident," his wife retorted.

"Accidents are planned. I need trustful allies and an ironclad scheme." Should he organize something, there was no reason for him to pay for the whole higher class. If they wanted their share, he would drag them with him. He did not want his head to end up like Brecken's.

"You will probably find allies everywhere now that the king has refused the alliance with the Windy Isles."

"He refused the hand, not the alliance." Evrardin still could not understand why the man had declined such an offer. The princess was probably the most beautiful match he could have gotten, and the dowry was worth its weight in gold. Maybe the man was as insane as Agroln.

One of his servants came to the door. "We have received a letter for you, my lord."

Evrardin rose and took the envelope. There was no name on it. "Did you see who left it?"

The servant shrugged. "It was a woman, my lord, but she had veils on her head. I would dare to say that she came from the slums or some whorehouse."

Puzzled, Evrardin opened the letter and read the missive. He smiled.

"I think I have the solution to all our problems, my dear." He took a candle and moved to the fireplace. Delicately, he lit the corner of the paper. As the flames consumed the letter, Evrardin savored the five small words written on it. *Down with the sapphire eyes.*

68

The charcoal brushed the paper with short strokes. Louis stumped it with the tips of his fingers. Though he was satisfied with the shades on the mouth and the curves of the neck and shoulders, he was sure something was wrong. He realized the tattoos were missing.

"What will happen to us if you succeed in your task?" Selen asked.

His friend lay on the grass in front of him, his hair spread around his body like a satin halo. The colorful flowers of the inner garden smelled sweet. Louis spotted bees and butterflies, but no birds were singing.

"I have no idea," Louis answered sincerely. He was so absorbed in the past and in his task that he never took the time to think of the future. He had dreams for his country and the people, but none for himself. He believed he was already lucky enough to have met the man of his dreams. He knew how precarious such relations could be. It was like being a rock on the shore, facing the blades of the waves under a storm. Two souls against the rest of the world. Therefore, he enjoyed every day as if it were his last. "What would you want?" he asked with a smile.

"I miss the life I had in my shack. It was primitive compared to the king's apartments, but I was free, and I felt at home," Selen said dreamily.

"I understand what you mean," Louis said. The solar was not his home, but he had not felt at home in Neolerim either. What was home, anyway? An apartment with blue curtains? A place where he could sleep in peace? If it was a place where love was, then he had had no home since childhood. Yet, if it was a place where he felt free, himself, and happy, he didn't remember having had a home at all. "When all is done, I want a home," Louis said. "But I have to tell you that I have never taken care of sheep."

They laughed. Louis drowned in Selen's laughter. He could not help but think of his previous life's soul mate, of all the flowers Louis had brought him, of their walks in the countryside, and when his love had once told him how he had run naked in a field of wheat. The memories made his heart ache. That was indeed the simple kind of and carefree life he longed for. If it could ever be more than a dream. "All right for the sheep, then," Louis said, smiling. "Selen?"

His friend turned his face towards him. The waving grass caressed his cheek.

"*Je t'aime.*"

The tenderness in Selen's smiling eyes answered his feelings.

Lissandro entered the yard. "I am pleased to see that you can also enjoy the fresh air," his friend exclaimed. Lissandro approached behind him. "It's beautiful. I had no idea you were so talented," he said, looking at the drawing.

"Don't exaggerate. It's not a Michelangelo artwork," Louis said.

"He would have enjoyed your model. You share his tastes for classical eroticism." Louis gave him a dirty look. "You know your model has some clothes on," Lissandro hurried to say.

"What?" Selen exclaimed.

"I was only joking," Lissandro laughed, "but you should come and look at that. It's you on all points." Selen rose and came to them.

"Am I that pretty?"

"You are," Louis said. "Unfortunately, I will have to burn it."

"But why?" Lissandro exclaimed.

"There can't be any evidence," Louis sighed.

"In that case, I will keep it on me. If not signed, it could have been drawn by anyone," Selen said. He took the paper, folded it, and put it in his tunic.

"How do you feel, Louis? Are you ready for the session?" Lissandro asked.

His friends had been so kind to him the last few days. He felt like he had burned his last sparks of energy with the princes, and he had gotten sick. For three days that had felt like an eternity, he had stayed in the solar, resting and writing. Lissandro had taken care of the papers and formalities while Selen had met the ministers. Though Louis was stubborn, his friends had had the last word for once, and he had felt his energy grow again. He felt blessed to have them by his side. "I am fine. I have prepared a speech, just in case. Once again, I have no idea who our guests will be. The king of the Frozen Mountains. It sounds like the title of a fairy tale."

"It sounds like a Wagnerian opera," Lissandro said.

"Do you like opera?" Louis asked with interest. "I love Italian opera. I tried to compose some stuff, but I suppose it all got lost. I miss music so much."

"You composed?" Lissandro asked, surprised. "Did you play any instrument?"

"I tried flute," Louis answered.

Lissandro burst out in laughter. "Hmm. I'm sorry. You should know that the best music came after your death," Lissandro said. "I can't play any instrument, but if I see a minstrel, I will sing a few airs that he can play for you. Beethoven's 'Ode to Joy' on hurdy-gurdy. It promises to be interesting."

"Shall we move?" Selen asked, holding out his hand to him. Louis grabbed it and rose.

"Show must go on!" Lissandro exclaimed.

"His Majesty Louis Domgeornan, first of his name, by the grace of God, King of Trevalden and the Crysas Peninsula and His Other Territories, Protector of the People, Guardian of…" the herald cried out.

Louis did not listen to the rest of those pompous titles. Those false courtesies made him wince inwardly. Every time, it felt like a slap to his face, reminding him how low he had fallen. Should anyone from his previous life be here today, Louis would have been ashamed to death. "I am Louis and only Louis," he muttered, "and I am but a man in the crowd." Should he ever forget it, he would stab himself.

He went to his throne and sat. The king's guards took their positions, five on each side of the dais. Selen and Lissandro took their places. As usual, the hall was crowded. On account of Louis's poor health, the sessions had been scarce lately, making each of them a special event. Besides, it was the first time a foreign king would present himself in person to him.

The crowd near the entrance moved to the side with haste. Behind him, the herald cried out the titles of the king of the Frozen Mountains. Louis straightened in his seat. The men walking down the main alley had none of the graceful appearance of the princes of the Windy Isles. They were warriors. The metal of their massive armours clattered as their boots pounded forward. Breaking with all good manners and protocol, they had kept their helmets and weapons on. They looked clean, yet their appearance was marked with battle wounds. Though their height was impressive, one man towered over them all. Heavy fur of what once may have been wolves hung from his shoulders like a cloak over his steel armour. Louis could not see the man's face under his half helmet, but his long, blond hair floated straight around his shoulders. In a leather gloved hand, he held leashes in an iron grip. Three shabby wolfhounds trotted by his side. None of the men had horns on their heads, yet Louis knew what he was facing. Louis squirmed, hoping they had come in peace. The tall man Louis had suspected to be the king handed the leashes to one of his soldiers and spoke.

"King Louis of Trevalden, I, King Thorkell of the Frozen Mountains, salute you and wish you a long and peaceful reign," the king said in a stentorian voice. As he talked, he removed his helmet. "But I fear that his Majesty has something that belongs to me."

Louis heard a shrill come from his left side. He turned his head and saw Lissandro bend over and fall to the ground.

"My son," King Thorkell said with an understanding look at Louis.

Keeping his calm, Louis rose, came forward, and spoke. "Your Majesty, I think this requires an explanation. Therefore, I suspend the session for the time being and propose to you that we settle this matter in private."

Once Louis had spoken, the herald declared the session over. The crowd broke into outraged whispers. Louis did not want to know now what kind of gossip would come out from this. Behind him, Selen rushed to Lissandro and carried him out of the hall. Louis stepped down to King Thorkell. "Follow me," he whispered in anger.

They gathered in the room where they used to hold the high council's sessions. While Selen helped Lissandro to regain consciousness, Louis talked to Folc.

"And don't let anyone enter this room until we are done," he told the boy.

Louis closed the door and strode towards the king, his hands spread in incomprehension. Louis did not know how to begin.

"I should have guessed that he may swoon," the king said, confused. His voice was low but kind. "Lilo has always had a fragile nature."

"Grimmr, is that you?" Lissandro asked, rising from his chair.

"Yes, it's me, love," the king said, looking at his friend with a smile.

"How did you find me?" Lissandro walked forward and embraced Grimmr.

"You shine like a beacon in the night. When I heard that three young men had defeated the evil King of Trevalden, I had no doubt you were one of them."

"If you came to this world with Lilo, how can it be that you are the king of the Frozen Mountains?" Louis inquired.

Grimmr approached him. "Ages of experience. I know how such kingdoms work.

"I used to be king once. It was easy to take over the throne. When my memories came back, I knew Lilo would appear somewhere," Grimmr said, looming over him. The man was probably a head and a half taller than Louis. "En passant, I am impressed by your work. To build all that on your own in a world you barely know. I knew you had it in you, but still."

"You know me?" Louis asked, surprised.

"I remembered your face when we were in the hall. In centuries of existence, you learn to know the place to be at the right time, and Europe had its eyes riveted on your capital. I saw you die on the scaffold. That was a scene," Grimmr said with awe. "Good to see you are back in one piece. Oh, and I'm sorry for your loss. He was a good man." He patted Louis on the shoulder with commiseration.

Louis realized that the man was probably of the same kind, or species, as Lissandro. An older sort maybe. This would explain his extended knowledge and his brutal conception of power. He could well have been a real Northman.

"And now that you have launched a scandal in my court, what are your plans?" Louis asked.

"Bringing Lissandro home, of course. I have a kingdom to rule."

Louis was taken aback. Not only had the man troubled a royal session, but he would take away one of his friends. "I oppose…" he retorted with anger.

"No. Louis, please," Lissandro implored. "He is my soul mate. If he goes, I can't stay."

It was as if the walls were falling down. "I can give you lands, a townhouse… whatever you want." Louis regretted his weak words at once, but he felt helpless.

Grimmr looked at him and half smiled. "I need to go, I'm sorry. You're clever. You can manage it as king. I can leave my men here if you fear for your security."

"I don't care about my security!" Louis snarled. "You don't understand." He pointed at the king. "I do not expect barbarians to appreciate my work. All your sort can do is sack and destroy civilizations, like the Goths falling on the glorious cities of Rome and Sparta." Never would Louis receive counsel from primitive Northmen.

Grimmr smirked. "I do understand. I have seen what utopias like yours do to the world. I have seen them being twisted and corrupted. It is not your fault. You are an idealist. Yet, you should aim for peace instead of changing the hearts. But what can you understand of life, you who only long to die?"

Louis stepped back with disgust. "I won't even answer to that." Upset, he leaned with his flank against the table. The world turned around him, and he had lost his grip on it. He felt Selen's arms fold around him gently.

"He doesn't know you. I know how life in the Frozen Mountain is, and we don't want something like that here," his soft-spoken love said. "Lissandro is my friend, and I will miss him dearly, but we must respect his choice."

Louis took one of Selen's hands in his. "You are right, but I feel…"

"Abandoned?" Selen whispered. "You are not. Every man has doubts, but in the end, comes a new dawn. We have a world to build."

Louis closed his eyes and clenched Selen's hand.

"My men and I will leave tomorrow. I don't want to bother your people," Grimmr said.

"Louis, will you let me go?" Lissandro inquired.

Louis opened his eyes. "I do not own you. You have always been free to choose."

"I know. But I know how you feel about the cause. I don't want you to see me as a coward or a traitor. I want to stay your friend."

Louis turned to him. "I won't. You will always be my friend." He smiled.

Lissandro smiled back. "Just don't go dying on me when I'm gone."

"I already died once for the cause," Louis said.

"You never died for the Revolution," Lissandro chuckled, "you died for love."

"What do you mean?" Louis asked, confused.

"No one told you to die. They did not ask for your head. If you wanted to help the cause, you could have lived, played your cards cleverly, and influenced the men and the laws. You had won the war, you had power, but you loved him so much that you sacrificed yourself and your dreams. Yes, choosing your friend was honorable, but was the cause not worth all sacrifices? You gave up and left your country at the mercy of lesser men. The little Corsican of your team imposed the military tyranny that you had feared. And look at you now. What stands in your way if not him?" Lissandro pointed at Selen. Louis just gaped. "But if you crushed your feelings, if you betrayed your friend, I would not have the respect and admiration I have for you today. So be yourself. Follow your heart to the end."

Louis had not uttered a word since Lissandro's talk. The words still resounded and spun in his head. Under his ear, he heard Selen's slow heartbeat. They lay on the bed, silent. A candle burned on the bedside table. Selen's hand delicately caressed his hair. Under him, his friend's peach skin was warm and comforting.

"Did I make the wrong choices?" Louis asked, tightening his embrace around his friend. Louis did not know if he should feel sad or not. He only felt confused.

"Did any of us say that?" Selen replied. "Everyone has to face difficult choices in his life. I think you made the noblest ones. And you should keep going that way."

Louis had done what he thought to be right. Yet, it did not mean it was the best decision. Lissandro and Grimmr saw him as an utopist, but he could not be the monster his opponents had said he was. "I know I don't fear killing the scum of this world, but did I kill innocents?" He had given the condemned a trial and a chance to prove their innocence. They had to punish not only the traitors but even those who had been indifferent; passivity, especially in wartime, was a crime as it let evil flourish. Cowards had paid. Criminals had been executed. He couldn't have killed the ones he wanted to protect.

"I do not approve killing in general, but these are exceptionally hard times. Think of how many innocents would have died should you have let the scum live," Selen answered.

Louis stayed silent. Those were exactly his thoughts.

"How will I do without Lilo? His counsel was wise. I need counselors I can trust. I can't have the power alone. It would make me a tyrant."

"You have me. You have Pembroke. You can do as Lissandro suggested and organize discussions with the guild masters. I have spoken a few times with Mauger, your keeper of seals. He seems to be an honest man. I am sure those discussions would please you," Selen said. His friend lay his face on his head. "Just don't give up," Selen breathed.

"You know I won't." Louis raised his head and smiled.

The Northmen had gathered on the esplanade, ready to depart. The morning sun was rising in the east over the mountains. The breeze was already warm. Lissandro's belongings had been packed and tied on a horse.

Lissandro and Selen hugged. In his hand, Selen held a small pouch Lissandro had given him. Selen's eyes were red with emotion. "You have a heart of gold and are the best friend a man can have," Lissandro said. "It would break my heart to know something happened to you. And please, watch over him," Lissandro said, pointing at Louis. "Temper his passions."

"I can hear you." Louis smiled.

"I hope you do," Lissandro said, walking towards him. "And I hope you will follow my last advice. I did not represent much at your court, but I was supportive. You can't manage if you're two or three. It will always look like tyranny. Strengthen your bonds with the people, find good counselors. Learn to trust."

"I will. The next time you come back, it will be a different city. A better one."

"I don't doubt that," Lissandro said, but his eyes were filled with sorrow. "Don't forget, follow your heart. But, please, don't die. I thank God for bringing me here to your side. To have me fight beside you. You are the bravest man I have ever met. I will miss you."

"You make it sound like a funeral oration," Louis told Lissandro.

"I only want you to know it." He threw himself into Louis's arms. "Give this world an age of glory," Lissandro whispered.

"Ride safely home, and come back to us, my friend," he whispered back and kissed Lissandro's cheek.

Lissandro mounted his horse. "You will always be welcome in the north."

"Au revoir, Lissandro," Louis said, smiling.

"Goodbye, Louis Antoine." His friend winked.

"Oh, sod off!"

Lissandro laughed out loud and kicked his horse. "Goodbye, Selen! Yee-haw!" he shouted and waved as his mount galloped towards the gate.

The gallery in the south aisle was empty and silent at that time of the night. Folc hurried through the dark. He knew the way by heart.

The guards had received melons for their supper. The king encouraged the soldiers to eat fruits and greens instead of the traditional pâtés and salted pork. Folc liked fruits, maybe a bit too much. His bowels had been painful, and he had stayed longer than usual in the garderobe. Now, he was late for his watch. If his comrade had left his post without waiting for him, the door to the king's apartments would be left unguarded. It could not happen, especially under his watch.

Folc turned around the corner of the staircase leading to the main gallery. He stopped. There was a light, and he heard someone talking. Usually, no one was to be seen past midnight. Had something happened? Though he had every reason to be here, Folc did not dare to go down the steps. There was something he did not like in this voice. He tiptoed closer.

"I will go there now. I want to hear what this man has to say," a croaky voice whispered. Folc bent his head and saw the profile of a man. He knew him to be one of Louis's ministers. Evrardin, the man's name was. The man twitched. Folc pulled his head back into the shadows.

"It may be a trap. I will come a little later. Besides, it's best we don't arrive together," another voice said. This one sounded clear, fruity.

All this smelled fishy. The light of the men's candle went down the staircase and disappeared. He heard footsteps take the main gallery. Folc was tempted to learn more. Yet, he had his watch. He went down the steps and looked into the main gallery. The door leading to the king's apartments was still guarded, but the man hopped from left to right with impatience. This meant that the guard was waiting for him to leave his post. Good. Unfortunately, he would have to wait the rest of the night. Folc went down the steps where the light had disappeared. He had abandoned his post, but he hoped Louis would forgive him.

One floor lower, a door opened on one of the alleys, giving way to the esplanade. The candle had been blown out, but Folc saw the black silhouette head towards the gate. It passed through it without alerting the guards. Folc removed his armour swiftly, hid it under a rose bush, and followed the man into the night.

The chase through the city was long. Fortunately, the man was not on a horse. Folc was glad to have followed him. The man's behavior was suspicious. He sneaked into alleys, weaving his way through drunkards and shady characters strolling in the dimly lit streets. Here and there, he turned around, searching the darkness with suspicion. His footsteps led him to the slums. The man checked his back once more and disappeared into a decrepit house.

In the moonlight, Folc observed the building. It was pitch black. The shutters on the ground floor were closed, nailed with planks. But the windows on the first floor were gaping black holes.

He went around the building. Behind lay a junkyard with rotten boards, trunks, and all kind of rubbish. It smelled foul, but Folc could not put a name to the stench. Careful with the rusted nails, he crept up on the boards. Folc climbed to the first floor, hoisting himself up to a window. He slipped inside and halted against the windowsill. Murmurs rose from the floor below. As he could not find an aperture in the floor, he made for the door on all fours. A faint light came from the staircase. The old wood squeaked. Folc stopped and progressed again. Under his fingers, he felt small seeds. He looked down. Dried corn and rat droppings. Light came from downstairs. Since no one could be seen, he stepped slowly down the stairs. The door leading to the room on the ground floor stood ajar. Folc sneaked inside and lurked from between casks.

In the light of a lantern, seven people were gathered around a low table. Their shadows swirled on the wall. They wore black cloaks and hoods. Folc could not see their faces, but he recognized one of the voices to be Evrardin's. Another voice was also familiar. He listened carefully.

70

Their hate was stronger than their fear. Although none knew him, the nobles had answered to Segar's invitation. There were six of them. One was missing. Segar had let the rage grow in their hearts, and now it was time to harvest the ripe fruits. The gathering place was an abandoned house on the docks that Jamys had inspected a few days ago. Behind the cheapest whorehouses, the area was murky and disreputable. The people roaming about minded their own business. Segar had been there early, but he had let the men gather in the room downstairs until half of them had arrived. Now, he stood in the middle of the circle, facing his guests. Even with their hoods on, Segar could tell who they were. He had observed their hands and gestures during the court sessions. He pushed back his hood with confidence.

"My dear lords, I am pleased to see that you were eager to meet me," Segar told the men in front of him. "Some of you may recognize me. Let me just say that I was in the Rebellion. I have observed the man for a long time. Your fortunes are not the only ones he has threatened. Maybe some of you want to share views on the matter?"

"If I am to say something, I want to see the face of my interlocutors," one man said.

"This is a pertinent request. Does anyone object to it?" Segar asked. No one raised his hand. "Well, then I suppose you can drop your hoods."

Slowly, the men pulled back their hoods and looked at each other. No one was surprised to meet familiar faces.

"You have managed to gather the upper crust of Nysa Serin." Evrardin smirked.

"Not all of it," a baby-faced man said. "Many have already lost their head in the gutter."

The men grumbled in approval.

"I lost my cousin last week," Honfroi exclaimed, his double chins wriggling. "How can a man be executed for having some good times with his maids?"

"Did he pay the tribute?" Evrardin inquired.

"He was going to, but the charges against him were only about rape. The judges said that there were no servants anymore. That everyone was free. As if such things could be."

"Unfortunately, there are. We, in the justice courts, have received new laws. I have heard that the king has taken advice from the commoners," a voice said.

The men grumbled with outrage. Segar stepped forward to take control of the conversation.

"Hush, hush, my lords. We need to keep our temper to organize ourselves well," Segar said. They turned towards him. "I propose that we listen to Lord Evrardin, who, as minister, will give us the latest news from the court." Segar sat, facing Evrardin.

Evrardin rose. "As you probably noticed, there has been some turmoil in the palace lately. Our king lost one of his counselors two weeks ago in troubling circumstances. Still, it did not stop him from carrying on with the reformation of the royal administration and justice. The king has had several meetings with the guild masters. As I understood it, he plans to write new laws. Considering the events since his enthronization, I fear that those new laws will turn against us. Therefore, we need to act—before it is too late."

While the man spoke, Segar felt a burning in his arms and chest again. The pain had not left him and kept stabbing him from time to time. It grew inside him. Parts of his arms had turned black and were covered with hard crust. He had tried to remove it, but he had just cut himself badly. He had never seen such disease before. Whatever happened to him, he could not die. Not before he had taken his revenge. He was within a hairbreadth of dethroning the swaggering bastard. His humiliation would be long and painful. Then, Segar would step forward. The power would be his and to all his kind.

"Thank you, my lord." Segar rose. "As you heard, it is a question of time until terror spreads inside our houses."

A man raised his hand. "I'm sorry to interrupt. As you know, I am a merchant, and I lost half of my goods when the taxes on exportation were enforced. I don't have the means to hire mercenaries anymore, but don't you lords have men at your orders?"

"We have thought about it, yet we can't summon commoners against the king. Especially a king they admire. What we would need is mercenaries," the baby-faced man said.

"And this is where I offer my help." Segar grinned.

"Offer?" Honfroi asked, dubious.

"Well, consider I have a personal interest in the matter," Segar said. "As you said, the commoners admire the king. The solution is easy. Make them learn to hate him."

"How?" the men asked.

"With gossips, lies, insults. It doesn't matter who he really is; it's the image we give of him that counts. We will make him the most despised king in the history of Trevalden. Once his reputation is destroyed, I have enough men to take over the castle. Now, to give weight to our arguments, I will give you one solid basis." Segar looked at the gleaming eyes of the men in front of him. They were ready. "My lords, our king is a bugger, and his pretty counselor is nothing more than his mistress."

The assembly roared, outraged. The high priest rose and faced the men.

"This is an infamy in the eyes of the Gods. I can and will have them burned for that!" the priest shouted.

"I knew that with his plump, soft lips, he was inclined to laziness and voluptuousness," a man with a strong, aquiline nose grumbled.

"Hum, physiognomy is charlatanism, Lord Noder," Evrardin said.

"My lords!" Segar called them back to him. "To succeed with our plans, we need proof, a witness. For that, we need access to the palace and a mole. You can help us with that, can't you, Lord Honfroi?"

The man grinned. "One of my pawns will checkmate the king."

They heard screams from behind their backs. Segar turned around. "I got you, little rat!" Hernays shouted.

The man came to them, holding a wiggling boy under his arm. "Good that I came a bit later. There were spies after all."

"Let me go!" the boy shouted.

Hernays dropped the boy in the middle of the circle. Segar recognized him at once.

"The little Folc! If it isn't a nice surprise. It seems we already have one fish in the net," Segar exclaimed.

"We must kill him," Honfroi said. "He is one of the king's guards. He will betray us."

"No. Not the little Folc. He is the puppy of the king's slut. He is worth more alive than dead," Segar said. "But preferably locked in a pit somewhere."

"I can take care of it," Hernays said. He knocked Folc out and threw him on his shoulder.

Segar turned to his guests. "I think the meeting is over. Everyone knows what to do. So be ready, my lords. Tomorrow, a king will fall."

71

"I'm sorry, but I see nothing," Brother Benedict said. The monk's cold hand held Selen's arm up as he looked at his armpit. "Let me see your neck again."

Selen bent his head and pushed his hair to the side. Brother Benedict pressed on his neck and shoulders with his thumbs.

"But I assure you that it hurts," Selen said.

"Where?" Brother Benedict asked, pushing Selen's torso backwards again.

"In my arms and chest. It feels like a stab, and it spreads from my hands to my heart." Selen did not dare to say that his arms gleamed as well. The man would accuse his eyes.

"You are far too young to have a stroke. And it's the most common disease to spread that way. Does the king suffer the same thing?"

"No. Why do you ask?" Selen looked at the monk with suspicion.

"I am a monk. I see things." Brother Benedict winked. "You share the same food, right? All I can recommend you is to eat more, especially meat. Poultry and fish should suffice. I know our lords usually eat too much rich food and fat, but to live on fruits and nuts won't keep you healthy, especially with your musculature. Do you still train?"

"I swim and train in the inner yard with the guards."

"All the more to follow a good diet," Brother Benedict said.

Selen put his tunic on again. He was not convinced with Brother Benedict's diagnosis. There must be more to it than food.

"I have heard the king was unwell. I have some tincture you can give him." Brother Benedict handed him a small flask. "Tell him he needs to see the sun more often. Take him to your training. You both are pale like corpses."

"I thank you for your time," Selen said, heading for the door. "By the way, have you seen Folc?"

The monk shrugged. "I'm sorry, no."

Selen left the workshop and walked through the inner garden. Folc had not presented himself to his post during the night. It was not like him to abandon his duties. Besides, the boy could not be found anywhere in the castle. Selen grew worried by the hour. He entered the solar.

Louis sat at his desk, drowning in mountains of papers as usual. Those sessions with the guild masters had proven effective on Louis's spirits. The commoners had come with interesting ideas for new laws. It was not the constitution his friend wanted, but it was already something.

Selen walked towards him. He picked up Louis's goblet and sipped some wine. "Brother Benedict says that you should eat a bit more than cherries."

"Why were you at Brother Benedict's place? Are you ill?" Louis asked without raising his head from his papers. Yet, he sounded concerned.

"Nothing to worry about." *Or, nothing you should worry about*, Selen thought. "What we should worry about is Folc's disappearance," Selen sighed.

Louis looked at him. "What are you talking about?"

"The boy was not at his post last night, and he has mysteriously vanished."

"I can't believe that Folc would have voluntarily abandoned his duties," Louis said, laying the quill on the board. "Something must have gone amiss, and he went to fix it." Louis took Selen's hand and kissed it. "Don't worry, the boy is clever and survived a war. He will be back."

"And if he won't?"

"Then, I will send every guard to search for him," Louis said sternly. "But let's wait until tomorrow."

Louis resumed his writing. Selen ran his fingers through Louis's hair, pushing it to the side. He placed his hands on his friend's shoulders and massaged them gently. His thumbs pressed on the small knots of muscles at the back of the skull and on the spine. Louis uttered a short, high-pitched moan that made Selen's groin stir. The quill stopped its dance on the sheet.

Selen released his grip and took the paper his friend was writing on. "May I read?"

"Of course," Louis answered and lay back on the chair.

"When a population set free from tyranny has written wise laws, its revolution is done; if these laws are adapted to the land, the revolution will hold," Selen read aloud. "There can only be a few laws, and only those who rule the land must be scared, never the people. Those who conspire or embezzle, those who oppress or corrupt will be condemned. Besides, each year, everyone will have to justify the use and the origin of his wealth. The right to property and revenues can't be made to the detriment of others. In nature, men love each other. In social life, they take care of each other." Selen put the paper back on the desk and sat astride Louis. "It seems that these discussions with the commoners inspire you," he whispered, looking into Louis's blue eyes.

"No. You inspire me." Louis smiled.

"Do I?" Selen grinned and traced a finger on the bulge in Louis's pants. "How do I inspire you now?" Louis put a hand on Selen's neck and pulled at Selen's lower lip with his lips. Selen opened his mouth and let Louis's tongue roll against his. There was something savage in the way his friend kissed. Louis always took his mouth in the most avid way, ravaging it with his tongue, as if he needed to taste the life essence in his breath. It aroused Selen, but it could make his jaws ache for hours. His hand pressed and rubbed Louis's crotch. His friend's pants were getting tight.

"Maybe I could write something inspiring," Selen said cheerfully. He rose and turned around to bend over the desk. With the quill in his hand, he tried to find something relevant to add to his friend's words. While he composed the words in his head, Selen felt Louis's hands on him, unlacing and pushing down his pants. His friend cupped his bare bottom firmly in his hands. "If you let me," Selen said, frowning as Louis pulled him backwards.

Selen had written a few words when the quill crossed the paragraph sidelong. Selen stood gaping. The rapturous feeling still lingered on his flesh. "That was mean." Selen turned his head and smiled lewdly.

Louis gazed at him, licking his lips. "Didn't it help?"

"Maybe you need a break," Selen suggested. His eyes narrowed. He stepped out of his pants, grabbed Louis by the waist, and carried him up.

"Put me down!" His friend laughed, holding on to Selen's shoulders.

Selen laughed as well and threw Louis onto the bed. He removed his tunic and untied his hair. As Louis rose on his knees, Selen knelt on the bed and embraced his friend.

"I love you," Selen whispered. They pressed their foreheads together. His face gleamed. His life had never been so happy.

While Louis removed his jerkin and shirt, Selen unlaced Louis's pants, rubbing his friend through the cloth at the same time. Louis pulled off his pants. Soon, both of them knelt naked, holding each other tight in a warm cuddle. Selen breathed in the scent of violet with a hint of woody amber on Louis's skin. They kissed and caressed. With the tips of his fingers, Selen played with Louis's earring. With the other hand, he grazed a finger on every detail of Louis's face.

"You are so beautiful," Selen breathed dreamily. His friend took the finger into his mouth and sucked on it, his tongue licking the sensitive pulp delicately. Selen emitted a little squeak. A shiver ran like lightning from his finger to his groin.

Louis let go of his finger. "No, my love, you are," he whispered. He bent his head and nibbled at Selen's neck and collarbone.

Selen tossed Louis on the side. Still kneeling, Selen stroked his length as if he were alone and let Louis stare at him. When he judged his friend had gaped long enough, Selen grazed his mouth down on Louis's chest, on his abdomen, and through the fuzz of dark hair, tracing a line of kisses around the swollen organ. Selen's tongue flicked on the sticky, moist head of his friend's erection and around the rim before swallowing it as far as he could. He heard how Louis enjoyed it. While he slid a hand between Louis's legs, Selen felt Louis's hand on one of his cheeks, pulling his bottom over him. Louis's mouth teased him in ravishing ways. Selen's muffled moans joined Louis's loud breathing as he felt the tips of Louis's fingers push inside him, sliding deep, until he turned slippery.

When his fingers felt that his friend was as ready as he was, Selen turned around. "Do you want me?" he whispered in Louis's ear.

Louis only smiled and lay on his side. Selen slipped behind him and pressed his chest against Louis's back. Selen would have never guessed that Louis fancied being taken so much. In front of Louis's crushing confidence, Selen had considered himself to be the vulnerable one. Yet, he could not be weak if Louis put him in charge of his body.

Louis turned his head to kiss him. Selen placed his erection against Louis's tight entrance. With a light push, the head popped inside with a delicious feeling. He took hold of Louis's leg and raised it over his hip. As Louis pressed himself onto him, smoothly working the length in, Selen uttered a deep moan. The feeling of Louis's tightness around him blew his mind every time. Never had he considered or desired to take someone before. Though he refused to stand on top of his love, Selen was grateful to Louis for giving him such sensations.

His hips rocked, trying to balance the bold part of him that craved to dig inside his love and holding back, which had proven a lot more difficult than he had thought. His attentions were rewarded and encouraged by soft moans. Selen's hand went from Louis's long leg to pinch a nipple. Selen loved to feel like one with his friend. He kissed the side of Louis's face. Louis had closed his eyes, his head dangled, and his open lips searched for his. Selen covered them with his mouth. The fire in him was intense. Selen's hand went down to Louis's loins and folded around him.

His friend's hand grabbed his wrist. "No. Stop," Louis murmured. Selen let go and looked into the sapphire eyes staring at him. Louis turned around. Selen gulped and bit his lip with expectation.

Louis pushed him firmly up and with his back against the high headboard. Selen did not resist the greedy assault. He grasped the wooden rim, as his legs hooked around Louis's waist.

"Tell me if it hurts," Louis whispered. "I mean, your back."

"Make a mess out of me," Selen whispered back, lustful.

Selen slammed his head back against the wall when Louis impaled him onto his hips. He felt Louis slide one hand behind his head, while the other hand supported his bottom, the fingers nailed into the flesh. His friend was needy. The moves of Louis's hips were lusty and fierce. Selen's short nails raked on the wood. Louis raised his head to reach his mouth. Selen approached his swollen, damp lips, but the frantic moves made his head twitch. Without thinking, he pulled at Louis's hair with one hand. Louis howled, yet his love did not complain and let Selen move his mouth against his.

Selen craved more. His brain was melting. "Louis, Louis… Faster. Cleave through me," Selen mewed, his eyes half closed.

His back slammed against the wood. Sweat covered his chest and neck. He looked at Louis. His friend's face was tense. He had bloody bite marks on his open lips. His long, sweaty hair fell on his brow and brushed his cheeks. Behind the curls, his eyelids twitched in blue sparks. Selen saw that Louis was desperately holding back his orgasm. He felt Louis's hand leave his head, and he shouted when it closed firmly around his erection to rub the wet head.

"I can't hold on," Louis breathed. Selen thought his friend had already held out longer than usual. He improved with each of their communions.

"Me neither," Selen gasped.

His heart was on the verge of exploding with every rub against his spot. Fire pooled in his loins, and his legs shook. His vision blurred. He heard Louis cry out and sensed him release inside of him with long spasms. Louis's head rubbed against Selen's sweaty chest as his body swayed. Yet, Louis did not pull away but kept moving, turning Selen's thighs wet. Louis stared at him, feeding on his pleasure, his stroking hand commanding Selen to come. For a few seconds, Selen was no more. He closed his eyes, opened his mouth wide to scream, and felt his seed splash over his chest. His whole body trembled. As his legs slid down, he clenched Louis's shoulders. Still catching his breath, his friend held him tightly.

"I love you," Selen murmured, nearly in a sob. He opened his eyes and was struck with terror.

One of the young maids stared right at him, shocked, with the water jar in her hands. The jar fell and exploded into pieces. The water gushed all over the floor. Louis swiveled his back in a fraction of a second and let Selen fall onto the bed. Selen's first reaction was to cover his mouth and to curl, to hide himself from the face of the world. He saw Louis grab his pants.

"Wait!" Louis shouted, but the maid was already gone.

Selen's brain came back to reality, and he swiftly made for his clothes as well. When he was dressed, Louis was already outside. Selen rushed for the door but stopped. He did not know if he should run outside as well. Should people see him, it would only confirm the girl's version. Still, he felt a trap, and Louis may be in danger. He ran out. There was no one in the garden. It was still a peaceful late afternoon. At least, it had been. The door leading to the gallery stood ajar. Louis knelt over the guard that lay on the ground.

"He is dead," Louis said. "Merde!" He hit the wall with his fist and slid down with his back against it, his head in his hands.

"No! Get up!" Selen shouted. He dragged Louis up again. "Think! It's her version against yours, and she killed a guard."

"Do you really think such a frail little girl could kill a royal guard?" Louis asked, shattered.

"Not for a second. But it's the only version that can save us," Selen said, looking straight at Louis.

Guards came their way. They hustled once they saw the guard on the floor.

"Your Majesty! What happened?" they cried out.

"Someone killed the guard. I saw a young maid run away," Louis said, stoic. "Search the palace. And I want one man to watch that door."

While Louis spoke, Selen backed slowly into the garden. He realized he was barefoot and disheveled. When he was sure that no one could see him, he hurried back into the solar and finished dressing.

"Where are you going?" Louis exclaimed when he came back.

"To the city. I need to find Folc," Selen answered, fastening his cloak.

"No. I won't let you go. It's too dangerous. This was a trap," Louis said, blocking him.

"I know. Yet, if they wanted us dead, they would have killed us. What they wanted was proof. I don't know why, but I know we have a few hours. You are the king. They can't throw you down so easily. This was Folc's watch, and they knew it. They have the boy somewhere."

"Take some guards with you, or let me come with you," Louis insisted.

"No, it's better I go out hiding under a cloak. You stay here and reinforce the palace. I will be back soon," Selen said.

"But where in the whole city do you think you can find the boy?"

"I think I know who is behind this," Selen responded. "The same as always."

It took only a few seconds for Louis to understand. "Segar Mills." His eyes were filled with rage.

"Please, let me go. I swear on the gods I will be back."

"Turn around and hurry back here as soon as you see trouble." Louis held his wrist tight.

Selen kissed Louis and left.

The city was peaceful as always. Whatever Segar schemed, it had not started yet. With his hood over his forehead, Selen strode towards the docks. The Crown controlled the high districts and the market area where each building had been listed. If the man hid somewhere, it was probably near the river, in the city slums. Selen would have to be careful not to be seen, or it could become dangerous for him. His decision to stroll around in this area may be foolish, but should the boy die because of him, he would not forgive himself.

Selen tried to think of which place would be best for Segar to hide the boy. Actually, it could be anywhere. Yet, Folc did not look like every boy. Maybe someone had seen him. A harlot leaned against a porch. She had a red gown and orange petticoats. Though she wore heavy makeup, she was still young and fair. Her huge bosom was pressed high in her corsage. Selen had never approached a harlot, but he thought that a woman may have noticed a young boy, and harlots used to stare at people. He tugged on his hood to hide his forehead and approached the girl.

"Excuse me," he said timidly.

"Can I do something for you, pretty one?" the girl said with a smoky voice. She caressed his chest with her hand. Selen squirmed but still faced the girl.

"I am searching for a boy."

"Oh, I see. Yes. It was obvious," she said, looking at him with a half smile.

Selen realized his mistake. "No, no. I mean…he is my brother." *Not plausible, but more realistic than my son*, Selen thought. "He is around fifteen and has freckles all over his face."

"I'm sorry, sweetheart. I have seen no boy with that description. Are you sure I can't do anything for you?" she carried on, intensifying her advances. "I could give you a very special price. How about a few things for free if you don't take the whole package? We don't see men like you around here."

"Thank you, but I'm not interested." Selen tried to twist off politely from her grip. "Do you know someone who can help me?"

"Hmm, there is a pimp up there on the street who owns quite a lot around here. But sweet men like you should not go there. The man is nasty."

"How can I find him?" Selen asked.

"He will find you if you step into his territory," she cooed, a hand still on his waist.

Selen thought it was time for him to leave. He thanked her again and kept on walking up the street. As he progressed, the smell of piss and rancid water increased in the air. The houses looked even worse. Some were abandoned, spiked shut. Others, full with casks, must be used as warehouses. He hoped he would not need to enter the taverns. They were gloomy, dirty, and probably crowded with prowlers. The perfect place for him to get trounced.

There were people going down the street. Probably workers who had finished their day. A group of men came from the other way towards him. They looked joyful and shared bawdy jokes. Selen lowered his head and pulled his cloak around him. The men did not care about him, but one of them stepped out of the group and pushed him roughly by accident. Selen fell onto the ground. His hood slipped off his head. As he tried to rise, he heard a shout in the crowd.

"That's him! This is the king's fag!" Selen looked up and saw an angry man in a grey frock. The man pointed at him and shouted and spluttered with exaltation. "He is an insult to the Holy Scriptures! A spit in the gods' faces!" The rest of the crowd turned towards Selen with disgust.

"You dirty whore! Sick vermin!" they shouted aggressively. Some spat towards him.

"Bugger! Suck my cock!" a man shouted, grabbing his crotch. A woman threw a fish head.

Selen felt terrorized. His heart beat faster. He knew no words could stop them, and it was too late to run. While reaching for his dagger, he shrank against the wall of a house. Killing himself would still be better than what they would do to him if he was alive. Yet, he could not do that. Louis was waiting for him. The group closed around him. Selen's hand tightened on his dagger. He would fight back. Shouts came from down the street.

"Get lost, you rascals!" a man shouted. A group of guards marched against the crowd. The angry mob did not linger against armed men. They spread into the alleys and disappeared.

"Are you all right, Selen?" Selen turned his head and saw Hernays standing next to him.

"Yes, thank you so much." He calmed down. "I should not be here. I was looking for Folc."

"Oh, I think I know where Folc is," the man said, grinning.

"You do?" Selen exclaimed with joy. "Can you lead me to him?"

"With pleasure," Hernays answered.

They went back down the street together and turned into an alley. If the main road had been dirty, there was no word to describe the pavement here. Selen spotted dead rats on the side. It reeked of excrement. He put a hand over his face. He wondered what Folc did in such a place. "Is it far?" Selen asked.

"No. It's just here." Hernays said.

The alley opened into a small yard. A decrepit house stood in front of them. The shutters had been nailed closed. Selen wondered if the building would collapse if someone entered it.

"He is inside," Hernays said. The man stepped on the porch and pushed the door open. The wood creaked. The place was dark, lit only by a lantern in the room on the left. It smelled musty and damp.

"Folc?" Selen said with a low voice. He felt insecure. Something was amiss. He entered the room to the left. There were casks and old chairs but he couldn't see anyone. Selen turned towards the exit. "There is nothing here—"

Hernays punched him in the stomach. Under the pang, Selen bent over and collapsed on the ground.

"Oh, yes. There you are," the man growled.

He kicked Selen hard in the chest, sending pain through his ribs. Selen coughed.

The man was strong. Why hadn't he killed him already? He needed to escape. He wouldn't find any help here. Hernays kicked again, walked behind him, and knelt. Short of breath, Selen tried to rise. Hernays slammed him on the back with his fist. Selen fell back on the floor with a groan.

"The king's fag, right? You have fooled us well. Let's see if I can make you squeak like the king," Hernays said. He grabbed Selen's arm, twisted it around his back, and shoved a vigorous hand between Selen's legs, pressing on his crotch. "Not bad, not bad at all."

Repulsive pig, Selen thought, repressing a scream. *That's why you keep me alive. I'll cut your hand.* Selen tried to reach for his dagger, but Hernays pinned him to the floor with another blow and cast the dagger away. "Don't be foolish now. You may even like it. Boys say I'm hung," Hernays grunted, his hand and thumb pressing harder onto Selen's lower parts.

"So remove your filthy hand and go fuck your horse," Selen grunted while looking around for something to grab. *At least get mad at me and do something foolish.*

As he searched, Selen scraped the floor with his nails, trying to escape the disgusting grip. He heard Hernays's panting behind him. His twisted arm hurt. On the floor, a long fragment of a board got loose. With all his strength, he swiveled and threw the pointy sliver sideway towards the man's face. The wood hit Hernays under the left eye, tearing out pieces of skin and sending splinters into the eye. Hernays screamed and pulled back his hand, placing it against his wound. Selen jumped free. With rage, he kicked his boot into the man's face. Blood spurted from Hernays's mouth and nose and spattered the wall. *It's not enough.* Selen went for another kick, but the man blocked his foot and pushed him backwards with a grunt. Selen fell down and hit the back of his head.

"You like it nasty. I will make it painful." Hernays rose, staggering.

Selen kicked him hard in the crotch. As Hernays leaned forward with his hands against his private parts, Selen jumped up and went for his dagger. Hernays grabbed him by the arm and punched his hip. The pain tore him apart. Selen cried out, hit the wall with his back before he slid down to the floor.

"I won't touch your face," the blond man panted. "I like my whores pretty."

Hernays stumbled in front of him and raised his fist to strike. Selen grabbed a plank with a nail in a cask that lay next to him and smashed it against Hernays's head. The nail ripped through the skin. The man yelled. Selen knocked him again. While Hernays crawled away with blood dripping from his face, Selen hurried to his dagger. He picked it up and came back. Hernays's face was only cuts and bruises, but his eyes still shone. Selen shoved his boot into the man's belly and knelt astride him.

"A whore?" Selen shouted, running his dagger into Hernays's right eye. "Do I look like a fucking whore?" He pulled out the dagger and pinned it in Hernays's throat. He panted. "Your sort will never touch me again."

As he rose, he heard muffled screams coming from the basement. Selen looked around and spotted a door under the stairs. He ran to it.

"Folc?" he exclaimed.

"I'm here!"

Selen slammed the door until it broke open. The boy rushed out and threw himself against him. "Selen!" Selen held him tight. "Selen. They want to kill you and Louis. I heard them. It's a plot!"

"Yes, I know. We are going back to the palace," Selen said. "But first, I have one thing to do."

They were back on the street. People came their way, curious. Selen tied the rope on the hook on the wall behind the pole.

"I think we should go," Folc suggested. "There are people coming."

Selen checked if the knot was strong. On the other end of the rope, Hernays's body swayed in the air. Blood trickled from the wound on his throat. *Now you're hung*, Selen thought. The man was bare-chested. On his belly, Selen had carved a word with his dagger. *Rapist*. As people gathered around, Selen shouted to them.

"This! This is the king's justice! This is what the king does to pigs like him!" He pointed at Hernays. "Remember it when your daughter or your wife gets ravished." He took Folc by the arm. "Now we get back to the palace," he whispered.

They proceeded through the city, Selen still hiding under his cloak. The streets were quiet. It did not look like a revolt had stirred up, at least not in the market district. Maybe Segar wanted to start with the slums. Those religious fanatics could raise a mob in a second. Despite what Louis thought, the people craved blood. Fortunately, it did not matter to them whose blood it was. Louis must strike the monks before they spread anger in the men's hearts.

They arrived on the esplanade.

"We should go inside. That way," Folc exclaimed.

"No. Follow me," Selen ordered him. They went to the stables. "Prepare a horse!" he shouted to a lad.

Once the mount was ready, Selen helped Folc get onto the saddle.

"But no! Why?" The boy struggled.

"You will ride far away from here. Go to Millhaven and stay at the court," Selen said.

"But you need me here. I can help. I am a king's guard!"

"You will be a dead king's guard if you don't run away from here. I don't want anything to happen to you. So get away and let me take care of the king," Selen snarled. He slapped the horse's rear.

He watched the boy ride away towards the esplanade. Now, they had no friends left in the palace. Selen hurried back to the solar.

72

The doors to the palace were secured and locked. Louis had summoned the king's guards. The men were gathered in the gallery, waiting for his orders. He did not even know if he could trust them anymore. Louis sat at his desk, his hands grabbing his hair. Selen had been away for far too long now. There must be something he could do.

The door opened. Selen rushed into the solar.

"Selen!" Louis rose and strode towards his friend. "Are you all right? You look… hurt." Selen's face was untouched, but he had blood on his clothes, and one of his hands on his ribs.

"I'm fine," Selen answered, panting. "I found Folc and sent him away from here. Louis, we need to go. The place is not safe."

Louis took Selen by the arm and made him sit on a couch. "Calm down. Is it your blood?"

Selen shook his head. "It is Hernays's. There are religious fanatics on the streets spreading words about us. Soon the slums will rise."

"The slums can't rise against me. All I did was for the most unfortunate of our people," Louis responded in denial.

Selen stared at him with a sad look. "I'm sorry, Louis. But you know how mobs are. And Segar and your ministers are behind them."

"I see. After all I did, they'll declare me an outlaw again. They will trash my name and cover it with filth." Louis did not care as much for his name as he cared for everything he had accomplished, all he could do for this land. Why did no one understand the goodness in his project? "Is virtue really a utopia?" he asked Selen with sorrow in his soul.

"No. It's not. I am convinced that there are many people who are grateful to you. But we have not extirpated enough of the evil that dwells in this city," Selen answered.

"Is it even possible?" Louis remembered the dragons in the assembly and the crowd that had spat on him.

"If you give up, no one will succeed." Selen took his hands in his. "Don't look sad and don't despair. I'll stand by you. I am your only king's guard. I won't let anyone hurt you."

Louis looked at Selen's smiling face. He caressed his cheek. No words could express his gratitude. "I love you." He rose. "I don't want it to end with us trapped in the palace like cowards. We won't show weakness or hesitation. Come."

Louis stepped out and went to the main gallery. "Open all the doors!" he shouted to the guards. "And prepare my horse, I'm riding to the city." He would speak to the crowd and see for himself if they still wanted him or not.

Louis and Selen headed north in the gallery, towards the stables. Selen, who strode at his side, halted. When Louis turned around to urge him to follow, Selen collapsed to his knees.

Louis hurried at his side. "What's wrong? Are you wounded?"

"It's burning…my chest," Selen breathed, a hand against his heart. He rolled up one sleeve. Though his skin was usually pale, his arm shone with a faint white light. "It hurts."

Louis remembered the white light he had felt on his skin before. He did not know if it was the same for Selen, but at least it had been harmless for him. Louis took hold of Selen and put an arm around his waist. "Courage, my love. Lean on me. Hang on a little more. We must go out."

Guards waited for them in the yard. Louis walked as straight and calmly as he could. Selen managed the few steps to his horse alone. They mounted their horses and rode to the esplanade.

They were passing in front of the great hall when a mob rushed from under the gatehouse. Louis wanted to talk to them but realized that it was more than just a mob. There were many of Segar's soldiers among them. He looked back. The guards blocked the way. *Their* way. He tried not to panic. The doors of the great hall opened.

A group of nobles and armed men rushed towards them. Louis's horse shied. Louis looked at the chaos around him. They were aggressive but still hesitant to harm their king. Louis looked at their faces. Faces of hostility and abhorrence he had seen before. All hope abandoned him. Would he die lynched by a mob this time? Yet, he felt no fear. Only sorrow for his dreams, shattered once again. But this time, his hands were not tied. He would fight them to the end. He reached for his sword.

Louis heard a scream behind him and turned. The men grabbed Selen by his hair and legs. His friend fell off his horse.

"Selen!" he shouted but got no answer. He jumped off his horse and drew his sword. Men came towards him with swords and spears. Swirling his sword, Louis pushed them away.

"Don't hurt the king! He's mine!" he heard Segar's voice say.

Louis looked towards where Selen had fallen. His friend had been dragged on the ground by a group of men. They kicked him with their feet, insulting him with crude words. Louis would rush towards him if only he could drive his assailants back.

Louis heard shouts come from the gatehouse. He turned his head and saw Folc with Pembroke and Josselin at the head of armed men and a crowd of commoners. The group attacked the heinous mob.

"In the name of the king!" Pembroke yelled.

"Over here, Louis!" Folc shouted, stretching out his hand towards him.

Louis refused to join them. Selen was still on the ground. One man stepped forward from the mob. Louis recognized him. Jamys. Segar's henchman. The tall man walked towards the group on Louis's right. He took Selen by the hair and dragged him to the edge of the cliff.

"No, no... No," Louis whispered, shaking his head. He threw a last, spinning blow at his attackers and hurried towards Jamys. The brute had seized Selen by the throat and hung him over the precipice. Selen was barely conscious. His hands scratched feebly at Jamys's wrist.

"Hold on, Selen!" Louis shouted. He ran his sword through the man's back, as vertically as he could to avoid hurting his friend. Jamys collapsed. Louis pulled him backwards with all his strength. As the man released his grip, Selen slid, grasping frantically at Jamys's clothes, then at the edge of the cliff. With horror, Louis saw Selen's hands disappear.

Louis crept towards the edge. The wind of the emptiness whipped against his face, through his hair. Down on the cliff, Selen hung on to a protruding stone.

Selen's hands trembled. Louis saw panic in Selen's green eyes. Louis tried to reach Selen. "Grab my hand!"

Selen stretched out his arm to reach Louis's hand. Too short. "I can't," Selen murmured.

Louis crept further until he could barely hold on to the edge. "Try again," he implored, breaking into tears.

Selen pulled harder on his arm and stretched out his hand. As his fingers grazed Louis's, a white light spread from Selen's arm into Louis's body. Yet, Louis barely cared. His legs tensed when he saw the look of despair in Selen's eyes. His mind screamed in denial.

"I love you," Selen whispered. The stone tumbled. Selen fell backwards with his arms stretched out, his long lilac hair floating around his face. The stone hit his brow. At the same time, Louis plunged over the cliff.

The fall was fast, but he managed to grab his love. Their entwined bodies swirled in the air, falling. He would not leave him; he never could. *The only reason one fights is for what one loves. I will die for love again*, Louis thought, *and join the stars.* "Together," Louis breathed, holding Selen tight.

He felt an excruciating pain in his back. As the roofs of the city's houses grew closer, Louis stretched his wings. And flew.

The side door of the great hall flung open. Louis stepped forward, carrying Selen in his arms. His long archangel wings were folded behind his back. He stepped onto the dais. Delicately, he laid Selen onto the ground. His friend breathed weakly. Louis cupped Selen's face in his hands. Tears ran down his cheeks.

"It is your wings I carry, my love," Louis whispered.

He swiveled his face towards the nave. His narrowed blue eyes burned with rage. The mob of nobles and armed men looked at him with disbelief. Louis stared only at one man. Outside on the esplanade, Segar Mills grinned at him.

Louis rose. Slowly, he walked down the central aisle, his torn tunic hanging around his waist, his giant wings floating gracefully behind him. The mob opened. The nobles stepped back and curled against the walls. When he crossed the threshold, the battling crowd outside fell silent. Louis faced Segar. The man's shirt was half torn, revealing black scales covering his skin to his neck. Sharp bones, or plates, protruded out of his shoulders. Though he had no armour, Segar was taller, stronger. His grin was barely human. Segar spoke.

"Behold! Killed by your hands, I rose up from the soil you rinsed in blood!"

Segar raised his arms high. His eyes sparkled with red. "I have split open your closet and turned your world upside down. Your dreams shattered, you're nothingness again." Segar laughed and stretched his arm wide. "Look around you! The time for glory and honour has passed away. They are a lost cause. But you are not. I can see the burning pride in your eyes. Join me in sin. Obey our Master!"

"Fool! I despise you and your kind. There is pain in my heart, but my tears are no weakness," Louis answered with scorn. "Although a shadow inside me sees no tomorrow, I want to believe there is hope. Hope for innocence and virtue."

"Virtue does not dwell in the hearts of men. The age of innocence and purity you long for never existed. Mankind follows my voice. Their flaws grow like weeds, and I feed their every need." Plates grew on Segar's back.

"You creep in the twilight, but this is the dawn of a new age!" Louis cried out, stepping forward. "Like a phoenix, mankind will be reborn from the ashes of the pyres I built for your minions." Out of the corner of his eye, he saw Folc run towards him. Louis made a sign for him to stop.

"Ah! I grow stronger every day!" Segar boasted. His teeth shone, sharp. "I roam the darkness of the hearts. Can you look around you and tell me you believe in virtue? War, corruption, suffering, and death rule this world."

"And I also see innocence and love. Justice and goodness will hold hell away from men. Evil will be crushed," Louis answered.

"Your justice? Theirs? Who can tell the wrong from the right? You? You play God with such an arrogance. I like it!" Segar raised his fist with delight. His fingers turned into claws. "Burn with me!" His words were poison foaming at his chops.

"Never!" Louis snapped.

"Do you know why I hate you?" Segar growled. "You believe the words you speak. There is freedom in your eyes." He spat the words. "But you can't escape your fate, and you are doomed."

"My fate lies in my hands. I am the master of my own will. You can have my body, put me to death, but you will never have my heart." While Louis spoke, his white wings spread wide in the wind.

"The world is mine. I will feed on your flesh, I will feast on your sins and on the hatred of the men." Segar threw himself at Louis with a roar.

"Folc!" Louis shouted. The boy handed him a sword. Louis rotated the hilt around his thumb, raised the sword like a spear, and threw it. It skewered Segar during his jump. The beast fell to its knees.

Louis walked towards him and pulled out the sword. "And forever, I will stand in your path, burning with vengeance. Now that you have knelt, return to hell." With one clean blow, he beheaded his foe.

Louis turned around. Every man standing on the esplanade knelt and bowed. He looked at them with contempt. They had taken weapon against goodness, but they bowed to the force. Yet, some had come to save him. He looked at Folc and half smiled. Louis dropped his sword and walked back towards the hall. As he entered the nave, his archangel wings withered away in sparks of light.

73

Slowly, Selen opened his eyes. His body hurt. He lay, probably on a bed. It was warm and soft. Once his vision had become clearer, he recognized the ceiling of the solar. He felt a weight on him, and someone held his hand. He bent his head as low as his neck allowed. Louis sat next to the bed. He had fallen asleep with his head on Selen's abdomen. Louis's hand cupped his. His friend looked tired. He had dark rings under his eyes, and his features were drawn. His mouth was slightly open. Selen heard him breathe.

Selen pulled his other hand from under the blankets. He felt pain all over. His body twitched. Louis opened his eyes. His friend smiled with relief. He clenched Selen's hand and buried his face against Selen's chest. "Selen," he murmured.

"Am I alive?" Selen asked. "I thought I fell."

"You did," Louis said, cupping his face. "But you are my angel. You gave me your wings." Louis smiled and sobbed. "The white light from your arms."

Selen remembered the light and how it had flown into Louis. "Angel wings?"

Louis nodded. "It was your light."

"What of the plot?" Selen asked, worried.

"It's over," Louis said. "They have been arrested. I will fix their execution. I've killed Segar Mills."

"And…what of the rumours?" Selen inquired.

"I will fix that too. We will fix it, together." Louis smiled. "How do you feel?"

"Alive. This is already a good start." Selen smiled. "How long did I sleep? How do I look?"

"You only slept the night. Brother Benedict examined you. He said you are covered with bruises, but besides your ribs, no bone is broken. Your face is all right. You probably protected it with your arms. You were lucky."

"Lissandro said I have a saint watching over me," Selen said.

Louis's face twitched. "No, I made you suffer. I endangered your life. I am sorry. I love you so much." His friend wept and lowered his head.

"I have chosen to be at your side until the end. Isn't that what you wrote? That friends should fight side by side and die together to be buried in the same grave?" Selen smiled.

"Yes. I did."

"And you jumped." Selen reached for Louis's face with his hand, whatever pain it caused. Louis's cheek was soft and wet with tears. "I love you," Selen whispered.

"You are the only reason I want to live." Louis's face came close to his. His friend touched Selen's opening lips with his in tiny sips. Selen tasted the salt on his friend's plump lips. Louis's touch was so soft that Selen thought he was kissed by an angel when he remembered it had been his wings. Selen would have taken a thousand of his kisses and a hundred more.

Someone knocked on the door. Louis dried his tears abruptly and composed himself. Selen made a sign that his friend looked neutral again. Louis got up and opened the door.

"You open your door yourself?" Selen heard Pembroke ask.

"Yes. I'm still not used to the etiquette," Louis answered. "Come in."

Pembroke stepped inside the solar. He was clad in black robes as usual. He noticed Selen in the bed.

"Oh! I... Oh," His face looked surprised and ill-at-ease. "So the rumours were true."

"It depends on how you present it," Louis said. "If I care about Selen, yes. But if I hear one more filthy word like the ones I heard yesterday, I will put their heads on spikes."

"Well. It's...unusual. Yet, I know your worth as men, and I won't judge. How do you plan to present it to the population? Or will you deny the whole thing?"

"I have not thought about it yet. I would like to focus on the prisoners first," Louis suggested. The two men took a seat.

"As they have been caught in the act of rebellion against their king in a time of peace, I think we could easily skip a trial," Louis said. "All the men present yesterday on the esplanade and their leaders will be executed. How many men did you arrest?"

"Over a hundred, Your Majesty," Pembroke replied. "Nobles, henchmen, religious fanatics. But also two of your ministers, the high priest, and members of the most prestigious families of Nysa Serin."

Selen thought that this would be a good cleansing. Should Louis put them to death, and he had no doubts of his friend's intentions, this would make sure that no one would ever be tempted to rebel again. It would be a fatal blow at their enemies.

"I will make no exception. Yet, for reasons of practicality and hygiene, you will hang half of them, the henchmen and the religious fanatics. We will behead only the nobles. Not that I want to do them a favour, but I know what a hundred heads in one day do to the pavement," Louis said. "I want a public execution. I will assist with it with the rest of the court. That should teach them."

"When do you want to have the execution organized, Your Majesty?"

"As soon as possible. Tomorrow, if Selen has the strength to stand up. I don't want to postpone these things. The blow must fall sharp and inflexible," Louis answered. "Now, there is another point I would like to approach. It's their wealth and goods. They have to pay, but we have to show justice and fairness. You will seize their wealth and properties for the Treasure, but—and I insist—you will leave enough for their widows and children to live decently. They have the right to keep one house and their personal belongings. I want no pillaging, no violence. I don't want to hear of raped women, and there won't be orphans and widows begging in the streets. Have I been clear?"

"I will see to that, Your Majesty," Pembroke said with approval in his voice. "Is there something else I can do?"

"We have lost three of our ministers. We need to replace them. I think that, considering the importance of the nobles in this false insurrection, the time is ripe to open the high council to commoners. I will send you a list of the guild masters who gave me the best impression. You and Mauger will introduce them to the functions. Maybe we can finally work together on the constitution. I want everyone in this city to feel concerned about their rights."

Selen was pleased to see that the shattered dreams of his friend were coming back to life again.

"I have a little question, Your Majesty," Pembroke said. "Can we know more about your…you know, feathers?"

Louis smiled. "I think you should ask God about that. It was his will."

The men rose. Pembroke took his leave and left the solar.

"Do you think you can endure standing up?" Louis asked.

Selen tried to sit in the bed. He felt as if he had been trampled by a horse. He groaned with pain.

"I did not mean now," Louis said, holding him back down. "Now, you must rest. I want you by my side during the execution. Not for the sight, of course, but to show we are united."

"Are you sure?" Selen inquired. This could only reinforce the rumours.

"If they don't accept us after that, nothing will ever change their minds, and I can't hold you in a cage. I would like, for once, not to limit my relationship to a single room. If you are ready."

"I'm ready," Selen said. "Louis, considering I nearly died, I want to know. Is your name Antoine?"

Louis's smile faded. His eyes lost their glow as if his friend had aged a hundred years. "My name is Louis Antoine Saint-Just. But please, don't use it. It is…loaded with memories. I was Antoine…" Louis paused, overwhelmed with feelings. He shifted his tearful eyes before looking at him again. "For you, I want to be Louis, only Louis. If you understand."

"I understand," Selen said. "I'm sorry."

"It's all right. Rest now," Louis said, laying a hand on him. "I'm here if you need anything."

Selen slipped under the covers again, looked at the sky through the window, and closed his eyes. The singing of the birds put him to sleep.

Even with his bruises on fire, Selen had managed the whole way from the palace to his chair on the dais without stumbling. Thousands of people were packed in the square. They looked pacific and attentive, as if they were attending an exceptional show of high intensity. They had come with their families, and many ate snacks. The gallows had been raised to the left of the dais. There were only three of them. Considering that it was the middle of summer, the bodies had been removed progressively to avoid the horrible stench of the excrement falling from the corpses. The last thirty condemned, clad in a plain, grey frocks, still hung from their ropes, swinging lightly with the wind. Some had their tongues drying out in the sun. These thirty had been left for the crowd to gaze upon. They would be cut down by the end of the day. Though it was still faint, the scent already reached Selen's nose. The scaffold for the beheadings and the dais were one single, huge platform. Louis wanted to have the sight so close that the rest of the nobles would feel the coldness of the blade grazing their frail necks. On the right, the forty condemned, packed by ten and also clad in the same frock, stood in a line. The herald stepped forward and shouted.

"In the name of his Majesty Louis Domgeornan, King of Trevalden and Protector of the People, the condemned men here have been found guilty of fomenting an insurrection against the king. Considering their status in the public service, their action is considered by law as criminal. They have been judged outlaws and usurpers of the king and the people's sovereignty and are thus condemned to death."

Selen could not help but notice that the status of high priest was now included in the public service.

The first man was pushed forward to the block. He was a middle-aged man with an aquiline nose and a large chin. His brow was covered with sweat. The man trembled and squeaked with a little voice that did not match his stature. When the guards pushed him down, the man soiled himself. The executioner's axe fell. Selen could not see the blow, but he saw the head roll and the blood squirt in long jets. The guards bore the body and threw it in the cart down the scaffold. One man picked up the head by the hair and cast it with the rest. The guards fetched the next condemned.

The process was long. The pain in Selen's back and broken ribs grew more severe. He twitched in his seat and stifled a groan.

"Are you all right?" Louis whispered with concern without turning his head.

"It hurts but I can hold," Selen answered. He looked sideways at his friend. Louis was calm and grim with determination. He sat cross-legged on his throne, with his head on his joined hands. His eyes narrowed. Only three prisoners were left, the high priest, Honfroi, and Evrardin. Louis had kept them for the end. His friend raised his hand.

"Hold on," Louis said.

The executioner stopped. Louis rose and approached the block. His black boots tramped on the blood-soaked boards. He held a hand towards the executioner. The man did not react at first, but then he handed his axe. Louis took it.

"It is time for the king to dispense justice himself," Louis exclaimed.

The guards pushed the high priest forward. Selen felt a bit frustrated that he could not see Louis's face from where he sat, but he saw the emotions on the priest's face. It was a mix of hatred, fear, and incomprehension. Though Louis did not have the dexterity of the executioner, it only took one blow to take the man's life. The head of the high priest fell on the boards. Louis pushed the body from the block with his foot and raised his hand towards Honfroi, announcing the fat man's turn. The execution was cleaner. The head fell heavily. Finally, it was Evrardin's turn. The minister knelt on the side of the block.

"Any last words?" Louis said low to the man.

"They hated me, but they will never love you." Evrardin smirked. "The people like heroes, but they despise goodness. They envy our money, because they share our flaws. Give them bits of what we have, and they will gladly bear a yoke." Louis cleft Evrardin's head.

"I said words, not a speech," Louis told the severed head.

Selen watched Louis put the axe against the block and walk forward to the edge of the scaffold. His friend gazed at the crowd. His long hair floated in the wind. The sides of his blue brocade tunic flapped against his legs. He shouted. His voice was clear and powerful.

"People of Trevalden! My people! Yesterday, men broke my heart. And I will only confide in you. As my function of king makes me the servant of the people, I owe you the truth, and I hope I will still be honored with your trust."

At the mention of truth, Selen leaned forward, as did the nobles around him. The truth was rarely something everyone wanted to hear.

"Those men have tried to divide our government. They wanted to spread chaos. Their jealousy and pettiness have pushed them to increase their influence and to concentrate the power in their hands only, leaving no right to live for anyone who did not fit in their schemes. They have corrupted the watch and the tribunals. They wanted to overthrow good people to make their domination unstoppable. Those men thought that *they* had made me king, that I owed them. And thus that I would follow their scheme. But I am not a traitor to my people. I serve my country. I speak in your name. My lips will always be sincere. Therefore, I present you the facts, as they are, though some would want them to be settled in the offices of the palace."

At the promise of spicy revelations, the atmosphere tensed. Selen felt worry grow in him and hoped his friend was not digging his grave.

"It is true that some of the nobles took the glory for the deeds of the Rebellion. That they felt offended by the new laws. They also wanted to corrupt the minds, thus, they spilled obscene words and thoughts among you. To force you to commit crimes that were against your interests. Selfishness ruled their hearts, and therefore, unfortunately, as they stood in the way of your happiness, they had to be tamed." Louis pointed at the bloody block behind him. "As long as I will reign, there won't be factions in the government. There will be no calumny, no lies, and no injustice. The force won't be law. The institutions we are working on will fix the guarantees of your rights and your freedom. Only justice and rightful laws will protect you. The power belongs to the people. It can never be in the hands of one single man. No one wants a tyrant. No one wishes another Agroln! I will fight for justice until the end. Yet, some of you may want to take me down. I leave you your own free will. I warn you, though, that factions mean destruction, death. As for me, I would prefer death than to be the accomplice of such criminals. A king must reign fairly—or die!"

Though the words had moved Selen's heart, he was not sure that the people had caught the meaning of his friend's words. Fighting the pain in his body and his fear of the crowd's reaction towards him, Selen rose from his seat and stepped forward. He passed near Evrardin's corpse. Droplets of blood stained the bottom of his white tunic as the wind swirled it against the block. He stopped at Louis's side. He looked at the people, ready to hear insults as lewd as the ones he had heard in the slums. Still, what he heard was different.

"Is it the man who kills rapists?" a woman asked.

A scarred man pointed at him. "I remember him! I fought under his command at the battle of the dam!" the man said with pride.

"He is the one working at the school," another voice said.

Selen smiled. As clearly and audibly as his friend had talked, he shouted.

"People of Trevalden! The days of glory are not over. But their future depends on you! Will you put down a government that has such high designs for your future? Whose king is so wise that he refuses the absolute power of his function? A king who wants to speak in your name? Who loves you?"

Their eyes on him, the people listened to his words carefully. Selen gave them time to ponder on them, yet not long enough to let his fears take over him.

"And this is not any king. It is your hero of the Rebellion. The victor of the Eryas Lowlands. The man who defeated Rylarth the dragon. A man so noble that he refuses to take the glory for his own victory, but instead, salutes the bravery of his soldiers."

He pointed at the man in the crowd who had fought at his side. The soldier nodded with approval and pride. Selen looked at the crowd again.

"Would you choose mayhem, violence, hunger, and death instead of him? Do you miss Agroln so much? A tyrant who tortured you in his chambers and killed your own children? The man standing in front of you today will give your children an education, work, and a good life in peace. Yes, he has spilled blood, and I know he will—but for the greater good only, and never without reason, never outside the law. He will never be like Agroln. Will you thank him with your hate? Will you kill a hero and give the power to a coward? Will you jeopardize your future when you can have the security of happiness? I believe in you, good people of Trevalden. I believe that freedom and love lie in your hearts. Therefore, we raise our hands for an era of justice, an era of peace, a golden era. For a new dawn. With your hero, your herald, your king!"

Selen grabbed Louis's hand and raised it in the air. The crowd acclaimed them with thundering roars of joy and applause. Selen smiled with relief. The people had made their choice. They were safe.

74

There were songs and dances, colors and laughs. The air smelled of flowers and melons. Roasted pork, exotic fruits, cakes, and wine had been distributed to the city's people. This time, the Crown had paid for the festivities. Musicians had been generously encouraged, and bards could be seen at every corner. The doors of the temples had been opened wide. Candles had been lit and incense burned to remember the fallen brothers. The days of darkness were over, but no one would forget.

They had dug a large hole in the main square. Selen stood on his knees in the earth, unlacing a small pouch. He poured the contents into the palm of his hand. Two small, green beans fell from the bag. He had cried with joy when Lissandro had given him this gift. His friend had had no idea of how precious these seeds were. They were more than trees; they were life itself. The sacred tree of the gods. It would bring prosperity and protection to the whole kingdom. Selen buried them in the center of the circle.

"Put your hand next to mine," Selen told Louis.

Louis knelt at his side and placed a hand on the earth, where the seeds lay.

"If there is one last spark of divine energy in us, and if it's the will of the gods, then it should be the accomplishment of our quest," Selen said.

Selen was right. A faint white light left their bodies and spread over the earth.

"It is over," Selen whispered solemnly. They rose and watched the soil. Two green sprouts grew from the earth. As they developed, they entwined. The saplings rose, always higher, turning into trees. Their knotty trunks grew strong, and their boughs expanded wide. Leaves budded and enfolded, green as emeralds. Orange flowers speckled the luxuriant foliage. Around them, people gazed and sighed with amazement.

"One day, when the people will be ready, it will talk to them," Selen said with awe.

"Why did you plant such a magical tree in the middle of the city?" Louis asked.

"For the Children of the Forest, for their sacrificed children, for their lost realm. So that the people of this city never forget that nature lies at the heart of all things," Selen answered with melancholy.

"Society is not the work of men. As violence and savagery is not in nature. Animals do not fight their own species. Like this tree, they only require affection and fulfilled natural needs. Like this tree, every living organism needs roots, a trunk, and branches. It needs unity within itself and with its environment to survive. What men need is to look closer at nature. It is a good choice of place indeed."

Louis smiled.

"Should we head back to the palace?" Selen asked. It would be the first court session after the dramatic events. They would need to face the court again. Louis wanted peace with the nobles. He would show them that unity was possible without the use of the force. It would take time for the wounds to heal, but Selen had faith in their dreams.

Selen and Louis met Folc in the main gallery. His armour of king's guard shone brightly. He was proud and radiant. "Are you ready to begin, Your Majesty?" the boy, no, the man, asked.

"I am ready, Captain Folc," Louis said with a smile.

"Then, I will inform the herald," Folc said. He looked at them with affection. "Good luck." Folc entered the great hall and closed the door behind him. Selen and Louis leaned against the wall near the door, waiting.

"Are you ready to be king?" Selen asked Louis. With the rumours and the hateful thoughts, Louis had had a hard time believing the people's reaction during the execution. He had prepared himself to die and had only wished a memorable and honorable end. Selen's intervention had come as a twist in Louis's final speech.

"You know, I don't want to make it a life task, but I accept to lead the people until they are ready to make a world of their own. Besides, the kingdom is too vast to impose a republic. It will take time. Maybe what they need for now is a good king." Louis half smiled.

Selen smiled back with complicity. He would not have called Louis's words a change of heart—he didn't wish for one—but it was a good start for moderation. "For freedom, equality, justice…"

"And love," Louis said, looking into Selen's eyes. He straightened and exhaled. "Are you ready?"

Selen took a deep breath. "I am," he answered, resolute. This session would be a leap of faith.

Louis opened the door. The two men entered the great hall together. The sunlight shone through the high windows. Standards of velvet azure and argent, Trevalden's colors, hung high on the walls. Their clothes matched the heraldry. Louis was clad in royal blue robes with ample sleeves, and Selen was in glimmering, ivory silk jacquards with matching pants and boots.

The long nave was crowded with new and old faces. There was something different in the men's attitude. Confusion had replaced anger and scorn. The nobles looked uncertain of their future. For once, they feared the people. The faction wars were over.

Selen sat down on his throne next to Louis. The imposing dragon skull had a proud place on the wall behind them. Louis laid his arm on the armrest and held his hand raised. Selen saw the smile in the corner of his lips and the light in his eyes. The leap of faith. Delicately, Selen placed his hand on Louis's. Instead of fear, he felt happiness. Instead of shame, he felt pride. He looked at the crowd and defied them with a kind smile. It would take time, yet Selen was patient. It was a new start. A new life. A second chance.

Thank you for reading my first novel, Rising from Dust! I hope you enjoyed it. I would gladly appreciate your comments. If you are curious to know more about the following events in Trevalden, feel free to join the official Facebook website called "Martine Carlsson".

CPSIA information can be obtained
at www.ICGtesting.com
Printed in the USA
LVHW050527210820
663741LV00014B/1540

9 789198 392357